YOU
CAN
KILL

YOU CAN KILL

REBECCA ZANETTI

ZEBRA BOOKS
Kensington Publishing Corp.
www.kensingtonbooks.com

ZEBRA BOOKS are published by

Kensington Publishing Corp.
900 Third Avenue
New York, NY 10022

All Kensington titles, imprints, and distributed lines are available at special quantity discounts for bulk purchases for sales promotion, premiums, fund-raising, and educational or institutional use.

Special book excerpts or customized printings can also be created to fit specific needs. For details, write or phone the office of the Kensington Sales Manager: Kensington Publishing Corp., 900 Third Avenue, New York, NY 10022. Attn. Sales Department. Phone: 1-800-221-2647.

ZEBRA BOOKS and the Zebra logo Reg. U.S. Pat. & TM Off.

First Printing: November 2024
ISBN-13: 978-1-4201-5693-5
ISBN-13: 978-1-4201-5694-2 (eBook)

10 9 8 7 6 5 4 3 2 1

Printed in the United States of America

This one is for Alicia Condon.

This book is our forty-third project together . . . and it's our last. We've shared drafts, deadlines, and drinks over twelve years, and I think we've created some wild worlds together. As you step into retirement, I just want to say that I'm going to miss this. Miss us. You've been an amazing editor, and I feel like we've become friends.

As you know, change and I are not friends. When you said I could drop by if I'm ever in the neighborhood (across the country), I hope you meant it. Because I consider any place east of the Rockies to be in the neighborhood of you.

Here's to all the stories we've created and to the new adventures waiting for you. May they be filled with joy. You deserve it.

Acknowledgments

From the bottom of my caffeinated heart, I want to thank all of the wonderful people who have helped get this book to readers:

As always, thank you to Big Tone for your support and understanding when I write while on the beach during our vacations. I love that you've never flinched at the darkness my mind can create (in books, of course), and have never lost sleep after my odd questions about the best way to bury a body or the most efficient murder weapon found on a golf course. Or at least for not showing it.

Thanks to Gabe Zanetti and Karlina Zanetti, two of the most creative and inspiring people in the world. I'm proud of the choices you've made and can't wait to see what you both do next. I love you.

Thank you to my agent, Caitlin Blasdell, who is a master at finding and destroying plot holes while also negotiating contracts with the precision of a chess master who sees the entire board at all times. Thanks also to Liza Dawson and the entire Dawson group.

Thank you to my editor, Alicia Condon, to whom I dedicated this book. Thanks for your hard work on this one as well as the forty-two that came before it. Nice job with the timeline, too. I think I had four Wednesdays in a row before you fixed it.

Thank you to the rest of the Kensington crew: Alexandra Nicolajsen, Steven Zacharias, Adam Zacharias, Alicia Condon, Elizabeth May, Lynn Cully, Jackie Dinas, Jane Nutter, Lauren Jernigan, Vida Engstrand, Barbara

Bennett, Justine Willis, Renee Rocco, Darla Freeman, Susanna Gruninger; Tami Kuras; Valeece Broadway-Smith, Andi Paris, Kristin McLaughlin, Shannon Gray-Winter, Kristen Vega, Carly Sommerstein, James Walsh, and Pam Joplin.

Thank you to Eva Hájková from Metafora/Grada publishing, the Czech publisher of the Laurel Snow series, who actually named this book. Thank you also to editor Karolina Stranska and editor-in-chief Magdalena Feldekova for working so hard on this series and for doing such a wonderful job. I truly enjoyed lunching with you in Prague.

Thanks to Corey Millard for always answering my questions regarding mining, crystals, and anything earth related every time I ask—for whichever series I'm work-ing on at the time.

Thank you to Anissa Beatty for handling my social media and for running Rebecca's Rebels, my FB street team, and thank you to Kristin Ashenfelter for wrangling TikTok for me.

Thanks to the Rebels: Kimberly Frost, Madison Fair-banks, Joan Lai, Heather Frost, Gabi Brockelsby, Leanna Feazel, Suzi Zuber, Karen Clementi, Asmaa Qayyum, and Jessica Mobbs for detailed beta reads, suggestions, and support.

Thanks to Writerspace for spreading the word about the books, and to Book Brush for creating such inspiring graphics and for providing what authors need so we can have more time to write.

Finally, thanks to my unwavering support crew: Gail and Jim English, Kathy and Herbie Zanetti, Debbie and Travis Smith, Stephanie and Don West, Jessica and Jonah Namson, and Chelli and Jason Younker.

Chapter 1

Icicles hung like sharpened spikes along the eaves of the hospital as FBI Special Agent in Charge Laurel Snow ducked her head against the biting wind and strode across the crunchy snow to enter the building. The door shut behind her with a grinding screech. She shivered and brushed snow off her shoulders. Winter had extended her reign into the beginning of April, which wasn't unusual for the sleepy town of Genesis Valley, and yet the chill factor seemed to be worsening.

Her footsteps echoed hollowly through the vacant waiting area, and she hastened at the sight of the unmanned reception area. The nurse was known to be a barracuda who liked to block people, so Laurel skirted the desk and hustled down the northern hallway.

Her phone buzzed, and she paused, lifting it to her ear. "Agent Snow."

"Hey, Laurel," Walter said. "I just got your message. Do you need me at the hospital?"

"No. You keep packing. I'm fully equipped to handle this."

Walter cleared his throat. As her second-in-command,

he'd been injured several times in the last few months, and she was pleased he and his girlfriend had won a vacation to a sunny and relaxing locale.

"I don't like that Jason Abbott wants to see you in the hospital. Do you have backup?" Walter asked.

Laurel's service weapon felt snug at the back of her waist. She looked down the empty hallway, noting one of the fluorescent lights buzzing in the far distance. "The Genesis Valley Police are guarding Jason Abbott," she said. "I have plenty of backup. Please continue your preparations for your time off."

Walter exhaled heavily through the phone. "I can't believe he tried to kill himself again."

Abbott's actions didn't fit with his pathology, but perhaps the lack of hope was enough to make the serial killer want to avoid trial. Laurel had gathered enough evidence against him that he would certainly be convicted of brutally murdering successful women, cutting off their hands, and leaving them frozen in icy graves. This was the second time he'd attempted suicide while awaiting trial.

"What did he say when he called?" Walter asked.

The buzzing from the far light increased by several decibels.

Laurel swallowed. "He called our office and said that he wanted to talk about additional victims." Apparently the hospital had let him use a phone, which was something she would address after she spoke with him. "He waived his right to an attorney as well."

Walter crunched on something, probably ice. "Isn't that surprising? He has a good lawyer."

"He's an angry narcissist who believes he's more intelligent than everybody else."

Walter snorted. "Even you?"

She leaned against the wall, trying to keep herself out of sight of the nurses. The place seemed deserted. "Especially me. I'll report back what I discover. You continue packing."

Walter chuckled. "All right, boss. Give me a call after you meet with the lunatic."

She clicked off and slid the phone into her pocket before looking in both directions and hurrying toward the end of the hall. Evading that nurse had become imperative. Laurel turned the corner in time to see a uniformed police officer step into room 113. Irritation clocked through her. As a dullard, the local sheriff might not be teaching his officers proper procedure. Unbuttoning her coat just in case she needed to reach for her weapon, she strode toward the doorway and walked inside.

"Officer, return to your post," she said to his broad back.

He stood looking down at the figure in the bed, his shoulders wide and his fists clenched at his sides. She could comprehend his anger. Jason Abbott was a brutal killer, and many people wanted him dead.

"Officer," she said.

He pivoted suddenly.

She recognized him, but it was too late.

He slammed her against the wall and shut the door, one hand clutching her throat, the other covering her mouth.

Jason Abbott.

She gulped several times, her hands loose at her sides, and then looked beyond him to the figure in the bed.

"The officer," he affirmed.

"Is he deceased?" she said against the palm over her mouth. He had her backed up to the wall, close enough that she couldn't quickly reach for her gun. The heavy metal bit into her back, just waiting for her to move into action.

He shook his head. "Not yet, but he's full of sedatives."

Jason stood at least a foot taller than she, and his dark blue eyes sparked with anger. Even furious, he was a handsome man, with his closely cut beard and his broad shoulders. Solid, with a high percentage of muscle mass compared to fat, he'd obviously been working out these months in jail.

She swallowed, refusing to show fear. He needed the fear and wanted it desperately. So she rolled her eyes.

He blinked and then slowly removed his hand.

Her throat ached, but she kept calm, glancing at the bandages covering his wrists. "You didn't cut very deeply."

"I didn't really want to die." He smiled. "However, *you* are going to meet your maker."

She considered viable plans of action and pivoted her hips twenty degrees, driving her knee up to his groin, impacting soft tissue. He instinctively bent over and emitted a low groan. She struck toward his eyes, trying to blind him. He dodged to the side, and she hit his mouth, his teeth scraping her knuckles with a painful slice.

Taking advantage of his movements, she retrieved her gun from the back of her waist.

He punched her wrist, and her hand smashed against the wall, pain careening up her entire arm. She dropped the gun.

Grunting, she rotated and punched him in the eye, and he fell back. Then she kicked him in the groin again. She started to yell, but he smashed her in the cheek. She flew toward the bed, impacted the side, and crashed down, screaming for help. Then he kicked her under the jaw. Her head snapped back against the bed again, and darkness fell across her vision.

"What is going on here?" a female voice yelled.

A body landed next to Laurel. She couldn't see. Her vision blurred.

"We aren't done." Jason Abbott's voice came from very far away.

A high shriek next to her made Laurel jump, and she blindly scrambled for her gun. Jason kicked her shoulder, and she careened across the room, slamming into the wall head first.

Then darkness fell.

"I'm relatively unharmed," Laurel protested again, sitting on the hospital bed as Fish and Wildlife Captain Huck Rivers ducked to look into her eyes.

The doctor tapped notes on a tablet while leaning against the wall. "You're going to be a little sore." He looked up, his blue eyes bloodshot and his grizzly gray eyebrows bushy. "You took a good hit to the cheek and the jaw, and your shoulder and forehead are bruised, but from the look of your knuckles, you inflicted damage as well."

She had kicked more than she'd punched, so her foot should hurt more than it did. She made a mental note to buy more of these type of boots. "How is the nurse?" Thank goodness the woman had arrived and screamed so loudly for help.

The doctor's lips tightened. "She has a broken jaw, unfortunately. Nurse Wallentrout isn't going to like that."

Huck winced. "No, she isn't."

"I owe her gratitude for her intervention." Laurel stared down at her phone, fighting panic. "We have a felony arrest warrant out for Jason Abbott, and all agencies are on the lookout for him."

Huck stood tall in front of her, his expression calm, but his eyes a glittering brown. Heightened color showed along his cheekbones, and his shoulders appeared an inch higher than usual, showing extreme tension. "Do you think he'll leave the state?"

Laurel rolled her neck from side to side in an attempt to ease the residual pain. "I'd like to think so, but he's angry. He's been locked up for months, and he wants revenge."

"On you?" Huck asked shortly.

She nodded. "On me, and most certainly on Abigail." On any professional woman who'd crossed him, which included Abigail, Laurel's half sister, who had experimented on Jason Abbott and probably pushed him into killing sooner than he would have otherwise.

"Do we have to warn her?" Huck asked wryly.

An unwilling smile tickled Laurel's lips. "I've already notified FBI Special Agent in Charge Norrs from the Seattle office."

Huck's dark eyebrows rose. "Are they still dating?"

"According to him, yes, they are. He unfortunately believes they are becoming serious and once again requested a dinner date with us."

Huck shoved his hands into his Fish and Wildlife jacket, his rugged face set in harsh lines. Tall and powerful, he looked ready to take on all attackers. "Not in a million fucking years."

She could not agree more but focused on the doctor. "I'm ten to eleven weeks pregnant, but I wasn't hit in the abdomen or lower extremities tonight. I feel well, except for an ache in my face. We have an appointment with an OB-GYN in two weeks to hear the heartbeat."

The doctor made another notation. "We can schedule you for an ultrasound tomorrow if you like, but if you're not spotting or feeling any ill effects, it probably isn't warranted. But peace of mind does matter."

She had a serial killer to catch. "Thank you, Doctor, but we'll wait for the regular appointment." She felt fine, and at this early stage, if something went wrong, there wasn't much that could be done about it.

"Are you sure you're okay?" Huck placed a heavy hand on her shoulder, swiping his thumb along her jawline and the slight ache there. As the father of the child, it was natural he'd be concerned.

"I am, and we need to find Jason now."

Huck looked over at the doctor. "How's the officer Abbott put into the hospital bed?"

The doctor shook his head. "Still out. The prisoner punched him several times and then somehow acquired a vial of sedative. We've performed blood tests, but I don't know which sedative was used yet. The officer's breathing is strong, so he's not in any danger, but it may take him awhile to wake up."

Laurel nodded. "We'll need to secure the CCTV from the hospital."

"Nester's already on it," Huck said. "I called him while you were being examined."

Nester served as the computer guru for Laurel's team, the Pacific Northwest Violent Crimes Unit. "Good."

Huck ran a hand through his hair. "You really think Abbott's going to stay in the area, don't you?"

"I do," she said softly. "He's been cooped up for too long. He'll want to kill again soon." Plus, he'd be very angry that he'd had to run when the nurse screamed and hadn't gotten to take his revenge on Laurel. So he'd be both furious and desperate to show how much more brilliant he was than all of the women he hated.

She stepped down and reached for her coat. "We have work to accomplish."

"I'm driving," Huck said.

"You always drive," she murmured, walking down the hallway and outside into a blistering wind.

"That I do," Huck said, opening his truck's passenger-side door for her.

Laurel climbed up into his truck and clipped her seat belt in place, her mind calculating details she'd memorized about Jason Abbott. Where would he stay? Where would he go? She had investigated him fully, and he didn't own real property. He'd be hiding out somewhere he felt safe.

"I'll need to interview Abigail. I'm certain he confided in her more than she admitted," she said.

Huck grunted in response.

Dr. Abigail Caine had experimented on Jason Abbott, encouraging him to engage in violent fantasies that ultimately led to his kills.

Laurel glanced back to see the dog crate that usually held Aeneas, Huck's Karelian Bear Dog. "Where's the dog?"

"I left him at home," Huck said. "He seemed content snoozing by the fire."

They made the remaining drive in silence, and Laurel sighed, her eyes heavy. The doctor didn't think she had a concussion, so she allowed herself to drop into a dreamless sleep. Jolting awake when Huck stopped the truck, she fumbled for her door to step out onto the crunchy ground and plod into his cabin.

"Are you hungry?" Huck asked, shutting the cottage door behind her.

"Not even remotely." She headed into the bedroom, ditching her clothes and crawling into bed.

His chuckle followed her. "I'll be with you in a little while."

Later, she instinctively felt the heat when he slipped into the bed, and she rolled over to let herself be warmed. Just before midnight, his phone trilled, and his office called him out to investigate a poaching case.

She snuggled deeper into the warm bed, letting her body heal. He returned sometime later, pulling her close, reporting that he hadn't found the poacher. Her dreams flashed a kaleidoscope of fist fights, chilly nights, dead women, and blistering storms. They both groaned when his phone alerted him again, and his office called him out to find a missing person. As an F&W captain, Huck normally took point on any search and rescue or poaching operation. He also served as the department's diving expert.

He kissed her cheek. "Go back to sleep."

Two calls in one night? She blinked. "Maybe you should come work with the FBI. We get more sleep."

His chuckle as he exited the room lightened her spirits, and she smiled, almost immediately dropping back into her dreams.

The buzzing of her phone jerked her awake early in the morning, and she lifted it to her ear, noting that Huck hadn't returned yet. Then she took a quick moment to hope that Jason Abbott had been found.

"Agent Snow," she whispered sleepily.

"Hey, boss," Walter said, his voice somber. "We have a body."

Chapter 2

The body lay yards from Iceberg River at the base of Snowblood Peak, face down, frozen to the unforgiving ground. Standing at the edge of the parking area, Laurel shivered and stared up at the mountainous peak with its jagged edges rising high into the fierce gray clouds. "We seem to have come full circle," she murmured.

FBI agent Walter Smudgeon shoved his hands in his jacket pockets, his gaze on the body. "The way up and the way down are one and the same."

Laurel looked over at her partner. "Heraclitus?"

Red tinged his broad cheeks. In his midfifties, he had intelligent hazel eyes and thinning gray hair that he'd lately begun to style with gel. "I've been reading a lot these days. Ena likes philosophy."

Fascinating. Walter had been shot in an earlier case, and he'd decided to invest in a longer existence, exercising his wounded body to a healthy muscle mass, dedicating himself to a new romantic interest, and apparently studying philosophy. Ena was a Fish and Wildlife officer who worked under Huck, and Walter seemed to adore her.

Laurel noted the state crime scene techs setting up a tent over the body, close to the broken ice. "Heraclitus also said that one cannot step twice in the same river."

"Huh," Walter said. "Haven't read that one. Those thoughts seem to contradict each other."

"They're compatible statements." Laurel angled her head for a better view. The victim had longish blond hair and was still fully dressed in a short black wool coat, dark jeans, and scuffed brown boots. She appeared to be a female in decent shape. "Everything flows and nothing stays."

Walter reached into his back pocket to draw out a pair of thick gloves. "Who said that?"

"Plato, but I believe he paraphrased Heraclitus."

Walter settled shiny and unscuffed snow boots on the icy ground. "So it's about the river? The movement of the water beneath the ice versus solid ground?"

Her current proximity to the victim prevented a detailed analysis of the possible crime scene. "Our perception is subjective, as is any conclusion when becoming philosophical."

He gestured for her to precede him. "Who said that?"

"Me." Having been given a wave from the crime scene tech dressed in thick white coveralls, Laurel gingerly picked her way across the rough terrain, her rugged boots finding purchase on the ice. "Philosophy involves asking questions with few true answers." Which had always irritated her to no end.

Every question should have an answer. In fact, each one most certainly did, even if she couldn't find it. She slipped, and Walter instantly grasped her arm, straightening her. "Thank you."

"No problem. You'd think we'd be finished with the snow and ice, considering it's April first," he grumbled, walking closer to her now.

She shrugged. "We're thousands of feet above ocean level, Walter." At least the snow might melt soon down in the town of Genesis Valley. "We're fortunate snow-mobilers found the body."

"Huh. The body is just a short distance away from the parking area. Somebody would've found her."

They reached the now-tented area just as the wind increased in force, blowing Laurel's hair away from her face. Her breath caught from the cold as she crouched to better study the body. "There are no obvious signs of murder, and she still has her hands." Jason Abbott had liked to cut off the hands of his victims, but he'd had an ax easily available each time.

Unlike now.

Fish and Wildlife Captain Monty Buckley stepped out of a rig in the parking area and strode toward them, his countenance pale from recent cancer radiation treatments. "I radioed Huck to fill him in as he drove. He's on his way now." Monty walked gingerly, his movements jerky.

Laurel stood. "Did Huck find the missing person?"

Monty shivered in the cold, even though he wore a heavy jacket and gloves. "Yeah. They found the old guy not too far from the retirement home, with hypothermia and possible frostbite. He's alive at least."

So Huck would be in a good mood. The man blamed himself when he couldn't save a victim, and even though that was irrational, Laurel could empathize.

Monty gestured to the body. "Her head and torso are

on federal land, and her waist and legs are on state land. This is a weird one, for sure. So I figured we'd share jurisdiction." He motioned toward a younger Fish and Wildlife officer taking photographs near the tree line. "Tso, get over here."

The man let his camera hang over his neck and walked toward them, his black eyes intense. Frozen chips of ice dotted his longish black hair, showing he'd been photographing the area within the trees. He wore an F&W jacket over jeans and thick boots. "I shot the full scene and took extra photographs of the cracked ice over the river. There's blood on the edges, and the techs captured samples before the ice melted." He smiled at Laurel. "You must be Laurel Snow. I've heard about you."

"I am." She held out a gloved hand to shake. Huck had mentioned the new officer, but she hadn't met him.

Monty provided the introductions. "Laurel Snow, please meet Qaletaga Tso, fresh from Arizona. You know? Where there's actually some sun and not constant winter?"

That might possibly be sarcasm, but Laurel couldn't read the tone. Perhaps Monty was dreaming of a trip to a warm beach resort. She and Huck had planned to vacation in Cabo, but work kept interrupting. The new officer appeared to be Native American, and if she remembered correctly, Qaletaga was a Hopi name. "It's nice to meet you."

Officer Tso released her and held out a hand to Walter. "You as well."

"Walter Smudgeon," Walter said. "I bet you miss the

sun. Like Monty, I'm seriously tired of the gray skies but am going to have to put my vacation on hold."

Tso grinned, showing perfectly symmetrical features. "Vacation?"

"Yeah." Walter sighed. "My girlfriend won a sunny two-week vacation from her church's raffle a week ago, and we had planned to leave this afternoon."

Laurel studied the victim. "You are maintaining your departure schedule." The man was recovering from multiple gunshot wounds, and although he appeared healthier than ever, he needed this break from murder. "I have backup, and if I need you, I'll call."

Walter frowned. "Fine. Welcome to the team, Qaletaga Tso."

"Thanks." Officer Tso stared up at Snowblood Peak. "I've recently taken up snowmobiling, so I'm enjoying myself in Washington State so far. I have my diving certification but have never plunged into icy waters like this." He looked over his shoulder at the frigid water. "I suppose since we found blood on the ice we'll need to do a dive?"

"That's up to Huck." Monty straightened as two of the techs brought over small flat shovels. "Good. They're going to turn her over. Let's see what we can find."

Laurel's stomach rolled. As the head of the FBI's PNVCU, she was accustomed to crime scenes. However, because she was eleven or so weeks pregnant, HCG and estrogen hormones were causing unexpected nausea. She drew in several frigid breaths and exhaled through her mouth, attempting to calm her autonomic nervous system to prevent her from vomiting all over Walter's new boots.

"You okay, boss?" Walter asked.

She must've paled. "Yes. The wind is chilly." She and Huck hadn't informed anybody about the pregnancy other than Laurel's mother. They'd agreed to keep the pregnancy a secret until she reached the safer second trimester. Although Huck's paternal overprotectiveness would probably alert the ones closest to them soon. She accepted that characteristic in him.

The team moved a foot away from the body to allow the techs to gingerly scrape away ice. "Monty? Detail the scene for me, please," Laurel said.

"The first is the cracking of the ice over the water with blood found on the edges," Monty said. "The action was deliberate, which could indicate that the deceased broke the ice and tried to jump in, but in that case . . ."

"Who pulled the body to the bank and away from the river?" Walter finished for him.

Monty nodded. "Exactly."

Laurel bent to study the body. Jason Abbott had been furious the night before—he might've killed the first victim he could find. "We'll proceed as if this is a homicide considering the blood on the ice and the fact that somebody dragged the body away from the water."

A truck rumbled from behind her, and she turned to see Huck pull to a stop and jump out. He opened the back door and let out his Karelian Bear Dog. Aeneas leaped gracefully to the ground, still wearing his search and rescue vest, his black-and-white markings adorable. Then the two walked toward them, both slightly wild and very sure-footed.

Huck's gaze swept her from head to toes, no doubt making sure she'd properly dressed for the weather. His protectiveness toward the female carrying his progeny was no doubt strongly rooted in biology and evolutionary psychology. Or perhaps that was just Huck.

He stood tall and broad, filling out his Fish and Wildlife jacket with natural muscle. His hair was a dark brown, his eyes a mellow topaz, his bone structure strong and symmetrical. He wore faded jeans and black boots, and the dog looked natural at his side. "You said we share jurisdiction with the FBI?"

Monty nodded. "Yeah."

Huck's focus had already moved to the cracked ice, and he headed toward the river.

Laurel shifted into motion, noting he slowed his pace until she reached his side. "What do you see?"

"The ice." They reached the edge of the bank, and he put his body slightly between her and the river. "Watch your step." Then he dropped to his haunches as Aeneas sat at his side. "Something sharp cut through this part." He pointed to several jagged edges. "There's blood."

"The techs collected samples." Officer Tso came up behind them. "Do we need to dive?"

Huck stood. "I don't want anybody going beneath that ice. The river is moving faster than you think." He turned to face Monty. "Let's use Polar Paul first, and then if it finds something, I'll consider a dive."

"Polar Paul?" Officer Tso asked.

Huck gestured Laurel ahead of him on the small trail, no doubt so he could catch her if she slipped. "Yeah. Our autonomous underwater vehicle which we just redesigned with enhanced insulation to deal with ice-cold bodies of water."

Laurel had never understood the need to name objects, but she appreciated the alliteration of "Polar" and "Paul." She strode across the ground to the tent covering the body. So far, they didn't have a cause of death. The bloody ice covering the woman's face was beginning to fall off in chunks.

Huck stepped up to Laurel's side. "You think Jason Abbott killed her?"

"It's certainly possible." Laurel squinted to see better. The victim's eyes were closed. "Is that foam around her mouth?"

Officer Tso leaned in and began clicking photographs. "It appears so. Isn't that a sign of drowning?"

Laurel looked back at the cracked ice. So the killer had brought the woman to the river, broken through the ice, and then drowned her in the freezing water? Abbott had been locked up—first in jail, and then in the hospital. Those situations could be suffocating to a man like him. Had he found a new way to kill? "I'd like to have Dr. Ortega at Tempest County perform the autopsy." The coroner was as meticulous as any she'd ever seen, and she trusted his judgment.

"Gotcha," Monty said.

More ice fell off the victim's face. She appeared to be in her early sixties or so with pale blue skin that could've resulted from the cold or drowning. Or both. "Is there any ID on the body?" Laurel asked.

The nearest tech shrugged. "The water on her clothing has frozen, so we should get her to the lab before trying to find a wallet."

Huck took a step closer to the body, his shoulders stiffening.

"Huck?" Laurel focused on him. His posture had gone rigid and his gaze intent. "Do you see something?"

Aeneas whined, ducking his head against Huck's knee, no doubt catching the captain's tension.

Huck swallowed. "I—I think I know her."

Laurel looked back at the woman. "How?"

His rugged face went slack. "I think that's my mother."

Chapter 3

Huck parked his truck to the far right of the lot fronting the Fish and Wildlife building to allow Aeneas to jump out and run along the trees. The snow had finally started to melt, leaving the ground damp with a few crocuses poking up here and there. He turned to stare at the building. Not too long ago, he would've fought coming to the office with every fiber of his being, but Laurel Snow had brought him out of his self-imposed exile. Mostly.

The two-story brick building held Staggers Ice Creamery in the center of the ground floor with its huge sign, newly replaced in bright yellow, fluorescent letters. Laurel and her FBI team occupied the second floor above the creamery.

The Washington State Fish and Wildlife offices staffed the two levels to the right. To the far left, the first floor was now being rented by Laurel's mom as a new storefront for her herbal teas. He figured Laurel wanted to get her mom out into the world a bit more, and with her tea subscription business becoming so lucrative, the next logical step was to create a storefront.

He didn't want to look above the tea shop, where Rachel Raprenzi now held her podcast, *The Killing Hour*. She was an ex-girlfriend, current reporter, and a constant pain in his ass.

Aeneas bounded out of the forest.

"All right, boy, let's deal with this." Huck strode forward and opened the glass door to the small vestibule shared by the Fish and Wildlife and FBI offices. He walked by the door to his office to reach a new, locked metal door. Squaring his shoulders, he pressed the red button to the side.

"Hey, Huck," Kate said through the intercom, and a buzzing sound echoed. He pulled open the door and let the dog run up the stairs before him. The new security system was very much needed.

He walked up the stairs slowly, ignoring the girlish cancan wallpaper on each side of him. Laurel's unit had been made permanent at least for a year, but cases kept getting in the way of decorating the place. He kind of liked the wallpaper and hoped they didn't get rid of it, but it wasn't exactly government issue. He reached the top of the stairs, where Kate Vuittron, the unit's administrator, sat behind a glass cabinet that had once served as a pastry display case.

"Hey, Kate," he said.

"Hi." She smiled, her eyes sparkling, a picture of her three teenaged daughters behind her on a small counter. Her blond hair flipped out around her shoulders, and she kept typing with one hand as she focused on him. "They're in the conference room. You can go on back."

"Thanks." He moved beyond her to a door that bisected the wall and maneuvered down the hallway to turn right into the conference room. A long table consisting of an ornate, gold-bronze, circular sculpture beneath a very worn, rough-looking, haphazardly placed door centered the room. The tabletop had been glass, but he'd broken it in March by tackling a murder suspect onto it.

Sitting in a white leather chair at the head of table, Laurel looked up.

"No glass top yet, huh?" he asked, moving inside.

She shook her head. "No, it's on back order. We might have to wait another month."

"Sorry about that."

She smiled. "You did save my life at the time, so no complaints."

He studied her, enchanted as always by her unusual looks. Her hair was a thick, dark, rare reddish brown—a true auburn, which would make her intriguing on its own. However, her eyes were truly unique. One green, one blue with a starburst of green in the iris, heterochromatic within a heterochromatic eye. He'd read somewhere that heterochromia was a sign of intelligence, and, considering she had been a child prodigy who'd attended college in her early teens and now held multiple advanced degrees, he figured it must be true.

"How do you want to handle this?" he asked.

She chewed on her bottom lip, a sure sign she was thinking. "We certainly have problems."

He barked out a laugh.

She caught herself. "Before we concentrate on the case, how are you?"

The question rocked him back on his heels. As a logical person, Laurel normally took a reasonable and rational approach and rarely asked about feelings.

"I have absolutely no idea," he admitted.

"How certain are you that the victim is your mother?"

He opened his mouth to answer and then shut it, thinking things through. "Not sure at all." The confession loosened the hot lump of coal that had settled in his stomach. "I've never met her," he said. "I've seen pictures of her from years ago, and when I saw that woman's face, I figured that's what she'd look like now. But again, it's been thirty-plus years since my father took pictures of her."

"So it's entirely possible that woman was not your mother."

Huck nodded. "Yeah, I guess I should send a DNA sample to Dr. Ortega, huh?"

"Affirmative."

Huck rubbed the back of his neck. "I have the report from Polar Paul. We didn't find anything of interest in Iceberg River."

Walter Smudgeon walked inside, several file folders in his hands. He tossed them onto the makeshift table. "What's the plan?" he asked. "If that's Huck's mom, we have a conflict of interest for, well, both of you." Walter stood to about five foot nine and had slimmed down recently, today sporting a new dark blue belt. He seemed to love buying belts these days. In addition, with his face thinner, he looked years younger than he had before being shot three times in the abdomen.

Huck had to protect his team. "Yeah, we're talking conflicts of interest without question. Monty will handle things at Fish and Wildlife if the victim is my mother, and I can step off the case."

The last thing Huck wanted to do was call in Deputy

Chief Mert Wright from Seattle. The guy was a moron, and Huck had thankfully avoided him the last couple of months. He looked at Laurel. "Considering we're dating, you might have to turn the case over to somebody else on your team."

Laurel pushed her hair over her shoulder. "I've already notified Special Agent in Charge Wayne Norrs from the Seattle office, in case he needs to assume command of the investigation. For now, let's proceed as if the victim is *not* your mother."

Huck shook his head. "I'd rather we didn't have to deal with Norrs. He worked the Broken Heart case with us well enough, but considering he's dating your half sister, I'd like to avoid being in his orbit."

"I agree," Laurel said. "But proper protocol dictates that I at least notify him. His office is occupied right now with several RICO cases as well as multiple drug cases, so he didn't sound eager to add to his caseload. For now, Walter, you need to get to Sea-Tac. You've earned this vacation."

"I have an hour." Walter pulled out a white leather chair and sat. "Nester," he called out.

"Yo," Nester called back, soon appearing in the doorway. "I heard we caught one at the base of Snowblood Peak."

Huck moved around to take a chair at the table. "We did. There's a chance it might be my mother."

Nester jolted. "Dude, I'm sorry about that."

Huck sat. "We don't have an ID yet, and frankly, it's probably farfetched. I never met her, so how would I know what she looks like now?"

"Good point." Nester worked as the computer guru for the FBI team. In his early twenties, the guy was intelligent and insightful. Tall and slim, he liked to snowboard on his days off, and based on the mangled boards he'd mounted to his office walls, he enjoyed taking risks. Rumor had it that he also dated quite a bit, and with his dark eyes, dark skin, and contagious sense of humor, that rumor was probably true. His expertise in tracking the untraceable by computer made him invaluable on any case. "What do you need from me?" he asked.

"I need you to do a deep dive on Huck's mother," Walter said.

"Delta Rivers," Huck murmured. "I have no idea if she kept Rivers as her surname."

He had long since dealt with the fact that his mother had given birth to him and dumped him on his dad more than thirty years ago; he didn't need to go into it now. His father had passed away from cancer a while back. He'd figured it would be just him and his dog until Laurel had come into his life. Would their child inherit Laurel's heterochromatic eyes and unusual intelligence, or be more down to earth and streetwise like him? He glanced over to make sure the color had returned to her pretty face.

"Also," Laurel said, "I know that the state police interviewed the two snowmobilers who found the body at the scene, but Nester, I'd like you to bring them in and get your own feel for them. Okay?"

His eyebrows rose. "Really?"

"Yes. You said you wanted field experience, and

Walter will be out on vacation, so let's start with this," Laurel said.

"Cool, thanks." Nester disappeared.

Huck frowned. "I thought you were getting two more agents."

Laurel lifted both hands. "We will at some point, but I'm not in any hurry. So right now, this is what we have."

Considering her group had put away three serial killers so far, Huck thought they were doing just fine. In combination with Fish and Wildlife, they could cover every aspect of a case.

"Did you ask Dr. Ortega to put a rush on the autopsy?" Walter asked.

Laurel nodded. "I couldn't reach him but left a message. Apparently there was a nightclub fire in his jurisdiction last night resulting in several deaths. Walter, why don't you start filling out a murder board since you now have forty-five minutes? Just leave that board closest to you alone."

The farthest board was turned over so nobody could see it, but Huck knew it showcased Laurel's half sister, Abigail Caine, and notations on her suspected crimes. Like Laurel, he was aware that Abigail, as brilliant as her sister, had motivated serial killer Jason Abbott to commit atrocious acts, and she'd helped another killer hide his deeds before that. Laurel wanted to put her away, and Huck was on board.

Walter dug photographs from the scene out from his file folder and began taping them to a board.

Huck's ears heated. That couldn't be his mother. She just looked like Delta. He had definitely jumped the gun and hadn't been thinking when he'd spoken. He'd been caught off guard. "You know, the likelihood of our victim being the woman who gave birth to me is unrealistic." His body finally relaxed. "I think I just reacted to the fact that she looks familiar."

Walter appraised him. "That's fine. But why don't we do some preliminary work and I'll interview you real quick?"

"Sure," Huck agreed.

Laurel looked away from the board. "You now have forty minutes."

Huck nodded. "The woman gave birth to me and left town. Haven't talked to her. Haven't met her. Don't know anything about her."

Walter grimaced at his empty notepad. "That was quick. Did your father tell you anything about her?"

Huck tried to remember. "Just that she was a free spirit and liked to drink beer. That's it."

Walter sighed. "How about we do that DNA test?"

"No problem." Huck's phone buzzed, and he read a text. "Rachel Raprenzi has the story about Jason Abbott escaping custody. I hate to say it, but I think I should go on her show and alert the public to this one. People have to know to be on the lookout."

His gut actually ached at the thought.

Chapter 4

Early afternoon, Laurel settled into her seat at the conference room table, careful not to catch her sweater on the rough edges. Walter and Ena had left for their vacation, and she calculated how to cover Walter's excellent legwork.

"Just one more sec." Nester typed rapidly on his laptop next to her.

She reached for her herbal tea and took a sip.

"Have you given up lattes?" he asked.

She looked down at the tea. "My mom insists I compare the new batches being released this spring. I promised to try one blend each day and give her my honest opinion." She probably needed to tell her team about her pregnancy, but not quite yet. Of course, they'd noticed she hadn't been drinking her normal lattes.

Moderate caffeine consumption was considered safe for most pregnant women. Yet she was aware that, as a stimulant, caffeine could cross the placenta, and a fetus couldn't metabolize it efficiently. So she erred on the side of caution. Plus, she enjoyed her mother's new blends and found herself agreeable to giving detailed notes at the end of every day.

"Here we go." Nester clicked his mouse again and gestured toward the screen mounted on the far wall. "I have gone through all of the jail's visitor logs for Jason Abbott. He was visited by both his ex-fiancée, Haylee Johnson, and Dr. Abigail Caine in the last week." Nester pointed to the screen. "Also, attorney Melissa Cutting, who happens to be Haylee's aunt, visited. As you know, visits with counsel are not recorded."

Laurel took another sip of the huckleberry-flavored brew. "I thought we put a ban on Abigail visiting Jason Abbott after his last suicide attempt."

"We did, but as his attorney, Melissa Cutting had it lifted."

Laurel took a deep breath. "We were not notified of this?"

Nester shook his head. "Nope. No one let us know."

That did not compute. "Why would Melissa do that? When you're finished here, call her and schedule an interview."

"Sure," Nester said. "Also, Fish and Wildlife has arranged for Haylee Johnson to be interviewed on Friday because that's the soonest she'd agree to meet. I'd bet dollars to doughnuts that Melissa Cutting will accompany Haylee as her attorney." He frowned, his dark eyes sparkling. "Dollars to doughnuts . . . Where do you think that phrase comes from?"

Laurel reached for a notepad near the center of the table and pulled the paper toward her. "I believe the phrase is an American idiom that originated in the late nineteenth century to do with a bet or wager in which the speaker is confident of the outcome."

"Of course." One side of Nester's upper lip quirked.

Laurel warmed to the subject. "The speaker of the

phrase is saying they're willing to bet something of higher value against lesser value. At that time, doughnuts were relatively inexpensive."

"Unlike now," Nester groused.

Laurel nodded. "Yes, I have noticed pastry price increases."

"The price of everything has increased lately, hasn't it?"

Unfortunately, he made a true statement. "Yes, and I don't see economic hope in the near future."

"Here's the first video." Nester clicked the button.

The visiting room of the Genesis city jail came into view, with Jason Abbott in an orange jumpsuit, his handcuffs attached to a bar on the table, sitting across from ex-girlfriend Haylee Johnson.

Teacup in hand, Laurel sat back to watch. Even after a couple months in jail, Jason Abbott appeared handsome with symmetrical features, dark hair, deep blue eyes, and a neatly trimmed beard. He looked as if he could be a double for Jamie Dornan, a young actor she'd seen in an older streaming British crime drama the previous week.

Across from Abbott, Haylee had her long blond hair up in an intricate twist and her blue eyes expertly lined and shadowed. For her visit, she wore a black dress with a row of pearls adorning her neck. "That's an odd outfit to visit somebody in jail," Laurel said.

"Yeah, she looks hot," Nester replied.

Laurel glanced at him. "Please expand on that statement."

He frowned. "Haylee is trying to appear . . . well, *something* for Jason."

"A black dress connotes class, as do the pearls,"

Laurel mused. "She's wearing a more adult-type outfit than she wore before he went to jail." If Laurel remembered correctly, Haylee had always sported jeans and a sweatshirt. "She's trying to impress him?"

"Yeah," Nester said. "Maybe she's trying to show him that she's more sophisticated, classier, and . . . I don't know, educated?"

Laurel's chin dropped. "Jason Abbott murdered highly successful women. Why in the world would Haylee want to look like one of them?"

Nester lifted his shoulder. "I don't know. I mean, she obviously wants his interest."

Laurel had spent much of her life studying various sciences, but there wasn't one that explained human behavior, not completely. She was coming as close as possible. "I don't understand this."

"Me neither," Nester said.

That was something at least. "Let's play the video," she said.

He clicked a button.

"How are you, Jason?" Haylee asked, her voice tinny on the recording.

"I'm fine. Lonely. I've missed you." His voice remained deep and soothing.

Laurel's stomach rolled. Jason had absolutely no interest in Haylee other than using her, and he never had. How could the woman not see that?

Haylee leaned toward him. "I've started school."

Jason perked up. "You have? What are you studying?"

She straightened her shoulders and pushed her breasts out. "I'm going to cosmetology school."

Nester frowned. "Isn't she a landscaper?"

"She worked in a greenhouse and had a green thumb," Laurel said. Haylee's lack of a formal education had seemed to bother the woman.

"Why does she want to impress him?" Nester asked.

Laurel shook her head. "I can't explain her motivations here."

Haylee hopped in her seat. "I thought that would make you happy."

Abbott smiled, slow and sure. "I love that you want to make me happy, Haylee."

The young woman clasped her hands together. "I've talked to my aunt, and it's a good field for me to pursue."

"Well then, I'm proud of you. If I ever get out of here, maybe I can help with your schooling."

"I would love that," the girl gushed. Apparently, she'd forgiven him for holding a gun to her head and threatening to kill her if the FBI didn't leave them alone. "Do you think you'll get out?"

"I do." Abbott turned his head to look directly at the camera. "I'm too smart for them to keep me in here. Besides, your aunt is an excellent attorney. How is your lawsuit against the FBI going?"

Haylee shifted in her seat. "My aunt isn't sure there's a great case there, because you did have a gun on me when I got hurt. But there's a chance we can prove that Laurel Snow or that terrible Abigail Caine was at fault. You were drugged at the time, correct?"

"Yes. Abigail had drugged me. I don't even remember trying to hurt you." Tears filled his eyes. "I'm so very sorry."

"What a liar," Nester muttered.

Laurel nodded. "He's proficient at it. Those look like

real tears." Abbott certainly knew how to mirror true emotions.

Haylee plucked at her pearls. "Please tell me you're not still thinking about Abigail. About either of them. What a terrible family they come from."

"Not at all," Jason said smoothly. "In fact, I've forgotten about both of them."

Haylee preened. "That's so good to hear."

Abbott looked at the camera again. "However, I doubt they've forgotten about me."

Laurel watched the rest of the video, not finding any clue other than Abbott's obvious stares at the camera. He'd already planned on escaping at that juncture.

Nester ended the video. "What do you think?"

The human brain would always remain a mystery. "I have no idea. What about you? Did you catch subtext or hints that I might've missed?" As hard as she tried, she still missed latent meanings and sarcasm. She lacked Huck's instincts when it came to people, but she had studied facial expressions and micro-expressions.

"I didn't see anything," Nester said. "I don't think Haylee would've been able to completely mask the truth if she knew Abbott planned to escape."

"I agree," Laurel said, somewhat relieved. "All right. Any more videos?"

Nester quickly typed. "Oh, yeah. Here is your wonderful sister."

"Half sister," Laurel corrected quickly.

"This video was taken two days before the one featuring Haylee."

Laurel watched as Abigail confidently strode into the interview room. Like Laurel, Abigail had natural auburn-colored hair and heterochromatic eyes. They'd inherited those traits from their father, whom Laurel still intended to see in prison somehow.

A trusted pastor in the local church, he had sexually assaulted Laurel's mother when she was only seventeen, resulting in Laurel, who hadn't known she had a half sister until just a few months ago.

For the meeting, Abigail wore a deep green skirt suit with a red power shirt beneath the jacket.

"Was this around Christmas time?" Nester chortled.

Laurel looked at him. "Excuse me?"

"The red and the green. What's up with the red and the green?"

"Oh." Laurel studied her half sister. She was more prone to wear black than green. "The red is for power. The pencil skirt is because it makes her look like a successful and professional female, which we know is one of Jason Abbott's triggers." Laurel studied the woman who looked so much like her. "The color green is known to have a calming effect, so perhaps she wants him to concentrate. Please amplify the audio."

Nester clicked several buttons.

"Jason, don't you look lovely in orange," Abigail drawled, gracefully taking a seat.

"What's up with the red and green?" He sneered. "Still in the Christmas spirit, even though it's long past?"

Her smile was catlike. "I'm more of an avenging angel than a whimsical one. However, I'm sorry I haven't had time to visit. But, you know, success takes precedence." She covered her mouth with her hand, showing sharpened red nails. "Oh, excuse me. You *don't* know. Success has always remained outside your purview, hasn't it?"

Jason paled but met her stare. "I'm not letting you mess with my head this time."

"Now, Jason, I just want to help you. I always have." She tapped her nails on the table.

"Right, you want to help me. You experimented on me! It's your fault those women died."

Abigail's eyebrows rose, and she leaned toward him as if unafraid of his outburst. "Really? I don't recall raping them, strangling them, or cutting off their hands. I believe that was you, correct?"

He gulped. "I never would've done those horrible things if I hadn't gone through all that behavioral therapy with you, or been on the drugs you shot into my system."

"Are you suggesting that you're just a little wind-up toy that I spun in the direction I wanted?" she asked. "Are you that weak?"

He straightened. "No, I'm not weak. You know I'm not weak."

"Yes, I do," Abigail said placatingly. "I think you're smarter than anyone gives you credit for. Definitely smarter than your mother ever thought."

Jason just stared at her.

"I can't believe you're still in here, in fact." Abigail looked around the dismal room. "Some birds are not meant to be caged, Jason. I would think you are one of them."

"I agree. My attorney is good, and I will get out of here." He leaned forward slightly. "Do you think you could help with my case?"

Abigail looked toward the door and then back, her face set in intriguing lines.

"Stop the video," Laurel said.

Nester froze it in place.

Laurel leaned forward. "Her eyebrows are drawn together and raised. Her eyelids have drooped, and the corners of her mouth are pulled down slightly." She looked at Nester. "Those micro-expressions show concern or sympathy, correct?"

Nester cocked his head and studied the screen. "Yeah, I'd say sympathy, maybe empathy. I thought she didn't feel those things as a, what? Psychopath, sociopath, narcissistic nut job?"

"I've never employed definitive labels," Laurel said. "But yes, she's proficient at simulating authenticity, isn't she?"

"Well, yeah. Don't people like her mirror real expressions, real feelings?"

"They do," Laurel agreed, taking another sip of her tea. She could study Abigail for years, but that wouldn't put her half sister in prison where she belonged. "Please proceed with the video."

Nester pressed the button, and the video continued.

"I wish I could help you," Abigail said. "But I think you need to help yourself."

Nester sucked in air. "Did she just say what I think she said?"

Laurel didn't reply.

"Help myself. What do you mean?" Jason asked.

"Come on, Jason, you can get out of here," Abigail said. "Just work with your attorney and study the law. You know what to do."

Nester coughed. "She just pretty much told him to escape, right?"

"Those weren't the words that she used," Laurel said. "She's telling him to learn the law."

Abigail leaned forward. "I am very sorry that you ended up in the hospital; I should have tried to visit you. I hope you're not still having such terrible suicidal thoughts. You belong on this earth. Jason. There's a lot of good you can still do."

"Thank you," Jason said, his body relaxing for the first time. "I appreciate that." His eyes gleamed in a different way.

"What's his expression?" Laurel asked Nester.

Nester paused the video again. "Um, interest? Like a light bulb just ignited above his head?"

"Yes. His eyes widened, his eyebrows rose, and his lips curved in a slight smile. Do you see those markers?"

"Yeah," Nester said. "Also, his head tilted slightly. She pretty much just told him how to escape, didn't she?"

"Not in a way that we'll ever be able to prove." Laurel looked at Nester, her mind reeling with this new information and trying to form a rational conclusion. "The question is, why would Abigail want Jason released from custody?"

Nester studied the screen. "So she can finally kill him?"

Chapter 5

He felt as if this entire place was bad touching him. Huck sat across a thick plexiglass table from Rachel Raprenzi as some tech fiddled with the microphone attached to the top of Huck's black T-shirt. He still wore his faded jeans.

"Can we do his makeup and hair?" the guy asked.

"Hell no," he answered before Rachel could.

She smiled, her eyes sparkling, excitement vibrating from her. "What do you think of the new studio?"

He wished it were anywhere but in the building where he worked. He looked around at the hardwood floor and wide-screen behind them with the words *The Killing Hour* scrolling by. "It looks like a newsroom."

"That's what we were going for." She placed her hands on the thick plexiglass. "We want the set to be more contemporary than most newsrooms but with a podcast feel. I'm excited that you're one of our first interviews here in the studio. We just got it all set up."

"Great," Huck said, his skin itching.

She leaned toward him. "I'm surprised you called me. I feel like you've avoided me since I came to town."

Of course he'd avoided her. They'd been engaged, and she had torn apart his personal life for a story. One of his cases—a kid—had been drowned in a river, and he'd spiraled into depression after that. Oh, he'd caught the killer, but a dead kid would always weigh on his conscience. That case had catapulted her into a much better career and him to the middle of a mountain with his dog.

Looking at her, he couldn't remember why they'd ever become engaged. Yeah, she was beautiful with her blond hair and sparkling eyes and fine bone structure, but there was nothing inside her other than ambition. Laurel Snow was ambitious as well, yet she would never use another person the way Rachel would. While Laurel could appear factual and possibly cold, she was anything but.

"Are you ready?" Rachel asked.

"I am." At least as ready as he'd ever be.

Her gaze flicked to his dark T-shirt. "You could have dressed up or worn your uniform."

"I'm in the middle of a case, Rachel," he said. "Sorry, it's not the optics you wanted." Perhaps he should have worn his uniform. He glanced back at his jacket hanging over the chair. "I can put on the Fish and Wildlife jacket, if that would help?"

Her gaze narrowed. "Why are you being so agreeable?"

"Because we need your assistance," he said smoothly.

She preened. "Oh, I like that." He'd figured she would, which was why he'd said it. "Yeah, put on the jacket."

"All right." He reached for his jacket and pulled it on, zipping up. The black rainproof coat had a Washington

State Fish and Wildlife Police patch on his left arm and a clear embroidered badge with a star over his left breast.

"Perfect," she said.

The tech guy moved in again and tugged the microphone off Huck's shirt to secure on the collar of the coat. "Let me at least do his hair."

Huck looked up. "You touch my hair, and I'll break your hand."

At least six feet tall with blond hair and impressive biceps, the guy grinned. "All right. I could have made you famous—or at least gotten you a date for the night." He sauntered away toward the control room.

Rachel stared at Huck. "Speaking of which, do you have a date tonight?"

He glanced at his watch. "We need to get going on this, or I'll call another podcast or channel or whatever."

"Fine." She nodded at the control room. They counted down, and then the red light above the door flickered to life. "Good evening. This is Rachel Raprenzi from *The Killing Hour*," she said. "Today we have Washington State Fish and Wildlife Captain Huck Rivers in our studio with us. Thank you for meeting with me," she said, a natural in front of the camera.

"You bet," Huck answered, urgency rushing through him. Time was way too short on this one. "We actually need the public's help."

Rachel smiled. "Yes. It's my understanding that the Witch Creek serial killer, Jason Abbott, escaped from police custody last night."

"Yes," Huck said. "Apparently, Mr. Abbott faked a suicide attempt and ended up in the hospital where he was able to effectuate an escape. We need the public's help in tracking him down before he hurts anybody." A picture of Jason Abbott came up on the wide screen between the two of them.

"How did he escape?" Rachel asked.

"Apparently, he overcame a Genesis Valley police officer, knocked him out, and put him in the hospital bed."

Rachel's gaze sharpened. "You're telling me that Jason Abbott just walked out of the hospital while in police custody?"

"Affirmative," Huck said, a lump of coal settling in his gut.

She looked away and then back as if uncomfortable. "My sources tell me that FBI agent Laurel Snow was also present. How did a serial killer overcome a trained FBI agent?"

Huck lowered his chin. "Jason Abbott is a killer who took two trained public servants by surprise."

"Whose fault was that?"

"We're not concerned with fault," Huck said. They needed to get a killer back behind bars. Now. "We're focused on finding this prisoner and getting him off the streets before anybody else is hurt. To which end, we're hoping the public will report anything they see. There's a number at the bottom of the screen you can call. We have a 24-hour hotline."

Rachel shook her head. "This is the man who was arrested for murder by strangulation and cutting off his victims' hands, correct?"

"Yes."

"Yet there was only one police officer guarding him? Was this the state police, Captain Rivers?"

Oh, he didn't like this direction. He needed the local

police force to work with him, but confirming the facts would be easy for Rachel to do, so he had to give her the truth. "No. It was the Genesis Valley Police."

Rachel tsked her tongue. "Why in the world would the local police be guarding such a dangerous individual? Shouldn't the FBI have had him in federal custody?"

Awareness clicked down Huck's spine. So that was going to be her angle. "Mr. Abbott was held in the local jail awaiting trial. It's a common procedure in Washington State."

"Yet, is it?" Rachel flicked her hand toward the photo of Jason Abbott on the screen. "Was this incredibly dangerous person kept local just so FBI agent Laurel Snow could gain access to him? I have visitor logs to show that both she and you have visited Abbott in jail several times."

"We have questioned him," Huck said. "It didn't matter where he was kept—we would have interviewed him any chance we got in order to gain justice for his victims. Surely you understand that, Rachel?"

She blinked twice in apparent surprise that he'd used her first name. "Of course I understand that, Captain," she returned. "Yet I find the custody arrangement odd and apparently a truly atrocious plan. Whose idea was keeping Jason Abbott in the local jail? Was it the FBI's?"

"I truly don't remember. All involved agencies agreed that Abbott would be kept at the Genesis city jail until trial."

"But he has escaped." She shook her head. "Sometimes I think the FBI just doesn't do its job. You're a state police officer, correct?"

He looked for the trap but couldn't quite nail it down.

How had he ever trusted this woman? "Yes. Fish and Wildlife officers are fully commissioned Washington State Police officers."

"Did you insist that Abbott be put in a more secure facility?"

"Abbott didn't escape the facility. He escaped the hospital."

"Which truly seems like a bad idea, don't you think? I mean, looking back? Tell me, Captain Rivers, are you still in a personal relationship with FBI agent Laurel Snow?"

Huck fell back on training and kept his face expressionless. Aha. So that was where she'd decided to pounce. "I don't believe my personal life is any of your concern, Ms. Raprenzi."

"It might be the public's concern," Rachel said, her smile reminding him of a stalking fox. "If that personal relationship led to the escape of one of the most dangerous serial killers ever found in Washington State. Were your decisions colored by your relationship?"

"I don't see how they could be," he said. "But I have to ask you, is this attack colored by yours?"

She reared back. "Excuse me?"

He peered at the camera. "I'm sure everybody knows that you and I were engaged at one point. Is this attack on Agent Snow one based on jealousy?" He lacked media training, but he knew people, and he knew how to get his point across.

"Of course not," Rachel said.

Huck smiled, putting every ounce of charm he'd ever had into it. Hopefully his expression would read as sincere and confident. "Well, good then. We agree that nobody is motivated by personal relationships in this matter, and we all agree that we'd very much like to put alleged serial killer Jason Abbott back into custody for his trial."

Rachel sat back. "Of course we do. *The Killing Hour* is delighted to provide this public service to the entire area of Genesis Valley. So I have to ask you, Captain, word is just coming through that a dead body was found at the base of Snowblood Peak near Iceberg River, correct?"

"That's correct," Huck said. Damn it. He hadn't known the media had gotten hold of the story yet.

Rachel's face fell into perfect lines of concern. "Was the victim a woman?"

"Yes, but she has not been identified yet," Huck said. "So that's all I can share at this time." The more he thought about it, the more the idea that the victim was his mother seemed farfetched. He had overreacted upon seeing the body, and he wished he had kept his damn mouth shut. All he needed was for Rachel to hear about his statement at the scene.

"Don't you find it a terrible coincidence that serial killer, I mean *alleged* serial killer, Jason Abbott, escapes a hospital and then a woman is murdered the same night?"

That would probably be the headline in the online edition come morning. "We actually don't know time of death," Huck said. "She could have been murdered before Abbott escaped."

Now disbelief filtered perfectly across Rachel's features. How did she do that? And how the hell had he fallen for it so long ago? "Wouldn't that just be a terrible coincidence?" she whispered.

"I can't comment on the body that was found," he said. "We don't have enough details."

"How was she killed?" Rachel persisted in asking.

He kept her gaze and avoided looking at the camera as he gave the truth. "I don't know."

"Did you view the scene?"

That scene had planted itself in his brain. "I did, and I still don't know the cause of death."

"Were her hands still attached to her body?" Rachel asked slyly.

Huck exhaled slowly. "Yes, her hands were attached, and I saw no signs of strangulation, which, as you know, was Jason Abbott's MO." Of course, strangulation and drowning both involved loss of breath until death resulted.

"Are you telling me there might be two killers out there?"

"I'm not telling you anything other than we found a body. We don't even know if there was foul play. There hasn't been an autopsy, so let's not speculate." He focused on the camera. "For now, I need everybody on alert, watching for Jason Abbott. Please call the number at the bottom of your screen even if you just suspect something. We need the public's help."

"All right," Rachel said. "We have to go to our sponsors now."

The red light above the door blinked off. Huck yanked the microphone off his jacket and tossed it onto the table.

"Thanks for your help, Rachel." He pushed his chair back.

"You really love her, don't you?"

Huck paused and then stood. "I don't know what you're talking about. I'm not discussing my personal life with you."

"Then how about you and I go for a drink to celebrate old times?" She leaned forward, revealing a nice amount of cleavage beneath her pink top. The sparkly and somehow professional material pared nicely with her black pencil skirt and high-heeled black pumps. "What do you say?"

"I say no," he said. "Thanks again for helping us with this case. The sooner we get Abbott back into custody, the better for everyone." He strode toward the door and paused, turning to look back. "Abbott's type is professional women with higher educational degrees, which you have. Be careful, Rachel. By recording this and going live with it, you'll definitely be brought to his attention."

Rachel smoothed her blond hair back from her face. "Huck, I didn't think you still cared."

He didn't. "I want every woman to be safe, and this interview will put you front and center." Well, behind Laurel Snow, Melissa Cutting, and most likely Dr. Abigail Caine. All three were better educated than Rachel, but there was no doubt Huck had just put a target on the reporter's back. "Be careful and watch your movements. If you feel like you're in trouble, call the police. My agency and the FBI are stretched pretty thin right now, but the Genesis Valley police force should be able to provide you with protection."

Rachel's chin lifted. "You mean the police force that just let Jason Abbott escape?"

"I imagine they're on much higher alert now," Huck said dryly. "But yeah, call them if you feel you're in danger."

She sat back and crossed her legs, hitching the pencil skirt up. "Now, Huck, we both know if I'm in danger, I'm going to call you. Right?"

He'd stopped answering her calls long ago, but as he glanced at the face of Jason Abbott still on the screen, he had to admit he had just put Rachel in danger.

If she called, he'd help her.

By the smile on her face, she knew it.

Chapter 6

Laurel pushed away the now-scraped-clean plate of her mom's pot roast dinner and patted her stomach. The cat she'd rescued last month, Fred Lacassagne, slept on her foot. "I ate too much."

Her mom chuckled, appearing at ease at the country-style kitchen table, one leg tucked beneath the other and her posture perfect. "You probably ate just the right amount. Although, you look tired."

"I am." Laurel stretched her neck. "It was a long day." She couldn't believe they'd found the body just that morning.

"I'm glad you came home tonight."

Laurel found peace in the quiet kitchen. "I haven't seen you for a few days and thought I should check in. Before I forget, the new huckleberry-rhubarb tea is my favorite so far."

"Nice to know." Deidre stood and reached for a notepad from the counter to scrawl notations across it. "What did you like best about that blend?"

"The concoction tasted like huckleberries and rhubarb pie while soothing my stomach."

Deidre stretched into a casual yoga pose. "Yes, there's some peppermint in there." She looked healthy with her trim physique, a clip holding her chin-length blond hair away from her face. She'd practiced yoga as long as Laurel could remember and even wore a yoga outfit most of the time. "I'm not sure about the in-person store, though."

Laurel shrugged. "Why don't you commit to a six-month experiment, and if you don't enjoy yourself, we can either hirc somebody else to manage the store or cut the lease short. The documents I drafted protect you either way."

"Of course they do." Deidre retook her seat. "How is Huck?" It was nice that her mother was finally warming toward Huck. She'd never been a fan of men in general, and Laurel couldn't blame her.

"He's doing well. He had to give an interview to a local podcast, so I'm sure he's in a grouchy mood." Which was one of the reasons she'd decided to stay the night at her mother's home.

Deidre speared a carrot from her plate. "He's not much in favor of the media, is he? Although, I don't blame him."

"Neither do I," Laurel said. "I'll call him later to see how the interview went."

"So"—Deidre cleared her throat—"have you two announced the pregnancy yet?"

Laurel took a sip of her sparkling water. "No. We'll wait until the second trimester. I'm not ready to share the news with anyone else yet."

Her mother studied her. "What's wrong?"

"Nothing is wrong," Laurel said, and then quickly

decided to be truthful. "I don't think I can be the mother that you are." There, she'd finally said the words.

Deidre shocked her by laughing. "Of course, you won't be the mother I am. You'll be the mother you are. You can't compare yourself to anybody else, Laurel. I believe you learned that a very long time ago."

The truth in that statement caught Laurel. "Yes, but children require affection and fun and goofiness and love. Everything I do comes from the brain, not the heart."

Deidre tilted her head. "So? Maybe your kid will be the same."

Laurel took another drink. "What if I'm more like Abigail than like you?" She wasn't one to express fears because there was no logic in doing so. Yet this one would not leave her alone.

Deidre slapped a palm on the weathered table. "That's one of the most ridiculous things I've ever heard. Abigail is a crazy psychopath, and you are a sweetheart, as am I." She grinned. "This baby will get the best of all of us, including Huck, who seems like a fairly sentimental guy." Not many people in town would consider Huck to be anywhere near sentimental, but Deidre saw things in people that Laurel never did.

"He has become rather overprotective. I imagine he'll be so with his child as well."

"I imagine so," Deidre said dryly. "I'm rather surprised he hasn't popped the question."

Laurel blinked. "Why would he do that?"

Deidre stared at her for a moment. "Because you're having a baby together. He seems like a rather old-fashioned guy. Isn't that what normally happens?"

Laurel gently nudged Fred off her foot, stood, and

took her plate to the sink. "I have no idea." She cared about the captain, but she'd never envisioned herself being married—or having a child for that matter. Yet here she stood, pregnant.

Her mom brought over her own plate and slipped an arm around Laurel's waist. "I didn't say that to cause you concern. The idea just popped into my head."

"I know." Laurel leaned into her mom.

"Plus, look at the bright side," Deidre said. "Hopefully, the baby will get Huck's height or even mine. I'm not sure why you're so short."

Laurel elbowed her, understanding intellectually that her mom was trying to lighten the mood. "I'm not short." Yet every available metric showed her to be shorter than the average woman. Such a silly and inconsequential thing should not bother her to the degree that it did. "I need to buy more heels."

Her mom chuckled. "Good one."

Laurel took a deep breath, noting her mother's clear eyes and strong posture. Now was a good time to discuss a difficult topic. "How are you doing now that Zeke Caine is back in town?" The pastor had raped Deidre, and it couldn't be easy knowing he was close. That he was Laurel's father.

Deidre's chin lowered. "I'm fine. Mostly because my daughter, the brilliant FBI agent, is going to discover one of his more recent crimes and put him away."

That was absolutely Laurel's plan. The statute of limitations had run out on the crime against her mother, but certainly the bastard had committed other ones. "I am going to do exactly that."

Deidre smiled. "I know. For now, why don't you go get started with your knitting and I'll do the dishes."

"I can do the dishes," Laurel said.

"Go." Deidre gently nudged her.

Laurel happily wandered to the back of the house where they'd set up a knitting room. In college she'd discovered a need for knitted boots and hats for premature babies and so had created a nonprofit organization that now served hospitals all over the country. To relax, she and her mother both knitted, and then sent the results to the warehouse for distribution. She sat in a comfortable recliner chair and reached for light blue yarn to begin a new set of booties. Her phone buzzed, and she pulled it from her back pocket. "Agent Snow."

"Hey, it's Huck. Did you get a good dinner?"

Her stomach felt full. "I had pot roast. You are welcome to come over and have a plate, if you like."

"Thanks," he muttered. "But I'm going to take the dog home. We both need to run for a while." Huck often jogged to keep in shape and stave off stress.

She pursed her lips. "You've been working out a lot lately."

"I need to run off the interview with Rachel," he retorted.

Realization rustled through Laurel's brain. "Oh." She had missed the inference in his words. "Do you believe the interview will be beneficial?"

"I do," he said. "Otherwise, I'd be putting my head through a wall right now. We managed to get Abbott's face on the screen as well as the number for the 24-hour hotline. I'm hopeful somebody will call in a good lead."

"As am I." She pressed the phone's speaker button

and began to knit. "My mother seems to think that the baby will inherit the good parts of all of us. What do you think?"

"I'm hoping the kid has my height," Huck returned easily.

Laurel snorted. "As am I, but you know we have no control over which chromosomes we pass on to offspring." Or was he trying to ease her mind? He might have been joking, but she really did want the child to have his height.

"I hope he or she has your eyes."

Laurel sat back, her fingers moving quickly. "I don't know if I do. People view me as an oddity, and it took me awhile to become accustomed to it. You have pretty eyes, Huck. They're more than brown, kind of amber. Maybe the baby should have your eyes."

"I don't think we get to choose. Remember?" Huck laughed. "It sounds like you and your mother had a nice talk."

"We did, but I still hold concerns that I lack the appropriate skills to be a good mother."

Huck scoffed. "As long as you stick around, you're better than the mother I got."

Was there pain in his voice? She couldn't tell. "I don't know why your mother left, but I imagine she regretted that decision her entire life."

"I don't know." Huck sighed. "Damn it."

Her fingers slowed. "What?"

"I have a car in front of me weaving all over the place. I think someone's been drinking." The sound of a siren echoed over the line as he no doubt flicked his on. "I have to go, Laurel. I'll give you a call tomorrow."

"Have a good night, Huck."

The sound of the gear shift being locked into Park clunked through the line. "You, too, and we'll worry about all of this later."

"I like that plan. Good night." She continued to knit, trying to banish her erratic concerns. Hopefully Huck would call in backup. Should she have suggested it?

The Cadillac in front of Huck had swerved over to the side and hit a dirty snowbank. He called in for backup from the county, finishing with, "I'm going to need somebody else to bring the driver in for processing. I have my truck with the dog in the back and am unable to transport." He clicked off just as a car rolled to a stop behind him. His hand on his weapon, he stretched out of the vehicle, turning.

"Hey, Huck, it's just me," Rachel Raprenzi called out, stepping out of her dark blue compact behind him.

"Get back in the vehicle," he said, using his best cop voice. "Now."

She faltered and then did as he said. Great, now the reporter was following him? He'd already called in the license number of the vehicle in front of him, and he walked toward the passenger door, angling his head to make sure there wasn't anybody in the back seat. He had to knock on the front door window. It slowly rolled down.

"What's wrong, Officer?" a female voice slurred.

He pointed his flashlight inside the vehicle to see the mayor's wife in the front seat, her eyes bloodshot and the smell of alcohol pouring from her. Just wonderful.

This was all he needed. "Do you know why I pulled you over?"

"I do not." She hiccupped. "I do know that you're messing with the wrong person, so I suggest you get back in your truck." She narrowed her gaze. "I know you, don't I?"

"Captain Huck Rivers," he said. "License and registration, please."

She snorted. "You know who I am. I'm Teri Bearing, the mayor's wife."

"Yes, I remember." Huck had interviewed her for an earlier case. At the time, she had seemed like a nice person. "Mrs. Bearing, have you been drinking tonight?"

"No," she said.

Right. She smelled as if she'd crashed into a liquor store. "License and registration, please."

"I am not going to put up with this indignity," she snapped. "Now get the hell away from my car."

He held on to his patience with both hands. "Mrs. Bearing, I need you to give me your license and your registration, and we'll go from there. All right?"

"No." She started to roll her window up.

He put a hand on top of the car. "If you don't give me those documents, I'm going to have to arrest you. Now, it's a cold night and I don't want to ask you to get out of the car quite yet, so how about you hand those over?"

"No." She opened her door suddenly, slamming the metal into his legs. He stepped back, anger whipping through him. Yet he kept his hands loose. She jumped out of the car, slid on the ice, and grabbed her door. "Now you listen to me. My husband runs this town. I'm not going to take this bullshit from you."

Dressed in a flashy white sweater and tight leather pants, her red-bottomed boots were causing her problems on the ice.

A light flashed to his right, and he noted Rachel approaching with the camera in her phone lit up. He gave her a look. "Get back in your vehicle. I'm not going to tell you again. I'll arrest you as well."

The reporter backed away.

Police lights swirled through the darkness as a county patrol officer rolled onto the scene. His hand on his weapon, the man stepped out of his vehicle. "We have a problem here?"

Huck nodded. "Yes. The driver was maneuvering erratically, and she refuses to hand over a license or her registration."

Mrs. Bearing punched him in the shoulder. "You're not even a real cop. You're Fish and Wildlife."

"Actually, ma'am, we are fully commissioned police officers," he said.

She glared at the other officer. "Then why'd you call for backup?"

"So somebody could take you in," Huck retorted. He didn't want her in the back of his truck with the dog, so it had been necessary.

The county cop hitched up his belt. "Ma'am, can we please have your license and registration?"

"Who are you?" she hissed.

"I am Deputy John McDonald from Tempest County," the guy said smoothly.

Huck nodded. "Huck Rivers."

"Pleasure," the deputy returned. "Ma'am, have you been drinking tonight? I smell alcohol."

Teri Bearing glared at him. "I'm the wife of the mayor here in Genesis Valley. I have not been drinking, which I just told this Fish and Wildlife officer. This is harassment, and I will not stand for it." She lifted a hand.

"Ma'am, if you hit me again, I'm going to arrest you for battery," Huck said, wanting nothing more than to get home.

She dropped her hand. "This is unreal. This will not be tolerated."

"All right, ma'am," the deputy said. "Hand over your license and registration."

"Fine." She leaned back into the car, grabbed the documents, and slapped them at the deputy. "I'll deal with you, not the Fish and Wildlife moron."

Huck looked at the sheriff's deputy, who shrugged. "Fine. I'll handle the rest of this if you want to be going."

"I really do," Huck said. "Are you sure you've got this?"

"Yes. We're going to run through a field sobriety test. And then, ma'am, I'm going to ask you to take a breathalyzer."

She stomped her foot. "I will not."

Huck paused. "I'll just stand over there by my rig." He seemed to agitate the woman for some reason, but he wasn't leaving the other officer without backup.

"Good plan," McDonald said.

Mrs. Bearing failed the field sobriety test and then the breathalyzer, so Deputy McDonald handcuffed her and led her to his car.

Huck leaned against his truck. "I'll call for a tow."

"Thanks," McDonald said. "I'll get her processed. I'm sure she'll be out in no time, though." He sounded sympathetic.

Huck turned to open his door.

"That was fun," Rachel said, popping up from the rear of his vehicle, her phone safely out of the way.

"I told you to get back in your vehicle."

She rocked back on her heels, smiling wildly. "They're gone now. I don't have to."

"Please tell me you didn't record that entire situation."

Her laugh sounded gleeful. "Of course, I recorded the unfortunate situation with the mayor's wife. Are you kidding me? This is going to make great copy. I'm going live with it in about an hour. Hopefully we can catch the mayor bailing his wife out."

Huck jumped into his truck. Just great.

Chapter 7

Midmorning, Laurel turned off *The Killing Hour*, which had shown Huck pulling over an obviously intoxicated Teri Bearing the night before. While politics had never interested Laurel, she could at least recognize a potential problem when one arose. Huck had performed his job, but the mayor was known to be a bulldog when it came to his family.

The office was too quiet without Walter. When had she begun to depend on him so much? She'd built an efficient team, and perhaps she didn't need to request additional agents. Her unit was able to cover every aspect of a case, and she could always rely on Fish and Wildlife, the Seattle FBI office, or even the local sheriff's office if necessary.

Perhaps she didn't want more people in her life.

Her phone buzzed, and she clicked a button. "Agent Snow."

"Hi," Abigail Caine said cheerfully. "How is my *little* sister?" The way she said it made Laurel think she was talking more about height than age. But that could be her own insecurities talking.

"Where's Jason Abbott, and when can you come in for an interview?" Laurel asked evenly. If anybody had a clue as to Abbott's whereabouts, it was the woman who'd suggested he escape.

Abigail sighed. "I don't know where he is right now, but I can assure you I know where he was an hour ago."

Laurel sat up straighter. "Excuse me?"

"The idiot walked right up to my door this morning and tried to break in. My alarm went off, and the security folks for my subdivision just notified me. I was teaching a class here at the school and didn't have my phone with me." Armed with several advanced degrees, Abigail taught classes at the Northern Washington Technical Institute.

What had been Jason's plan? To break in and wait for Abigail to return home? "Where is Jason now?" Laurel asked.

"No clue. My security camera caught him trying to break into my house, and I'm having the security people forward the information to you." Abigail's tone remained calm. Nearly bored. "The guy thought he'd break in and just wait for me to get home? Moron. Thinks he's smarter than my alarm system. He took off into the forest by my house, and the guys couldn't find him. They did notify the local police, who are investigating."

Laurel's desk phone buzzed. "Hold on for a moment." She answered. "Hi, Kate."

"Hi. Sheriff York is on the phone," Kate said.

Laurel sighed. "Abigail, I have to go. For now, you comprehend that Jason Abbott blames you for his lot in life and wants to kill you."

"I'm well aware," Abigail drawled. "I'm requesting FBI protection."

"My current resources allow for me to secure you in a safe house, but I'm unable to provide protection in any other scenario. We have a scarcity of agents." In fact, she'd love to squire Abigail safely away from her right now.

Abigail sighed. "I don't want to put my life on hold, and I guess my agent Norrs can protect me well enough."

Laurel paused in reaching for her other phone. "Why are you still dating Norrs?" In her experience, Abigail discarded men after she had finished using them. So she still must have a use for the FBI agent.

"Wayne is phenomenal in bed. We're quite the item now, you know."

A headache loomed at the base of Laurel's neck. So Abigail had more machinations in store for the FBI and Laurel's team. "Say hi to him and come in for an interview before I have you picked up by officers." She clicked off and answered the other phone. "Agent Snow."

"Hi. It's Sheriff York. Jason Abbott tried to break into Dr. Caine's home an hour ago."

"I've heard. Is there any chance you traced his movements?"

York coughed. "No."

Wonderful.

After a full day of searching fruitlessly for Jason Abbott, Laurel wished she'd gone on vacation with Walter. He'd texted twice with pictures of Ena drinking fruity cocktails by the beach. She was happy for him. Also a little envious.

With snow once again falling lazily outside in the darkness, Laurel sat on Huck's sofa and stared at the crackling fire. They'd picked up deli sandwiches on the way to his cabin after work. She blew on her tea, both hands around the mug, as Huck shoveled the driveway outside in the snow.

The puzzle of why Abigail would want Jason Abbott free led to one conclusion. She wanted to kill him.

Why?

What did he still know about Abigail that he hadn't already shared with Laurel and Huck? Or even with his attorney in an attempt to gain him favor with the court?

Her phone buzzed, and she jolted before grasping it. "Agent Snow."

"Hi, Laurel. It's Pedro. I'm sorry it has taken me so long to return your call. There was a terrible nightclub fire that has us all working overtime."

"Dr. Ortega. Thank you for returning my phone call. I'm sorry the nightclub fire took so many lives." She'd dealt with burned bodies before, and the smell never quite left. "I wanted to check on the victim from Iceberg River."

He coughed. "Sorry to cough at you. We're all fighting something here. I hope to get to your victim tomorrow or the next day, and I did receive the DNA sample from Captain Rivers."

Anticipation licked through her. "And?"

"It's in line along with the rest of the samples. I hope my lab is able to get to it soon." He came across muffled for a moment. "I apologize, but I need to get back to work. We'll talk soon."

"Of course. Thank you." She clicked off the line. So much for gleaning answers for either case. The fire shifted its color but failed to provide clarity. She dozed off until Huck and Aeneas entered the one-bedroom cabin, both shaking off snow.

She forced herself to awaken. "It appears to be snowing even harder than earlier." The local meteorologists had been largely mistaken about the weather that week.

"Yeah." Huck removed his boots and hung up his heavy jacket as Aeneas ran into the kitchen and started eating out of his dog bowl.

Huck padded over in his worn white socks with a hole in the right one. He sat next to her on the sofa and extended his jean-clad legs, crossing his ankles on the sofa table and pushing magazines out of his way. "What a night."

She leaned into him, careful of her tea. "Heavier snowfall is expected?"

"Looks like it. Windy night, too."

Laurel stared into the flames, her mind unsettled.

He tugged on her hair. "What's going on in that big brain?"

"My brain is of normal size," she said quietly. "I'm attempting to uncover Abigail's motivations. Why she'd want Jason Abbott out of prison."

"Huh. Sounds like a waste of time to me. Her motivations lack logic, and you're all logic."

She jerked and then settled. "I see."

"Hey." He turned his head to study her. "I said something wrong. What was it?"

How did he do that? She wasn't even looking at him. "The logic. That's not how you raise a baby. They need love. Hearts and kisses and whimsy."

His dark eyebrows rose, but he remained silent for several beats. "The heart is an organ, correct?"

She frowned. "Of course it is."

"Then how can love, an actual emotion, truly come from an organ in the middle of our chests?" He settled more comfortably against the sofa, still holding her close.

"I don't know."

He chuckled. "That's a statement I don't hear from you very often. If love or emotion doesn't come from the middle of our chests, why can't it come from our brains? There's a lot about the brain that we don't understand, right?"

"That's true," she whispered.

"So maybe those big thoughts you have are love. The way *you* love."

She blinked. That made sense.

"Perhaps you use more of your brain than others, or maybe your brain is just more efficient. Either way, doesn't that mean you'll be able to love better than most people?" He wriggled his toes toward the roaring fire, no doubt warming them. "So give yourself a break and stop worrying about it. You will love this baby exactly as he or she needs to be loved, and you're going to be a great mom. I promise."

There was no actual way he could make that promise, yet somehow his statement did make her feel better. "You're eminently likeable," she murmured.

"Yeah?" He grasped her waist and lifted her, easily planting her on his lap.

His casual strength stopped her breath in her lungs. Her body was reacting naturally to an obvious overture from a strong and capable male, yet he affected her heart, too. That little organ that shouldn't feel anything. She leaned in and kissed him, enjoying the way his fingers flexed on her hips. "I like your strength, as well."

He took over the kiss, his lips firm and his tongue seeking. Smooth movements had her shirt and bra flying across the room, and she chuckled.

Palming her breasts, he nipped along her neck, biting her earlobe. "Are you sure this is okay?"

She ran both of her hands through his thick hair, pulling so she could give him a little bite. The man probably needed sleep, but he was questioning her well-being. "Please clarify your question."

He leaned back, both hands on her breasts, his brown eyes liquid soft. "You and me. Right now with the baby and how you're feeling."

She caressed the sides of his neck, filling her palms with the strong cords. "I don't understand. We're already pregnant."

"Yeah, but . . . You haven't been feeling well. Are you up to this?"

"You mean sex?"

He nodded, slightly tweaking her nipples.

Liquid fire rushed down to her core, and she pressed against him. "I'm perfectly healthy, Huck. Surely you took anatomy or biology in junior high?" She wanted to laugh, but his expression remained so serious, she was afraid she might hurt his feelings.

"Yes, Agent Snow," he said with some exasperation. "I even passed both the biology and anatomy classes. But this is the first baby I've ever been responsible for, you haven't been feeling well, and she's inside you, so I figure I should at least ask."

Sometimes the grumpy captain was just too sweet to understand. "She?"

He shrugged. "Yeah. Why not?"

There was no way to know the sex of the child. "I promise that I am more than up to a bout of sex with you." The idea that he was so concerned when he obviously knew there was no need sent her desire even higher. Everything was different with Huck. She'd never realized that emotions, the real kind, could cause arousal. The more familiar she became with him, the more she started to trust him, the more she wanted him. Whatever they had went beyond the physical, and that was new to her.

"What are you thinking?" He unbuttoned her pants.

She reached for the hem of his shirt and dragged the heavy material over his head. "Just that you're sexy when you're all protective."

He leaned in and licked her nipple, causing her body to tremble. "That's probably a good thing, because my nature, according to you, is protective."

In a nutshell. She'd never required protection from a man, but this one wasn't giving her a choice. It was an interesting conundrum considering their chosen professions.

He slid his hand inside her pants and found her, entering her with two fingers.

She gasped and leaned against him as need coursed through her.

"There we go," he murmured, wrapping one arm

around her waist and standing. "Let's get you out of your head." He skirted the sofa table and strode into the lone bedroom, leaving the crackling fire behind them.

"You're the only person in the entire world who's managed that feat," she said as he laid her down and tugged her slacks off.

He grinned, unzipping his jeans and shoving them to the floor before removing his socks. "I like that."

She'd figured he would. Everyone wanted to feel special. Huck Rivers actually was unique. She reached for him, and he dropped to his knees, his mouth finding her sex.

He was also exceptionally good at this.

She closed her eyes as he quickly drove her up with his talented mouth and tongue, and she cried out his name as the orgasm roared through her. Softening, she came down, mumbling about true talent. Her brain remained fuzzy.

He levered himself over her and slowly entered her, his gaze intense.

She dug her nails into his rigid triceps, widening her legs. "Everything is perfect, Huck," she whispered, somehow knowing he needed reassurance. She couldn't read people, but she was beginning to understand his needs. Maybe it was her brain or perhaps her heart, but she wanted to truly know him. To let him completely understand her.

He entered her fully and then kissed her, going deep. "You're good?"

"I feel wonderful," she said honestly, wrapping her legs around his waist. They barely reached, but if she wiggled, she could link her ankles together.

He groaned and pulled out, only to push back in. Gingerly. Almost hesitantly.

She clapped both hands on the sides of his rugged face and yanked him in for a hard kiss. At the end, she nipped his bottom lip.

His eyes sparked, and she watched, entranced.

Then he pulled out again and shoved back in, setting up a hard hammering that beat the headboard against the wall. Desire ripped through her as hormones clashed and nerves ignited, forcing her to close her eyes and hold on to his arms. Pleasure whipped through her, zinging through every erogenous zone.

He changed the angle of his thrusts, and she detonated. The orgasm rolled wave after wave through her, and she rode them, letting vivid colors fill her mind. He continued to pound, finally grinding against her and shuddering with what felt like a powerful climax.

Still inside her, he lifted his head, his sleepy eyes studying her. "You still good?"

She grinned, her body satiated. "Yes. For now. We're just getting started, correct?"

His lips touched hers as he spoke. "Definitely."

They made love again and then drifted off to sleep only to awaken once more with the captain raring to go. That orgasm had her holding her breath, and then she dropped into a deep sleep.

The buzzing of a phone pulled her groggily from a REM cycle in which she was searching for river rocks to decorate a patio. "Agent Snow," she yawned into the phone.

"It's Nester," the agent said, his voice raised. "My

sister was hit by a truck jogging this morning in Seattle. I have to go. I have to."

She sat up, pushing her hair out of her face. "Of course." Calculating the workload without Walter and Nester, she forced herself from the warm bed, her feet landing on the chilly wooden floor. "Go to Seattle."

Huck switched on a light, his eyebrows raised.

Nester gulped, and the sound of a vehicle starting came over the line. "I can work remotely. I promise I will."

"I know." She looked out at the dawn barely breaking through the clouds and shivered. Jason Abbott hunted women even now, and she'd find him on her own if necessary.

It felt as if fate were on his side.

Chapter 8

Morning brought more freezing rain with it. Dr. Abigail Caine turned off the heater in her vehicle as she glanced at the Glock 17 sitting beside her on the passenger seat. She'd purchased the weapon the day before at a garage sale in a rural city even smaller than Genesis Valley. While she owned a couple of legally purchased weapons, she found that buying one or two untraceable guns was always a good thing.

She increased the volume of her radio as she watched the rather quiet Staggers Ice Creamery building. Laurel currently worked like a good little public servant safely in her office, so Abigail pulled out of the parking area and drove away down Jagged Rock Road and through the town of Genesis Valley. That insipid reporter, Rachel Raprenzi, came on the radio with *The Killing Hour*, detailing once again the arrest of the mayor's wife. Abigail smiled and turned the volume up even more.

She'd worked on an annual fundraiser with Teri Bearing, and the woman was truly a pain in the ass. She always had a clipboard, check marks, and no problem letting everybody else do the work. The woman had also been a little too nosy about Abigail's life.

The idea of her being handcuffed and fingerprinted was a delight. The woman drank like a fish. Stupid people bothered Abigail. Her own IQ blew off the charts and always made her the most intelligent person in any room. However, Laurel remained a question mark. Was it possible that her half sister had a higher IQ? Abigail chuckled. Of course not. Her phone dinged, and she pressed the button on the dash. "Dr. Caine."

"Dr. Caine, this is Dr. Rudolph from Northern Washington Technical Institute. Where you work."

She rolled her eyes and tapped her red-painted nails on the steering wheel. "What can I do for you, Richard?"

"I'm wondering why you canceled your Computational Neuroscience class this morning," he snarled. "In addition, I believe you have a cognitive science upper division class this afternoon."

She drove out of the city hub toward unincorporated land, noting the snow-laden branches of the pine trees around her. When would winter end? "I have my neuroscience students working on projects." She fully intended to teach her afternoon class in person on campus. "I don't believe I asked for your input on my syllabi or schedule."

He cleared his throat. "May I remind you that I'm your boss?"

She chuckled. "May I remind you that you had an affair with a seventeen-year-old coed two years ago?"

Heavy silence hung over the line. "If you think I'll allow you to blackmail me any longer—"

"Stop it, Richard." She did not have time for his

nonsense. "Just think of the headlines and piss off." She ended the call. As the best teacher at the institute, her students often reached glorious careers. Her neuroscience students actually currently worked on several important projects, and she'd given them the day to do so.

Of course, protecting Laurel came above all else.

Abigail turned down another snowy winter road. Laurel didn't appreciate the effort Abigail expended, but someday she would. The woman was a fascination. They looked similar enough to be twins, although Abigail had at least four inches of height on her sister.

Unfortunately, Huck Rivers kept getting in the way. Someday it would just be Abigail and Laurel touring the world. Thinking of the things she could show her sister delighted her. Of course, Laurel needed to get on board. The baby would help. The baby would be a little genius like them, and Laurel would require Abigail's help.

She pulled down the long drive of the Genesis Valley Community Church, unsurprised to see two vans overloaded with heavy equipment and satellites parked near the front. Their father planned a megachurch, no doubt, so he could make millions. She appreciated his quest for money because with money came power, or at least freedom. Yet, he deserved neither.

She drove halfway down the drive and pulled over to see him emerge from the church and check the vans, shaking hands with the men who stepped out. It was quite unfortunate he hadn't died when she'd repeatedly stabbed him last month. She had had him close to meeting his maker when Laurel had intervened and saved his life. That was one wrong for which Laurel should pay. How could she have saved that bastard?

Abigail shook her head.

As if sensing he was being watched, her father looked up and spotted her. An expression crossed his face that she couldn't quite read. He said something to the men and then walked toward her, wearing a heavy down jacket that no doubt protected his chilly heart from the even colder wind. His bald head had to be freezing, however.

She took great pleasure in the thought and rolled down her window.

He arrived while the men behind him unpacked the many satellite dishes. "Abigail, what are you doing here?"

She smiled. "I'm checking on things. I know what you're up to."

He looked back at the workers. "Yes, I'm going to save souls across this great land of ours."

"Oh, please. You don't care about souls; you care about coffers."

He smiled, and an unwilling chill wandered down her back. "Don't forget I can always suddenly remember who tried to murder me a short time ago."

She waved a hand in the air. "I wouldn't, but you feel free to do what you must."

"I always do." His chin lowered.

She looked away. "I've been keeping an eye on my sister and her friends. What a coincidence it is that Walter Smudgeon and Ena Ilemeto won a two-week trip to the Caribbean."

"Did they?" Zeke asked. "I know the church had a raffle, but I was unaware who won. I don't handle that kind of thing any longer. Pastor John would be the person to talk to, and I believe you have his phone number."

"I surely do," Abigail said. "Yet today, Nester Lewis, Laurel's genius computer guru, rushed off to Seattle. Apparently, a truck barreled into his sister during her morning jog.

Zeke's eyes widened. "That's horrible. I will certainly add her to my prayers."

"You're attempting to isolate Laurel," Abigail said. The idea of Zeke driving to Seattle and running over the computer genius's sister showed impressive dedication. "She won't turn to you even if she's all alone. You need to understand that salient fact."

Zeke wiped rain off his head. "My dear daughter, the imagination you have. I had nothing to do with the raffle, and I certainly haven't been to Seattle to hit anybody with a truck."

She hadn't been keeping a close enough eye on him. "We'll see about that. I'm not a big believer in coincidences."

"Neither am I." Zeke stepped away from her vehicle. "However, like many of my parishioners, I am a big believer in fate."

After a shitty day, darkness without any moon pushed against her home's windows as if trying to get inside. Teri Bearing finished the last drop of inexpensive sparkling blush wine, her head swimming and irritation filling her every pore. Her husband was such a complete asshole. It wasn't her fault she'd gotten pulled over two nights before. It had been the officer's fault. He'd been a complete dick, just wanting to make some point about her, and maybe get his name in the paper.

Pushing away the bottle, she walked over to her wine rack to find it empty. She had stayed at home by herself, hiding away from reporters who'd staked out her front lawn until finally they'd given up and gone away. That was lucky—she couldn't have anyone following her tonight.

That hag, Rachel Raprenzi, had taken delight in streaming *The Killing Hour* with images and actual recordings of the arrest. Rachel had caught Teri actually assaulting that stupid Fish and Wildlife officer.

Her youngest son was staying the night with a friend, and she'd told Saul she had made plans to spend a couple days at a spa in Seattle. He'd stormed out at the news. No doubt he was out playing poker and getting drunk. He had no right to be so angry with her. He'd barely spoken to her since he'd bailed her out. She could not believe this.

It would be a true pleasure making that Fish and Wildlife officer's life a living hell, but that joy would have to wait. Tonight, she needed companionship. Love. Adoration. Maybe some fucking fun in the snow. She'd dressed carefully, showing her best attributes. Her pants were pressed, pink linen and her sweater white cashmere. She wore pearls in her ears and at her throat because she was the mayor's wife, damn it. They'd regret hurting her like this. All of them.

Yanking on her boots and a long wool coat, she grabbed her handbag before hurrying out to her car. She didn't have far to go. Pausing, she darted back inside to grab a knit cap to cover her hair and a scarf to protect the bottom of her face. The reporters had given up, but she didn't want to take any chances.

Muttering about men in general, she ran to her vehicle, backed out of the drive, and hit the mailbox. Damn it. She had told Saul not to put it there.

Grunting, she put the car in Drive and moved forward before backing into the street again. The car slid on the ice. Her head swam, but she took several deep breaths. She was fine and a better driver than any of them.

She slowly made it out of their subdivision and then turned onto the country road. She swerved and corrected, her car sliding across ice.

A vehicle behind her rapidly closed the distance. Morons shouldn't be driving this time of night. Blinding lights filled her mirror, and she blinked. What a jerk. She pushed the mirror out of the way and sped up.

The vehicle behind her sped up as well. She could barely see. She slowed down. Fine, they could just pass her. The driver behind her hit the brakes and slid.

She laughed and increased her speed. If they wanted to play, she'd play. The truck sped up again, and the lights blinded her. Jackass. She hit her brakes.

The vehicle slammed into her. She spun wildly around and came to a pause, rage boiling through her. She opened her door, already screaming at the motherfucker who had dared to hit her.

A blur of motion came from the other vehicle and hit her so fast and so hard, she flew back against her car. The attacker punched her several times, and she shut her eyes, lifting her hands up to protect her face. Pain roared through her head, and her hat fell down her shoulder. The attacker grabbed her hair and slammed her head against the vehicle.

The world went dark as unconsciousness stole her away.

Teri came to with her hands bound behind her back and a blindfold over her eyes. Jerking awake, she tried to move, but she was in some sort of container in a moving vehicle. One bouncing over potholes.

Scrambling to remove the blindfold, she failed and started screaming until her throat hurt. Finally, she gasped. "Let me go. Don't you understand? Do you know who I am?" She gingerly turned onto her side, her knees up to her chest.

The enclosure was too small for much movement. Her fingers, secured behind her back, touched some sort of rigid metal wire. Was she in a box? She moved her head, again trying to dislodge the blindfold, and again failing. The driver breathed evenly in the front seat. She was in the back? "You have to let me go. I won't tell anybody," she whimpered.

No answer.

She pleaded and threatened for a good five minutes until they rolled to a stop. Her heart thundered in her ears. The vehicle remained in idle, and she heard a door open and shut. Then silence. She instinctively knew she was alone.

A door opened, and a rush of cool air burst against her legs. Metal clattered and then strong arms grabbed her hips and yanked her out of the crate. She flew down and fell on hard ice, her hands tied painfully behind her back. She tried to struggle, and but her attacker grabbed her hair, pulling her over rocky, icy ground.

Bruises flared to life along her body, and she flailed, fighting, trying to scream. A rough rag was instantly shoved into her mouth. She tried to spit it out, material lodged down her throat. She started to gag.

The freezing cold bit into her, and her pants tore on the icy ground. Then her attacker released her hair, and she fell, hitting the back of her head, her fingernails digging into the ice at her back. She groaned and tried to roll to her side.

The sound of ice cracking filled the night, and she jerked. What was happening? A person grunted, and more ice cracked, the sound deafening.

She shivered from the brutal cold and tried to kick her legs out, rolling onto her butt and then kicking wildly with her feet. Her boots glanced off the ice, and she tried to crab walk away. Her fingers had gone numb, and her body was following suit. Then rough hands grabbed her shoulders again and pulled her in a different direction.

She fought wildly but couldn't get anywhere.

Her attacker ripped the gag out of her mouth and then tossed her onto her stomach, where she slid down at least a foot over rough ice. Pain pounded through her ribcage. She shook her shoulders wildly, trying to pull her hands free of the ropes. The scent of pine filled her nose. Her body shuddered from the cold.

A hard hand on the back of her head then shoved her down. Glacial water slammed against her face, and she opened her mouth to scream, gulping down ice and freezing cold water. She struggled and tried to spit it out, her body convulsing. That brutal hand pushed her farther down, and she jerked her head up, fighting to breathe, only to have her head hit the underside of the ice.

Pain ripped through her skull.

She swallowed more water, coughing and convulsing, until her limbs became too heavy to move. Her lungs froze. Darkness, when it came this time, felt warm.

Chapter 9

Laurel yawned in the passenger seat of Huck's truck, her muscles aching with fatigue. The call had come in around dawn, a mere two hours after Huck had made it to his cabin after an all-night search and rescue operation following a witness's report that they'd noticed an elderly man wandering out by Orphan's Peak. Huck hadn't found the guy after searching for hours.

As the sun slowly pierced the cold fog, he drove to the site of another body. Her eyes felt scratchy and her feet chilled as she perched in her heated seat while Huck drove the truck. "I'm sorry you didn't find your lost person last night."

Huck shrugged. "The witness could've seen shadows in the trees. We don't have any missing persons reports, so I'm not too concerned. Am tired, though."

She didn't blame him. "Hopefully you can sleep tonight."

"I can only dream." He turned toward the Genesis Valley Community Church, outside the incorporated town. The wooden structure had gorgeous stained-glass windows, several wings, and a freshly painted looming steeple. The structure appeared as if taken from a magazine featuring typical country churches, except with more mass.

"Are you all right?" Huck asked.

"I am." The truth was she would rather turn around and drive in the other direction than face Zeke Caine again. "Considering the condition of this body sounds similar to the Iceberg River victim, we should let Monty take the lead."

"I didn't call Monty in." Huck pulled to a stop near the side of the church. "It's early and cold, and I think he's fighting a bug."

She pulled on her gloves. "He needs to be more careful after those radiation treatments. I wish he would take some time off."

"As do I." Huck opened his door, looking tough and strong in the morning light. "But he's stubborn."

That seemed to be the way of the Fish and Wildlife crew.

Opening her door, she stepped down, noting sounds of activity coming from behind the church. Fields stretched out on either side of them to the tree lines, and she headed to the side of the church that often held tented festivals. She walked toward the frigid-looking river behind the building, noting that the crime scene techs had already erected a tent. She nodded at Officer Tso when he emerged from a stand of trees to her right.

"Hi, Captain Rivers and Agent Snow." Tso made his way through calf-high snow to reach them, his face set in somber lines. "I've been taking pictures of the scene.

They're trying to get any evidence they can from the body and the surrounding area before they flip her over."

"Hi, Officer." She took a deep breath, chilling her lungs as she walked toward the tented area. Silent River flowed behind the church, and beyond, Orphan's Peak loomed over the entire area. Huck had once mentioned that it was difficult to climb, but he'd done so to rescue stranded campers.

She glanced over her shoulder at him. "Is that where you were looking for that elderly person last night?"

Huck jerked his chin toward the other side of the crusted-over river. "We searched on that side near the base of the cliff and farther to the east. We didn't see anything. I certainly didn't hear anything." He frowned. "More importantly, Aeneas didn't alert."

She scrutinized the wide river winding between her and Orphan's Peak. "Would he have alerted if something was happening on this side of the river and while focusing on the search perimeters across the water?"

"I don't know, especially since the wind howled loudly and drowned out most sounds," Huck said as they reached the tent.

The wind increased in force, beating against her face and chilling her skin. Even though she wore gloves, she stuck her hands in her pockets to view the newest body.

The victim lay face down, her body mainly covered by a long, black wool coat that reached brown snow boots. Ice had frozen to her, and she was similarly adhered to the ground as the first victim. Laurel squinted to see better. This person also appeared to be a blond female.

Huck strode toward the river, and Laurel followed, stepping gingerly in the thick snow.

"The ice is cracked open." He dropped to his haunches near the edge. "Just like at the other scene."

Laurel looked over her shoulder at the victim again. Had somebody actually broken the ice of the river, forced her head under the water, and drowned her before dragging her here to freeze to the ground? "This scene is too similar to the first one that any possibility of accidental death for either is statistically improbable, if not impossible. So we proceed now as if we have two homicides, even without official autopsy reports. Can we turn her over now?"

The techs chipped with ice shovels around the body, careful to avoid disturbing any evidence.

"Yeah, we're about ready," the first guy said. "Hold on." He used his shovel as a lever and shifted to the side as a woman with dark brown hair, fully encased in heavy white coveralls, did the same. They gently turned over the corpse.

Ice had frozen all over the woman's face, and blood was crusted around her mouth.

Laurel looked closely but couldn't see an obvious cause of death. "Put a flashlight closer to her face, would you?"

"Sure," the first tech said, gingerly releasing his shovel and reaching for a flashlight in his back pocket. He flicked it toward the woman's face.

Laurel gasped and took a step back.

Huck grasped her arm. "Is that Teri Bearing?"

Laurel swallowed. "The facial characteristics resemble Mrs. Bearing. It's difficult to tell with all the water frozen around her face, but . . . I believe so." Laurel stepped closer. "Can you see if her left hand is free?"

The tech gently lifted it. "Barely. I don't want to move her too much till we get all this ice off her."

"That's all right." Laurel crouched down to look closer. "I believe that's Teri Bearing's wedding band." She had met the mayor's wife during an earlier case.

"Huh," Huck said. "She must have bailed out of jail after I arrested her."

"Yes," Officer Tso said. "I actually saw the video from *The Killing Hour* when she left the station. Rachel Raprenzi followed her and tried to get a statement. And boy, all Mrs. Bearing wanted to talk about was you."

Huck straightened. "What'd she say about me?"

"She went on and on about Fish and Wildlife picking on people and acting like they were real cops and said that you pushed her hard against the car. That her new mission in life was to get you fired."

Huck looked at Laurel. "Did you know this?"

"No. I try not to watch Rachel's podcast," Laurel said. "But the entire arrest is on video, isn't it? When you pulled her over?"

"Yes," Huck said. "Not only did I have a camera on, but I'm sure the deputy sheriff did as well. I didn't touch her."

Laurel believed that implicitly. "Please take the body to Dr. Ortega. Hopefully he can perform our autopsies quickly since we have two victims with similar MOs." She scanned the area. "The snow fell all night?"

"Yes," Huck said. "The wind also made a mess. I don't see any footprints."

She looked toward the Silent River again. "Can you tell what cracked the ice?"

He shook his head. "That's doubtful, but I'll try. Tso, take a bunch of pictures of the opening, will you?"

"I already did," Officer Tso said. "But I'll take more now that it's getting lighter out here." He ambled toward the river, his footsteps sure.

Laurel kept her hands in her pockets. "Who found the body?" Everybody looked around. "Who's managing the scene?"

"That would be me," Genesis Valley Sheriff Upton York said, emerging from the back of the church. "I was talking to a witness inside. I took over the scene since I arrived first."

"We're on unincorporated land, so this isn't your jurisdiction," Huck said.

Laurel nodded.

The sheriff shrugged. Snow fell onto his receding hairline, and he brushed it off. He looked square and tough in his dark jacket, and his brown eyes remained passionless. "The pastor called me in, and here I am."

Unfortunately, Laurel and Huck were both down members of their respective teams, so they might actually need help with legwork. "Who found the body?" Laurel asked.

The sheriff nodded back at the church. "A guy named Tim Kohnex. He was walking his dog."

Laurel frowned. "He was walking his dog in the dark?"

"Yeah. Guy says he has trouble sleeping and often takes walks to watch the sun come up."

"Where does he live?" Huck asked.

Sheriff York pointed east. "Down the river, maybe five miles."

Laurel looked toward the winding river. "Is he a member of the church?"

"Everybody around here is a member of the church," York said. "He's inside."

Laurel looked at Huck. "Let's interview the witness." Empirically, the first victim was not Huck's mother, and since she hadn't been identified as of yet, a conflict of interest hadn't been established.

"I agree," Huck said.

Laurel started to walk and then paused. "Adhering to all sense of caution, perhaps I should speak with the witness alone."

"You're not going in there without me," he said quietly enough that only she heard.

She appreciated his discretion in masking his overprotectiveness. "I can face Zeke Caine."

"I'm sure you can," Huck agreed, walking toward the church.

She sighed. The most prudent plan would be to shield Huck from the case on the chance that his mother was the first victim. However, she did appreciate his effort to remain near should she find herself confronted by her father.

A small door stood ajar in the east wing of the church, and she paused to admire the large windows of the main building, some stained glass, some translucent, which looked out to the river and the snowy peaks.

Huck fully opened the door and gestured her inside. As she walked in, heat immediately surrounded her. The warmth felt glorious, but her face tingled in pain from the cold outside. She needed to keep a hat in her pocket. The local meteorologists had claimed that spring had arrived, but perhaps winter had not let up her cold grip on the world quite yet.

Laurel walked into the sprawling gathering room east of the main part of the church where round tables had been set up, each surrounded by gray plastic chairs. At one, a man sat next to a wet dog, a steaming Styrofoam cup in his hands. She hadn't realized people still used Styrofoam. He appeared to be in his early fifties with blondish-brown hair and matching mustache and beard. His deep blue eyes appeared clear and focused.

He stood when he caught sight of her. "Hello. Hi. How are you?"

She cocked her head. The man had to be at least 6'7", if not 8". He stood taller than Huck, who was at least 6'4", and had angled and symmetrically good-looking features. Rugged and tough. "Mr. Kohnex?"

"Tim. Call me Tim. This is Buster." Buster appeared to be a wet border collie trying to stay awake. The dog sneezed twice and shut his eyes with his nose on his paws.

Kohnex stared at her. "I've never met anybody with two different-colored eyes before. Doesn't that mean you have two spirits?"

"I'm familiar with that legend but grant it no credence." Laurel looked around, surprised to find the gathering room vacant.

He followed her gaze. "The pastor went to get more coffee."

A chill ran down her spine. "I see. Mr. Kohnex, can you tell us about your morning?"

"Sure. Buster couldn't sleep, so we decided to walk along the river and catch the sunrise. It was snowing all night, so I wasn't sure that we'd see anything beyond the clouds. But sometimes it's still pretty even when there are clouds, you know, like in life?"

Laurel tried to warm her toes by curling them inside her boots. "You can sit back down if you like."

"Only if you sit as well." He gave her a charming smile.

Her feet were freezing, and she wouldn't mind sitting for a moment. Plus, it was a proficient tactic to relax him. "That would be more comfortable."

She sat, and Huck took the other seat at the round table. Behind him, a white counter ran along one side of the wall piled high with various platters and empty drink dispensers. The place held a whiff of cookies, no doubt because the congregation gathered there after services and for events.

"You're a member of the church?" Huck asked.

"I am," Kohnex said. "I moved to Genesis Valley about seven years ago, and I joined the church right away."

Laurel's feet tingled as warmth seeped back into them. "Where did you live before you came to Genesis Valley?"

"I lived in Texas. I coached boys basketball and invested some of my money in an upstart oil company. With my guidance, we hit it rich, and so I retired and moved up here because I like the slower pace, love ice fishing, and enjoy the snow. Though this is the first time I've ever found a dead body in it." He shook his head, his eyes somber. "I knew something was going to happen this week, but I hoped I was wrong."

Laurel studied him. "You knew something would happen?"

"Oh, yes. I have the sense. I get feelings sometimes.

It's hard to explain. Flashes of . . . I don't know. I guess you'd call it awareness. I knew I was going to be touched by evil this week. I can't think of a better way to say it." He kept eye contact as he spoke, something that was rarer than most people realized.

"I see," Laurel said. "Did you know from which direction that evil would come?"

Kohnex wiped a large hand down his face. "Not at all. Buster and I take walks all the time, but I had an inkling that something was going to happen today. Now I'm not entirely sure if it was finding the dead body or meeting you, Agent Snow."

Laurel kept her face calm. "Meeting me?"

"Yes. I've imagined you before. The dual-colored eyes, the wild scarlet hair."

She'd never considered her hair wild or all that scarlet. It was more brown, tinged with some red. "I see." How convinced was he of his delusions? "Perhaps you've just seen me on the news? We've had a few newsworthy cases lately."

"I don't watch the news," Kohnex said. "Don't you believe in things you can't see?"

"Rarely," Laurel said. "Did you recognize the body?"

He shuddered. "No, I just saw a body lying in the snow next to the river. So I ran into the church and called the police."

"Where did you say the pastor had gone?" Laurel asked.

"He went to get more coffee." Kohnex sat with confidence, his long legs stretched out beneath the table.

Huck unzipped his parka. "You called the police after running inside. Was the pastor already here?"

"No. After dialing 911, I called Pastor Zeke, and he arrived in about fifteen minutes. He wanted to go out there and say a prayer over the body, but I told him that we should wait until you arrived because we didn't want to contaminate the crime scene."

Huck leaned back and made his chair squeak. "So you know something about forensics."

Kohnex waved a hand in the air. "Just what I've seen on TV. I used to watch that *CSI* show until it got a little boring. But, you know, everybody knows not to contaminate a crime scene."

"What makes you think it was a crime?" Huck asked abruptly.

"Well"—Kohnex sat back—"I heard about the other lady found by Iceberg River. The details were pretty graphic—that she was frozen face down, and this woman was on her belly and frozen, too, so I just figured. Plus, the place felt like murder. Like evil had been there. Do you believe in coincidences, Agent Snow?"

"No," Laurel said. "These feelings you get, have they led to you to any other crimes?"

He ducked his head. "Yes, but not often. I've called in anonymous tips after having a vision, but usually people don't believe me. I learned that a long time ago, so I don't say anything. But since I'm here, I thought I should."

"Is there anything else you'd like to add?" Laurel asked. He actually seemed to believe he held psychic powers.

Kohnex leaned down and stroked his dog, as if seeking comfort. "Just that this killer . . . I could sense him.

He's been here before. He knew the woman, and he's just getting started."

A rustle sounded, and Zeke Caine strode into the room.

Kohnex brightened. "Pastor, the FBI is here."

Zeke looked directly at Laurel. "I can see that. How are you, my wayward daughter?"

Chapter 10

Huck kicked his chair away from the table and to the side, putting him squarely between Laurel and Zeke Caine. "Pastor Caine, we have questions for you."

Zeke kept his gaze on Laurel and walked toward them with a coffee pot in one hand and several Styrofoam cups in the other. "Yes, I assume you do." The now bald pastor had apparently once had the same auburn-colored hair as Laurel and Abigail, as well as their heterochromatic eyes, but he wore blue contacts to mask them.

Kohnex stilled. "You're Agent Snow's father?"

"I am," the pastor said.

Kohnex looked from one to the other. "There's bad blood between you." His dog whined, and he leaned down to pet him again, for the first time appearing uneasy.

"Laurel, it's good to see you." The pastor ignored Kohnex. "I know you've called several times to speak with me, but I needed space after our first rather unfortunate interaction."

Huck kept his face expressionless. He hadn't realized that Laurel had reached out to her father. There was no doubt in his mind that she planned to put the man in prison, and he believed she'd eventually succeed.

"Yes. Last time we spoke, you were in the hospital after being brutally attacked," Laurel said. "Yet, for some reason, you won't tell me who assaulted you."

They all knew who'd stabbed him. Abigail Caine, his other daughter, had attacked him.

A calculating smile lifted the pastor's lips. He probably stood a little under six feet tall and appeared broad and in fairly decent shape for his age.

Huck wondered how many punches he could take before he fell. Probably two. Maybe one if Huck aimed perfectly. "Where were you last night?"

The pastor finally looked at him. "Captain Rivers, it's good to see you. We should probably go out and have a drink since you're dating my daughter, don't you think?"

Huck had faced predators his entire life, and until now, he'd considered Abigail Caine to be the most dangerous of them all. This guy could give her a run for her money. At least it explained where Abigail had inherited the crazy gene. "I'm not going to ask you again. Where were you last night?"

The pastor placed the coffee pot and cups on the table, stepping between Huck and Kohnex. "I worked here until about nine at night, and then it's absolutely none of your business where I spent my evening."

"There was a body found out by the river behind your church," Huck drawled, standing to his full height. "So you can either come into the office with me for a more formal interview, or you can stop being a jackass."

Kohnex gasped. "I feel dissent here," he said. "Maybe we should all take a deep breath."

Oh, yeah, there was definitely dissent here.

Laurel cleared her throat. "Where were you, Pastor Caine?"

He honed in on her. "You mean 'Father,' don't you?"

"I absolutely do not," she said.

He sighed. "Fine. I was with a friend all night."

"Does your friend have a name?" Huck asked.

Zeke sighed. "I really wish to leave her out of this, if you don't mind."

Huck just stared at him and crossed his arms.

"Very well," the pastor said. "Her name is Uma Carrington, and she owns the Little Tin Box, which is the antiques store right around the corner from the Center Diner."

Laurel didn't so much as move. "Is she older than eighteen?"

Zeke smiled again, all charm. "I believe she's in her late twenties. You can't believe every story your mother tells you."

"No," Huck said before Laurel could get in a word. "We're not going there, and we're not talking about anything other than this case. If you have a problem with that, I'll put you in cuffs and take you out of here right now."

Zeke drew in air and focused on Huck. "Aren't you the overprotective lover?"

Towering over the man, Huck stepped closer. "You're going to want to watch yourself, Pastor Caine. You really are." He let his voice lower to pure threat. "Now, we would like her phone number."

The pastor easily rattled it off, taking a discreet step away from Huck.

Huck remained in place. For now. "What do you know about the woman found frozen on your church grounds?"

"I arrived here in time to be told to stay inside the church," Zeke said. "I didn't even get to see who's out there."

"It's probably Teri Bearing, the mayor's wife," Kohnex said suddenly.

Huck twisted toward him. "How did you know that?"

"I was listening at the door," Kohnex said. "But I had a feeling she was somebody prominent in town. Even though she hadn't been turned over and I couldn't see her face, there was something about her. I don't think you'd call it an aura, more like an essence." He tapped his bottom lip and stared off into the distance. Then he looked back at Laurel. "Like you two. I knew before the pastor used that unfortunate word that you and the captain were tied together. Strong bonds there."

Huck didn't have time for this bullshit.

"You've been through chilly storms together, haven't you?" Kohnex asked.

Laurel barely kept from rolling her eyes. It was close. Huck saw her lids twitch, but she managed to restrain herself. He liked that about her a lot.

She removed her gloves. "Pastor Caine, you were with Ms. Carrington from nine last night until when?"

"Until I got the call from Timmy," the pastor said. "He said he found a body, and I came here right away. This is not good for me or the church. Tonight was supposed to be our first live service. I'm taking the church national. It's going to be a megachurch, Laurel. But we can't hold a live service when there's a dead body out back, and now it seems it's the mayor's wife? What a disaster."

"Well, gee, Pastor," Huck drawled. "I'm real sorry to ruin your day."

The pastor put both hands on his hips. He wore black slacks and a white button-down shirt, even though he'd been called out of somebody's bed to get to the church. Did he always dress up?

Laurel cleared her throat. "Let's all remember that we do not have a positive identification for the victim yet."

Zeke focused once again on Huck. "Didn't you have an altercation with the mayor's wife recently?"

"How do you know that?" Laurel asked quietly.

The pastor kept his gaze on Huck this time. "I pay attention when one of my girls is dating somebody. I try to learn everything I can about them. I've got more Google alerts on you than you can imagine, and I quite enjoy *The Killing Hour*. That Rachel Raprenzi is fascinating. I think she still is enamored with you."

"Ah, Rachel," Kohnex said. "I watch her, too. Yes. I can see a connection between the two of you." He gasped suddenly and grabbed his throat, turning toward Laurel. "Something's coming for you. Oh, my. It's a force. A force that wants just you. You're in grave danger."

Huck might actually have to hit this guy. "She's an FBI agent. Stop making things up."

"I'm not. I can see it. I can sense it from two different directions actually. And one . . ." He leaned in. "Is very close to you," he whispered. "Do you have a sibling?"

"No," Laurel said shortly.

Kohnex looked down at his dog. "I think that you do. There's a familial essence, a connection to the danger."

He peered into the distance again, and his tone deepened. "Somebody wants to harm you, Agent Snow. You need to be very careful."

Yep. Huck was going to have to clock him. He sighed. "Do you have any connection to Teri Bearing, Pastor Caine?" He emphasized the "Pastor" this time.

Zeke shrugged. "The Bearings attend the church, so I know Teri and the mayor and their kids. They joined long before I left on my sabbatical, and they're still members now. I think they were actually looking forward to the live sermon tonight. The mayor wished to give a brief talk about the community, you know, to bring in people."

"Where is Pastor John?" Laurel asked, referencing the pastor who'd taken over for Zeke when he'd disappeared for years.

"Oh, my. Did I forget to call him?" Zeke asked. "I saw him when I left last night, but he may have stayed here all night. I don't know."

There was no doubt in Huck's mind that Zeke Caine knew Pastor John's location at all times. Pastor John had been the one to set up this live national sermon service. He couldn't have been too happy when Zeke had returned and taken over. "Does Pastor John still live in the church cabin to the west?"

"No," Zeke said. "John purchased one of the cabins farther down to the east, a distance from Timmy's place. There's a series of them that were built by a family named Bollington at least thirty or forty years ago. They've each been individually sold through the years."

Huck glanced toward the outside door. "Just down this river?"

"Yes. He purchased it a month ago, I think. But I have no idea what time he left the church last night." Zeke pressed one hand against his cheek. "You don't suppose Pastor John killed Teri, do you?"

"Why would I suppose that?" Huck asked.

Zeke looked away and then back. "I don't know. But they were seeing each other."

"Define *seeing*," Huck said.

The pastor shook his head. "I really shouldn't. I'm not one to engage in gossip."

"This is a murder investigation, Pastor Caine," Laurel said.

"You mean 'Father.'" Zeke's tone sounded indulgent.

Her voice remained sure and strong. "I really don't."

Huck cleared his throat. "How long have Pastor John and Mrs. Bearing been seeing each other?"

"Maybe for a couple of months, from what I understand." Zeke looked properly somber.

Huck lowered his chin. "Are you breaking the confessional right now?"

"Oh, no, no. This is just normal gossip," Zeke said. "I'm not breaking the confession at all. I wouldn't do that."

"All right. From whom did you hear this gossip?" Laurel asked.

Zeke lifted his hands. "I really don't know. I can't say. Besides, if I did hear something in confession, and it wasn't about the confessor, then I'm not breaking the confessional."

Huck tried to hold on to his patience. "Somebody in confession told you about Pastor John and Teri Bearing?"

"Yes. I can't reveal the identities of those persons

because I gleaned the information during confession, although I can tell you about the actual affair because that wasn't what was confessed."

Huck glanced at Laurel. She shrugged.

He didn't know either. "I thought just Catholics have confession."

"No, not at all. I think it's important to lift sins off the chest, and we hold confession here once a week," Zeke said. "Although, Tim, I do note that you haven't been to confession recently. Should you attend?"

Kohnex shook his head. "No. Anything I've done is between me and God."

Laurel focused on Kohnex. "Tim, did you know Mrs. Bearing?"

Kohnex nodded. "I did. We attend the same church, but outside of church we weren't friends. She had a darkness around her, an aura of . . . I don't know. If I had to pick one word, it'd be 'melancholy.' But in the last couple of months her aura had lightened to a pink, almost a sparkling-champagne pink. So I figured whatever had been weighing on her had lifted. Maybe she had fallen in love."

"Did you hear that she was dating Pastor John?" Huck asked.

Kohnex scratched his chin. "I did not. But I don't hear confessions. At least not formally."

"Formally?" Pastor Caine asked.

Kohnex shrugged. "Sometimes the wind whispers her secrets to me, and then I know."

"So you and the wind, huh?" Huck asked.

Kohnex nodded solemnly. "Yeah, my talent used to help with basketball games. I would know which players to put where and which plays to call. Then the wind murmured to me when I invested in that oil company. Lately, I've got to tell you, she's been crooning a lot."

"Saying what?" Laurel asked.

"Beware," Kohnex whispered, his eyes widening.

Laurel tucked her gloves into her jacket pocket. "Beware of what?"

Kohnex looked back at his dog. "She hasn't told me yet."

What was this guy's deal? "Where were you last night?" Huck asked.

"I told you. I was home, and then I took my dog for a walk." Kohnex smiled at the dog.

"I see. What about Sunday night?" Laurel asked.

Kohnex pursed his lips. "Same. I don't go many places, Agent Snow. I was home with my dog. We had macaroni and cheese. I watched the television and went to bed. That's pretty much what I do. Every once in a while I get online and play around with the stock market, but all I seem to do is make more money."

The pastor frowned. "We really do need to get you involved with the church's basketball team, Tim. It's not good for you to be out in your cabin with your dog at all times."

"How close is your cabin to Pastor John's?" Laurel asked.

Kohnex shrugged. "I don't know, maybe a mile. We can't see each other, you know? We're in the middle of the woods, but he's the next home to the east of me, I believe."

Laurel glanced down at her phone. "Officers report

that Pastor John is not present at his cabin. Where is he, Pastor Caine?"

Zeke held out both hands in a helpless gesture. "Heck if I know."

Huck kept his focus on Kohnex. "Do you like blondes?"

A small smile played over Kohnex's face. "Yes, I like really athletic blondes, you know? Ones who golf and are tall. I wouldn't want to waste this frame on a short girl."

"Do you have a girlfriend?" Huck asked.

Kohnex scratched a mark on his neck. "No. I've been talking to this really hot chick from Arizona named Jeanie, but we've only talked and Zoomed. She's not looking for anything serious, and neither am I."

Huck needed to do a deep dive on this guy. "I need her number."

"Absolutely," Kohnex said. "She knows you're calling."

"How would she know?" Huck asked. This guy lived in his own universe.

Kohnex shrugged. "She knows things, too."

"Great. We'll be in touch with both of you," Huck said.

Laurel pushed back her chair and stood. "Pastor Caine, where have you been the last several years? It's my understanding that you took off five years ago, showed up a year ago for a short time, and then left again. Where did you go?"

"I was on walkabout," Zeke said. "I believe I told you that before."

"Yes, and I would like to hear more details now." Laurel faced her father squarely.

Huck took a step back so he wouldn't obscure her line of sight.

Zeke's superior smile might get him punched. "I really can't go into details. I went on a personal spiritual journey, and where I was doesn't matter to you."

"You didn't take a phone with you?" Laurel asked.

"No, I did not." He winked. "Sometimes a man just doesn't want to be found, Laurel."

Chapter 11

Laurel finished a very late and uninspiring lunch of a Cobb salad from the deli down the street as she sat in her office and thought through the two deaths. Sheriff York had delivered a preliminary notification to Teri Bearing's family since he had a relationship with them. The mayor had provided a positive identification from a picture. Even so, due to the victim's facial trauma, they awaited final confirmation from the coroner, and they'd all agreed to refrain from making public announcements until then.

Laurel had called to set up a time to interview the Bearings, reaching a voice mail. Saul and his two sons had disappeared, saying they needed time to grieve—and the damn sheriff had let them go.

That didn't work since Laurel needed to interview them, so Huck had issued a BOLO for them to no avail as of yet.

Also, so far, nobody had found Pastor John Govern, so she issued a BOLO for him as well. These witnesses needed to be tracked down. Now. Her desk phone rang. "Hey, Kate."

"Hi. Dr. Caine is here to see you," Kate said, her voice almost robotic.

"Thank you. You can send her back." Laurel preferred to deal with Abigail with a desk between them, instead of in the conference room. She angled her head but couldn't see down the hallway.

"Hello, dear sister." Abigail strode inside. She had grown her auburn hair out to her shoulders, and today had the thick strands flipped back in a sassy style. Her heterochromatic eyes sparkled. "How kind of you to invite me to an early supper."

"We're not going to supper. Please take a seat." Laurel gestured to one of the two leather guest chairs.

"You are so boring," Abigail muttered, shutting the door and then sitting. She wore a black, high-end-looking pantsuit with a white silk shirt beneath the jacket. The accompanying emerald necklace and earring set appeared genuine. "I already heard that Jason Abbott has once again eluded the police, and I am taking precautions to keep myself safe. No, I still do not know where he is. Are we done?"

"No, we are not finished with this interview. I watched the video of your visit with Jason last week."

Abigail's eyes crinkled. "Did you, now? I bet I appeared delightful on the big screen." She looked around. "Shall we watch it together?"

"I've seen enough," Laurel said. "Why in the world would you want Jason Abbott out on the street?"

Abigail's eyes widened, so very much like Laurel's that her stomach dropped. "Out on the street? I do not want that maniac free. He wants to kill you or me. Most likely me, and that won't do."

Laurel tried to study Abigail's facial expressions for hints of falsehood but couldn't determine any telltale signs. "Could you stop playing games for one minute? I watched the video of the last time you visited him in jail. I know you gave him the idea to escape. Yet your motivation for such a puerile act escapes me."

Abigail's chin slightly lowered and her lips lifted in an almost flirty smile, or at least what Laurel would consider flirty. "It really galls you when you fail to understand something, doesn't it?"

That statement held truth. "Are you planning to kill Jason Abbott?"

Abigail tapped her fingers on the desk. "I cannot believe you're still using this old door as a desktop. Do I have to go ahead and just buy you a desk myself?" Her smile widened. "I do have plenty of funds, as you know." She owned a marijuana farm outside of town, and apparently the business remained lucrative.

"What is your plan, Abigail? I think you're underestimating Abbott," Laurel said.

"Nonsense. It would be impossible to underestimate that dullard," Abigail said. "I wish you wouldn't worry so much." She held out her hand as if admiring her blood-red nails. "Although, I do like your showing how much you care about me."

"I'm concerned because he will kill innocent women, unlike you. Women who did not disturb his brain patterns until he felt free to act on his killing urges," Laurel said evenly.

Abigail straightened on the chair. "I'm bored with this discussion. Let's dish. How's the baby, anyway? You don't look any different. I expected you to be all glowy."

How annoying that Abigail had somehow guessed about Laurel's pregnancy before Laurel herself even had. Laurel wished she could've lied better when Abigail had dropped the bombshell. "Dr. Caine, we are here to discuss Jason Abbott."

Abigail threw back her head and laughed, the sound so much like Laurel's natural laugh that nausea rolled through Laurel's belly.

"You just called me Dr. Caine. I think we're way past that, don't you?" Abigail's dual-colored eyes sparkled. "Speaking of the Caine name, have you talked to dear old Dad?"

"Only as he relates to my current case," Laurel said. "I'm dealing with one sociopath at a time."

Abigail's heterochromatic eyes glowed in the office lights. "Sociopath, is it? I thought you diagnosed me as a malignant narcissist."

"I haven't diagnosed you with any certainty. You could be a psychopath for all I know, or care," Laurel said. "Have you spoken to Zeke Caine?"

"No," Abigail said. "I'm keeping my distance. You have to know he won't keep his distance from either you or me."

"I'm hoping he'll be too busy with the church to bother me," Laurel said. "So you haven't spoken to him, and you remain unaware of his movements during the last five years?" It was too late to arrest and charge him with the attack on her mother, but experience told her that he'd have additional victims out there.

"I neither know nor care where dear old Dad has been, and neither should you," Abigail said, her jaw firming.

"He's not going to leave us alone. At some point, you and I are going to have to combine forces to handle him."

Laurel swallowed. "Handle him? Would you like to elaborate?"

"I truly would not." Abigail met her stare evenly.

During Laurel's last case, in which prominent men had been murdered by stabbing, Zeke Caine had been a possible victim. There wasn't a doubt in Laurel's mind that Abigail had tried to kill him by copying the murderer's modus operandi. "Someday he will identify you as the person who stabbed him that night in March."

Abigail crossed her legs. "Do you think so? Then why hasn't he?"

"I don't know." There was the disastrous possibility that Zeke Caine liked to play deadly games as much as Abigail did. "Do you?"

Abigail chuckled softly. "All you had to do was let him bleed out that night. Why didn't you?"

Laurel had come upon their father and saved his life. "I want him behind bars paying for his crimes. Not dead. Are you admitting you stabbed him?"

"Of course not." Abigail winked as if truly enjoying the interview. "We both know that if I committed a crime, which I have not done, you'd never be able to prove it. Isn't it time you stopped pursuing me and became my sister?"

Laurel studied Abigail, wanting more than ever to get into her head. "Why did you stab him?"

"I didn't. Stop asking me about Zeke Caine, Laurel."

At the moment, Laurel required Abigail's assistance, so she chose to abandon that line of questioning. "Tell me where you think Jason Abbott would go."

Abigail tugged on one sparkling earring. "Who knows. By the way, speaking of Abbott, I saw the interview that our good old Captain Rivers gave to Rachel Raprenzi. She still has the hots for him, you know?"

"I care little what she feels," Laurel said. "The purpose of the interview was to notify the public about Jason Abbott's escape. You knew him better than anybody. If you're not involved with his escape, then help me. Where would he go?"

Abigail tapped one red fingernail on her chin. "You know, as your big sister, I could take care of that reporter for you."

Laurel believed the woman would do just that if asked. "Again, I wish for her to be left alone by you. If anything happens to Rachel, I will arrest you immediately." The gun at the back of her waist provided necessary reassurance right now. "We both know you threatened her before, and I have no doubt she'd be happy to testify against you."

"If you had any proof whatsoever that I threatened that perceptually challenged twat, I'd already be booked."

An unfortunately true statement. "Let's return to the subject of your jail visit with Jason Abbott. Where is he right now?"

Abigail flicked an invisible piece of lint off her shoulder. "This is so tedious. I couldn't care less where he is. Let's talk about us. Let's talk about the baby inside you. The one who will probably be a genius. What are we going to do with her?"

Laurel would keep Abigail far away from this baby. "You and I do not have a relationship."

"Of course we do. We're sisters," Abigail returned.

"This baby is going to need both of us. Do you think she'll have our eyes?"

Laurel had never met anybody more able to talk in circles than Abigail. The talent would be impressive if it wasn't so irritating. "Where would Jason go?"

Abigail tossed a hand through the air. "Would you give it up? I have no idea. Did you check with that insipid fiancée of his? Haylee, whatever it was?"

Abigail knew Haylee's name as well as Laurel did. She had an eidetic memory and didn't forget anything. "You know her last name."

"I choose not to spend any time on that twit. If anybody helped him escape, it would be her."

Laurel failed to discern an underlying tone in Abigail's voice. It was too bad Huck wasn't available right now, but then again, perhaps Abigail wouldn't speak so freely around him. "How would Haylee have assisted Jason Abbott?"

"Who cares?" Abigail murmured. "At least things are about to get interesting around here again."

Abigail's lack of emotion should not surprise Laurel, yet it did. "Just tell me why you'd want him out of jail if you have no plans to end his life."

"I have no wish to harm Abbott," Abigail said briskly. "If I'd wanted him dead, he'd be dead. I didn't need him to escape to take care of him. Surely you understand that much about me."

As a point, it was a good one. Abigail could probably engineer any situation that she wanted. "So, why do you want him free?" It just didn't make any sense.

"Again, I couldn't care less. As of now, I'm bored with this discussion." Abigail dug into her overlarge purse and brought out a notebook. "I'm writing you a song."

Laurel blinked. "Excuse me?"

"Since you're knocked up, I'm sure the good captain will propose soon."

"We have no plans for marriage."

Abigail continued as if Laurel hadn't spoken. "As your maid of honor, I'll need to give a speech, and I saw one online where the maid of honor sang a song that she'd written. I enjoyed it. A lot of interesting words rhyme with Huck."

Laurel shook her head. "You and I do not have a personal relationship."

"Of course we do. I very strongly advise that you stop saying that." Abigail lost all semblance of a smile. "You really don't want to be my enemy, especially since we share a common one."

"Zeke Caine?" Laurel recognized the truth in her statement. "I don't need your assistance ensuring Zeke sees justice. You and I don't have a scintilla of feeling in common."

Abigail stood. "That's where you're wrong, dear sister. You'll need me more than you realize. Soon."

Chapter 12

After a night at her mom's spent dreaming about chasing Jason Abbott through icy water and over snow-filled peaks, Laurel finished her breakfast burrito sitting in her FBI office. The Bearing family still hadn't been located, nor had Pastor John, and she fought irritation as she glared at the rough surface in front of her. Like the conference table, her desk was an old, repurposed door. She leaned to the side and yelled down the hallway. "Kate, are you any closer to acquiring a desk for me?"

"I'm working on it," Kate called back. "The requisition forms have been a pain, and the FBI holds on to money as long as it can. You need a drawer?"

Laurel looked at the basket holding pens and notepads near her left foot. "I require a couple of drawers. Would you put a priority on that one, please?"

"Of course. I'll do my best."

Laurel crumpled the burrito wrapper and tossed it into the garbage. She didn't want to apply pressure on Kate, but she really needed a drawer. She turned to her computer and typed her notes from Jason Abbott's two recorded jail interviews as a rustle sounded down the hall.

Huck soon filled her doorway. "Mornin'."

"Good morning." She gestured toward one of her two leather guest chairs. "Have a seat."

He dropped into one, his shoulders slightly slumped. "Thanks. No luck on finding the three Bearing men, but we finally tracked down the location of Pastor John Govern."

"Where was he?"

"Apparently the junior pastor left very early Thursday to go snowmobiling with a group from the church and should return sometime Sunday night, and we have no idea where. They just took off into the Cascades and let the wind lead them," Huck said. "I find it irritating that Pastor Caine didn't give us that information."

Good point. "Perhaps he didn't know."

"It was a church event," Huck said. "I have no doubt Pastor Caine knew all about it. I have half a mind to drag him into interrogation and ask him why he wants to hinder our investigation."

That might be interesting to watch. For now, she couldn't read Huck's expression. "Are you all right?"

He rolled his neck. "No. Rachel Raprenzi won't stop posting the video of me pulling over Teri Bearing, our latest victim."

She blinked. "Why?"

"She likes to mess with me."

Laurel winced. "I'm sorry."

Huck dug his fingers into the side of his neck as if the muscles had knotted. "She'd love to show some sort of improper relationship between you and me."

So the news of the pregnancy would be opportune for the reporter. "For now, we need to focus on finding Jason Abbott as well as the Bearings." Laurel would worry about Rachel's personal interest in them later. "I spoke with Dr. Ortega's assistant a few minutes ago about our first victim, the one found by Iceberg River."

Huck straightened. "Was she my mother?"

"Dr. Ortega is still working to identify bodies and determine the different causes of death from the Seattle nightclub fire. His assistant expressed uncertainty when he'd be able to send us the autopsy results."

Huck shrugged out of his jacket and draped it over the chair, flexing the muscles in his chest. "That's okay. Honestly, the more I think about it, the more I realize it just doesn't make sense that the vic is my mother. I shouldn't have said anything."

"Your instincts are often correct."

His gaze softened. "I thought you weren't a big believer in instincts."

"I lack natural instincts, but I believe in yours," she said honestly.

His smile made him look younger. "That's the sweetest thing you've ever said to me."

"It is not," she countered. She could think of many sweet things she had said to him.

"It was sweet. Speaking of sweetness, are you excited about our upcoming appointment with the OB-GYN?"

She had conducted copious research to find the most qualified doctor. "Yes."

"Will we be able to hear the heartbeat?"

She nodded. "Affirmative. I'll be more than twelve

weeks along, and a Doppler fetal monitor should be able to pick up the baby's heartbeat."

Huck grinned full-on this time. "Do you think it's a boy or a girl?"

"I have absolutely no idea."

"Yeah, but do you feel anything? Do you have any sort of mother's intuition?"

Mother's intuition. What if she couldn't relate to the baby as her own mother had to her? She didn't have those emotions, or she didn't know how to express them. She reached for a pen to tap on the worn door. "Did you know that while many cultures have myths and old wives' tales about mothers being able to sense something about their unborn babies, none of it is scientifically verifiable? I have no better chance of guessing than do you."

"Then I guess it's a boy," he said instantly.

She sat back, intrigued. "Why?"

He shrugged. "Gut feeling."

There was no possible way he could know that fact. She crossed her arms. "We'll see."

"Are you ready to tell anybody yet?"

"No. You?"

He shook his head. "No. I figure it's nobody's business but ours."

She liked that. "Did Rachel ask you out again?"

His chin lifted. "Why? You jealous?"

She considered the question. Was she jealous? "No. I'm fairly confident in our relationship. I'm not jealous, just curious."

"I like that about you," he said. He often surprised her with that statement.

She never understood to what he referred. "Please clarify."

He shook his head. "Nope. I just like you."

She might never fully understand him, but she did trust him. Believing in somebody besides her mom was new for her, especially since her own father was such an abomination. She's been spared pain in her childhood by not learning of him until recently.

Huck sobered. "Have you been able to reach Abigail Caine?"

"Yes. She came in earlier for an interview. I believe she knew that Jason Abbott would escape."

Huck ran a rough hand through his hair, ruffling the thick mass. "Why would she do that? She has to know that he wants her dead."

"She's a narcissist who lacks the ability to feel fear," Laurel said. "If Abbott attempts to harm her, I'm sure she's confident she can handle him."

"Why would she want him free?"

Laurel looked out the window to find a light snow falling. When had it started to snow again? "She obviously wanted Jason Abbott to escape, so she definitely has a plan." What that plan might be, Laurel had absolutely no idea.

Kate poked her head in the doorway. "Nester called and said his sister is doing well in the hospital. Broken leg in three places and a concussion. No clue who hit her, though."

"I'm glad she's going to be all right," Laurel said.

Kate nodded. "Melissa Cutting and Haylee Johnson are here as promised. Do you want them in the conference room, or do you want them down at Fish and Wildlife?"

"Let's interview them here," Laurel said. "Is that all right with you, Huck?"

"Sure." Huck stood and waited until Laurel crossed around the desk to walk in front of him. Today she wore heeled boots, so she felt a little bit taller than her normal 5'2". She'd paired black slacks with a green sweater, and she had her badge at her waist.

"Do you want to lead or want me to?" Huck asked.

She shrugged. "Let's both ask questions."

"Sounds good." He pressed his hand to the small of her back, and she felt his warmth all the way to her toes.

Regaining her composure, because she wasn't a woman who lost her composure, she walked down the hallway and into the conference room. "Thank you for coming in, Ms. Johnson," she said, noting Haylee pouring a glass of water.

Melissa Cutting sat next to her niece and across the table from the door. For the meeting today, she wore a high-end pantsuit with subtle gold and diamond jewelry. In her early fifties, Melissa had thick brown hair that curled around her shoulders, a smoothly botoxed forehead, and fully filled lips. She played with a thick emerald ring around her right finger. "We heard that Jason Abbott escaped," she said without preamble.

"Yes." Laurel looked at Haylee, who today had dressed back to form in a gray sweatshirt and faded jeans, her blond hair pulled up in a ponytail. "Did you know Jason was going to escape?"

"No." Haylee shook her head wildly. "I had no idea. I'm so glad he's out, though."

Huck pulled out a chair for Laurel and then sat next to her across from the other two. "Why is that? Do you want him to kill more people?"

Haylee flattened her hands on the rough wooden door serving as a table. "You have him all wrong. He is not a killer. What happened is all Abigail Caine's fault because of those experiments she conducted on him."

Laurel tilted her head, studying the young woman. Her facial expression showed markers of truth. Did she really believe that nonsense? "He cut the hands off women after raping and strangling them," she said slowly. "Nobody else in the world can make somebody do something like that. He is a bad person, and if he gets near you again, he will hurt you."

Haylee's eyes flashed. "You're just mad because I'm suing you."

"I couldn't care less about your lawsuit," Laurel said honestly. "The suit lacks merit. I'm surprised it hasn't been dismissed already."

Melissa Cutting smiled, her teeth perfectly aligned. "We think we have a good case, and I'm greatly looking forward to your deposition next month. You were reckless and unprofessional, considering your sister was involved in the whole situation. We will prevail, Agent Snow."

"I disagree based on the law and the facts," Laurel said easily. "However, I don't have time to worry about that right now. We need to concentrate on finding Jason Abbott before he murders somebody else." If he was killing women by drowning them, he had just struck twice, so hopefully he'd take some time to cool off. If he wasn't the current killer, he would murder soon. She focused more directly on Melissa Cutting. "Why did you move to dismiss our injunction against Dr. Abigail Caine visiting Jason Abbott?"

Haylee swung to face her aunt. "You did what?"

Melissa met Laurel's gaze evenly. "I represent Jason Abbott, and he requested Dr. Caine's visit. He has the right to see anybody he wishes, especially when it comes to his defense." She glanced at her niece. "Dr. Abigail Caine is how we get him free, Haylee. Now, control yourself."

Haylee gulped and looked down at the rough table.

Huck cleared his throat. "Ms. Cutting, you perfectly match the description of his former victims. Please tell me you understand the risk and are taking precautions to protect your safety."

"I'm taking precautions," Melissa said. "But I represent Jason Abbott, so he has no need or wish to hurt me."

Laurel shook her head. "You do not understand the compulsions that drive him. If that craving builds up in him again, he will come after you, absent, of course, another potential victim."

"I hope he gets to Abigail Caine," Haylee burst out.

"Haylee!" Melissa said, drawing back.

Haylee sank in her chair. In her early twenties, she suddenly looked much younger. "I don't care. Jason would not have hurt anybody without that woman. Surely you understand that." She glared at Laurel.

"No," Laurel said. How could the woman be so lacking in self-preservation? "I do think that Dr. Caine accelerated tendencies that wouldn't have manifested themselves so soon otherwise, but anybody who would brutally kill the way Jason did was going to kill at some point. You need to understand that." Jason would eventually murder Haylee if the woman didn't begin to take precautions. "You have to understand."

"I don't know what to think." Haylee flattened her hands on the table.

Huck studied the two women. "Where were you both the night Jason Abbott escaped from custody?"

Melissa drew back. "Excuse me?"

"We just need to clear you, Ms. Cutting. You're Jason Abbott's lawyer."

Melissa swallowed. "I was home working on a brief."

"Alone?" Laurel asked.

"Yes. If I needed an alibi, I would have created one. I had no idea Jason Abbott was going to escape from the hospital." Melissa leaned forward. "In fact, I didn't know he was in the hospital. The jail failed to inform my law firm about that."

Laurel couldn't read whether the attorney was telling the truth or not. She looked at Haylee. "Where were you?"

Haylee shuffled in her seat. "I was home, studying for a test on hair coloring. I've been taking beauty classes." She studied Laurel. "You could use a blunter cut. You have wonderful bone structure."

A blunt cut? Maybe. "Do you live together?" Laurel asked.

"Not anymore," Haylee said. "I have my own apartment on the other side of Genesis Valley."

Laurel studied her. She'd been keeping tabs on Haylee since Abbott's arrest, so Laurel had already known the answer to the question, but she had wondered if Haylee would tell the truth.

"Do you have a roommate?" Huck asked.

"No."

Huck settled back in his chair, looking intimidating as he did so. "Can anybody corroborate your story?"

Haylee looked at her aunt.

Melissa shook her head. "We're finished with this line of questioning, other than to affirm that we had no idea Jason was going to escape, and we certainly did not facilitate his actions. He has not been in touch with either one of us."

"Will you submit to a phone dump?" Huck asked.

Melissa's jaw tightened. "No. I have communications with several clients that could be considered privileged, including the identity of said clients. Surely you understand that?"

"I do." Huck looked at Haylee. "What about you? You're not an attorney."

Haylee sighed. "You need a warrant, right?"

Laurel mentally clicked through an affidavit. "Haylee, I can obtain a warrant for your phone based on your relationship with Jason Abbott and the threat to the public now that he's on the loose. This would be a lot easier if you just cooperated."

Haylee looked at her aunt. "Do I have to?"

Melissa shook her head. "No, but I do believe that Agent Snow can obtain a warrant for your phone."

Haylee shrugged. "Okay, you can have my phone. But there's nothing interesting on it."

The interview continued for another hour, but Laurel failed to glean additional information from either woman.

Finally, she ended the interview. Melissa and Haylee stood and walked toward the door.

At the entranceway, Haylee turned around, her movements hesitant. "Agent Snow?"

"Yes?" Laurel asked.

"I want to believe that Jason has changed and does regret what happened. He was drugged by your sister, and I think he wasn't in his right mind that entire time. However, if Jason truly wants anybody dead, you have to know that it's you, right?"

Chapter 13

After lunch at the Center Diner, where Laurel ate too much apple pie, she returned to her office and sat on the worn wood of her temporary conference table, staring at two glass murder boards. The one on the left held images from the Jason Abbott case and the one on the right, the new river cases.

Were they connected? Had Jason drowned those two blonde victims? She didn't like the timing of his escape with the occurrence of the newest murders. Drowning and strangulation involved similar violence and loss of breath leading to death.

Kate crossed into the room and handed her an herbal tea. "Here."

"Thank you."

Kate pulled out a chair and dropped into it, looking at the boards. "These are definitely murders, right? Any chance this isn't a serial killer?"

"Yes, these are homicides. Two deaths do not a serial make," Laurel said, repeating a phrase she'd learned at Quantico.

Kate stretched out. "What's your gut feeling?"

"I don't have gut feelings. However, there's a ritualistic aspect to these murders that indicate the killer's compunction to continue."

"They're definitely not one-offs, are they?" Kate asked, drinking her coffee.

Laurel tried never to use guesswork, but these deaths were too similar to miss the implications. "It's doubtful." She glanced at her watch. "I wish we had completed autopsies from Dr. Ortega."

"Do you want me to call him?" Kate offered. "It's too quiet around here without Walter and Nester."

"No. Thank you, though. Dr. Ortega must be overwhelmed right now. I know he'll get to us as soon as he can." But she needed to verify the cause of death in these murders.

"You think the victims were drowned?" Kate asked.

"Yes, but I won't make any suppositions until we have facts."

Kate turned to face the boards. "Who found the victim we're pretty sure is Teri Bearing?"

"A man named Tim Kohnex. Nester's conducting a full background check on the man right now, working remotely. He's also still trying to find where Zeke Caine has been traveling the past several years."

Kate nodded. "I heard Huck mention that this Kohnex fella thinks he's psychic."

"He believes the wind whispers to him," Laurel said. "I guess that could be considered psychic. I don't know."

"What was your take on him?"

She hadn't read much from his facial expressions. "He seemed . . . interesting," she said. "Maybe lonely. He likes his dog. I find it odd that he goes walking by the river before the sun comes up. That's perilous, no matter how well you know the terrain."

"You think he could be our guy instead of Jason Abbott?"

"I have no idea, and we need to keep an open mind about these killings. Kohnex is tall and strong. If these women were drowned somehow, I would say he has the strength to do it."

Kate eyed the picture of Kohnex Laurel had taped to the murder board after returning to the office. "Did he seem serial killer-ish to you?"

"I don't know what that means."

"Right," Kate said, looking over at the board that prominently featured Jason Abbott. "Any news on Abbott's whereabouts?"

Frustration crawled like ants beneath her skin. "No," Laurel said. "I think it was good that we got word out to the public, but so far no leads have panned out."

Kate snorted. "Yeah, I guess."

There was an inflection in her tone, but Laurel couldn't grasp its meaning. "Am I missing something?"

"No." Kate placed her cup on the worn table. "After Huck's interview, I guess half of the calls to the hotline have been to request his phone number."

Laurel tilted her head. "The callers won't give the information to the dispatch? They want to speak directly to the officer in charge?"

"Um, no," Kate said. "They want his number."

It took Laurel a second, and then realization hit. "They're romantically interested in the captain."

"Yeah, Laurel," Kate said dryly. "One lady wanted to know his address so she could mail her bra to him."

Laurel frowned. "Her bra? What would he do with her bra?"

"I don't know. Use it as a slingshot?" Kate chuckled. "Anyway, dispatch is getting a kick out of the multiple requests to meet the captain."

"Oh." Laurel focused back at Jason Abbott's mugshot. Even there, on the day he'd been arrested, his gaze was direct and his stature confident.

"You don't have to be jealous, Laurel," Kate said.

She paused. "Jealous of what?"

Kate studied her for a moment. "Forget it."

Sometimes people just didn't make any sense, or more likely Laurel was missing something again. But right now, she had to concentrate on her job. There wasn't time to deal with anything else.

Nausea rolled up in her stomach, and she sucked in oxygen. Oh, no. She was okay. Oh, wait. No, she wasn't. Lunging from where she was sitting, she grabbed the wastepaper basket from the corner of the room and lost her lunch and all of the pie.

"Whoa, boss." Kate grasped her hair to pull it away from her face. "Whoa."

Laurel retched harder, her body convulsing.

"How much pie did you eat?"

Laurel coughed and then straightened, standing with both arms around the bucket. "Sorry, I must've eaten something unpleasant."

"You look pale, Laurel. You should to sit down."

"No, I'm all right. I need to brush my teeth."

She stumbled out of the conference room and down to her office where she kept a toiletry kit. Supposedly morning sickness abated after the first trimester, and she had great hopes that she would stop vomiting at that time. Although she understood from her research that it was entirely possible she'd be this nauseated through the entire pregnancy.

Taking the tin garbage can with her, she rinsed the thick metal out in the bathroom before washing her face and brushing her teeth. Her throat felt raw, so after returning the wastebasket to the conference room, she walked down to the kitchen and made herself a cup of soothing chamomile tea. Hopefully that would help.

Huck appeared in the doorway. "Hey, Kate said you puked all over. Are you okay?"

Laurel finished stirring the tea. "Yes, I vomited, but I'm all right. I lost all the pie, though."

He chuckled. "Isn't that supposed to go away soon?"

She turned and looked at him. His eyebrows were lifted and his gaze intent. "Is that concern on your face?"

"Yeah. That's concern on my face."

She took a sip of the tea, letting the chamomile soothe her throat. "There's a chance the nausea will dissipate after twelve weeks, but there's no bright line in the sand."

Huck smiled, still looking concerned. "Where does that phrase come from anyway, 'bright line in the sand'?"

"Oh," she said, sipping again. "The 'bright' part is new. It used to be just a line in the sand. You know, to delineate a limit. I think, according to popular lore, it was used during the Battle of the Alamo in 1836."

"Is that a fact?" Huck leaned against the doorframe.

"Yes. Apparently Lieutenant Colonel William Travis drew a line in the sand with a sword and asked those willing to stay and defend the fort to step over the line."

"Did everybody step over the line?"

She warmed to the subject. "Everybody but one man."

"Who's the guy who didn't step over the line?"

Laurel ran through what she remembered. "Keep in mind all of this may have been embellished or invented as a good story, but supposedly a man named Louis Moses Rose did not cross the line. This is just folklore."

"I do like how you quote folklore," he said. "You did a good job facing down Zeke Caine yesterday."

"Thank you. You excelled at refraining from punching him in the face."

Huck grinned. "See, you can read people well."

"No, I didn't read that at all. I just know you." It was surprising how much warmth she felt at being able to make that statement.

He cleared his throat. "We should have a dump on Haylee's phone in a day or so."

"Good. Although Jason Abbott is too smart to call Haylee, unless he wants us to know he called her," Laurel said. "I wish we could obtain Melissa Cutting's phone records."

Huck shook his head. "She's an attorney and has a lot of clients. There's just no way."

How irritating. "I know. I don't suppose Abbott would have told her anything of merit anyway. I think Melissa would have communicated a concern to us."

"You do?"

"Affirmative. I know she's representing him, and she's receiving good press from the case, but he is a serial killer, and she must care about her niece some," Laurel said.

Huck nodded. "We're nowhere on Abbott and so far

nowhere on the two blondes found by the rivers. What did you think of that Tim Kohnex?"

"He sounded lonely," Laurel said. "Kate asked me the same thing about Kohnex."

"Do you think he really believes he's psychic?"

Laurel shrugged. "I don't know. Do you?"

"Yeah," Huck said. "I think he believes it. Do you believe in psychics?"

She shook her head. "There's no empirical evidence that psychics can read thoughts or know of events before they happen. I think a lot of people put dots together. A good charlatan can do that. A talented performer at a circus or a fair can do that. It's all about reading people, which I do not know how to do, but there are some phenomenally talented grifters out there who are capable of it."

"You think Kohnex's a grifter?"

They'd likely find out soon enough. "I think he might really believe," Laurel said.

"In that case, could he be dangerous?" Huck asked.

Anybody could be dangerous. "It depends what his delusions tell him. What do your instincts say about him?"

"I'm not sure," Huck said. "I found him difficult to read."

That was a rarity for the captain.

"Or," Huck acknowledged, "maybe I was just focused on Zeke Caine being in the same room with you. I didn't like it."

Laurel moved toward him. "I didn't like it either, but I need to discover where he has been during his travels. I want to put him in prison, Huck."

"I know." He rubbed the whiskers on his rugged chin.

"How many people have you seen in the last two weeks who have worn red shoes?"

She tried to take a moment away from thinking about murder. "That's a game I play with the deputy director of the FBI."

"Yeah, but it's a fun game."

Her stomach finally settled. "In the last two weeks, I would say probably twenty-eight."

"Probably?"

Sometimes she liked to sound as if she was being thoughtful about something when the number just popped into her head. "Okay. Most certainly twenty-eight."

"That seems like a lot for the small town of Genesis Valley."

"I spoke to a kindergarten class about spring and summer safety, and little red boots appeared to be in style." She looked out the window at the softly falling snow. "Although I should've stressed winter safety since that early spring doesn't appear to be arriving."

He grinned. "True. I'm sure the kids had fun with you."

"Actually"—she frowned—"could I take Aeneas with me next time I visit a classroom? I'm not sure they had fun. They looked confused most of the time, and their teacher had to interpret my words for them."

"Yes, you can take the dog next time."

That would be a relief. "I've learned that children like animals and warm to the person with them instantly."

"Which is why many predators have animals," Huck said, somberly.

"Yeah, I thought of that, too," Laurel said. "I wouldn't use Aeneas in a predatory manner, of course."

Huck chuckled. "Of course. For now, why don't we bug Dr. Ortega again?"

"We shouldn't," she said. "I just spoke to his assistant this morning. Is there any chance Pastor John has returned from his snowmobile trip?"

"No. He probably won't return until Sunday night, from what we've been told. Unfortunately, nobody knows the route they took since it was some sort of unstructured ride."

How unfortunate. She aspired to expedite the work on this case. Had Pastor John truly engaged in an adulterous affair with Mrs. Bearing? Laurel walked past Huck and turned toward her office. "We need to speak with him."

"True. I also want to interview the Bearing family, but they're off grieving somewhere unknown. I called the sheriff again, and he claims he doesn't know where they are, but I'm not sure I believe him. The BOLO hasn't helped any."

"That's unfortunate," Laurel noted. The mayor had two sons: one an adult attorney and the other a teenager still living at home.

Huck scrubbed both hands down his face. "I know the mayor identified the vic as his wife, but I saw the face of that victim. There was a lot of ice and damage, and even the bones seemed crushed—is there a chance it wasn't her?"

"That's unlikely. I didn't recognize the wool coat, not that I know Mrs. Bearing very well. But my first thought when they turned over the body was that it was her, and I believe her wedding ring looked familiar." Laurel crossed around her desk and lifted the phone to dial the ME's office.

"Dr. Ortega," he answered.

Laurel blinked. "Oh. Hi, Dr. Ortega. I'm surprised to have reached you personally."

"Oh, Snow. Yes. Agent Snow, I was just going to call you."

She put him on speakerphone. "I'm here with Captain Huck Rivers. Do you have any news for us?"

"I wanted to let you know that I will be performing autopsies on both bodies you sent to me later today."

"Oh, good," she said.

He sneezed. "I have positively identified both victims. The second one is, not surprisingly, Teri Bearing. We had her prints on file. Also, we managed to run the DNA of the first victim, even though I haven't completed the autopsy yet."

Huck straightened in the doorway. "What did you find?"

"I found a match to you, Captain Rivers," Dr. Ortega said.

Laurel stiffened. "Please extrapolate."

"I analyzed the DNA samples from the victim and Captain Rivers using short tandem repeat markers across numerous loci, including analysis of mitochondrial DNA sequences."

That made sense. "Those are passed from mother to offspring, correct?" Laurel confirmed.

"Correct," Dr. Ortega affirmed.

"What is your conclusion?" She wanted to hold her breath.

The sound of papers rustling came over the line. "The DNA analysis conclusively supports the assertion that

Captain Rivers is the biological son of the first victim. The probability of maternity is 99.99 percent."

Huck didn't move. He didn't even shift his weight.

Laurel searched for a method to provide him comfort, but nothing came to mind. "Thank you, Dr. Ortega. Please let me know when you have the autopsies completed."

"I will. Per protocol, I've notified both of your superiors." Ortega cleared his throat. "Huck?"

Huck looked at the phone. "Hi, Dr. Ortega."

"I'm very sorry for your loss."

Huck's eyes darkened. "Thank you, Doctor. I appreciate it."

Chapter 14

After a long afternoon of failing to make progress on her cases or track down the Bearing men or Pastor John, Laurel tightened her seat belt in Kate's vehicle. "Thank you for the ride home."

"Sure thing," Kate said cheerfully, her headlights on bright. "So Huck got called out on this too-dark and cold night?"

"Yes. He said he'd be a couple of hours." Sometimes Laurel almost forgot that they didn't actually work together. "Now that we know the Iceberg River victim is his mother, we have to take him off this case anyway." She'd miss working with him.

Kate nodded. "Why did you want me to call Sheriff York for you earlier? I thought we all agreed that he's a pain in the butt."

Laurel sighed. "We needed his help since we're down two agents. Plus, since he has familiarity with the mayor and the Bearing family, I believe he knows where they are and can bring them in." So Laurel could schedule time to interview all of them. Since Dr. Ortega had positively identified Mrs. Bearing as the second victim, the sheriff had no choice but to cooperate. If he could only locate Pastor John, he'd actually be of use. Fish and Wildlife were searching for the snowmobiling group, but they only had so many available officers right now, and the Cascades were vast.

Kate's Volkswagen Bug slid on the ice. "Oops." She corrected and slowed down.

"I thought you planned to purchase a winter vehicle."

Kate shrugged. "Vic's will is still being contested by that twit, Kirsti, so the funds he left for the girls haven't exactly arrived yet."

Kate's ex-husband had been murdered by a serial killer earlier that year, and unfortunately, his last will and testament was being challenged by the very young woman for whom he'd left Kate and the girls.

"How are your girls doing?" Laurel asked.

Kate pushed hair out of her eyes. "They're great. Vida is still perfecting her soccer skills for the upcoming season. She's all into geometry. Val is working hard on her photography projects while playing basketball, and Viv is getting ready for lacrosse. It's the first time she's played, and she's pretty excited. She's still dating Ryan."

"That's good. I'm glad they're doing well."

Kate's girls were twelve, fourteen, and sixteen—all cute blondes like their mom.

"We'll have to get together for dinner soon," Kate said. "They miss seeing you."

Laurel had found herself exceedingly preoccupied with numerous commitments lately. "I agree. And don't worry, my vehicle is at Huck's cabin, so I can drive myself tomorrow if he's out on another mission." He'd been called in right around dinnertime to help plant warning flags up near peaks ripe for avalanches. It was a good thing he enjoyed working outside with his dog.

"No problem. If you want a ride, I'm happy to pick you up."

Laurel shook her head. "Thanks, but I'm ready to drive. I do have a new car."

Kate pulled up to Huck's cabin. "Do you want me to help you shovel the drive?"

"Huck enjoys unwinding when he returns home by excavating the entire area. I'll just clear the walkway for now," Laurel said. "You say hi to your girls for me."

"I will." Kate waited until Laurel stood safely to the side of the metal building before backing down the driveway.

Laurel removed the biggest shovel from the shop and made quick work of the walkway before hurrying inside the cabin and shedding her coat and boots. Huck had given her a key not too long ago, and she was starting to feel at home. That feeling should have caused her some concern because she'd never been at home with anybody but her mother.

Her stomach grumbled, and she moved to the kitchen, glancing toward the quiet living room. Huck, per usual, had already stacked kindling and logs in the hearth, so she decided to make a fire before eating. She struck a match, and the logs instantly ignited. There was nothing like a wood-burning fire in the winter. She should add one to the barndominium she planned to build on her mother's property.

She looked out at the light snow still falling. Like

everyone else around her, she was more than ready for spring.

Something in the snow on the deck outside caught her attention, and she moved closer to the sliding glass door. Her breath caught in her throat. She dodged back to the kitchen and grabbed her weapon out of her purse, then shoved on her boots before hurrying to the door and opening it.

She flicked on the outside porch light. Black dahlias had been scattered all over the deck and down onto the grass beside the winding river, their dark red petals stark against the snow and ice. She shivered and pointed her gun in every direction. Black dahlias had been Jason Abbott's calling card.

She tugged her phone from her pocket to call in the trespass to both Fish and Wildlife and the local sheriff's office. She needed this scene processed now.

"Jason?" she yelled toward the forest after she'd clicked off. "Why don't you show courage and move into the light? Let's talk."

The wind whistled eerily through the trees, shaking branches and scattering piles of snow on the ground. She squinted in every direction but could see only darkness. He would've wanted to watch her find the dahlias. In case he was still watching, she kept her face perfectly calm.

"This is actually fairly boring," she called out. "Really? Flowers?"

Her phone buzzed, and she lifted it to her ear. "Agent Snow."

"Did you like my gift?" Abbott asked.

She kept her guard up, making sure to put her back to

the door, just in case. She hadn't searched the entire cabin. While there was no sign of a break-in, she wasn't going to risk another fight with him.

"You mean these stupid flowers?" She forced derision into her tone.

He was silent. "Black dahlias. They symbolize betrayal. Women like you betray."

"Please," she muttered, trying to sound both insolent and bored. "This is the best you've got? Flowers? Show yourself, Jason. Let's finally have this out."

"Laurel, at least be a little appreciative. I can't just find these like I could before. In fact, this is my last batch." He sounded sad about that.

She took a deep breath. "Are you drowning women now instead of strangling them?"

He chuckled. "I'm adaptable, it's true. I'm just getting started. You know I love the long game."

That was a falsehood. He had difficulties with impulse control. She decided to take a page out of Abigail's book. "I've talked to several professional women in the area, and we're all consentient about you."

"What?" he asked.

She could play his game better than he could, and she wasn't even a game player. "Come on. We both know that you are fearful of educated women and not up to sesquipedalian discussion."

He remained silent.

She could utilize even larger words with him, but she figured she'd angered him enough.

"You think I'm stupid?" he snapped.

"I do think you're stupid," she agreed. "I think you're an absolute moron." She eyed the tree line carefully. If he hid out there, he wouldn't be able to keep from rushing her, yet no movement showed.

"You have no idea who I am," he hissed.

She chuckled, and the sound carried on the wind. "I know exactly who you are. You're a little boy who likes to throw tantrums by tossing flowers around. You're silly, Jason. Pathetic."

"Enjoy your evening, Agent Snow," he snarled. "I'm coming for you soon."

Upon rushing home, Huck had searched the entire area around his cabin until finally joining her in bed, having found no evidence left by Jason Abbott. After a night of fitful dreams that involved drowning, Laurel worked overtime in her quiet office, concerned more bodies would be found soon. She poured through the case files on Jason Abbott, a cup of tea on her desk and a half-eaten breakfast burrito in the garbage. The local police had also searched for Abbott in the area around Huck's cabin to no avail, not that she'd expected a glowing arrow pointing to his location.

Huck was currently being interviewed by FBI Agent Norrs and Fish and Wildlife Deputy Chief Wright, and she wished she could be there with him. For him.

Kate appeared in the doorway and brought her a can of ginger ale. "Here you go. This sometimes helps. I heard you throwing up again."

Laurel looked up, still feeling nauseated. "I'm fine. You didn't have to come in on a Saturday."

"If you're working, so am I." Kate smiled, dressed

down in brown jeans and a pretty pink sweater. "How far along are you?"

Laurel blinked and sat back.

Kate shrugged. "I puked with both Viv and Val for months. I recognize the look."

"Oh." Laurel accepted the ginger ale, instantly realizing she couldn't keep this secret from Kate, and lying to her friend held little appeal. Plus, Kate had experienced pregnancy three times and no doubt held much wisdom. "Approximately eleven weeks."

A broad smile spread across Kate's face. "Congratulations, Laurel. I think that's fantastic news."

Laurel opened the soda and took a drink. She'd try anything to get rid of this feeling. "Thank you. I'm worried."

"Of course, you're worried," Kate said. "That's the primary function of a mom. Trust me, I'm always worried. Everything will be fine."

Laurel appreciated the support. "Thank you. I hope so."

"Does that explain why Huck has been hovering lately?"

Laurel took another drink. "Has he been hovering? He's been overprotective, but I've become accustomed to that."

"He has been standing guard around you more than usual," Kate said. "It's a good thing. You have to let him be a part of this."

"I am," Laurel said.

Kate tapped on the door frame. "Good. If you need anything, let me know. I'm sure you'll have questions."

"I'm sure I will. I've been studying and reading up on

pregnancy, but I might have real-life questions," she mused.

Kate chuckled. "All right. I'm here for you." She turned and sauntered out of view.

Laurel looked back at the case file, trying to find any sort of pattern that would lead to a clue where Abbott might be right now. Nothing stood out. She'd had the techs try to trace the phone call from the previous night, but Abbott hadn't been on the line long enough. She also had Nester working from Seattle, analyzing possible vacant properties in the area where Abbott might be squatting. So far, he had not found any viable possibilities.

Her desk phone buzzed, and she saw that it was Kate calling. "Hey, Kate. You were just here."

"Laurel Snow. Did you just make a joke?"

Laurel sat back. "Not really."

"It sounded like one," Kate said. "Rachel Raprenzi from *The Killing Hour* keeps calling, wanting more details about the victims found by the rivers."

The woman certainly was persistent. "Tell her no comment," Laurel said.

"Also, whether you have an update on the Abbott case," Kate continued.

They already had the hotline going, so there was no need to utilize *The Killing Hour* again. At least for now. "Tell her no comment for now."

"Okay, gotcha. Oh. Um, Sheriff York just buzzed in downstairs. Want me to ignore him?"

Laurel sighed. "No. Let him up."

"I guess." Kate clicked off.

Minutes later, Sheriff York walked into Laurel's

office. "I figured I'd update you in person on this fine Saturday since neither one of us is getting a day off anytime soon." He had dark circles under his eyes.

"Hi, Sheriff," she said. "I assume you've found the Bearing men?"

He wiped a hand across his brow. "No. I thought they'd headed out to a friend's cabin near Snowblood peak, but I was wrong. Saul owns a private plane, and I checked, and it's gone."

Laurel blinked. "You allowed the husband of a murder victim to fly out of town?"

His face reddened. "No. I thought they needed a day or two in order to grieve, which is what I'm sure they're doing."

She reached for her phone and texted Nester to track Saul Bearing's plane somehow and then search outlying states for property owned by the Bearings. "When you did speak with the mayor, did you get any information?"

"They all thought Mrs. Bearing had headed out to a spa vacation in Seattle the night she went missing. We're trying to track down any spa where she might've had a reservation, but so far we haven't found anything."

So perhaps she'd lied to her family about her whereabouts, which made sense due to her alleged affair with Pastor John. "What about dumping her phone?"

"We're working on the warrant now."

Laurel took another sip of the bubbly soda, noting her stomach starting to settle. "Did you bring up any alleged affairs to the mayor in those brief moments you spent with him before allowing him to leave the jurisdiction?"

"Are you being sarcastic?"

She stiffened. "No."

His gaze narrowed. "No. We didn't have much time to talk."

She'd prefer to speak with Pastor John before Mayor Bearing, but at this point, she just wanted to find her damn witnesses. Taking a deep breath, she forced herself to sound anything but sarcastic. "I appreciate you initially providing the notification of death to the Bearing family. I know how difficult that can be, and you've been helpful since we're down two agents right now." She required his continued assistance right now, so she forced herself to say the words.

"No problem. I'm sorry we haven't found Pastor John Govern yet. They stupidly didn't take radios with them, so they could be anywhere in the mountains."

Heat clashed down Laurel's throat. How frustrating. She wanted to interview him before the mayor. "Keep the BOLOs on everyone active."

"You got to know Pastor John a little bit, didn't you? During your first case here?"

She thought back. "I interviewed him a few times and he invited me on a date that I refused, but I wouldn't say that I know him." He was a charismatic leader, and the person responsible for securing the TV deal for the church.

York glanced down at the stacks of paper in front of Laurel. "You think Jason Abbott's responsible for these newest killings?"

"I don't know," she said. "I can envision him trying to play games with us by switching his MO. Drowning and leaving a victim covered in ice is similar to strangling and leaving a victim in an ice block." But she worked with facts and not conjecture.

York patted his belly. "I was studying the two recent deaths and noticed something interesting. Your first case, when you arrived in town, had crime scenes at Snow-blood Peak, where the first victim in this case was found. We also found a victim in our latest case at the church."

Laurel straightened. "You're correct. We should see if Fish and Wildlife cameras can be set close to areas where we've found the victims of recent cases, especially those near a body of water."

York nodded. "I'll talk to Fish and Wildlife, but the new bodies weren't exactly where the earlier crimes took place. Nobody has that many cameras."

He made a good point. "Let's have Fish and Wildlife place the cameras on roads leading to former dump sites," she said thoughtfully. "Then if we get a body, at least we'll have a photo of the vehicle the killer is using."

York straightened. "Do you think we'll get another homicide?"

She looked out at the gray day outside. "We need to proceed with that probability. We have two kills within, what? Three days. That's quick, Sheriff York. That's a very fast turnaround."

"Do you think we're looking at another one tomorrow?"

"I hope not. Both of our current victims were blondes, in fairly decent shape, and found frozen. Your investigators need to search for any commonalities between them, especially if their lives intersected at some point." She had Nester doing the same.

York nodded. "Got it. You know, there's another connection they have."

Laurel looked up. "What's that?"

"Huck Rivers. The first vic was his mom, and the second was filmed hitting and threatening him."

Laurel blinked. The sheriff was correct.

Chapter 15

Already in a bad mood, Huck sat in his own interrogation room across from FBI Special Agent in Charge
Wayne Norrs and Fish and Wildlife Deputy Chief Mert
Wright. Aeneas had deserted him and headed toward his
dog bed in the corner of Huck's office upstairs. While
Huck felt some sort of an affinity with Norrs because
he'd seemed like a decent guy during the last case they'd
worked together, his back teeth gritted together at facing
Mert Wright again.

Norrs was wide and stocky with a bald head and intelligent piercing blue eyes. He had a boxer's face, complete with a nose that had no doubt taken a punch or two
during his life. In comparison, Mert Wright was in his
midsixties with a beer gut, beady brown eyes, and a
bald head.

"I can't believe the clusterfuck you've gotten us into
this time, Rivers," Wright snapped.

Huck kept his expression stoic and tried to focus. He
could not believe Jason Abbott had called Laurel the
night before.

Norrs cut Wright a look. "I don't think it's the captain's fault his mother was found dead at the base of a mountain, Deputy Chief. Maybe go easy."

Wright pushed back in his chair. "Go easy? What are we going to do when the news gets ahold of this?"

"Deal with it," Huck said somberly.

Norrs cleared his throat. "I think I'll take the lead on this. First, Captain Rivers, I have to tell you that we did notify the local sheriff about the identity of the first victim. Sheriff York gave me his word that he'd keep that under wraps."

Huck sighed. "York doesn't like me. I'm sure he'll announce that the vic was my mother."

"No," Norrs said. "He's still feeling the heat from allowing Jason Abbott to escape. He'll keep his mouth shut."

Perhaps he would. Who knew? "Okay."

Norrs sat back. "Captain, when was the last time you spoke with your mother?"

Huck agreed with Norrs taking the lead. "I've never spoken to my mother."

"Never?" Wright asked incredulously, his thin eyebrows lifting into his bald forehead.

"Never," Huck said easily. "Never met the woman. She didn't want to have kids but got pregnant. Agreed to have me and then left me with my dad. He seemed fine with it."

Wright leaned forward, his beady eyes narrowing. "You're telling me you never once in your entire life talked to your mother?"

"Not once," Huck said.

Norrs cocked his head. "Did you ever try to find her?

You have enough military and police contacts that you could have most likely tracked her down."

"No, I never tried to find her. She left." As far as Huck was concerned, she hadn't wanted a life with him. "She made her choice, and I wasn't going to hunt her down and ask her why. Some people don't want kids."

Unlike him. He definitely wanted the baby Laurel was carrying, without question. They might have to keep that news under wraps until this case was over, however.

Norrs tapped a pen on the scratched metal table between them. "What about your father? Did he ever talk to her?"

"Not to my knowledge," Huck said. "I think he would've told me had she ever reached out or if he had ever called her. He wasn't big on secrets."

Wright shook his head. "So then she suddenly appears here dead?"

"Imagine my surprise," Huck said dryly. "I have no idea what she was doing here. I don't know where she came from or where she's been the last thirty-two years. Until she turned up murdered, I figured she didn't want to know me."

"Do you care?" Norrs asked.

Huck's chest hitched. "Yeah, I care. It's my job. When somebody's killed in my territory, when they're murdered, it's my job to figure out who did it." Plus, she had been his mother. He'd find out who killed her and put them in prison.

"It's not your job this time," Wright snapped. "You are off the case."

Norrs nodded. "I concur. You can't be involved with

this case, Captain Rivers, even though you hadn't seen or heard from Delta Rivers your entire life."

"That's fine," Huck said. "We have enough going on to keep me busy."

"True." Norrs had dark circles under his eyes. Apparently, he had been working around the clock.

Huck cut a look at Wright. "Monty Buckley is more than capable of running the investigation. You didn't need to come in from Seattle. When was the last time you actually investigated a case?" The guy was a paper pusher.

Wright's face turned red. "Watch yourself."

"There wasn't a phone or any identification with the body," Huck said. "Have you been able to trace my mother's movements?"

"You're off the case," Norrs repeated evenly. "Your father must have told you something about your mother."

Huck thought back. "He told me that she was a free spirit who liked to drink beer. That she didn't want to be tied down and definitely didn't want a family."

"How did they meet?" Norrs asked.

Huck didn't have many details. His dad wasn't exactly one to wax on about anything. "I think river rafting. My dad was a guide on weekends to make extra money in the summers, and I believe he said that a group she was in had rented the rafts."

"What group?" Wright asked.

Those kinds of details would have been irrelevant to his father. "I have absolutely no idea," Huck said.

"You're telling me that this woman abandoned you, and yet your father still gave you her name as your middle name? Huck Delta Rivers?" Norrs asked smoothly.

Huck grinned. "I think he figured I might want to take a part of her through life since I wouldn't have *her* with me. But you should also know that Huck comes from his dog Huckleberry, who died before I was born. So maybe my dad just had trouble thinking up names."

Wright crossed his arms. "Being abandoned like that, you must feel rage or anger toward her."

Huck lifted his shoulders. "Not really. She didn't actually exist in my mind, you know? My dad told me about her, and that was it. She was a fleeting thought." He didn't know how to explain it. "My upbringing was fine, and I wondered once in a while about her, but that's as far as it went. We all make our choices in life, and she made hers."

Norrs leaned forward. "So when she was no longer just a thought, when she showed up in your town, how did that make you feel?"

It was a good question, and Huck could see where Norrs wanted to go with it. "Considering she was dead when I saw her for the first time, it felt weird," Huck admitted.

"It's our understanding that you recognized her immediately," Wright pushed.

Huck nodded. "I did. I'd seen pictures, of course, but it's been more than three decades. She didn't age much." He hadn't really thought about it. "There were definitely wrinkles and some changes, but I recognized her," he said. "Then I figured I was wrong, because why would she be here? If she were here, why didn't she call me or at least try to meet up?"

Norrs took a notebook out of his jacket pocket and

started scribbling on the paper. "You're telling us that she did not contact you in any way?"

Huck shook his head. "You can dump my phone. I know you're probably already dumping the office phones. If she called me, we did not connect. I get a lot of spam callers, and if I don't recognize the number, I don't pick up." That was pretty common in law enforcement as far as he knew. "If she'd ever left a message, we'd have something to talk about. But my guess is she didn't call me." Why hadn't she? Yeah, he wished she had called him. He couldn't help but be curious about her.

"How do you know that she didn't try to contact you?" Norrs asked.

Huck shrugged. "Fish and Wildlife has been in the news quite a bit lately in connection with the different serial killer cases in Washington State. If she wanted to get ahold of me, she could've found me easily." He had to wonder what she was doing in town and why she hadn't reached out. Did she still have friends in the vicinity? If so, nobody had ever mentioned that fact to him.

Norrs looked down at his papers. "Where were you the night Delta Rivers was murdered?"

"I was home," Huck said. "Well, after a search of the farming district for a poacher who shot too close to residences."

Wright scratched at a scab on his chin. "You were called in to search for a poacher?"

"Yes," Huck said. "There are several residences over in the farming land. One called in a report that somebody was trying to shoot deer way too close to their house."

"Did you catch the person?" Wright asked.

Huck shook his head. "No. I took the report and searched, but we didn't find anybody. You can check the call-in logs and you can interview the people I spoke with. A nice family named the Martinellis."

Norrs shifted. "Did you find evidence of possible poaching?

"Yes. I spoke with the Martinellis, and somebody definitely shot too close to their house. They hit the siding, in fact. Feel free to talk to them." He cracked his neck. "In addition, I took pictures and documented the scene. You can review the entire casc file at your leisure."

"We definitely will," Wright said. "You could've been the poacher, right? I mean, if you wanted to set up an alibi, that's an easy one."

Huck frowned. "I wouldn't shoot close to a house like that."

Wright snorted. "Do you have a burner phone?"

"No."

Wright scratched beneath his left eye. "Okay, Captain. Now we're going to sit here and you're going to recount every minute of your past week."

Norrs nodded. "I think it's necessary, too. What time were you called out by the Martinellis?"

Huck scrubbed both hands down his face. When had he last shaved? "I think it was around midnight, but double-check the call logs for an exact time."

"My assistant is going through all of the records right now," Norrs said. "How long did it take for you to reach the farm?"

"It's a thirty-minute drive from my place, but it was

cloudless and very cold that night, which means the roads became iced over, so I might've taken more time. Then I spent at least an hour speaking with them, investigating the damage, and taking notes and pictures." It had been freezing that night, and he'd fitted Aeneas with a heavy coat before taking him out to search.

Wright studied him, obviously looking for a question to ask.

Norrs ignored Huck's boss. "How long did you search the vicinity?"

The guy knew what he was doing. "I searched for a couple of hours at least," Huck said. "The Martinellis have about fifty acres that abut forest land, so it took a while."

Wright frowned. "If they have fifty acres, why the hell would anybody shoot close to their house? Especially so late at night?"

Huck dug deep to keep his temper in check. "Because they were poaching, Deputy Chief. They must've followed a good-sized buck via the moonlight, since it was clear and freezing, and then decided to take a shot too close to the house. Since it was so late, maybe they figured nobody would bother getting out of bed to contact us."

It irritated the hell out of him that anybody would shoot that close to a dwelling. Especially at night. There had been kids sleeping peacefully in their beds. He would keep looking for the poacher. Anybody dumb enough to make that mistake would make another.

Wright threw up both hands. "Did anybody see this huge-assed buck?"

"Just the poacher," Huck said.

"Then why couldn't you or your dog find the shooter?"

Huck shrugged. "Aeneas tracked a scent to a nearby logging road, and my guess is that the shooter had a vehicle there. Dogs can't track vehicles." Although he'd searched the entire area just to make sure.

Norrs nodded. "After you failed to find the poacher, what did you do?"

"I took my dog and headed home to sleep around three in the morning."

Norrs focused on him. "Can anybody confirm your timeline? Exactly when you returned to your home?"

Huck didn't like this at all. "Yes. Special Agent in Charge Laurel Snow can confirm what time I returned home."

Wright's beady eyes gleamed. "So you and the FBI agent are sleeping together. That's a terrible conflict of interest."

"Sometimes our cases cross, but there's no conflict," Huck retorted. "I understand that I need to recuse myself from this case, but you're crazy if you take Laurel off it."

"She's that good?" Wright sneered.

Huck didn't give a crap that the man was his boss. He was about to be punched in the face.

Norrs cocked his head. "As for Teri Bearing's murder, you were out on a call that night across the river from the church where her body was found, right? We have your GPS, Captain."

Huck remained stoic while his body flooded with adrenaline. "Yes. We received a call, an anonymous one, about an elderly man wandering in the snowy forest."

"Did you find him?" Wright asked.

"No." Huck drew in air. "Laurel was with me in bed when the call came in."

Wright picked at a pimple on his chin. "You could've called Fish and Wildlife, gotten back in bed, and then received the call from the office."

Huck didn't have time for this. "I didn't do that. Again, I'm off the case but Laurel should stay on if you want to find this killer." Although he'd rather send her on a vacation somewhere warm, but he knew better. She was dedicated to the point of being obsessive.

Wright scoffed. "Nobody is that good. She can't be."

"You're wrong," Agent Norrs answered for Huck. "Laurel Snow is that good when it comes to catching serial killers. There's a reason she heads the Pacific Northwest Violent Crimes Unit. I'll go speak with her after this interview."

Wright pivoted to face him. "You think she'll tell the truth? That she wouldn't lie for her boyfriend and provide an alibi for *two murders*?"

Norrs frowned. "I do think she'd tell the truth, and what is there to lie about? The captain just admitted he was searching the forest, alone with his dog, within the approximate time frame of Delta Rivers being murdered and to searching along the river, with his dog, within the time frame of Teri Bearing's murder. GPS shows that both searches were within a stone's throw of the murdered and scenes."

Well, shit.

Chapter 16

After a frustrating day without her team, Laurel gratefully climbed up into Huck's truck after work. Maybe they should take Sunday off. She turned on the seat warmer. "You know, I could drive once in a while. I did just buy a new Nissan Murano." Her former SUV had been riddled with bullet holes she was fairly certain had been fired by Abigail after she'd stabbed Zeke Caine.

"You can drive anytime you want," he said.

Laurel looked at him beneath her lashes. "You always try to drive."

He shrugged. "I'm a good driver."

"More like a control freak," she muttered. Yet it was true. His reflexes were seconds faster than hers, and he was more accustomed to driving on the winter roads.

Plus, while she might not admit it, she did like to relax and think through her cases without having to concentrate on the road. But still, she had purchased the new Nissan, and she should drive it more. Right now might be a better time to focus on him, however. "How are you feeling?" she asked gingerly.

"Feeling? Fine."

Perhaps she had asked the wrong question. "You have recently discovered that your mother, who abandoned you when you were a baby, was found dead in your own backyard. I wonder if that fact pattern raised certain feelings within you."

He barked out a laugh. "'*That* fact pattern'?"

"Yes." She truly lacked the ability to do this. "I'm concerned about your welfare."

He reached over and took her hand. "I appreciate your concern. I really do. But I never considered Delta to be family. She had me, she left. Dad was my family."

"Still, I felt the lack of a father growing up," she said, although she had truly been better off without him, considering Zeke Caine had turned out to be her father. "So, you must have felt the absence of a mother."

He shrugged. "Sure. There were other moms who volunteered at the school, and I had friends whose moms would cut off the crust of their sandwiches when I was young. Then in high school when I played football, there was the night everybody gave their away jersey to their mom to wear. So, yeah, I guess I missed having a mom, but Dad and I did all right. So did you and your mom."

Laurel nodded. Perhaps that was one of the qualities that drew them together. They had both grown up without one parent. "Yet it must feel odd that she's dead."

He looked out the window. It had finally stopped snowing, and the moon had already begun to climb into the sky.

"I guess. I didn't know if she was alive or dead for thirty-two years. So, I suppose I am wishing she'd

reached out while she was here, so we could've met."
His hands remained relaxed on the steering wheel as he
capably maneuvered the country roads. "I think it's odd
that she was found here in my hometown. Why did she
come back to Genesis Valley after all this time?"

"That question has been traversing my thoughts as
well. Are you certain she didn't try to contact you?"

He shook his head. "I suppose I get spam calls like
everybody else, but I ignore them. If people don't leave
a message, then I pay little attention."

"What about at the office?"

He took the turn down Birch Tree Road toward his
cabin. "They have a deputy scouring through all of the
call logs, but nothing so far. We'll need to see if she had
a cell phone and conduct a background check on her."

Laurel took a deep breath. "There's no *we*. You've
been taken off the case, and I am probably next."

She could maintain a professional distance from the
emotions of the case and still investigate it. However, she
didn't want to do anything to put the case in jeopardy,
and an apparent conflict of interest would do just that.
"Special Agent Norrs informed me that he's going to
join the case as soon as he wraps up his three other
ones." So she had a little time to find Jason Abbott,
whether or not he was their current killer.

Huck parked the truck near his sturdy metal shop. "I
need to run with Aeneas for a while. He's been cooped
up all day. Why don't you go inside and get warm?"

"I'd love to be warm." She stepped out of the vehicle.
"I'll heat up stew. It's in the freezer. My mom sent it
over last week."

"Sounds good. Come on, Aeneas." He opened the back door to release the animal.

Laurel carefully picked her way across the still-icy ground and entered the cabin, removed her jacket and boots, and then started a fire. Once again, Huck had placed paper, kindling, and wood in a perfect formation, so all she had to do was light the match. Starting a fire was easy for her, because she could visualize the geometric proportions necessary, but it was nice that Huck took care of the preparations.

Her phone buzzed, and she lifted it to her ear, walking over to the sofa. "Agent Snow."

"Hi, Agent Snow. It's Dr. Ortega."

"Hi." She sat on the sofa and tucked one leg under her. "How are you?"

He coughed. "Tired. But I have the autopsy results for both of your recent victims."

Laurel watched the fire. "Thank you for calling. What did you find?"

"Starting with Delta Rivers, I found multiple contusions and abrasions on the upper limbs and right side of the head."

"Okay," Laurel said. "Somebody grabbed her arms and her head."

"Yes," Dr. Ortega affirmed. "Specifically, there are clusters of bruises on both forearms consistent with being forcefully gripped, and also an abrasion on the right cheekbone, maybe from blunt force trauma."

That made sense with Laurel's theory of the case. "So somebody grabbed her arms and her head, and either hit her in the face or smashed her face into a hard surface such as ice."

"That's what I surmise. No internal injuries or fractures noted, and the skin around the wrists was damaged. I collected fiber samples that look like rope and sent them to the lab"

So the killing was more about restraint than inflicting bodily injury. "What about cause of death?"

"Petechial hemorrhage is present in the conjunctiva of both eyes, indicative of asphyxia."

"What about her lungs?" Laurel asked.

He cleared his throat and then coughed several times, sounding as if he was coming down with a cold. The man had probably been working around the clock. "The lungs are edematous and congested, with foam present in the airways consistent with drowning."

Laurel clicked through what she remembered about the victim. "What about a microscopic examination?"

Keys tapped across the line. "The presence of diatoms was confirmed in lung tissue samples supporting the diagnosis of drowning."

Laurel had figured that would be the case, but one never knew. "Any additional findings?"

"Yes, the toxicology report is pending, but blood analysis shows signs consistent with hypothermia, including elevated levels of cold-induced enzymes."

Laurel nodded. "That makes sense because the river is freezing. Please give me the conclusion."

Dr. Ortega cleared his throat. "Cause of death is determined to be drowning with evidence of premortem physical altercation, including bruising consistent with forceful restraint and signs of blunt force trauma to the head. The manner of death is classified as homicide."

Laurel leaned back and rubbed a hand over her eye.

"What do you think? It sounds like she fought with somebody, and then they shoved her head down into the freezing water until she drowned."

"Unfortunately," Dr. Ortega said, "that's exactly what it sounds like. The thing is, especially at the Iceberg River, they would've had to cut a hole in that ice, even on the edge, to be able to do this. There was scraping on the top of her scalp as if her head was actually shoved beneath the ice."

"That's a very brutal killing," Laurel murmured. "What about Teri Bearing's autopsy?"

The doctor clicked keys again. "Everything's pretty much the same as the first victim except for height and weight. Same manner of death—definite drowning."

"Any other injuries?"

"Affirmative. Contusions on the body and same on the skull that might've caused loss of consciousness, as well as damage from the probable ropes around the wrists," he said.

Laurel looked up at the ceiling. "It would take a perpetrator with impressive strength to be able to hold a victim down like that."

"Maybe," Dr. Ortega said, sounding exhausted. "It would depend on leverage."

That was an excellent point. Especially on the freezing banks of both rivers, if the victims' hands were bound for some time. Even if their hands had been freed, it would have been difficult for either of them to find purchase with arms or elbows or hands to shove themselves back up, particularly if somebody had pushed their heads beneath the ice.

"Thank you for your dedicated work. I appreciate it," Laurel said.

"Any time. I hope you catch this guy before I get another body. Good night, Agent Snow." He ended the call.

Another body? So did she. The wind howled against the windows, and she shivered. Was Jason Abbott this killer? Or did she have two monsters out there?

Chapter 17

Val Vuittron could not make the bank shot. Frustration made her hands shake as she tried again and missed.

"It's okay." Her pal Lonni slapped her on the back. "Take a deep breath. This is just open gym, dude."

Val looked at her friend. "Did you just call me dude?"

Lonni grinned, showing new blue rubber bands in her braces. She had curly black hair and sparkling brown eyes. Her skin was a deep brown with peach highlights, and she was an excellent point guard. "Yes. Relax. We're just goofing off. We have a lot of time until the spring tournaments."

"Yeah, but I want to win this year." They played three-on-three in the street, and last year she'd nearly broken her ankle. Her mom had freaked and made her wear a brace for the rest of the tournament. Sometimes it seemed like her mom working with Laurel and the FBI calmed her, and other times, Kate had to triple-check the locks on the doors before going to sleep.

Lonni tossed the ball and hit the backboard, making a basket. "We will, but part of this game is having fun."

"Are you a philosopher now?" Val snorted. "I need some water. I'll be right back."

"I'll just keep hitting threes," Lonni said cheerfully.

Val chuckled and wove through the other girls practicing. They'd set up a game, four against four, later, but right now they were just goofing off. She enjoyed open gym, and she liked having found a game that neither her older nor younger sister played.

Plus, she loved postponing homework. Anything that would put off studying for the physics test she had on Monday, which she'd have to do the second she got home. At least she had all day tomorrow to figure out how to solve projectile motion problems.

She moved out of the gym to the darkened hallway and reached the water fountain, taking several big drinks, careful not to put her mouth on the metal. She'd forgotten her water bottle again, probably in the back of her mom's car.

"Hey there, can you help me? I've lost my dog," a man said.

She yelped and turned to look at him. "Excuse me?"

Empty and chilly, the hallway felt dark, although the gym was close by. She glanced toward the brighter lights and measured the distance.

"Yeah." He shook his head. "I'm so sorry, but I saw some girls leave the door open a few minutes ago. My dog ran inside the school. I have no idea where I am. I've never been in here."

"Oh," she said. Lost dog. It could happen. She squinted to see him in the barely there light. The guy was good looking. He was about six feet tall, cleanly shaven, and had sparkling eyes. A battered ball cap covered shorter dark hair. In his hands, he held a leash. But it was a little after dinnertime on a Saturday night, so was it odd that he was out with his dog? She wasn't sure.

"I just let him off leash for a minute," the guy said. "I'm sorry to bug you." He looked toward the gym. "I know you're busy. Just point me toward the best place to look."

She glanced down the hallway. "I'd look in the cafeteria. If you go down and take a right, you should be able to reach it." Dogs could probably smell old chicken casserole and burgers, which had been the offerings that week.

"Thanks."

She frowned. Weren't most of the outdoor doors locked? It was possible somebody had left the door a little bit ajar. She'd seen it happen before. But she also imagined most of her friends would stop a dog or at least chase him if they saw him enter. She edged toward the gym.

"I'm sorry." The guy held both hands up and backed away. "I didn't mean to scare you. This is weird."

"No, it's not weird." She felt stupid. "Not if you're really looking for your dog."

He was hot, his tight body dressed in a light black coat and jeans. He had to be in his, what, early twenties? She might only be fourteen, but she recognized a hottie when she saw one.

He pushed the cap further up his head. "I'll let you get back to it," he said. "I'm sorry about this."

"No, really. I didn't mean to . . ."

"Be smart?" he asked, chuckling. "You are. I'm a

strange man in a hallway. You should be on alert. And the whole dog thing, isn't that something serial killers use?"

She giggled. That trick was exactly something serial killers used.

The guy was charming and seriously cute with a dimple. "Do you want to help me look for the dog?" he asked.

The hair on her back rose again. "No, I don't think so, but I'm happy to call the janitor or even the principal." Her phone was in the gym. Damn it.

He moved toward her then.

Heat flashed through her ears, making them ring. She backed away.

"Now, Val, you've finally grown a brain, huh?"

He knew her name. Chills went through her, and her stomach dropped. Her knees trembled. She could kick him and she could run. He had that leash in his hands, but no weapon. What was that old saying? You charge the guy with the gun, and you run from the guy with a knife? She could get to the gym and safety.

He leaned in. "I know who you are."

She swallowed. "Yeah, I figured that out when you said my name."

He edged slightly between her and the gym.

She could hear the basketballs bouncing and girls laughing. "What do you want?" Her voice trembled.

He reached out and ran a finger down her face. "Don't you worry. You're too young and unaccomplished for me. For now, anyway."

She reacted as she'd been taught, trying to knee him in the nuts. He slapped her knee down and pushed her against the fountain, hard. She cried out as her hip hit the metal.

"Then again, you are awfully pretty."

Lonni moved through the doorway. "Come on. We're going to play—" She stopped.

Val's stomach clenched, and she pushed the man, running toward Lonni and screaming for help.

"Say hi to your mom and Laurel for me, will you?" he yelled, running away.

Val reached Lonni and shoved her back into the gym. "We need to call the police."

Laurel handed Val a warm cup of tea from the microwave.

The girl huddled beneath a blanket on her sofa with her mom's arm around her. "Yeah, that's definitely him," she said, looking at the picture of Jason Abbott on the sofa table in front of her. "But he shaved his beard. I didn't recognize him. I never really looked at his pictures in the paper, to be honest. He's really good looking." She sounded lost.

Stark pale, Kate sat next to her while Val's sisters sat on the floor near the sofa. Kate looked up, her pupils wide. "I can't believe he got that close to her. Laurel, what are we going to do?"

Laurel shook her head. She knew Jason Abbott wanted to play games, but she'd never thought he'd go after one of the girls.

Val gulped. "He said I was too young and unaccomplished for him. What does that mean?"

Laurel shook her head and looked at Kate, who was

not too young or unaccomplished. She was actually a professional woman and exactly the kind of victim for Jason. "How do you four feel about taking a vacation?"

Kate blinked. "Laurel, I can't leave you."

"The whole team is gone, so maybe we all need a break," Laurel said. "I'll request temporary workers. Kate, until I catch him, until I find him, none of you are safe."

Val sniffed. "I don't feel safe."

Laurel truly hadn't thought he would do something like this. "I don't think I'm underestimating him," she said absently. "He's obviously had time in jail to build new fantasies."

The drowning did make sense to her. The victim was truly helpless with her head held beneath the water, and he'd always liked frozen bodies.

She had the local police trying to track down where he'd acquired the dahlias that he'd placed around Huck's cabin. This cat-and-mouse game he was playing had to end, but first, she needed to make sure that Kate and her girls found safety.

The sheriff had just left after taking Val's statement, and the entire school had been alerted by the principal.

"Do we know how he got into the building?" Kate asked.

Laurel shook her head. "Not yet. The police are looking into it. They haven't seen any evidence of broken windows or locks, so it's entirely possible someone just left the door ajar."

"It happens a lot," Val said. "We feel pretty safe, and no one was really worried. To be honest, I wasn't that scared when he first started talking to me."

Laurel took a deep breath as Kate visibly shuddered, holding her daughter closer.

"It's all right," Laurel said. "This weather isn't good for any of us. Walter's in the Caribbean. Nester's stuck in Seattle, but I'm sure he'll be returning any day. So it's on me. I want to send you all to this wonderful resort in North Carolina. I visited there during a case once, and I don't know if you know this, but the weather in North Carolina is perfect this time of year."

Val perked up, her face still pale and her eyes red from crying. "Did you say perfect . . . as in sunny?"

"Yes. The resort where I'm sending you is in an area where it's in the midseventies right now on the ocean. You are going to love it." Laurel forced a smile.

Kate gulped. "I can't let you spend money like that."

Laurel waved a hand in the air. "Kate, please. I've invested well through the years, and I haven't had anything to spend money on. This is important. Abbott is after me and is going to target anybody close to me. I can't let anything happen to you and the girls."

"I don't know," Kate murmured.

The idea of being without Kate left Laurel with a sense of isolation she hadn't experienced in a long time, but she hid that feeling from her only friend. "Really, you need to go."

"What about school?" Val asked.

Laurel looked at her. "I'll go speak to each one of your teachers and flash my badge if need be."

Viv snorted, watching her younger sister. "I think that's okay. A note from mom should do it. But I wouldn't worry about it, considering a serial killer just talked to

Val in the hallway tonight. I'm sure we could pretty much do anything we want for the next couple of weeks."

"Good." Laurel reached for her phone. "I have a travel agent I work with out of DC. I'm texting her now, and she will make the arrangements for you to leave first thing tomorrow morning."

"It's three hours later in DC right now." Kate's chin lowered.

Laurel immediately received a text back. "That's okay. Janice never sleeps. She said she'll have excellent arrangements to us within the hour."

"Okay," Kate said, relief crossing her face. "I guess we need to pack." She looked around. "Laurel, thank you for coming over so quickly."

Laurel studied the smooth leather sofa. "Happy to help. I'm staying the night."

"Oh," Kate said. "You don't need to do that."

"Yes, I do," Laurel said grimly, her weapon at the ready in her purse. She didn't believe Jason Abbott would make a move on Kate or the girls tonight, but she would never underestimate him again.

A knock sounded on the door, and they all jolted.

Laurel swung to her feet, grabbing her purse.

"Hey, it's me," Huck called out.

"Thank goodness." Vida, the youngest, jumped up.

Laurel walked toward the door and opened it so Huck could come inside, several pizzas in hand.

"I brought pizza," he said, his gaze dark but his smile wide. He shut the door.

Vida went to help him. "I'll get sodas out of the fridge. I think we have paper plates as well."

"That's good." Huck looked around. "I take it we're staying here tonight?"

Laurel took all day Sunday off with Huck after seeing Kate and the girls off at the airport. They watched old movies, played gin rummy, and hung out with Aeneas. She missed her cat but wasn't comfortable bringing him over to Huck's yet. Plus, Deidre loved spending time with Fred. The downtime was good for Laurel's mental health to allow her subconscious to work on the myriad of problems in her cases.

Plus, Fish and Wildlife officers were keeping watch over Deidre all weekend, which relaxed Laurel even more.

However, Monday morning her frontal lobe was back to being fully engaged. She worked the morning away, making phone calls, arranging her schedule, and seeking a connection between Delta Rivers and Teri Bearing. When she failed utterly at that, she turned to the Jason Abbott case and reviewed his files again, trying to find any sort of clue as to where he might be. She also finally tracked down Uma Carrington, Zeke Caine's alibi for Teri Bearing's murder, and arranged to speak to the woman in person the following afternoon.

Agent Norrs had assigned his executive assistant to cover for Kate at the front reception desk. Her name was Sherry Layton, and Laurel had met her during a previous case. The white-haired woman seemed both professional and efficient.

Laurel missed Kate already. The office even felt

colder somehow. Laurel's cell phone buzzed, and she pressed the speaker. "Agent Snow."

"Agent Snow, you absolutely must leave my girlfriend alone," Zeke Caine said, his voice rough.

Laurel's stomach dropped, and she sat back in her chair, looking at the phone on the desk. "Uma Carrington is your alibi for the killing of a woman right outside your church. I have no choice but to speak with her."

Zeke sighed heavily through the phone. "I'd think you would trust me. I am your father."

"You raped my mother," Laurel retorted instantly and then took a deep breath to calm herself. Emotions would just get in the way of dealing with this narcissistic jackass.

"I am sorry to snap at you," Zeke said. "I've been trying to get ahold of your mother, but she won't return my calls. I think we need to have a family meeting."

Laurel stiffened to the point that her neck popped. "You will, under no circumstances, try to contact my mother again. Do you understand me?" Why hadn't Deidre told Laurel of these attempts? If her mother had some outlandish notion that Laurel needed to be protected because she was pregnant, Laurel needed to disabuse her of that idea right now. Clearly, Laurel needed to find a way to get Deidre out of Genesis Valley for a short time.

"Come on, Laurel, you're back in town. I'm back in town. It's time we cleared the air. Your mom needs to tell the truth."

"You will not contact her again. I will obtain a restraining order if necessary, and I have no doubt that would greatly hinder your attempts to preach to the world via television. Do you understand me?"

Silence ticked over the line for several moments. "I'm not somebody you want to threaten, daughter," he said.

A chill slicked through her. "That declaration did not constitute a threat. That was an unequivocal assurance. My mother shall remain entirely beyond your reach."

"Ah, Laurel," he said. "This is not the route you want to take with me."

She crossed her arms and forced herself to remain calm. "I have no idea where you've been on your little walkabout, but I will trace your path. I know that you left victims in your wake, and Zeke, I'm going to find them."

Now a hiss came over the line. "I am always two steps ahead of everybody, daughter. So you go ahead and ignore my warnings. But when your world starts crumbling, remember that you had a choice. Remember this moment."

"Are you threatening an FBI agent?" she asked calmly.

His chuckle was dark. "Absolutely not. I'm just talking to the daughter I didn't know existed for most of her life. If this had gone differently, I would've protected you from Abigail. Now you are on your own, and believe me, you have no idea what lies in the heart of the woman who shares your DNA."

Laurel looked out her window at the chilly day. "I can read Abigail just fine. In fact, I believe the two of you, at your cores, are the same."

He laughed this time, somehow making even that sound threatening. "Not even close, Laurel. Oh, Abigail's dangerous, but she's a puppy playing in a dog's world."

"I take it you're the dog?" Laurel asked instantly.

"We'll see when I have my teeth around your neck." He chuckled again. "Figuratively, of course. I would never hurt anybody in this world, but daughter, you should have chosen the path of being my ally. Now you'll learn more about me than you ever wanted to know." He clicked off.

Laurel sat back and looked at her phone before turning and vomiting violently into her waste basket.

Chapter 18

Early afternoon, Laurel sat in her conference room next to Fish and Wildlife Captain Monty Buckley, whose face had turned nearly as pale as his white hair. He'd been thrilled to tell her that they'd located Pastor John, who was being brought in for an interview. Right now.

"Are you sure you want to be here?" she asked. "You haven't given yourself enough time to recover from the radiation treatments."

Monty coughed. "I'm happy to be anywhere and am so thankful I no longer have cancer. I just have a little bug that I caught because my defenses are down." His hand shook when he reached for his cup of coffee.

"I think you should go home," she said. "Monty, you and my mother have started becoming friends, and I know it would hurt her greatly if anything happened to you."

He straightened his shoulders. "I need to be here, Laurel. Huck can't be."

"We're working the case together, but that doesn't mean we both have to be at every interview. Right now, Fish and Wildlife is tracking down the movements of

Mrs. Bearing while Nester is doing the same for Delta
Rivers, working remotely. Our organizations work well
together, Monty. We can cover for each other."

He looked at the door and then back. "Are you sure?"

"Yes. Why don't you take the afternoon off, get some
sleep?"

He faltered and then stood. "I really could use some
sleep."

"I will send you my notes after I meet with Pastor
John, okay?"

Monty smiled, and the tension around his eyebrows,
forehead, and mouth had eased. "Okay, sounds good. If
anything happens on the case, call me in." He walked
shakily out the door.

Silence pounded around the office after he left. Even
the wind sounded mournful outside. Laurel called Nester.

He answered immediately. "Hi, boss."

"How's your sister?" she asked.

"Good. She's going to be okay."

What a relief. "I'm so glad. Have you had a chance to
conduct my searches?"

"Yep. I've been running searches for you and also for
my sister. I will find the truck that hit her." The rapid
clacking of keys came across the line. "I have not found
Saul Bearing or either of his sons."

She drew in a deep breath. "We have the local police
interviewing everyone at the mayor's office as well as
the elder son's law firm, and nobody has a clue where
they've gone." Perhaps the mayor had killed his wife.

"How infuriating. About Delta Rivers. So far, I have
not found a cell phone account for her. However, I did
track her movements and see that she arrived in town

just one day before her body was found. She flew in from Santa Fe."

Laurel straightened. "Did she travel solo?"

"Yep. I'm still trying to find out more information."

Laurel bit back frustration. Nester was doing his best. "Thank you. Call me when you have more." She clicked off.

Movement sounded and Sherry brought back Pastor John Govern.

"Pastor John. Hello." Laurel stood and shook his hand. "We've had a BOLO out on you for days."

"I heard. Sorry about that. We snowmobiled where faith took us and just returned a short time ago." Pastor John looked at the rough wooden door. "I take it something happened to your conference table?"

"The glass shattered in an unfortunate incident. We're using the door until we obtain a new top." Laurel studied the pastor. He had to be in his midthirties with short, curly brown hair, deep brown skin, and lighter brown eyes behind wire-rimmed glasses. He had shaved today, showing a hard cut jaw. He stood to about Huck's height but was slimmer than the captain.

"It's good to see you again," the pastor said, settling into the seat.

"Thank you. You, too," Laurel said. "Perhaps next time you venture into the Cascades, you should take a radio with you, Pastor John."

He waved a hand in the air. "Maybe. And it's John. Just John, remember? You're not a member of the congregation . . . unless that has changed?"

"No," she said. "That has not changed."

"Then call me John." The pastor smiled, showing a perfect row of teeth. "I apologize for not being available before now, since I've heard all the news. I cannot believe somebody brutally killed Mrs. Bearing and left her body behind my church."

Laurel watched his facial expressions closely. "Did you know Mrs. Bearing?"

"Of course. The Bearings are members of our church," Pastor John said. "I, um, I see them every Sunday." He looked away slowly and took several deep breaths.

She deliberately switched topics. "About Zeke Caine, just how long was he missing? A year, two years, five years? When we first talked, it was my understanding he'd been gone for a year. But now I understand he's actually been missing for five years? Please explain."

Pastor John took off his glasses and wiped them on the bottom of his blue sweater. "I don't know. He was gone between three and five years. They all kind of blurred together. I could look back at the exact date I took over."

"Then why did you initially tell us it was one year?" Laurel asked.

"It felt like a year. I don't know," Pastor John said. "The last few months have been very difficult for everybody in this community."

Laurel didn't think that was it. "You saw Pastor Caine during that time, didn't you?"

Pastor John flushed. "Yes. I saw him a year before you arrived in town, but he had taken a sabbatical before that, so when you add it all together it's, like, five years."

"Why didn't you tell us you'd seen him?"

Pastor John shrugged. "He just arrived in town for one day, and he said he didn't want to be bothered by anybody and was on a spiritual quest. I felt he was speaking to me as clergy and not as friends, so I kept his confidence."

"When was he here?" Laurel asked.

"Why does it matter?" Pastor John said. "You've solved the earlier serial killings. He maybe was here . . . I don't know. I don't remember the exact date. Maybe the August or September the year before."

"He didn't tell you why he returned to town?"

Pastor John shook his head. "No. I think he came to get money he had stashed in his cabin, to be honest. He hinted at it but didn't say so. But honestly, it doesn't matter. You weren't here in town. There were no crimes. Pastor Caine just came to get money. He was on a spiritual quest. That's all there is to it."

Laurel didn't like the fuzziness of the timeline, but she had to admit the pastor had a point. It didn't really matter if Zeke Caine had been missing for one year or five years. Nobody had abducted him, and he had every right to travel anywhere he wanted. "Do you know where he was at any point during the time he was gone?" She had to find more of his victims.

"I really don't," Pastor John said, meeting her gaze. "Is that why I'm here today?"

"No. You're here to talk to me about Mrs. Bearing."

Pastor John leaned back in an obvious tell. "Oh. I'm very sad when one of our parishioners has passed on, and I will definitely go meet with the family."

"You might not want to do that."

The pastor blinked. "Why not? I understand that Zeke has taken over a lot of church duties, but I'm closer to the Bearings than Zeke is right now."

Laurel cleared her throat. "Pastor John, were you having an affair with Teri Bearing?"

Pastor John's mouth fell open slightly, and his forehead creased. He clasped his hands in his lap, and his left eye twitched. "Um, I don't think that's any of your business."

"Were you or were you not having an affair? Please keep in mind that it is a crime to lie to a federal agent," Laurel said.

Pastor John's chin hit his chest. "Yes, Teri and I had been having an affair for two months, but we'd only been sleeping together for two weeks."

"Explain that to me."

The pastor looked away and then back. "We'd been talking quite a bit on the phone and at the church for, I would say, the last couple of months as friends, but then it grew into something more two weeks ago. It grew into a lot more."

"Where?" Laurel asked.

Pastor John blinked. "I don't think that is relevant."

"You don't get to decide what's relevant," she said quietly.

He sighed. "At the church."

Laurel frowned. "When I first met you, you were having an affair with a twenty-year-old who attended your church. You're a charismatic person, but you've got to be smarter than this."

Pastor John looked away. "Teri was going to leave her husband. I think we had the real deal."

"You thought you had the real deal with Lisa Scotford," Laurel returned, referring to a victim from their first case who had been dating Pastor John.

The pastor wiped his shaking hand across his forehead. "I'm just looking for somebody to love, and they keep getting killed."

Laurel winced. That was an awful and yet true statement. Pastor John had actually been one of her suspects in Lisa's death, but he'd been cleared. "Where were you Wednesday night into Thursday morning?"

Pastor John shifted in his chair. "I was home in the new cabin I bought."

"Alone?"

Pastor John nodded. "Yes. Teri was supposed to come over late that night and then go on the snowmobile trip with me. She told her husband she'd planned a spa vacation in Seattle for a few days, but we'd made plans to be together instead."

"What time did she arrive?" Laurel asked.

Pastor John shook his head. "She didn't arrive. She never came. I called her several times, but she didn't answer." He looked down at his hands. "I figured maybe she'd changed her mind about the affair, and it wasn't like I could call her husband. I can't believe she was being killed at that time."

"How do you know what time she was killed?" Laurel asked instantly, missing Walter. Interviews were easier when they could bounce their questions off each other.

Pastor John shrugged. "I heard that Teri's body was

found early in the morning, so I figured somebody murdered her that night. That also explains why she didn't call me back." He swallowed. "I had to leave very early Thursday on my snowmobile trip and just returned a couple of hours ago."

Laurel studied him but couldn't determine if he was lying.

His nostrils flared. "If you have Teri's phone, I'm sure all my messages are on it, showing that I was looking for her."

"Her phone wasn't with the body. Neither was her handbag, if she had one," Laurel said.

"What about her vehicle?" Pastor John asked.

Laurel couldn't read his expression. "It was found abandoned by the side of the road after an apparent car accident. We've sent paint samples to the lab." Unfortunately, the results would take more than a month to come back.

"That's good."

Laurel studied the pastor. "Did Mayor Bearing have any idea about your affair?"

Pastor John shook his head. "No, no. Saul had no idea that Teri and I had fallen in love."

"In eight weeks?"

Pastor John flushed. "Yes. It was quick, but we had a lot in common—even with the age gap. We both were looking for . . . I don't know, excitement and a good future. She was tired of just being the mayor's wife."

Laurel tuned into the inflection in Pastor John's tone. "Would you clarify that statement? What did she want to be?"

Pastor John looked around and then back at Laurel, tears gathering in his eyes. "You know it was my work that got us national attention so we could take the church to a much wider congregation?"

"Yes," Laurel said. "What does that have to do with Teri Bearing?"

Pastor John's jaw tightened. "We were going to take the TV contract away from your father."

"He's not my father," Laurel retorted instantly. "Please refer to him as Zeke Caine or Pastor Caine or Zeke."

"I'm sorry," Pastor John said. "I know he's been a terrible father to you."

"He hasn't been a father to me at all," Laurel said. "Please return to the topic at hand."

Pastor John cleared his voice. "I'm sorry about that. Teri and I were going to arrange production of a series of sermons to pitch to the TV folks to show them that I am the charismatic leader who should represent our church across this vast land of ours. She was going to help me write and produce a proposal."

"Did Pastor Caine know about this?"

Pastor John sighed. "I don't know. He's a smart man and might've put it together. But I don't see him killing Teri." He looked into the distance.

Laurel stiffened. "What are you thinking?"

He shrugged. "Nothing I should be. Zeke is a pastor. But there's a darkness . . ." He shook his head. "Forget it."

Laurel didn't require suppositions. "Where were you last Sunday night into Monday morning?"

Pastor John jerked. "When the first victim was killed?"

"Yes," Laurel said.

He cleared his throat. "At my cabin with Teri all night." He sagged against the chair. "Who is now dead."

"Do you know a woman by the name of Delta Rivers?"

Pastor John shook his head. "Never heard of her."

She drew a picture of Delta from her file folder. It showed the woman on the autopsy table, a closeup of her face with her eyes closed. "This is she. Have you ever seen her before?"

Pastor John cocked his head. "Hm. No. I don't think so."

"Are you absolutely positive that the mayor didn't know about your affair?"

Pastor John nodded. "Saul was planning an anniversary trip for the two of them to Thailand this coming spring. He had no idea."

"Do you know him very well?" Laurel asked.

"I've been his pastor for years, and he's a faithful member of the church."

Faithful. How interesting that Pastor John used that word. "Are you aware that he owns a plane?"

"Yes. It's a smaller one, and he liked to fly over the rivers. Why?"

"He's gone," Laurel said flatly. "Do you have any idea where he'd go? If he owns property outside of Washington State?"

Lines dug grooves into the sides of the pastor's mouth. "No. I have no idea. Teri and I were wrapped up in our own world." His voice cracked on the last word.

"Does Saul Bearing have a temper?"

"Definitely," Pastor John said. "All of the Bearing

men do. Saul and both of his kids. I wouldn't call them dangerous, though."

Jealousy and betrayal could make anybody dangerous. "What do you think he would've done if he'd discovered his wife was sleeping with his pastor?" Laurel asked quietly.

Pastor John swallowed. "I honestly have no idea."

Chapter 19

After work, Huck found Laurel sitting on the top of her makeshift conference table facing the three white boards. She was dressed in dark jeans and a white sweater, her auburn hair curling down her back. "You changed your clothes," he noted.

She looked over her shoulder. "Yeah. I spilled tea down my front. Sometimes I get clumsy when my mind becomes so busy."

He looked at the boards in front of her. "What's going on?"

She sighed. "You're no longer involved with this case." But she didn't make a move to turn any of the boards over.

"It doesn't mean I can't look." He crossed around and sat on the table next to her. Then he shifted back, lifted her up, and put her on the table between his legs, wrapping his arms around her waist. She leaned back against him, and her spicy strawberry scent filled his senses.

He looked over her head at the drowning victims' case. She had placed pictures of the victims at the crime scenes at the top, with persons of interest at the bottom.

That included the mayor, Pastor John, Tim Kohnex, Jason Abbott, Pastor Zeke, and him. "That's quite the picture you have of me."

She nodded, the top of her head bumping the bottom of his chin. "I know. I've included anyone who might be involved. The problem is, we don't know enough about your mom to know who would want her dead. I'm hoping Nester will have a more complete picture of her life tomorrow. He's working remotely from Seattle and is doing a good job so far—even though we haven't been able to find the mayor or his sons."

"We'll find them. To be honest, I'd like to know more about my mother," Huck admitted. "Everybody on that board has some sort of connection to Teri Bearing. I'm the only one who has a connection to Delta Rivers."

"That we know of," Laurel said. "The victims could be randomly chosen as well. For now, take a look at the two crime scenes, more specifically the ice."

He studied the pictures of the ice.

"In each case, something different was used to chip it away. See how the ice at Delta Rivers's scene is more . . . I don't know. What would you call it? Rougher and more chiseled. But the ice that was cut or chipped away at the second scene has smoother edges."

He nodded. "It's possible a spud bar was used in the ice by my mother's body."

"A spud bar?" Laurel asked. "I don't know what that is."

She sounded surprised. The woman was a walking encyclopedia, so he grinned, careful to hide his amusement from her. "A spud bar is a long heavy metal rod that has a chiseled end. It's used for chipping or breaking through thin ice. We have several around here. Most people do." He studied the cuts in the ice near Teri Bearing's body. "That looks more like somebody just smashed the ice, maybe with a hammer or some sort of smooth implement. Possibly a sledgehammer."

"Would a regular hammer do that?"

"Sure."

She placed her hand over his against her waist. "So we either have a killer who doesn't care how the ice is broken or . . ." She let the word hang.

"The thing is," Huck murmured, "there aren't a lot of defensive bruises on the victims. He subdued them pretty easily and could have cut or chipped a hole in the ice while also maintaining control. Do you have the toxicology results back?"

"Not yet," Laurel said. "You think they were drugged?"

He shook his head. "I don't know. The other option is that the killer prepared the sites before taking the victims there."

Laurel nodded. "In that case, the fact that he used two different implements surprises me. Serial killers like the ritual."

"Maybe the ice isn't important."

She was quiet for several moments. "So he doesn't care how the ice is broken. It's the manner of drowning them that matters—in the freezing cold water?"

Huck shrugged. "This is more your purview than mine, but maybe it just doesn't matter to him."

"That remains a possibility."

He looked at the list of suspects that she had kindly labeled "persons of interest," probably because his picture was there. "You think Jason Abbott would do this?"

"I don't think there's a limit to Jason Abbott's need to kill," she mused.

Huck studied the pictures of the crime scene, which included the bodies. "Would he change his MO like that?"

"Yes," Laurel said. "It's not unusual for a serial killer to change their MO for various reasons. They adapt to avoid detection, or their fantasies evolve."

"Huh," Huck said. "I didn't know that."

"Sure," she said, her voice quiet. "Ted Bundy initially lured female victims with charm, but later changed his approach to breaking into victims' homes. He evolved as he experimented with different ways to gain control."

Sometimes it shocked him, the knowledge that Laurel possessed. He had difficulty sleeping at night because of some of his cases. He couldn't imagine dealing with the images she'd witnessed in her young life.

She patted his hand. "There are several other serial killers who changed, so it's entirely possible that Jason Abbott is another one."

"I thought cutting off the hands was a big deal to him."

"It was and might still be," Laurel said, "but he's been locked up for months. There's something about the cold water and the drowning that I can see appealing to him, the absolute control over a victim while she sucks in frigid water and tries to breathe."

"In which case, my mother would be, what? Just an opportunistic killing?"

Laurel put her hands on Huck's thighs. "Yes. We have two women right now—both blondes, but that might be a coincidence. Maybe Delta was in the wrong place at the wrong time."

"Why would she be here at all?" Huck asked.

Laurel shrugged. "I don't know. I'm hoping Nester can figure that out. She flew in by herself from Santa Fe."

"Really?" Her palms were warm against his legs.

"Yes. I need to ask you—we keep calling her your mother. Do you want me to call her Delta or Ms. Rivers or Delta Rivers?"

He thought about it. "I know it bothers you when anybody refers to Pastor Caine as your father, but honestly, I don't really care." It surprised him that he meant it. He felt curiosity about Delta Rivers, and he would find the person who'd killed her. He owed her that much. She was who she was, and technically, she had been his mother. Even if he'd never met her. "Do you think Abbott would've needed to kill as soon as he had the chance?"

"I don't know," Laurel said. "He was locked up for a few months building fantasies in his head. Frankly, I'm surprised he stayed in this location. The smart move would've been to head to Seattle or any big city with a large homeless population where it would be easy to hide."

"The fact that he called you concerns me," Huck said. "I think he stayed here to deal with you and probably Abigail." Laurel's stomach audibly growled. Huck chuckled and lifted her up to stand. "I'm starving. Let's go eat."

"I have time for sustenance since we haven't found Saul Bearing yet."

Huck stood and slung an arm over her shoulders. "We have to get some protein in you. We can talk about whichever case you want."

She surprisingly let him take some of her weight. "How about we refrain from talking about cases tonight? Let's enjoy our dinner and engage in normal conversation."

"Huh," he said. He wasn't entirely sure either one of them knew how to do that.

Laurel followed the hostess, winding around tables toward a two-top by the window at Alberto's on the River with Huck's hand at her lower back. He felt like a solid and sure presence behind her, which she needed right now.

"Laurel?"

She stopped cold and turned to see Abigail sitting across from Special Agent Wayne Norrs. "Abigail, hello."

Huck stepped up beside her. "Hey, Norrs."

Agent Norrs placed his crystal glass on the table. "Hi, Huck. Sorry about the interview on Saturday. I didn't intend for it to go that long."

"Not a problem. You have to do your job," Huck said.

"I'm glad you stayed on the case, Laurel," Norrs said.

She noticed a small smile playing on Abigail's face. Obviously Norrs remained unaware of Laurel's pregnancy, or he would've insisted she recuse herself. Why hadn't Abigail told Norrs about the pregnancy? If she thought it was something to hold over Laurel's head, she was misinterpreting the situation entirely. Yet, it was none of the special agent's business, so Laurel felt no need to enlighten him, especially since she wanted to remain on the case and discover who had killed both

Huck's mother and Teri Bearing. Nobody deserved to die like that.

"You must join us," Abigail said.

"Oh, no, thank you," Laurel murmured. "We just want a quiet night out."

Norrs snapped his fingers, and the waiter hurried over. "We have a big enough table. This is actually a four-top. Can we have the two chairs back?"

"Actually, we have things to discuss," Huck murmured, "but we appreciate the offer." His tone remained polite but firm.

Abigail's eyes flared. "Now, Huck, I know you're not a pococurante participant here, so please just have dinner with us."

Laurel tried very hard not to roll her eyes. Abigail often used her extensive vocabulary to stab at Huck, but from what Laurel could tell, he honestly could not care less. "You're right, Abigail. Huck is neither indifferent nor unconcerned," she said. "But we have matters to discuss."

"We're family," Abigail said, smiling widely. "Any matters the two of you might want to discuss are better served here at the table with us. You do understand me, correct?"

"I really don't," Laurel said, meaning it. What was Abigail talking about?

Huck pressed his palm against the small of her back again, as if providing comfort. "I think she's threatening you with blackmail, sweetheart."

Agent Norrs frowned and looked from Laurel to Abigail. "Excuse me?"

Abigail arranged her face in perfect lines of what

Laurel interpreted to be shock. "I would never do such a thing. What are you talking about, Captain Rivers? I don't understand why you're being so intransigent."

Laurel shook her head. "He's not stubborn or uncompromising. And why would you blackmail me? I've done nothing wrong."

Agent Norrs looked from Abigail to Huck. "Yeah. What are you talking about?"

"Ask your girlfriend," Huck said shortly, before taking Laurel's hand. "Come on, we're seated over by the window."

He turned and started walking, leaving Laurel no choice but to follow him, which was good because nausea kept rising from her belly and she'd come close to throwing up all over Abigail and Norrs. The thought cheered her immensely, although then she'd probably have to explain why she'd vomited. Huck pulled out her chair, and she sat, looking outside at the darkness. Once he had settled himself, she leaned toward him. "Why do you think Abigail hasn't told Agent Norrs about the pregnancy?"

Huck shook his head. "I have no idea, but she seems to hold on to all information until she needs it."

"Like trying to blackmail us into sitting with them for dinner?"

Huck grasped his napkin, shook it out, and put it on his lap. "Exactly."

Laurel looked over at the other couple, who seemed to be enjoying their conversation. "I don't understand her at all."

"Me neither." Huck smiled as the waitress brought

them waters and took their drink orders. Laurel requested a ginger ale. "Are you comfortable staying?" Huck asked. "We could order our food to go."

Laurel placed her napkin on her lap. "Absolutely not. We're not going to be driven away because of those two."

A bottle of wine was soon delivered to the table. Huck looked at the waitress. "We didn't order wine."

"Oh, no. This is from your sister." The young woman smiled at Laurel.

Huck's jaw clenched in that way it did when he was irritated. "Tell her thank you, but neither of us is drinking tonight. We both have to be up early to work."

"Are you sure?" The waitress faltered. "This is a 2005 Chateau Margaux."

"It sounds delicious," Huck said. "But again, we both have to work early." Disappointment darkened the young woman's face, and Huck smiled again. "But tell you what. Why don't you open it and pour it for them? They're just too frugal to order it for themselves. I insist."

"Really?" the waitress asked.

"Yeah. Open it first and then take it over and tell them thank you, but we want them to enjoy it."

Her eyes lit up. "How lovely." She took the wine away.

Laurel frowned. "Abigail knows that I won't drink wine right now."

"I'm well aware of that," Huck said. "That's why she sent the wine over."

Laurel played with her fork. "I don't understand why she plays such games."

"Because she's a nut job," Huck countered.

Laurel chuckled, feeling better than she had all day. "I don't think that's the clinical term, Captain, but I believe I agree." She looked at Abigail, who stared back, her face flushed and her chin down. Definitely angry.

Laurel turned back to face Huck. What would Abigail do now?

Chapter 20

Closer to nighttime than she'd planned, Deidre Snow finished loading her car at the grocery store, thrilled that she'd found new organic gnocchi. Recipes played through her head. There were so many sauces she could create, and the idea put a happy hop into her step. She wanted to make dinner for Monty Buckley soon, and a filling and mild meal was exactly what he needed.

She slid into her SUV and drove away from the grocery store, noting that it had finally stopped snowing. The groundhog had not seen his shadow this year, but she figured he must have been drunk, because there was no way winter was ending early. She flicked on her headlights to combat the early darkness.

It had been nice of Laurel to have officers watch her home at night. She had slept soundly and knew they'd be outside her place again tonight. Thank goodness.

As she drove out of the center of Genesis Valley, a truck roared up behind her, its headlights on high. There were so many idiots on the roads these days. She slowed down so he could pass her. He edged closer. Her heart started to beat faster, so she sped up. The truck kept pace, its headlights so bright, she couldn't see the driver.

She slowed down again, and so did he. She looked around, but she'd already left the town behind, so she sped up and took a wild right onto a country road.

He followed her.

She fumbled for her phone and pressed speed dial.

"Hi, Mom," Laurel said through the Bluetooth in the dash. "Huck and I are just leaving a restaurant. It's freezing. How was the grocery store?"

"Somebody's following me. They have big, bright lights," she burst out, her hands shaking on the steering wheel.

Laurel's voice remained calm. "Where are you?"

"I just turned off Larneys Road," Deidre said. "I don't know. There are trees everywhere. I don't know where to go. What should I do? I sped up and he followed, and I slowed down and he did the same."

"Take a deep breath," Laurel said. "We're headed out to the truck. I need to put you on hold just for a second, okay?"

"All right." Deidre gripped the steering wheel tighter.

The truck behind her hit her back bumper. She screamed, but Laurel was already on hold. She would have to handle this.

There was another turnoff coming up, and she'd swerve suddenly. She waited until the last second and turned, going around a farm field. Damn it, why hadn't she looked in her rearview when she'd been in town? Or had the truck come after town?

"All right, I'm back," Laurel said. "I called the local

police. They know your location and are headed toward you. Do not leave your car."

"I know," Deidre said, panicking.

The truck had caught up with her again and hit her once more. Her vehicle slid on the icy road. She screamed.

"What happened?" Laurel asked, wind whistling through the phone. "We're coming. I promise, Mom."

"He hit me twice," Deidre said. "He's trying to hit my back bumper."

"I need you to stay on the best roads you can. If you take a right about two miles from where you are, it'll bring you back to Birch Tree Road, okay?"

Tears filled Deidre's eyes, and she blinked them away. "Is it the killer? Is it Jason Abbott? Is it Zeke Caine? What about your half sister? Or even a stranger who wants to rob me?" Horrific scenarios spun wildly through her head.

"It doesn't matter who it is. What matters is that you're in control and you're driving safely, okay?"

Deidre held her breath. "All right."

"Don't hold your breath," Laurel said.

Deidre sped up and looked in her rearview mirror. "Okay." All she could see were lights.

"Tell me about the vehicle behind you," Laurel said.

"I can't see anything but big headlights," Deidre gasped, in the grip of a panic attack.

"Focus, Mom. You're okay."

Deidre couldn't breathe. Was she having a heart attack? "I see the turnoff."

"Take it, but don't go off the road."

Deidre slowed down just enough and then turned. The truck immediately followed, sliding behind her.

"Now, I want you to press the gas pedal down. Hard," Laurel said.

Deidre followed orders, speeding up as the vehicle behind her did the same. "It's a big truck. The headlights are huge."

"Keep going. Three miles ahead, you'll be back on Birch Tree Road. I want you to take a left. Drive back toward town."

"Okay," Deidre said, and then yelped as the truck hit her again. Her SUV fishtailed wildly, but she'd grown up driving in the mountains of Washington State and she quickly corrected, hitting the gas. "I'm about to turn onto Birch Tree Road."

Sirens echoed in the distance. She took a left and fishtailed, nearly going off the road, but she made it back on. At least this road had been graveled. She swallowed and could barely breathe. Her lungs weren't working.

The sirens got louder. The truck spun around and drove in the other direction. She could see its taillights.

"They're going the other way." She let out a huge breath and her lungs stuttered.

"Keep driving. I've almost reached you, and the police should be there soon."

Deidre squinted to see red-and-blue lights spiraling into the sky around the nearest bend. "I hear sirens and can see lights in the distance."

"Don't stop until you get to the police," Laurel ordered.

"I won't," Deidre said, her body sagging. She couldn't believe this. What was she going to do now? She'd never leave her house again.

* * *

Laurel and Huck had stayed with Deidre all night. She'd been shaken for a while but had later calmed down. There were officers searching for the truck, but Deidre hadn't been able to give them much of a description.

Now Laurel had officers on her mother twenty-four hours a day. She might have to hire private security soon—or speed up her mother's travel schedule.

Back at the office, first thing in the morning, Tim Kohnex was waiting in the vestibule in front of Laurel's door as she walked inside the FBI building, finishing off a jelly doughnut.

Beside her, Huck paused. "Mr. Kohnex?"

"Hi." Kohnex pushed away from the wall. "I needed to talk to you."

Laurel wiped her hands on a napkin. "Do you have information regarding Mrs. Bearing?"

"I do." Kohnex looked around, his eyes flicking back and forth.

Laurel looked up to his face. "All right. Why don't you accompany me to the conference room upstairs?"

"I'll go with you," Huck said congenially.

"No, that's okay." Laurel looked at him. "You're not part of this case, Huck. We have to draw the line somewhere." Considering they planned to go on an ice-breaking excursion soon, she felt slightly hypocritical. But she needed to at least try to keep up a wall between Huck and the investigation.

Huck hesitated by the door to the Fish and Wildlife office, and she tried to read his expression. Was that concern?

The door buzzed and she opened it.

"Hello, Agent Snow," Agent Norrs called down. "I'm

working in your office today to get caught up. There's a man waiting in the vestibule for you, and I thought if you wanted to interview him, Sherry could get the conference room ready."

Huck's shoulders visibly relaxed. "Hi, Norrs."

"Hi, Captain," Norrs called back. "I see you purchased doughnuts. Did you bring me any?"

"Sure." Huck handed the box to Laurel, after filching one maple bar. "Share with Norrs. Even though he's investigating me for murder, I like that he's here to provide backup."

Laurel pulled open her door. "Follow me, Mr. Kohnex." She walked up the stairs.

"Nice wallpaper," Kohnex said from behind her.

She sometimes forgot that the nude cancan dancers lined the hallway up. "Yes, we probably need to update this place," she said, reaching the top of the stairs. "Hello, Sherry."

"Hello, Laurel." Sherry craned her neck to look at the doughnut box.

"Here you go." Laurel placed it on the display counter, feeling disjointed without Kate there. "Make sure Agent Norrs gets one."

Norrs appeared in the doorway. "I will make sure Agent Norrs gets one." He flipped open the box and pounced on a round pastry with sprinkles. "I never get doughnuts anymore. Which one do you want, Sherry?"

She took a chocolate one.

"Mr. Kohnex?" Laurel asked.

He shook his head. "I don't eat doughnuts. Do you have any scotch?"

Sherry snickered. "It's eight o'clock in the morning."

"Oh." He looked around. "Still, no doughnut."

Laurel walked through the open doorway. "This way, Mr. Kohnex." She led him into the conference room. "Make yourself comfortable. I'll be back in a moment." She strode down to her office and dropped her coat and briefcase before taking a notebook and returning to the conference room, where Sherry had already left a pitcher of water.

"Would you like coffee or tea?" Laurel asked.

Kohnex shook his head. "I don't do caffeine either."

"How about water?" She nodded to the pitcher.

He frowned. "Is it from a mineral well?"

"I believe we pour our water from the tap," Laurel said.

"Then no water." He kicked back in his chair, his arms long and his legs extending far beneath the table. He seemed to be in good shape. How marvelous it would be to be 6'7". Laurel could only imagine.

She sat down just as Agent Norrs strode inside, wiping the sprinkles off his shirt, and took a seat. Laurel introduced them. "Mr. Kohnex says he has evidence regarding Mrs. Bearing's murder."

Kohnex took a deep breath. "I've tortured myself whether to tell you this or not, but . . ." He looked up at the ceiling, and then down. "I walked in on Pastor John and Mrs. Bearing in his office a week ago. They were naked."

Norrs made a notation. "What did they do?"

"They hurriedly got dressed. They were both very embarrassed, but there wasn't much they could say." He lifted his shoulders. "I knew something was different about the pastor. His aura had completely changed, but the wind didn't whisper this one to me. However, I don't think he killed her."

Laurel sat back. "Why not?"

"His aura doesn't show evil. He's a nice guy."

Norrs cleared his voice. "I guess he's not that nice, considering he was having an affair with the mayor's wife."

"I see." Kohnex leaned back. "I had a dream about you, Agent Snow."

The hair rose on the back of her neck. "Was it a good dream?"

"It was not a good dream," Kohnex said. "You were running. There was snow and ice, and it was cold and frightening. I think you need to be very careful."

Agent Norrs leaned forward, looking like a stubborn bulldog. "Is that a threat?"

"No." Kohnex's eyes opened wide. "It's a warning. I'm telling you, the fates are whispering to me to warn you."

"Whispering?" Agent Norrs asked.

Kohnex nodded. "Yes, they want you protected, but there is a force after you." He shook his head and then stopped abruptly, staring down at the wooden table. "There are actually two forces after you, Agent Snow." He lifted his head and his pupils dilated. "You have to be very careful. It's not just your life you need to protect."

She barely stopped herself from reacting. "What do you mean? Please clarify."

He shook his head. "That's all I know, except . . ." He

clasped his hands together. "I don't want you to take this the wrong way."

He had something worse to say? Laurel studied him. "What is it?"

"There's going to be another body found by a river."

Laurel already knew that there would be another body if she didn't catch this killer. "Do you know when?"

"Very soon," he said instantly.

Agent Norrs gave her a look. Laurel nodded. They definitely needed to investigate Kohnex more deeply than they had so far. "How do you know?"

"I had a dream," Kohnex said.

"Who is the victim?" Agent Norrs asked.

Kohnex shook his head. "I don't know. All I see is a blond woman face down near a river."

"Pretty much what you saw when you found Teri Bearing?" Agent Norrs grunted.

Kohnex nodded.

"Is there anything else?" Laurel asked.

"No. I just want to help. I hope you'll let me help. Too many times, nobody does," Kohnex said, his voice rough.

Sherry poked her head in. "Hi, a younger blond woman is out front freaking out, and the reporter from next door just ran outside."

Laurel briefly closed her eyes. This was all she needed. "I'll go." She stood.

"Right," Agent Norrs said. "Mr. Kohnex, you can stay here with me and run me through everywhere you've been during the last couple of weeks, minute by minute."

Kohnex stretched his long legs out even farther, his lips turning down. "This is why I don't like to help. Now

I'm a suspect when you should be looking everywhere but at me."

"We'll look everywhere," Agent Norrs said, clapping him on the shoulder. "But for now, let's take a look at you."

Chapter 21

Laurel tucked her gun at the back of her waist and drew on a jacket over her light sweater before walking through the office and down the stairway with the cancan girls seeming to dance next to her. She burst into the vestibule and then took a deep breath before stepping outside into the chilly, windy day.

Haylee stood next to one of the vehicles with Rachel Raprenzi holding out a microphone as a beefy camera guy recorded them.

"There she is," Haylee yelled, spittle flying from her mouth as she pointed at Laurel. "There she is. All of this is her fault. She's the killer. Don't you get it? Don't you get it?"

Laurel frowned. "Haylee, are you okay?"

The girl wore a torn sweatshirt and jeans with muddy tennis shoes. Her blond hair was partly up in a ponytail and partly falling wild around her face. Her eyes were wide and she hiccupped. "No, I'm not okay. You set up my fiancé for murder, and now he's out free and won't talk to me. I can't find him. I'm sure you've killed him."

Laurel cocked her head to the side. "Have you been drinking, Haylee?"

"I have to drink all the time." The young woman threw up her hands. "You've ruined my life."

Rachel pressed closer. "You said that you believe Agent Snow is a killer. Could you expand on that allegation?"

Laurel turned and faced the reporter. "Keep in mind slander laws, Ms. Raprenzi."

"This isn't slander," Haylee yelled, her face turning red. "I saw you."

"What did you see?" Rachel asked quickly.

Tears fell from Haylee's eyes, and she wiped her nose on her sleeve. "I was there. I was out at the church. I saw her drive by. I did."

"What are you talking about?" Laurel asked, forgetting the camera for a moment. She'd deal with that later.

Haylee shook her head wildly. "Your hair is impossible to miss, that red. I saw you."

The cold started to seep through Laurel's clothing to her skin. "Haylee, why don't you come inside for an interview?"

"No," the girl yelled. "Don't you see? She'll just kill me, too."

This was becoming tedious.

Rachel stepped closer to Haylee as if trying to protect the woman, a small smile playing on her lips. "Now, Ms. Johnson, take a deep breath. We need to be careful about slander here. Without going into supposition, tell me what you saw and what you're talking about."

Haylee blinked. "Supposition?"

"Guessing," Rachel said instantly. "Without guessing."

"Oh, okay." Haylee's brow smoothed out. "Early

Thursday morning of last week, I couldn't sleep. I've been just driving around the mountains and town trying to find Jason. He was an avid camper, and so I hoped that I would come upon one of his campsites."

"Go on," Rachel said encouragingly.

Haylee looked at Laurel and then sidled closer to the reporter. "I drove outside the city over by the church. Jason and I used to go there once in a while, and I feel a sense of comfort there. I saw Agent Snow drive by. It was the day Mrs. Bearing's body was found. It was still dark out."

Rachel looked at Laurel and then back at Haylee. "Are you positive?"

"I know her hair. I mean, look at her. It's red."

"It's not red," Laurel retorted. "My hair color is brown with an undertone of red."

"It's red," Haylee and Rachel said in unison.

Laurel looked at the cameraman. She probably should excuse herself from this situation, but she wanted more information. "You're saying you were close by when the second victim was left by the river near the church?"

Haylee faltered. "I didn't see the victim. I just saw you drive by and turn down the church driveway."

"What was I driving, allegedly?" Laurel asked.

Haylee swallowed. "A truck."

"What kind of truck?" Rachel asked.

Haylee shook her head. "It was an old battered one, like half the farmers around here own. People borrow them all the time, right?"

Rachel kept her face in noncommittal lines, but her eyes glowed. "Yes, that's true. Anybody can get a truck, and I believe Agent Snow's family owns a farm."

Haylee shrugged. "I don't know anything about that. All I know is I saw her driving down the church road when it was still dark, before the mayor's dead wife was found."

Rachel cocked her head. "Didn't Mrs. Bearing get into an altercation with Captain Huck Rivers a day or two before she died?"

"I have no comment on that," Laurel said.

Rachel stepped closer. "Aren't you and Captain Huck Rivers in a relationship? You wouldn't just go kill somebody who smacked him, would you, Laurel?"

"Of course not," Laurel said. "I would be very careful what you say right now, Ms. Raprenzi."

"Don't let her threaten you," Haylee whispered sadly. "She and her crazy sister probably kill people all the time. You know Abigail Caine experimented on Jason? He never, ever would've even thought of killing anybody if she hadn't messed with his head."

Rachel pushed the microphone closer to Haylee. "Now, Ms. Johnson, we do need to be careful because of slander. Do you have any proof of this?"

Tears welled in Haylee's eyes again. "Don't you see? They destroyed all the proof, the FBI and Abigail Caine, but I can show you his records of when he underwent treatment by Dr. Caine, how he felt before, and then how he felt after. Worse yet, she shot stuff into his veins that made him feel powerful. Jason believed he could protect himself from evil women."

Laurel pivoted toward her. "Records? Did you say that Jason Abbott kept records?"

Haylee faltered. "I'm not giving his diaries to you."

Laurel would require a subpoena to get them. His

diaries might lead her to where Abbott hid right now, and they should provide important evidence for his trial. "Haylee, you've been questioned many times, but you haven't mentioned these diaries once. You know you're hindering an investigation and possibly obstructing justice."

"See," Haylee sniffed. "All she does is threaten. Believe me, you do not want to be on her bad side." She sneered, her eyes narrowing. "People who get there end up dead."

Laurel straightened. "You need to come in for a formal interview right now." She reached for the woman's arm.

"No!" Haylee yanked free and pushed Laurel.

The cameraman angled his camera to the side, trained on them.

Laurel cleared her throat. "Ms. Johnson, you have just made yourself a material witness in two separate ongoing FBI cases, both with rapidly clicking timelines. In addition, you just committed battery against an FBI agent. So either come in voluntarily right now for an interview, or I'll have no choice but to take you into custody."

Haylee swung around wildly and then stopped, straightening her shoulders. "Fine." She looked at the camera. "Make sure I come out of this, okay? She definitely wants me dead."

The smile Rachel Raprenzi flashed showed too much teeth. "We'll wait right here, Haylee. We promise."

Haylee slouched in the chair across from Laurel's desk, looking like a surly teenager.

Laurel crossed her legs, wishing Agent Norrs and Tim

Kohnex had vacated the conference room. "Would you like anything to drink?"

Haylee huffed and looked over to the side wall.

Laurel rarely became impatient because it was a waste of energy and brain power. At the moment, however, she had to fight the inclination. "Haylee, you are in your twenties. Stop acting like a petulant child."

"Petulant," Haylee snapped out. "You're fucking evil."

"Let's move past the name calling and the churlishness, shall we? Tell me about the diaries."

"No."

How could the young woman still want to protect Jason Abbott? "Where are they?"

"I'm not going to tell you."

"Haylee," Laurel said. "You just admitted on camera that you are in possession of these diaries, and that you might be able to identify a witness to the killing near the church. On camera," she stressed. "So if you don't work with me, I can have you arrested and charged with hindering an investigation and obstruction of justice."

"Well . . . then—" Haylee started.

Laurel held up a finger. "In addition, if you lie to me, it's a crime because I'm a federal agent."

"Ha," Haylee said. "That's not true. I know I have a right not to incriminate myself."

Sometimes Laurel truly despaired about the current educational system. "Yes, but I'm not asking you about yourself. According to 18 US Code 1001, it is a crime to knowingly and willingly make any materially false statement to any branch of the government of the United States. This means you can't lie to a federal agent."

"I can lie to the cops anytime I want."

Oh, spare her. Laurel took a deep breath. "That's the local police, and actually, you should be careful there, too. I'm talking about the federal government. Lying to me can result in fines and imprisonment. Do you want to go to jail?"

"No," Haylee said.

They had reached a consensus of direction. "Good. Where are the diaries?"

"They're at my place."

So at least they remained safe for now. "I want you to turn them over."

"Get a warrant."

Laurel had already asked Sherry to draw up a request for a warrant. "Why are you trying to protect Jason Abbott? He is a cold-blooded murderer."

"Because of your sister."

All right. They were not going to get anywhere with this line of questioning. "Tell me about the woman you saw in the truck."

"It was you. I saw your hair. I saw you drive. It was you. You were the woman in the truck."

Laurel considered questions that would elicit truthful answers and could settle on only one. "Is it possible the woman you saw was Abigail Caine?"

Haylee's jaw dropped open. "Well, um, I guess."

How could she not have already thought of that? "Do you have any idea why Dr. Caine would want to murder Mrs. Bearing?"

Haylee gulped. "I don't know. I mean, I heard Mrs. Bearing was doing the nasty with Pastor John, and didn't Dr. Caine used to date him? Could that be a reason?"

Not for most people, but who knew with Abigail.

"Are you currently under the influence of any alcohol or drugs?" Laurel asked abruptly.

Haylee put both elbows on the table and leaned forward. "Are you calling me stupid?"

Laurel had refrained from actually saying the words. "No, I'm just asking if anything is impairing your judgment."

"No," Haylee snapped.

Laurel harbored reservations about that assertion. "Tell me about the truck."

"I saw an old and battered farm truck. I don't know. Maybe like a yellowish cream. One of the millions we see around here."

"It was still dark outside. How did you see the driver's hair?"

Haylee cocked her head as if trying to remember. "From the dash lights and, plus, my headlights. I just figured you went to murder people. Are you a killer?"

"No," Laurel said.

Haylee snorted. "Maybe not, but that evil sister of yours definitely is."

Chapter 22

After a delicious lunch of decadent macaroni and cheese, Laurel walked into the conference room and set down her sparkling water. Upon concluding his interview with Tim Kohnex, Agent Norrs had left to liaise with the local police sheriff, and she surprised herself by wishing he'd stayed. The office was too quiet with her entire team gone. She shivered, feeling alone. "Sherry, I'd like an update on that warrant for Abbott's diaries in about an hour," she called out. They encountered difficulty securing a judge's signature.

"You've got it," Sherry called back. "That appointment with Ms. Carrington is in a few minutes."

Meeting Zeke Caine's new lover should be interesting. "Thank you. Please also call Nester and see if he's found a trace of Saul Bearing or his sons."

"Sure."

Laurel stared at the boards and at Jason Abbott's mugshot for several minutes.

Movement sounded down the hallway, and Sherry escorted a young woman in. "Special Agent in Charge Laurel Snow, this is Ms. Uma Carrington."

"Hi, Ms. Carrington," Laurel said, flipping the board over to reveal the unadorned side. "Thank you for agreeing to meet with me."

"Hi." The woman walked into the conference room.

Laurel motioned to one of the chairs. "Take a seat."

"Thank you." Ms. Carrington pulled out a chair and sat. She had angled bone structure, dark brown eyes, and long brown hair with very obvious and lovely blond streaks. Did Zeke like blondes? Like to kill them?

"Would you like a glass of water, Ms. Carrington?" Laurel asked.

She shook her head. "Call me Uma."

Laurel studied her. "Uma is one of the names of the goddess Parvati, a principal deity of Hinduism. I think the word means light or tranquility."

"Or fame," Uma said, smiling fully now. "In Hindu mythology, she is also known as the goddess of love and devotion." She lifted one dark eyebrow. "You've done your research."

"I like to read," Laurel noted. "I read that somewhere years ago."

"Ah," Uma said, settling back in the chair. She appeared comfortable in a long green skirt with a white-and-green sweater. Her earrings dangled in colorful beads of red, white, and green. "Pastor Caine said you needed to speak with me?"

That was an interesting way to speak about her boyfriend. "Yes. He alleges that the two of you are in a relationship?"

"Yes," Uma said, her high cheekbones accentuated perfectly with shadow and blush. "We have been dating for a couple of months now, I suppose."

Laurel leaned forward. "If you don't mind my asking, how old are you?"

Uma laughed. "I don't mind at all. I'm twenty-four." She brushed her hair back from her face. "I know there's an age gap, but I find Zeke to be knowledgeable and, frankly, a lot of fun. He has a zest for life you don't see in people my age sometimes."

"I see," Laurel said. The woman appeared intelligent and yet apparently had no idea that Zeke Caine was a predator. She supposed he could be charming when necessary and wondered if she should warn the young woman. "Could you please tell me where you were last Wednesday into Thursday morning?"

"Of course," Uma said. "I made dinner, a chicken cacciatore, on Wednesday night for Zeke and myself. Then we stayed in and watched a movie."

Laurel couldn't see Zeke as being the domestic type. "What movie?"

Uma waved a hand in the air. "There was an old movie marathon on one of the channels. So we caught the end of *Shawshank Redemption* and then watched *Back to the Future*. It was a lovely and perfectly mellow evening."

"And then?"

She shrugged. "After the movies, we went to bed."

"All night?" Laurel asked.

Uma met her gaze, her brown eyes wide. "Yes. The pastor stayed all night. In the morning, he cooked banana pancakes for me and then left once he received a phone call about the body found at the church who turned out to be poor Mrs. Bearing. He did not leave all night."

Laurel tapped her fingers on the table. "Can you be sure that Zeke didn't leave all night?"

"Of course I am certain, or I wouldn't say so. I'm a very light sleeper, Agent Snow. If Zeke had left, I would've heard him. He was with me all night." The woman showed no obvious signs of falsehood. Her brow remained clear, her body relaxed, and her voice level.

"Are you familiar with Teri Bearing?" Laurel asked.

Uma placed her hands on the table and clasped them together. Her nails were cut short with white tips. "Of course, I know Teri. We attend the same church. I'm very sorry to hear that she was the victim found by the river. She's always been very nice to me."

Laurel couldn't detect a lie in the words. "Do you know of anybody who would want to kill her?"

"Oh, no. Not at all. I suppose her husband wasn't too happy with her, considering she was sleeping with Pastor John." Uma shook her head sadly. "I could not believe it when Zeke told me that last week."

Laurel leaned forward. "Zeke told you that last week?"

"Yes." Uma winced. "It's not a huge secret, to be honest. They haven't hidden it very well. I'm surprised her husband didn't know. Perhaps he did."

Laurel needed to see Saul Bearing sooner rather than later. "What do you do for a living, Uma?"

"I just finished college and received my nursing degree after years of studying," Uma said, her face lighting up. "I start work next week at the hospital and can't wait."

"Congratulations." Laurel reached for her glass. "Have you ever met or heard of a woman named Delta Rivers?"

Uma pursed her lips, as if thinking. "No, I haven't. Why? Is that the name of the first victim?"

Laurel took a sip of her sparkling water. "I can't reveal that information at this time. Are you sure you've never heard that name?"

"I'm positive."

Laurel pulled a picture of Delta out of her file folder. It had been taken during the autopsy. "This isn't an ideal picture, but would you please double-check?"

Uma pulled the photograph toward her and cocked her head. "No, I'm sorry. She doesn't look familiar at all." Then she peered closer. "Maybe. It's difficult to tell from this. There was a woman at the church who met with Zeke a week or so ago. She had blond hair, and I didn't recognize her. But I just can't tell from this picture."

Laurel's instincts started to hum. "There was a woman you didn't recognize?"

"Yes, but you have to realize that is not uncommon. People come from Seattle all the time to meet with both Pastor Zeke and Pastor John regarding our outreach programs. I just figured she was one of those folks, maybe from the food bank."

Laurel nodded. "That's more than likely." Yet she needed to follow up on this. "The church doesn't have security cameras, does it?"

"Oh, no. Not at the church," Uma said, as if shocked by the very idea.

How unfortunate. They really could use some CCTV. Laurel couldn't think of any more questions. Unfortunately, the woman seemed like a good alibi for Zeke Caine. "I appreciate your coming in today," Laurel said.

Uma leaned forward. "I was hoping I could also talk to you about your father."

"We can't get into personal matters here, Ms. Carrington. I'm sorry."

Uma focused fully on Laurel. "No, really. He cares about you deeply and wants a relationship with you. He doesn't understand why you won't see the good in him."

Laurel pushed back her chair and stood. "That's because there isn't good in him, Uma. He's a predator and he harms women. He's a narcissist and probably a sociopath."

Uma stood and wrung her hands together. "You're wrong."

Laurel stared at her dispassionately. "Do what you will with the information I've given to you. But if you're as smart as you appear, you'll run fast and hard in the other direction." She showed the woman to the door and then returned to her office, her mind clicking travel arrangements into place. She called her mom's warehouse and spoke to the employees before phoning her local travel agent.

"What's going on?" Agent Norrs asked, walking inside and dropping into a chair. "Did I hear you making plans to head to Asia?"

Laurel rolled her shoulders, unsure of how much to reveal. Norrs seemed to be a good agent with poor taste in women, and he didn't have her trust. She missed her team, flashing back to being a child prodigy—all alone amongst her peers. "I'm rearranging a planned buying trip for my mother so she leaves tomorrow."

Agent Norrs kicked out his legs. "Sounds like a good idea. Is it because the killer is murdering blondes?"

"That might be a coincidence since we only have two victims." Hopefully they wouldn't get any more. "I'm more concerned that Zeke Caine wants to speak with my mother. With both of us rejecting his overtures, he could become even more dangerous than he obviously is right now. A malignant narcissist or sociopath with his kind of ego can't take such disrespect, and I'm concerned he'll strike out at her."

Norrs rubbed his smooth-shaven chin. "You think he'd actually hurt your mom because she doesn't want to talk to him?"

"Without question," Laurel said. "He has no moral compass, and I want her safe while I track his movements of the last few years. There's a reason he won't share where he's been, and I have no doubt he's victimized more people. I also need to figure out a way to talk to the female members of his congregation without being shut out. We haven't hit on a method for doing that yet."

Norrs whistled. "I spoke to your sister, and she truly doesn't like your father. At all. She'd really like to meet us for dinner tonight."

"I am unavailable this evening," Laurel said.

He sighed. "I'm going to keep trying. For now, that was quite the scene outside with Haylee Johnson. The news keeps streaming it."

Laurel pressed the palm of her hand into her eyebrow and gently rubbed it, hoping the increased supply of blood to the area would ward off her oncoming headache. "Yes, Haylee Johnson needs help. Make sure we have somebody on her at all times."

"Fish and Wildlife is trailing her, but their resources

are limited," Agent Norrs said. "Do you think she's in danger?"

"We all are, Agent Norrs."

Nester called in early that afternoon with news that he had tracked down the mayor in Montana and was working with the Montana field office to get the man on a plane back home. "There's a storm preventing the small plane from flying right now, but the mayor said he'd head out tomorrow morning and meet you at his house late afternoon."

"Make sure agents escort him to his plane, and also be clear that if he doesn't fly right here, I'll have him arrested for hindering an investigation," she said.

"No problem, boss."

Finally. She had a few choice words for the mayor. She and Huck could practice breaking ice on the rivers in the morning, and then she would interview the Bearings. She believed his son, the attorney, would also be present. "Have you found anything else about Mrs. Bearing's movements?" She placed her phone on speaker.

"No, and I can't find any spa where she had a reservation," Nester said. "I'm thinking she just lied to her husband and never made reservations since she planned to stay with Pastor John for a couple of days and go on that snowmobile trip. They certainly weren't hiding their affair."

Laurel sipped her herbal tea. "Have we found anybody to corroborate Pastor John's alibi that night?"

"No," Nester said. "So far, we haven't found anybody who saw him that night, and we don't have any CCTV that far out. I'm still working on it, though. He said he was home alone, so tracing his path to and from the church isn't going to be easy."

The pastor seemed to blur the lines between his professional and personal lives too often. Of course, Laurel was dating Huck. But an FBI agent and a Fish and Wildlife officer had a different relationship than a pastor and his parishioner. "What else have you discovered?"

"I've just started a background check on Tim Kohnex. Everything he told you so far checks out. He was a basketball coach after he played for Alabama. The guy was pretty good, then blew out his knee. During his time in Arizona, he notified police about crimes several times, but it was all kind of floofy."

"I need clarification on the word 'floofy.'"

Nester sneezed. "Floofy—meaning it's like he knew stuff afterwards. You know, like when he came in and told you that another blonde would be murdered by the river. Anybody who's watched a show about a serial killer pretty much knows if two blondes have been found killed in a ritualistic manner, a third will be found soon. That kind of thing. Where he could claim he had a vision, but also where most people could have guessed at it."

"That was my insight when I spoke with him." Even though his apparent intensity had given her pause. She wasn't an imaginative person, but anybody could get caught up once in a while. "Keep researching him. I'd like to know his movements around both murders. See if we can tie him to Delta Rivers or at least to the crime scene by the Iceberg River."

"You've got it," Nester said. "Also, the toxicology reports came back on both victims."

Laurel rubbed a knot in her neck. "Were drugs discovered in their systems?"

"No drugs. They were both clean of drugs other than the alcohol in Mrs. Bearing's system. She was over the limit to drive safely but not to the point where she would've lost consciousness."

Laurel relived the scenes in her mind. "So the killer either had the ice already prepared or subdued the victims and cut a hole in it without allowing them to escape."

"My guess is he scoped the places out in advance."

"Agreed," Laurel said. "Which gives us another chance to place the perpetrator at the scenes. He would've had to have been there at least once before. No doubt he scouted the areas several times."

Nester hummed softly. "The church is an odd choice, isn't it? People come and go from there a lot. Do you think this guy has a problem with religion?"

"I don't know," Laurel said. "The only tie we have between the two crime scenes is that we had earlier crime scenes in the same vicinities."

"That's creepy as hell," Nester muttered.

He wasn't wrong.

She sighed. "Maybe we need to speak to the public again. What have you discovered about Delta Rivers?"

"Fascinating woman. I traced her most recent location to a commune in Santa Fe. It's a place called Trust the Land, and according to the woman I spoke with, Delta Rivers lived there for the last fifteen years."

How intriguing. "That's a long time. It's a commune?"

"Yes. The commune is a cohousing community that

exists on the precepts of sustainability, cooperative living, and family creation. I think by that they mean you choose your family. There's a common house, kitchen, all that stuff, and they grow their own food. It sounds like they're a bunch of artists as well, and Delta was one of them."

Laurel rearranged her schedule in her mind. "How well did this woman with whom you spoke know Delta?"

"Extremely well. Her name is Opal Garcia, and she's the current president of the commune. I'm running a background check on her now. It should be completed in about an hour."

"Excellent," Laurel said. "Did she say she'd meet with me?"

Nester chuckled. "I figured you'd ask, and she said she would be happy to see you on Saturday. They have some ritual deal going on this week that has something to do with Delta River's death, and the co-op is closed to the public, so she won't see you till then."

Finally they'd found a lead Laurel could pursue. "Would you make flight arrangements for me?"

"I already did," Nester said.

Huck would want to accompany her, and he absolutely could not.

She dreaded that fight.

Chapter 23

Laurel wearily climbed the stairs to her mother's house and unlocked the door, stepping inside and nodding to the two patrol officers in their car by the fence. They'd watch the house all night. "Mom," she called out, kicking off her boots and outerwear. Fred rushed up and rubbed against her legs, and she leaned down to pet him.

"I'm in the kitchen." Deidre peered around the corner. "I made spaghetti. It's pretty simple. I didn't even put anything interesting in the sauce."

Laurel walked that way, rolling her shoulders. "That sounds delicious." She couldn't remember ever being this tired. She'd fought off serial killers before, and she'd run through woods and icy snow while being shot at, but pregnancy . . . That took a toll. She reached the kitchen and sank onto one of the wooden chairs. "How are you?"

"I'm much better. I just wish I could've told you who drove that darn truck." Deidre dished up two plates to bring to the table. "I've decided to concentrate on work. Our preorders for the spring and summer blends are way up. When I say 'way up,' I mean you'd better find somewhere to invest the earnings."

Laurel tugged her hair out of its clip. "I've found several places to invest. Just let me know how much I have to play with."

Deidre flopped onto her seat, wearing a tight-fitting black yoga outfit with a white tank top beneath her jacket. "Not that we're rich. I know we keep investing our profits, but still, it's nice to be able to buy shoes if I want to buy shoes."

"I concur." As the smell of fresh tomato paste hit Laurel, her stomach rumbled. She reached for a fork and instantly dug in. "I need to talk to you."

"Ruh-roh. Are you moving out?" Deidre poured herself a glass of cabernet.

Laurel's eyebrows lifted. "You want me to move out?"

"No, I don't want you to move out. I figured once you'd finished building your barndominium that you would, but with this weather, your plans have been put on hold, haven't they?"

"They have," Laurel said. She was converting an old barn down the road into a home for herself. With the baby coming, perhaps she should discuss the matter with Huck. They could build something together. His cabin wasn't big enough for a baby, but then again, they hadn't discussed fully moving in together.

Deidre watched her thoughtfully and then sipped her wine. "There are a lot of thoughts crossing your face. Maybe you and Captain Rivers need to sit down and have a nice talk."

"I suppose so," Laurel said thoughtfully. "We haven't planned much."

"You haven't known about the baby for long. Give yourself a break."

The last thing in the world Laurel wanted to do was take the smile off her mom's face, but they really did need to talk. "Zeke Caine called me earlier today and said that he has been phoning you."

Deidre paused with a fork halfway to her mouth and then set it down, still with pasta entwined through the prongs. "Yes. He has called the office several times, and I have ignored him."

"He doesn't have your personal cell phone number?"

"Not yet, but if I remember, he's rather persistent." Deidre paled.

Laurel stood up and fetched a glass of water before reseating herself. "He's dangerous."

"I know," Deidre burst out. "I've wondered if he was in the truck that tried to run me off the road."

As had Laurel. Of course, it could've been Jason Abbott. Or another killer she hadn't met yet. She pushed the pasta around her plate with her fork. "I was thinking that perhaps you should travel sooner rather than later to Asia."

Deidre blinked. "Laurel, I'm leaving in two weeks."

"Yes, I know, but harvest times for tea leaves and the other ingredients you love started a week ago and will continue for months."

Deidre stared at her over the rim of her wineglass. "You want me out of town, Laurel Snow."

"I really do," Laurel agreed. "Things are heating up around Zeke Caine and Abigail, and I have another serial killer in the area targeting women—so far blondes. Mom, you're blond." She shook her head. "My experience and judgment indicate you're in peril. My stress level would decrease if you moved up your travel plans."

Deidre reached for her fork and plopped the mass of pasta into her mouth, chewing while staring at her the whole time. "I'll need to talk to Dolores."

"I appreciate that, Mom. I'll pay for any fees incurred by changing plans."

Deidre waved a hand in the air. "I have as much money as you do, Laurel Snow. I can afford my own fees. Plus, they're all a write-off." She leaned forward. "I don't feel right leaving you here alone with your entire team out of town."

Laurel couldn't deny the sense of isolation right now, but she needed to abandon emotions and start strategizing. She took a bite of the perfectly seasoned pasta. She'd never understood how her mom created such delectable meals. No matter how many times Laurel attempted to measure ingredients and spices, she never achieved the same results. Deidre rarely used recipes and haphazardly tossed in ingredients.

"I'm not alone, Mom. I'm an FBI agent." One without a team in place.

"You promise you'll stay with Huck or he'll stay here?"

Laurel's shoulders finally relaxed now that her mom had agreed to leave town. "Of course."

Deidre grinned. "Are you actually working on instinct here, like a gut feeling?"

"Oh, no." Laurel hurried to assure her mother. "I'm calculating risks and odds and what I know about Zeke Caine, Jason Abbott, Abigail Caine, and whoever the serial killer might be if it's not Abbott."

"Do you think it's Abbott?"

Laurel looked down at her half-finished dinner. "I really don't know." How irritating.

"How soon do you want me to leave?"

"Tomorrow works for me," Laurel said.

Deidre's jaw dropped. "Laurel, I can't leave tomorrow."

"Sure, you can. I already looked into it." She forced a smile. "In fact, I have you and Dolores booked at a luxury spa in Arizona for three days before you take the long flight to Asia to obtain the best tea ingredients in the world."

Deidre took a big gulp of her wine. "I believe that's bribery."

"It's on me, and I already prepaid. The spa does not offer refunds."

Deidre's mouth opened. "Laurel Snow, that is blackmail."

Laurel accepted the label without hesitation. "Guilty of blackmail and bribery in one night. That's a new one for me."

"That's a new one for me, too." Deidre pushed away from the table and stood. "I have to pack."

"I am happy to help, and I already contacted Dolores. A car service will collect her and then arrive here tomorrow morning at five o'clock."

Deidre threw both hands up. "Five in the morning? Laurel, I can't possibly—"

"Yes, you can. I already talked to your employees. Sally and June are more than happy to take over. They were planning to do it in two weeks anyway, so we're just starting a bit earlier."

Deidre put both hands on her trim hips. "What did you bribe them with?"

Laurel blanched. "Thousand-dollar bonuses each week."

Deidre shook her head. "I taught you too well."

Laurel warmed. "That's kind of you to say. I can afford it, Mom, and having you out of town eases my mind while I work these cases."

"That does matter to me." Deidre leaned in and kissed her forehead. "Although you have to promise me you'll be safe."

"I promise. I've been trained by the best."

Deidre leaned back. "Come help me pack. Are you sure you can solve these cases in two weeks? Because I'm not moving abroad."

"Absolutely. By the time you get home, it will be safe for you. I promise," Laurel said, ignoring the ball of dread in her stomach.

She had to find this killer.

After helping her mother pack, Laurel snuggled down in bed, her body exhausted and her mind spinning. Fred curled into her side, sleeping contentedly. Laurel normally had more control over herself than this, but the two cases weighed heavily on her. There was no doubt there would be another victim soon if she didn't find the river killer, and probably yet another victim if she didn't find Jason Abbott. Unless the cases were one and the same, which was entirely possible. Her phone buzzed and she pulled it from the table. "Agent Snow."

"Hey, it's Huck." His low voice rumbled over the line.

She burrowed deeper into the blankets. "What are you doing calling me at this hour?"

"We had a sighting of Jason Abbott about a half an hour ago."

She sat up in bed. "Where?"

"I already checked it out. He wasn't there, and I have Fish and Wildlife officers as well as Genesis Valley police officers canvassing the entire area. Do not get out of bed. You need sleep."

She thought through her options and couldn't find a way to help with any such search. "Tell me about the sighting." She lay back down, pulling the covers up to ward off the chilly night.

"Abbott broke into a mom-and-pop convenience store a block away from the Center Diner."

She thought about the area. "I've been in there. I stopped for a slushie one day."

"You bought a slushie?"

"Yes. The purple ones are delicious. Do you have him on camera?"

Huck whistled, no doubt for his dog. "We do. I have the CCTV feed right now. We can look it over tomorrow, but basically he broke into a back door and stole a bunch of food."

"How did he look?"

"Fine. He was wearing black jeans, a dark sweatshirt, and a hat, but it's undeniably him—with a newly shaved jaw."

Her heart beat faster. "Did he look at the camera?"

Aeneas barked in the background. "I already fed you," Huck called out. "Laurel's not coming here tonight. Relax. The dog's looking for you."

She blinked into the darkness. "I doubt that's what he's barking about."

"You'd be surprised. He's really cranky when you're not around," Huck said as clothing rustled. "So am I."

She missed them both. "When I met you, your default setting was grumpy."

He chuckled. "I think that's fair to say, and I like the phraseology."

"Me, too," she said. "I heard it from Nester last week. Back to the case. So, Jason Abbott looked healthy but hungry. What did he steal?"

"He hit the cash register, which held about five hundred dollars, and then took food and water. He was wearing a backpack, and he filled it."

"He doesn't care that we saw him," Laurel mused. The man had narcissistic personality disorder, most likely. That made sense with what she knew about Jason Abbott. "We're still waiting on the results from dumping Haylee Johnson's phone. I wish we could obtain a tap on Abigail's phone. I know he'll reach out to her."

"Do we have enough for a warrant?"

She thought through all the facts she could accurately attest to in an affidavit. "We do not for Abigail, unfortunately. I could reach out and ask her."

"I wouldn't," Huck said. "She'll just play a game with you. You won't know if she's telling the truth or not."

Unfortunately, that was true, and Laurel didn't have the energy to deal with her half sister right now. "Jason robbed a convenience store miles away from the Genesis Valley Community Church, where Teri Bearing's body was found. Have we found any witnesses who might've seen him in that area lately?"

"Not yet," Huck said. "I have the canvassing officers reporting in every fifteen minutes, and if anybody gets a hit, they're to call me immediately. Thus far we don't have a damn thing." He cleared his throat. "I've been taken off my mom's case, but I can argue that the Jason Abbott case is separate right now. Kind of."

They had no proof that Abbott was committing the river killings. Yet. She wiggled her toes in the now-warming sheets. "We have more than we did yesterday. At least we know that Jason Abbott is still in the vicinity. Have you gleaned any news from the tail we've had on Haylee Johnson?"

"Not a word," Huck said. "I had them check in an hour ago, and she's been in her apartment outside Genesis Valley all day and night."

Laurel sighed. "I can't believe Abbott hasn't contacted her."

"Obviously not, because he had to rob a place to get food and money. He has to know that we're watching her."

Yes, but Abbott believed he was smarter than everyone else. "He'll want to outfox us by contacting her. He's probably biding his time, though." She enjoyed employing both colloquialisms.

"Most likely," Huck agreed. "How did your plan with your mom go?"

"Successfully," Laurel said. "She's leaving tomorrow morning with Dolores for the spa, and then they'll fly to Asia and meet with all of the growers. I have her staff rearranging her visits and timelines so she doesn't have to worry about it."

"You're a good daughter. I take it you and your damn cat will be moving in with me?"

She rolled over and curled onto her side. "Fred and I can stay here if you want. He doesn't like it when you swear at him."

"That cat couldn't care less," Huck said, chuckling. "I would very much appreciate it if you both moved in here. I don't like you being alone there, even though, yes, you are a trained FBI agent."

She sighed. "I am sleeping very soundly these days, and I wouldn't mind backup." As if on cue, Fred stretched against her, purring loudly. "Should we talk about a more permanent arrangement?" She winced. Personal matters were not her forte.

"I've been thinking about that," Huck said. "We have several options."

The sound of something popping came across the line, and it took her a second to identify it as a log in his fire. She missed his fire and wished she relaxed in front of it right now. Her mom's place just wasn't as warm. "List our options, please."

"We could expand my place and build a second level, or if you prefer, we could redesign that barndominium that you have planned."

She petted the cat and scratched behind his ears. "I was thinking the same thing. I would like to remain here on the family property closer to my mom, especially once the baby's born." She had no doubt Deidre would provide valuable babysitting. Plus, her mom was the most loving person she knew, and a baby would need that.

"That's fine by me," Huck said. "We can go over the plans. I will need a shop, though. You know that, right?"

She calculated the available space and mentally designed where each building should be erected. "We have acres upon acres of land here. You can have the biggest shop ever built."

"Now, that sounds like a good plan. I'm glad we're creating a future together, Laurel."

"As am I," she said, drowsiness hitting her. "All we have to do is find a couple of serial killers, and then we're in the clear."

He sighed. "Right. Just that."

Chapter 24

The sun hadn't risen yet as Laurel helped lug her mom's heavy suitcase out of the farmhouse.

"You stop that right now." Deidre rushed to grab the suitcase. "I've got it."

Laurel tried to strengthen her grip while also waving to the two officers in the patrol car near the driveway. These were local police officers from Genesis Valley, and she appreciated their diligence. "Mom, I'm pregnant, not injured. I can help you."

"No, I have it." Deidre gently pushed her away.

A black town car rolled to a stop on the well-lit driveway, and her mom's second-in-command, Dolores, jumped out of the back. "I can't believe this. This is insane." She ran toward them, her dark hair curled around her head. She was broad-shouldered and tall, and she elbowed both women out of the way. "I've got it. I've got it."

A man emerged from the front of the vehicle and hurried toward them. He wore a full suit with a bow tie. "I can help you, ladies," he said gently, prying the suitcase out of Dolores's hands.

"That's very nice of you, Charlie." She patted his arm

and nearly knocked him over. Then she reached for Laurel and gathered her in for a hug. For the journey, she wore black pants and a thick gray sweater with several scarves knotted around her throat and jangly silver bracelets up her arm. "This is so kind of you. I've never been to a spa like this. I did my research, and they read your aura, and they do your tarot cards, and then you get a massage." She hopped once. She was in her midforties, her dark eyes lit up and her wide face liberally spread with makeup. "I'm just so excited. This is so much fun."

Deidre smoothed back her hair. "You're going to need to dial it down a bit, Dolores. It's five in the morning."

"Oh, you." Dolores tossed a hand toward Deidre. "Cheer up. The unexpected is often fun."

Laurel shook her head. "No, it usually isn't. However, in this instance, I think you'll both enjoy the spa."

Deidre reached for her carry-on bag. "I don't know, Laurel. What about—"

"It's all taken into account, Mom," Laurel said. "Your employees can handle the shipments from the warehouse. We haven't opened your shop yet, so there's no reason for you not to enjoy yourself. You love this trip every year, and now it's starting out with a spa weekend."

Dolores clapped her hands together loudly. "A spa, a real fancy type of spa. You know movie stars go there, Deidre. We may see somebody famous."

Deidre sighed. "We're not going to see anybody famous."

"You might," Laurel countered. "I heard many actresses go to detox at this place. I think you're going to love it."

Deidre pulled her in for a hug. "All right, Laurel. I'll leave town, but you be careful, okay? Promise me."

"Of course I'll be careful."

They both stiffened as headlights showed down the driveway.

"Who would be here at this time of morning?" Dolores asked, turning and making all of her jewelry jangle.

Laurel narrowed her eyes at seeing Monty Buckley's Fish and Wildlife truck. "Perhaps Monty is coming to say goodbye to you."

"How thoughtful," Dolores said. "He likes you, Deidre."

Monty slowly exited his truck. "Huck told me where to find you, Laurel."

"Is everything all right?" Laurel asked.

He shook his head. "Not really. There has been a new development in the case." He looked at Deidre and then Dolores. "We can discuss it after these two get on their way."

"Oh, no," Deidre said.

"That's okay, Mom." Laurel gave her another hug and ushered her toward the town car. "You need to get to the airport to catch your flight. It's quite a drive. I'll miss you, but I love you, and I want you to have fun."

Monty moved in and reached for Deidre's hands. "Have a wonderful time, and when you return, I'll be a hundred percent. We'll party like the kids do."

Deidre smiled at him. "Take care of my girl, Monty."

"You know I will," Monty said cheerfully.

Laurel barely kept from rolling her eyes but safely deposited her mother and Dolores in the vehicle. Then she watched as it slowly drove away. "What development in the case?"

Monty's shoulders hunched. "We have another body."

Laurel ran back toward the house. "I need a heavier jacket and my weapon. Tell me what happened."

Monty hustled after her. "We received a distress call from a personal locator beacon about an hour ago."

She barreled inside. "Please tell me it wasn't out at Witch Creek."

"It was out at Witch Creek." He coughed.

"Damn it." She kicked off her slippers and yanked on her heavier boots and a thick parka before fetching her weapon and a travel mug containing warm tea. "Would you like me to brew you a coffee?"

"No, I've got one," Monty said.

She put her hood over her hair and followed him outside, stopping to lock the door before walking down and climbing into his truck as Monty slid into the driver's seat. "All right, give me the details."

He sighed and started the engine. "Somebody hit a personal locator button signaling an emergency that notified Fish and Wildlife. Two of their officers went to investigate, and they found a body next to Witch Creek. All I could get from them is that she's blond and frozen to the ground, face down."

"So being blond seems to be a pattern." Dread slid through Laurel. "Jason Abbott's first victim was found next to Witch Creek, and she'd engaged a PLB, so somebody is referencing the crime scenes from our previous cases. This is no longer a possible coincidence. Has Huck been notified?"

Monty turned down the country road. "Negative. I decided not to call Huck. He'd head out there immediately, and we have to shield him from this investigation."

"I understand," Laurel said. "Yet he's the best tracker we have in the state."

"I know," Monty said. "But we'll have to do this one without him."

She took a sip of the herbal tea.

"Your mom called last night and said this trip was a whirlwind created by you. What's going on?"

She shrugged. "My mother was already scheduled to travel to Asia, as she does every year, to buy supplies for her tea business. I merely talked her into moving the trip up a couple of weeks."

Monty flipped on the heater, and her toes instantly started to warm. "That's a good idea with everything going on around here. We have someone killing blondes. Plus Abbott might be the murderer, and you know he wants to hunt you."

"I know he's coming for us regardless of whether these are his kills or not," Laurel said. "So, yes, I pushed her out of the country." It was an apt description and she'd take it.

"I don't blame you," Monty said cheerfully.

"Thanks."

They drove to the edge of state forest land, where they met up with a young female officer waiting next to a fully enclosed UTV. "This is the easiest way to get out there," she said, winking at Monty. "Long time, no see."

He chuckled. "Very funny. Agent Snow, please meet Officer Jill Jordan."

Laurel didn't know what they were joking about. She climbed into the back of the UTV. "Nice to meet you."

Officer Jordan drove, while Monty sat next to her.

"You sure you don't want the front?" he asked for the third time, turning around to look at her.

"I'm good, Monty. Thank you." The modern UTVs were lovely, with heated seats and warmth all around her. She stared out at the light dusting of snow on every tree. "How long does the snow usually last in this area?"

Officer Jordan drove quickly. "It's Washington State. Sometimes we lose the snow in the mountains in February, and sometimes it's still here in June." She turned around a series of pine trees to follow a barely visible trail. "As my *obasan* used to say, 'Even on snow, three years.'"

Monty turned to Laurel. "I suppose you know what that means."

Laurel nodded. "It's a Japanese saying that even something as fleeting as snow can last for a long time, metaphorically hinting that impacts or consequences can endure longer than expected."

"Very good," Officer Jordan said.

"Oh," Monty muttered. "Like Jason Abbott. He's lasting longer in our lives than we ever expected."

The young officer nodded. "Exactly."

Laurel angled her head to see the officer. "Your grandmother sounds like a wise woman."

"She was," Officer Jordan said. "She always found the beauty in life. That's a rare gift, you know. She was a big believer in *ichigo ichie*."

"Ah. One time, one meeting," Laurel murmured. "I agree."

Monty looked over at the officer. "You're Japanese?"

"Yes. My mother is half-Japanese," Officer Jordan said. "I look like my dad's family. They're Scottish." She sighed. "Unfortunately, I didn't inherit the dark red hair."

She glanced at Laurel before focusing back on the trail. "Your hair is gorgeous."

"Thank you." It was the proper response, but Laurel had never understood why. She had no control over her chromosomal pairs. Her phone buzzed, and she pulled it free of her pocket, surprised to still be receiving cell service, and unsurprised to see the identity of the caller. "Good morning, Captain."

The sounds of a fire crackled across the line. "I heard we have another body. Are you headed to the scene?" Huck asked.

"I am, with Monty and Officer Jordan in a UTV," Laurel said. "You have been removed from this case."

Huck sighed. "I know, but I heard that the vic was found by Witch Creek. I know that area better than anybody." Aeneas whined through the line. "I should head out there."

"We both know you can't. If you want to be busy this morning, try to track down a judge to sign the warrant for Haylee's apartment, would you? We have been unsuccessful with that." She covered the phone with her hand. "Monty, somebody in your office notified Huck about this case, and you need to put a stop to it. He has to be shielded completely."

Monty turned. "I'll raise a ruckus when I return to the office." He grimaced over his shoulder at Laurel before focusing on the trail again. "Everyone likes and respects him so much, they all want Huck to stay on the case."

"It won't help in the long run," Officer Jordan said. "In fact, once we catch the killer, it'll screw up the entire case against the murderer. You have to know that."

Monty sighed. "I do. May I have the phone?"

Laurel handed her phone up to him.

Monty visibly straightened his shoulders. "Hi, Captain Rivers. If you interfere again, I'll have you put on disciplinary leave."

Laurel leaned closer to hear.

Monty sighed. "Thank you for understanding, and yes, that was really difficult to say. Is Aeneas enjoying those new dog treats I found in Snohomish last week?"

Laurel settled back against her seat as Monty and Huck engaged in small talk until Monty lost service. He handed back the phone. "He's okay."

"Good." Laurel leaned against the side of the UTV and closed her eyes, surprised by how tired she remained even after sleeping for several hours. She may have dozed off until they reached an area with a couple of obvious camping spots. She stepped out, and the wind chill slapped her wide awake. "This isn't where we found Abbott's Witch Creek victim."

"No," Monty said. "We're about . . . I don't know. What would you say, Jills? Maybe half a mile north of that scene?"

"So, he chooses the same body of water but not the exact same location," Laurel said. "I wonder if that's by design. Is the ice heavier here? We need to check that out, Officer Jordan. Please take pictures of the ice in this location and then the ice where Jason Abbott's first victim was found, all right?"

"No problem, Agent Snow," Officer Jordan said. "This baby will drive anywhere. I'm happy to do that."

They required additional backup for this case. "Thank you."

Dawn was just lightening the sky and the forest

around Laurel as she followed Monty between the trees toward Witch Creek. Icicles hung from the surrounding branches, and fresh snow covered the trail they followed. Many sets of boots showed near the tree line, no doubt as officers tried to preserve the trail, but Laurel couldn't discern any prints.

This killer seemed both methodical and lucky with the weather.

Monty looked back at her. "Do you think that the killer has changed his MO? I mean, initially there were three days between kills, and now seven days?"

Laurel's boots sank into the snow near a tamarack shivering in the wind. "No. I think he's careful and has to wait for the easiest time to take a victim. Based on what we know so far about Delta Rivers, she was a victim of opportunity, so we have to surmise the same for all of them right now—until we track her movements better to see if she somehow was stalked." There were too many unanswered questions about Huck's mother.

The wind cracked between the trees in bursts, pushing Laurel forward. Silence drummed around them as if the forest held its breath, allowing the wind to triumph.

She shivered, shoving her gloved hands into her pockets and ducking her head. Tucking her chin inside her jacket, she stepped in Monty's footprints, unsure why they stayed off the main trail. There were no prints. Period.

Finally, they emerged onto a crusted-over beach area complete with two worn and weathered picnic tables near the tree line. Ice covered them both.

Fish and Wildlife officers had already set up several spotlights as well as a tent over the body. From the look of the scene, the state crime lab techs had been at work for at least thirty minutes.

The creek stretched wide at this point with the other side showing a drop-off between the trees and the creek. Ice spread across the water, which bubbled in protest against it in several areas, not quite breaking through.

Laurel neared the body. She could barely make out blond hair beneath a bubble of ice that encased the victim's head and stretched down her entire length. She wore a long, gray trench coat with bright red boots. Awareness began to tick down Laurel's body, and she shivered, making sure her coat was zipped up to the very top. She should've remembered to wear a scarf. Stepping to the side, she studied the creek.

She angled closer, noting that the hole this time held sharper edges, like the first crime scene, so perhaps an ice spud pole had been used again. "We need pictures of the ice close up and far away, and I'd love to get a molding of those indents if it's possible."

"I'll try," the nearest tech said. "Officer Tso has taken photographs of the entire area. The ice has already melted quite a bit, but I'll do my best."

She nodded. "Thanks, Jeremy." She'd met him at a previous crime scene. He appeared to be in his early thirties with light blond hair and a serious countenance. Beneath the white hood of his suit, he wore a white knit hat.

"You bet, Agent Snow." Jeremy sat back. "We can turn her over now. I think we have her as secured as we can." They'd scraped all around the body. Had the killer poured water over her to obtain this amount of ice? That seemed most probable.

Laurel and Monty stepped closer. As the techs gently began to roll the body over, the ice cracked.

"Make sure you sample everything around her," Monty said.

Jeremy looked up with a "no kidding" expression on his face. Laurel had caught that with no difficulty. Either he was being very obvious or she was becoming more proficient at reading facial expressions.

"Here we go." Jeremy gently smoothed his ice shovel to the side.

Laurel bent down, and then her breath caught as she recognized the victim beneath the icy veneer. "That's Haylee Johnson."

Chapter 25

Late afternoon, the cottonwoods loomed high above them as if stretching toward the foggy sky which mercilessly pelted them with icy rain. Laurel tucked her hair more firmly underneath her knit cap and shivered as she followed Huck's makeshift trail toward the river behind his cabin.

"I can do this," he said quietly. "I'll take several pictures."

"You shouldn't even be involved to this degree," she said, accepting that this field observation would equip her better than any other method.

At least they had eaten a warm meal before engaging in this pursuit. She'd finished up at Haylee Johnson's crime scene and headed back to Huck's for this experiment.

Aeneas bounded along happily next to her, sinking in the snow and then leaping out to sink down again. She wanted to grab him and put him onto the trail, but obviously, he was having fun, uncaring of the freezing rain thanks to the waterproof parka covering his slim body. She tucked her face deeper into her coat, the hammer and screwdriver heavy in her hand. Finally, they reached the river.

Huck turned and looked her over. "It's probably too cold out here for you."

She'd bundled up as much as possible with two pairs of socks, thick boots, long underwear, jeans, a sweater, and the heaviest parka he owned. The coat hung loosely on her, yet provided a surprising amount of warmth.

"I'm fine." She nodded at the implements in his hands. "Let's expedite this assessment."

"All right. We have a sledgehammer, an ax, and a spud bar," he noted. "You have a regular hammer and a screwdriver. Should you record this?"

She placed both the hammer and the screwdriver on an ice-covered rock. "Yes."

Water dripped down his face. "Did Ortega say how soon he'd get to the autopsy for Haylee Johnson?"

"No, but he said he'd put a rush on her." Laurel's heart ached for the young woman. "Fish and Wildlife had a tail on her from our office to her apartment, and they said she hadn't left."

"Obviously, she went out the back and eluded them," Huck said. "Monty has people pushing the warrant for her place right now. Hopefully they'll find a judge this afternoon."

One could hope. "I really need to get into her apartment," Laurel said.

Huck set down the sledgehammer and ax while holding the spud bar. "Agreed. Monty has two officers on the apartment now, making sure nobody goes in, and this time, they're covering the back as well."

His tone held a grittiness that she couldn't quite read,

but she figured it didn't bode well for the officers who had lost Haylee the night before. Of course, it had been dark, so it probably wouldn't have been too difficult to avoid them if the young woman had tried. Had she gone to meet Jason Abbott? If so, had he drowned her in that freezing river?

Laurel pulled out her phone and clicked Record. "Captain Rivers is breaking the ice with what is called a spud bar." She looked closer at the implement. It had a long handle and a chisel at the end. There wasn't a lot to it.

He moved to the iced-over river, chose a spot, lifted the rod, and swung down. Ice cracked and snapped, flying in every direction. He continued with the device until he'd created a hole comparable in size to the one used to drown the victims.

Laurel recorded the action and then leaned closer, making sure to get every edge. The edges appeared to her to be more jagged than the ones found at either the Delta Rivers or the Haylee Johnson crime scene. Teri Bearing's crime scene had had smooth edges around the ice hole.

"I see," Laurel said. "That's not exactly right." They'd compare the pictures later, but so far the results weren't as expected.

"Let's try the ax." Huck placed the bar against a tree and reached for his ax.

Laurel's heartbeat began to thrum. If the killer had used an ax to break the ice, the recent murders would be tied much closer to Jason Abbott. He liked to use an ax on his victim's wrists, but what if he had turned that fantasy to the ice instead? Finally, she could see an actual tie between the current victims and Abbott.

Huck walked down the river a little way to another completely iced-over spot, hefted the ax, and swung it at the ice. He did so several times until he'd created the right-sized opening.

Laurel recorded him and moved closer, shivering in the freezing cold, her eyelashes feeling iced over. She leaned down to ensure the entire hole appeared onscreen. "Those indents are too wide and far apart." Disappointment clashed through her.

Huck nodded. "I know. I tried to hack closer and then farther away from each hit, but I'm not seeing the same pattern."

"I'm not either, but we'll compare. What if we used a smaller ax?"

"Maybe," Huck said doubtfully. "I can acquire one later today."

They then tested the sledgehammer, the smaller hammer, and finally, the screwdriver. Nothing created holes similar to those used to drown the victims. The indentations were too far apart and not symmetrical enough.

Laurel stopped recording and leaned against a bare tree, her feet numb. "I can't believe none of those worked."

"Perhaps the smaller ax? We need something sharp that will create even cuts."

She tried to think through what she remembered from each scene. "How do you get an even distribution of cut marks if you're hacking at ice?"

Huck's head jerked up. "Wait a minute—I have an idea. Do you want to come inside?"

She looked back toward the trail and couldn't imagine trudging down it again. "How about I stay here with Aeneas and you hurry?"

"Good plan." He grabbed the various weapons and moved into a jog. "Stay, Aeneas," he said.

Aeneas yipped happily, standing by Laurel in his heavy coat with even his ears covered.

"Thanks," she said.

Aeneas nudged her leg and then moved over to sniff at the various holes in the ice. The wind died down, leaving the area silently frozen. Craggy rocks jutted up from the river through the ice, showing a dangerous path from one bank to the other. Laurel trembled and tried to force warmth to her extremities.

Huck soon appeared, running easily along the trail, his hands empty.

"You didn't bring anything?" she asked.

"Oh, yeah, I did." He looked down at his boots.

She glanced down to see a rubber webbing over the top of his boots and buckled around the back. "What is that?"

He lifted his boot. "I'm wearing crampons."

She stared at the steel spikes extending from his boots. "Crampons?"

"Yeah," Huck said. "We use them for walking across ice and up glaciers or icy mountains to rescue people. I didn't even think of these."

She'd seen climbers using them on a documentary set in Iceland. "Aren't they made to grip the ice?"

"Yeah." Huck walked toward an untouched ice field over the river. "Keep in mind, all of these kills have been near the shore where the ice isn't as thick. They haven't been in the middle of a body of water."

He gingerly stepped onto the ice, easily keeping his balance.

She drew out her phone to record him.

He lifted one powerful leg and smashed it down on the ice. It cracked but didn't break. "Huh," he murmured. Then he started jumping up and down with both feet. One foot crashed through, and he leaned back, immediately kicking and stomping hard to form a circle. Then he stepped off the ice.

Laurel gasped and moved closer, making sure to capture the entire area before zeroing in on the hole. "That's it," she whispered. "The cuts are symmetrical and deep." She looked up at him. "That took a lot of strength and power."

"And anger," he said. "I could see somebody in a frenzy doing this."

She gulped and backed away from the dangerous hole in the ice. "So can I." So the killer used crampons with the first and third murder, but not the second. Was he unprepared for some reason?

Huck's phone trilled, and he pulled it from his pocket to press to his ear. "Rivers." He listened, his gaze lighting. "Good, thanks." He clicked off.

"What is it?" Laurel asked, shivering violently now.

"The warrant for Haylee Johnson's apartment just came in. Let's get some hot tea in you, and we'll go search her place."

Laurel needed to get her hands on those diaries. "You may not accompany me, Huck." She had no notion of who was providing him information about the case, but he couldn't be involved. She'd have to search Haylee's apartment with Monty.

Pressing a button on her phone, she lifted the device to her ear.

"Hey, boss," Nester answered. "Before you ask, the Bearings are set to land in about an hour."

"Good work, Nester. Huck will have Fish and Wildlife meet them at their plane." She clicked off.

Huck's eyebrows rose. "I will?"

She smiled. "Please? Then have an officer stay on them all night. I'll interview them tomorrow morning. The mayor is not to leave his home until I speak with him." Tonight, she would read those diaries.

Finally, she could track down Jason Abbott before he killed again.

Haylee Johnson had lived in a sad, one-bedroom apartment approximately twenty minutes away from the Genesis Valley Community Church in unincorporated land. The building held twenty apartments and had been erected probably in the seventies. The green shag carpet felt sticky against Laurel's boots, and the smell from dirty dishes stacked in the sink made her stomach roil. The heat had been turned low, most likely because the young woman lacked income. She truly had lost every-thing when Jason Abbott had been arrested.

Monty turned on all the lights, but the apartment re-mained rather dark. He opened the drawers in the kitchen and pulled them out, looking inside with his flashlight. "Thanks for meeting me here. I'm surprised Haylee's aunt let her live like this. Melissa Cutting is a partner in a big law firm. She's loaded, right?"

Laurel rifled through a stack of unpaid bills on the counter between the small living room and the dingy-looking kitchen. "Based on the jewelry and clothing Melissa prefers, I'd say she has plenty of disposable income. She should have helped her niece more."

"I don't know," Officer Tso called from the bedroom where he rifled through drawers. "Haylee seemed pretty stuck on a serial killer. Melissa Cutting probably didn't like that about her niece."

Officer Jordan looked through a stack of magazines on the table.

Laurel didn't know any of these people well besides Monty, and she barely knew him. Her team was gone. She was the sole FBI agent in the search. It had been a long time since she'd felt this isolated and alone.

Monty moved to the fridge and opened the freezer. "Got them." He pulled out three frozen-looking plastic bags and gingerly extracted a journal from one.

"Good job." Laurel peered closer, disappointment clouding through her. She'd have to wait until they defrosted to read. "They're frozen, so let's deliver them to the lab."

Monty slid the journal back into the bag. "Officer Tso?"

"Coming, boss," Tso said, lumbering over to plunk an aluminum evidence locker on the counter. "This thing's heavy." He opened the lid.

Monty gingerly placed the three journals into the locker and then shut it, twisting the lock. "We'll keep looking for evidence that Abbott has been here, but you take this to the state crime lab now."

Laurel straightened her back. They'd need at least another hour to go through the rest of Haylee's apartment before they'd be finished. "Ask the techs to send me scanned copies as soon as possible without damaging the journals." She calculated how long it would take for them to thaw out. "They should be able to have something for me by tomorrow."

"They're behind at the lab," Monty reminded her.

"I don't care. We need these now. Abbott's on the loose, and we have to consider the possibility that he is not the killer of the three drowning victims." If not, she had no idea how the news of Haylee's death would affect him. While the media hadn't learned of the woman's death yet, too many people knew the truth. It wouldn't be long before the public was made aware.

She shrugged off the unease she felt at missing her team as well as Huck.

Monty opened the fridge and started scouting through the contents, his movements slow and his face pale. "I don't like that Haylee physically accosted you in front of the news media and now she's dead. Rachel's going to be a problem."

"Rachel is always a problem." Laurel moved toward a bookshelf in the living room.

Officer Tso patted the evidence box. "I should get going with this. Do you need me for the rest of the search?"

"No," Laurel said. They'd found what they needed. She doubted seriously that Jason Abbott had set foot in this apartment.

Monty nodded. "Take Officer Jordan with you. She's working on serious overtime."

The brunette rubbed a spot of dust off her chin. "I could use a break. Thanks."

Laurel looked around. "Let's make sure that Abbott hasn't been here." She was finding it difficult to read him and follow his path or trace his movements. Hopefully, the journals would illuminate her.

"I'll put a rush on these pages," Officer Tso said, following Officer Jordan out the door.

Laurel wished she could have opened one to read a passage or two, but since they were frozen, she couldn't risk it. Finally, she was a step closer to finding Jason Abbott.

Soon.

Chapter 26

Qaletega turned down the seat warmer in Jill's SUV as she drove competently along the country road with trees flying by on either side. The clouds had parted to let the moon shine down, and the night could be considered romantic. In profile, she looked both strong and delicate at the same time. Her dark lashes were impossibly long, framing her pretty brown eyes.

"Stop staring at me," she said, her lips twitching. "We just met."

"I can't help it. You're beautiful." They'd met a week ago, and he'd instantly been smitten. He searched for a safe topic of conversation. "I have to tell you, I am sick of winter."

She looked out at the drilling rain. "Then you're in the wrong place. Winter could last for months yet."

"I read it's going to be an early spring. It's April. I imagine we'll have sun soon." He took vitamin D supplements as suggested by his doctor, but it wasn't the same as warm sunshine. He was fumbling this conversation, but he'd never been that smooth with the ladies.

"We might have a long summer, too. Tons and tons of sun for us both." Now he was just babbling.

She chuckled, having taken off her Fish and Wildlife jacket. He tried not to notice the way she filled out her uniform.

"Why did you become a Fish and Wildlife officer?" he asked.

Her dark gaze flicked to him and then returned to the road. "To protect wildlife. I've always wanted to do so."

He liked that about her. "Same with me, and I always wanted to be a cop. So the two dreams combine in this job."

"I get it."

It had been a long time since he'd felt this comfortable around anybody. His last girlfriend had dumped him at least a year ago because he was too nice, according to her. What in the world did that mean? Too nice? Who could be too nice?

A loud bang echoed and the vehicle rocked. "What the hell?" They swerved on the ice, and Jill corrected, pulling over to the side as the rear end fishtailed. "I think we popped the front right tire."

Qaletaga glanced out at the icy rocks on the road. "More than likely. It happened to me just the other night. Stay here. I've got it."

"I can change my own tire," she protested.

"I know. Let me be a gentleman. All right?"

She sat back, her pretty face softening. "Of course, you can be a gentleman. If you want to change a tire, you go right ahead."

Freezing rain poured down out there, and if he could at least keep her warm, he would try. He smiled at her just as a man emerged from the trees, his face covered, a weapon pointed at them. The guy reached her window in no time and knocked on it.

"Open the window." Qaletaga kept his hands within sight. His heart beat wildly.

She slid it down, her other hand remaining on the steering wheel.

"I don't want to hurt anybody," the guy said. Dressed in all black, he wore a balaclava over his head that covered everything but his eyes.

"Not a problem," Qaletaga said easily, his hand nonchalantly dropping to the side of his thigh. He'd never shot anybody before, but he was prepared. Probably.

Bullets instantly pinged against the hood of the vehicle. Jill jumped and moved toward him.

"It's okay," he said, his hands up now. He angled his head but could only see the tree line.

"Yeah, I've got a sniper backing me up," the guy said.

Qaletaga knew that voice from watching videos of the man's interviews to prepare for this case. It was Jason Abbott. "What do you want?"

"I want the evidence in the back hatch. Open it, and keep in mind, my sniper can hit anything from this distance. We aimed for the tire, and then we aimed for your hood. We could take out your head easily."

"This is a bad idea," Qaletaga warned, his adrenaline flowing. "I know you're Jason Abbott." Who else would want the journals?

"I think this is a good idea. Now." Abbott pressed the gun to Jill's head. She gingerly leaned forward and clicked the button to open the back hatch. "I could shoot you from any position, and so can my sniper. Don't move," Abbott ordered, walking around to the rear of the vehicle and hefting out the evidence locker. He walked a small distance from the vehicle and set it down near the tree line.

Qaletaga looked up and down the road. So far nobody was coming.

"Get out of the vehicle," Abbott ordered, pulling off his face cover.

"You got what you wanted. Now leave," Qaletaga said.

Abbott pointed the gun at Jill. "Now."

"Listen, Abbott, you're not hiding yourself very well. We've already called it in," Qaletaga said.

"You haven't called anything in." Abbott jerked open Jill's door and yanked her out. She cried out and fell. He shoved her toward the trees and then pointed the weapon at her. She lifted her hands.

"Get out of the vehicle," Abbott snapped.

Qaletaga pushed himself out of her door and walked toward her, trying to put his body between Abbott and Jill.

"Sit next to her," Abbott snapped. "So you recognized me."

"It's a little bit obvious, Jason," Jill said.

Qaletaga had to admire her grit. Her voice didn't even shake.

Jason smiled, and Qaletaga could see the charm women had found in him. Even dressed in all black, committing multiple felonies, the guy looked at ease with his dark hair swept back and his eyes calm.

"Killing cops is a bad idea," Qaletaga said.

"No shit," Abbott replied, looking toward the tree line. "However, my sniper does like to see heads blow like watermelons."

Qaletaga had to think of a way to get Jill out of there. "Let her go. You can keep me."

Abbott chuckled. "I don't want either one of you." He kept his weapon pointed at Jill. "Throw your phones in my direction."

Qaletaga reached into his pocket as Jill did the same, and they tossed their phones at Abbott.

Abbott grabbed both of them and immediately turned them off, before shoving them in his pocket. "Now your weapons."

Qaletaga threw his gun toward Abbott, and Jill did the same. Abbott picked them up and placed them in his other pocket.

"And your other weapons."

"That's all I have," Jill said.

Abbott's chin lowered. "Don't make me shoot you."

"That's really all she has." Qaletaga reached into his boot for his Glock 43 and lobbed it over.

"Nice," Abbott said.

Qaletaga looked toward the tree line and still couldn't see anybody. "Who are you working with?"

"Nobody you know." Abbott winked.

Jill cleared her throat. "I'm sorry about Haylee Johnson. I know you were close."

"We were engaged," Jason said congenially. "She was a means to an end. I'm not surprised."

Qaletaga scooted closer to Jill. "So you know that Haylee's dead?"

"Yeppers," Abbott said. "It's already hit *The Killing Hour*. Rachel Raprenzi reported on it ten minutes ago."

So Jason had been in a vehicle just ten minutes ago, which meant that whatever vehicle he had now behind that tree line was close to the road. Were there roads out there? There had to be. Qaletaga made several notes in his head. They were going to find this asshole.

"Did you kill her?" Jill asked.

Abbott studied them for a moment. "Did I? All right, who has the handcuffs?" Neither moved. "Come on. You both have handcuffs. Right now, pull them out."

Qaletaga pulled his cuffs from the back of his waist as Jill did the same. Hope filled Qaletaga. Maybe Abbott didn't want to kill them. The guy probably didn't want the FBI and the Washington State Police all descending into Genesis Valley at once.

"This way." Abbott motioned them toward the vehicle, where he had Jill secure Qaletaga to the back passenger-side door handle with the cuffs. Abbott then did the same to Jill before he leaned in and fired his weapon several times.

Jill jumped. Qaletaga looked over his shoulder to see the demolished radio.

"I imagine somebody will be along eventually," Abbott said cheerfully. "I hope you don't freeze to death in the meantime."

With that, he turned and strode toward the locker, easily lifted it, and then continued his way into the woods. Qaletaga watched him go, squinting to see better between the trees. Several shots rang out, hitting the front tire and then the back.

Jill jumped. "Holy shit."

Qaletaga glared. "The sniper is a decent shot."

The wind whistled toward them, blowing snow. He looked up and down the road and then fought against the restraints, trying to break the handle. A truck sounded in the distance as Abbott must've reached his vehicle, which sounded like it wasn't that far away.

Sighing, Qaletaga studied Jill. "Are you okay?"

She looked at him, her cheeks red from the cold and fire in her eyes. "Yeah, but I'm really wishing we had tried to at least read a couple of those journals, even though they were frozen."

Shots rang out from the trees, and pain exploded in Qaletaga's leg. Darkness swam around his vision, but he focused long enough to see Jason Abbott, his face partially shrouded by darkness, as he fired a handgun at them.

Jill screamed.

Huck burst through the doors of the hospital, sliding on the wet floor as he caught sight of Laurel and Monty sitting in chairs in the waiting room. They were both too pale. "How are they?"

Laurel stood and moved toward him. "Officer Tso is out of surgery and breathing on his own, while Officer Jordan is still in surgery." She took his hand and led him over to the seating area. "They were both shot in the legs, and Officer Jordan in the chest."

Huck sat, fury roaring through his veins. "The evidence box?"

"Gone," Monty said wearily. "I should've taken it. Not had those two kids do it." His hands shook as he rubbed them down his face.

A white-haired doctor in blue scrubs emerged through the swinging doors. "Officer Tso wants to speak with a Captain Buckley."

Monty stood. "I'll be right back."

Huck's legs bunched.

Monty planted a hand on his shoulder. "You're off this case, remember? Stay here." He hitched across the waiting area and through the doors, appearing years older than he had yesterday.

Huck leaned his head back against the wall. "What do we know?"

Laurel shook her head. "Nothing. A passerby saw both officers cuffed to the door and bleeding. He called it in." She plucked at a string on her coat, her voice soft. "The man's name is Jorge Lewiston, and he checks out. We have CCTV of him leaving the Center Diner and then calling in the shooting, completely panicked."

Huck swallowed. "We know who did this."

"We're not making assumptions," she said, her blue-and-green eyes sparking.

Fair enough.

Monty soon emerged, his chin up. "Qaletaga identified Jason Abbott as the shooter. He had an accomplice who acted as a sharpshooter during the robbery but didn't hit anybody."

"An accomplice?" Huck looked down at Laurel's flushed face. "Who would want those journals as much as Jason Abbott?"

Laurel rubbed her right temple. "Abigail isn't that reckless. Is she?"

Huck couldn't figure out who else it could be. Jason Abbott didn't have money to hire anybody. "Is Abigail that crazy?" Was it possible? If so, she was probably dead right now as well. "How's Tso?"

Monty dropped into a chair as if his body weighed too

much to remain upright. "He's going to be okay. Several gunshot wounds but nothing life threatening. Also, Officer Jordan is out of surgery. The doctor said the bullet in her chest actually hit the right side and damaged several ribs, but her prognosis is good as well."

Relief slammed through Huck. Yet he couldn't escape the thought that it could've been Laurel on the operating table.

There was a predator out there killing people, and he'd take the killer down even if that meant losing his own freedom.

He needed to find Jason Abbott. Now.

Chapter 27

After a fairly sleepless night, en route to interview the Bearing men, Laurel sat in the front seat of Huck's truck finishing a phone call with Monty. "So both officers are still listed in serious condition? But out of intensive care?"

"Yes," Monty said. "We have folks back in the woods, and we've already found where Abbott was keeping his vehicle. We're trying to trace it by CCTV right now."

Laurel's eyes felt as if she'd rubbed salt in them. She'd tried to sleep but couldn't calm herself enough. Huck hadn't fared much better. "Good. We should have somebody reach out to Melissa Cutting to see if she knows anything about this. Although she is Jason's attorney, she must inform law enforcement if she has knowledge of an ensuing crime."

Monty cleared his throat. "We're both down too many team members right now. I might have to ask the locals to help out. Who notified Ms. Cutting about Haylee's death?"

"We had the Seattle FBI contact her," Laurel said. "I surmised they could reach her before we could, and I was worried about the news reporting on the death."

"Good call," Monty said. "Rachel Raprenzi already has it."

Just fantastic. Rachel must have a source within either the FBI or Fish and Wildlife. Or both. "Be gentle when you reach out to Ms. Cutting because of her niece's death, but let her know that Abbott has now committed several additional felonies. She needs to reveal the truth if she has any idea where he is or who any of his known associates might be."

Monty cleared his throat. "There's only one I can think of, and I've been trying. The crazy doctor who experimented on him."

Laurel shook her head. "Abbott wants Abigail dead, and survival is always her prime motivation. I did try to phone her, but my call went to voicemail. My guess is that she's lying low."

"Smart woman," Monty said. "I'll call you as soon as I have anything. Good luck with the interview."

"Thank you." She clicked off.

Huck looked tall and strong in the driver's seat. "There's a chance Abigail wanted those journals back even more than Jason Abbott did."

"That's true," Laurel said. "If they contain details of how she experimented on him, I might finally be able to build a case against her." At the same time, Abbott needed to kill soon, and Abigail fit his profile. Was she reckless or overconfident to the point that she felt she could control Abbott?

Huck shook his head. "Those two getting together again is like putting two cobras in a burlap bag and shaking it up."

"I know," Laurel said, looking at the Bearings' stately

brick home on Royal Drive as Huck rolled to a stop in front.

He glanced at her. "I should go inside with you to interview the mayor."

"You can't," she said shortly. "You've been taken off this case. You probably shouldn't have driven me here, but I do appreciate the ride." Her whole body felt exhausted.

He glanced back at the dog snoring in his crate. "While you're inside the mayor's house, I'll start calling outfitting places in the area and see if anybody's bought crampons during the last year."

"I'm sure a lot of people have bought crampons."

"Me too, but it's the only thing I can do right now, so I'm going to do it."

She nudged his arm. "Thanks." She zipped up her coat. "What do you think about attending church services tomorrow? They're having a special service on Friday as a dry run for the first big, televised sermon. I read about the plans in the news."

He turned to look at her. "Why would we do that?"

"I want to put some pressure on Pastor John." He was a suspect, and observing his reaction to seeing the two of them in his congregation might be helpful. "I wouldn't mind seeing Zeke Caine's reaction either. Also, it'd be interesting to study how they relate to each other." With that, she stepped out of the vehicle and walked up to the front door to ring the bell. Saul Bearing instantly opened the door.

"Agent Snow, please come in," he said.

The mayor had silver-gray hair and pale blue eyes with dark circles slashed beneath them. For their meeting today, he wore pressed black slacks and a blue polo shirt. "Please sit down." He gestured toward a flowered sofa.

"Thank you." She slipped off her boots and removed her coat to hang over her arm before walking through the elegant living room to sit on the sofa. "I'm very sorry for your loss, Mayor Bearing," she said, unable to think of more comforting words.

He crossed around and fell onto the matching floral chair. "It's just too much. What with my sister-in-law Sharon dying just months ago and now Teri." He shook his head. "This is supposed to be a safe place to live. How do we have all of these murders?"

"I don't know." Laurel would never forget the sight of Sharon's frozen body at the cabin after Jason Abbott had brutally murdered her and then cut off her hands. Those hands had been found down by the lake near the cabin where Sharon had stayed. It had been owned by the mayor, actually.

The mayor scrubbed both hands down his face. "They say we have more serial killers in Washington State than anywhere else. Is that true?"

"No," Laurel said. "I believe the last time I checked, California had more active serial killers. However, Washington State has been associated with several high-profile serial killers such as Jason Abbott, Frank Zello, Ted Bundy, Gary Ridgway, and Robert Yates."

"So we just get more bad press?" the mayor asked.

Laurel nodded. "I suppose so."

The kitchen door opened, and Steve Bearing walked inside. "Hey, this interview didn't start without me, did it?"

"No," his father said. "We were talking about serial killers in general."

Steve took the other floral chair. His thick blond hair was swept away from his face, and his blue eyes appeared serious behind round black glasses. "I'm here in a representative capacity for my father."

"That is so noted," Laurel said, unsurprised that the young attorney wanted to protect his dad. "I'm very interested in finding the person who killed your mother, and I'm sorry for your loss, Mr. Bearing."

Steve looked away and then back. "As am I. Who in the hell would do such a terrible thing?"

"I don't know, but I will find out," Laurel said. "I need to ask you a few questions."

"Go ahead," Saul said wearily.

"Why in the world did you leave town during an active murder investigation, especially considering your wife was the victim?" Her voice remained level.

Saul flushed. "I had to get out of here. My cousin owns a cabin in the Flathead Lake area, and the boys and I went to grieve. We didn't know anything about her murder. Still don't." His voice cracked on the end, and his facial micro expressions showed signs of truth.

She tried to find the kindest approach with him. "Do you know at which spa your wife planned to stay during the time she disappeared?"

Saul ran a shaking hand over his eyes. "Apparently she didn't really have a reservation anywhere. I think she was lying to me."

Laurel sat back. "Why would you think that?"

He shook his head. "She'd been going off lately and not telling me where or why. I thought maybe she was moonlighting in Seattle, helping the homeless or something. She liked to have her secrets."

Laurel had read once that the spouse always knew deep down when their partner became unfaithful. Just how much did Saul know? "I hate to say this, but I have to ask you a difficult question. Are you aware that Mrs. Bearing was having an affair with Pastor John Govern from Genesis Valley Community Church?"

Saul paled and pushed himself even farther back in the chair.

"What are you saying?" Steve Bearing jumped to his feet. "That's a damn lie. You take that back right now. If you spew such slander about my mother publicly, I will destroy you."

She calmly studied both men. Whereas Saul had turned pale, red infused Steve's face. They appeared to be genuine reactions of shock. "As I said, I'm very sorry, but Pastor John has confirmed the fact, as have several other parishioners."

Saul shut his eyes and leaned his head back on the chair.

Steve dropped back onto his seat. "Dad, did you know this?"

Saul's jaw went slack. "No. I figured something was going on with her, and I did wonder if it might be an affair. She seemed happy and secretive, and she'd lost some weight." Saul stared down at his knees. "That's a fucking cliché, isn't it?"

"Stop talking," Steve said, sobering. "Right now, this interview is over."

"No, it isn't," Laurel said. "I really want to find who killed your mother. Where were you last Wednesday night, Mayor?"

He looked at her as if not quite seeing her. "Last

Wednesday night?" He looked away. "I don't know. Let's see. Oh, yeah, that was a charity bowl-a-thon for the children's center. I was there until a little after midnight. The event was covered by the local news."

"And then?" she asked.

He gestured around the opulent room. "I came home. I went to bed."

"Did you call your wife that night?"

He sighed. "No. She seemed more than happy to be leaving for the spa, and frankly, I was tired after bowling. We hadn't been talking much for a while, and after her arrest, it just got worse."

"Were you angry about that?" Laurel asked.

Steve Bearing leaned forward. "Watch yourself, Agent Snow."

"No," Saul said, ignoring his son. "I wasn't angry. I was just, I don't know, tired." He sighed. "I should have talked to her, or I should have tried to figure out what was going on, but I've been so busy. Life is exhausting sometimes." He looked at his son. "I didn't know she was having an affair. But don't be angry at her. She's gone, Steve."

"I'm not angry," Steve said, the pitch and volume of his voice rising.

Saul nodded. "Whatever went wrong, it was on both of us. I wish she'd talked to me though, instead of turning to . . ." He jolted. "Did you say Pastor John?" His voice rose.

"Yes," Laurel said.

Steve slammed his hands on his legs. "That bastard. He was in a position of trust, and he took advantage of somebody in need." He looked at his father. "You don't suppose she went to him for counseling and then he seduced her?"

Saul nodded vigorously. "I'm sure that's what happened. With me so distant, she was vulnerable, she was lost, and instead of talking to me, she went to a trusted clergyman. I'm going to kill him."

"Whoa." Laurel held up a hand. "Mayor, I need you to take that back. I can't have you threatening Pastor John."

Saul swallowed and took a deep, shaky breath. "You're right. I'm not going to kill anybody, but you can bet your ass I'm going to sue that bastard and that whole church."

Steve looked at his dad and then at Laurel. "Does Pastor John have an alibi for the night of the murder?"

Laurel cleared her throat. "I can't discuss the case with you, but I can assure you that we're looking at all possible suspects. Mayor Bearing, can anybody confirm that you were here all night Wednesday into Thursday morning?"

Saul's shoulders sagged. "No. I was by myself. Unlike my wife, I don't have a lover. I go to work. I come home. I engage in activities like bowling for the city. We don't have any live-in help."

"What about your younger son?" Laurel asked.

Saul shook his head. "Tommy was at a sleepover Wednesday night after his basketball game. On Thursday, he was at school when the sheriff arrived to notify me of Teri's possible death."

None of that sounded helpful. "Where is Tommy now?"

"Sleeping," Steve said. "He finally crashed an hour ago—hasn't slept in days. I can awaken him if you like, but he doesn't know anything more. I'd prefer you let him sleep."

She'd need to speak with Tommy, but right now, she believed Steve. "Please have him call me when he's up and around. Preferably later today or tomorrow." Laurel looked around. "Do you have security cameras?"

"We have one with our doorbell in front," Saul said.

But not in the back or even on the garage, so Saul could have easily slipped out and returned without anybody seeing him.

"We are going to canvass the neighborhood to see if anybody saw you," she said gently.

"I don't care," Saul said. "I didn't kill my wife. If I had found out about the affair, I would've talked to her. I would've tried to make things right. I certainly wouldn't have murdered her."

Laurel nodded, noting the deep lines extending from his eyes. They could be a result of sorrow, or they could be guilt. "Have you ever met a woman named Delta Rivers?"

"No," Saul said. "Why? Is she one of the victims?"

"I can't discuss that," she said. "How about Haylee Johnson?"

Saul frowned. "Haylee Johnson. That name is familiar, but I can't think of who she might be."

His son leaned forward, his eyes glittering behind the stylish glasses. "You do know the name. She was the woman dating Jason Abbott, the serial killer who murdered Aunt Sharon."

"Oh," Saul said. "That's right. I remember the name, but I never met the woman. Why?"

Steve looked up at a family portrait over the fireplace

that depicted the four Bearing family members. "Haylee Johnson's body was found yesterday. She's another victim of this guy. I heard about it on *The Killing Hour*."

"She's another victim?" Saul asked. "What could Teri and that woman possibly have in common?"

Steve pushed his glasses up his nose. "According to *The Killing Hour*, Fish and Wildlife Officer Huck Rivers is a suspect in the killings. Rachel Raprenzi cited a confidential source, but she's asking more questions than providing answers. You know him, Agent Snow. What do you think?"

"I don't think he's the killer," she said.

But could she prove it?

Chapter 28

Laurel finished drying a plate and handed it to Huck to put away in his cupboard.

"Another wild night," he murmured, looking over his shoulder toward the crackling fire.

Laurel's entire body felt as if it had been through a meat grinder. "This suits me. Thanks for making dinner."

He chuckled. "I'll make scrambled eggs anytime you want."

That had been exactly what she needed.

"Go sit down by the fire," he said. "Do you want ice cream for dessert?"

She perked up. "Absolutely. I didn't know you had ice cream."

"I bought a carton the other day. Do you want chocolate or butterscotch topping?"

"I'll take both." Yet another advantage to being pregnant—no guilt about eating sugar. She walked over to sit on the sofa and extended her feet the way Huck always did, then leaned back to shut her eyes. A wet nose instantly pushed against her hand, and she started petting the dog. Taking that as encouragement, he hopped up onto the sofa and spread himself across her lap.

She opened her eyes and looked down. "I'm pretty certain you're not supposed to be up here, buddy."

He closed his eyes and pretended he was asleep. She wasn't in charge of training him, so she would leave any correction to Huck. Plus, it felt good to have the dog on her lap. She looked over to the corner where Fred stretched out on Aeneas's bed by the fireplace. The cat opened one eye, seemed to judge everything was good, and went back to sleep. He sure had made himself comfortable at Huck's with very minimal fuss.

"Have you heard from your mom?" Huck asked from the kitchen.

"Yes. She and Dolores are having an absolute ball at the spa. They had their pictures taken and their auras read from the photographs." The procedure hadn't made any sense to her, but as long as Deidre and Dolores enjoyed themselves, she was happy. More importantly, they were far away from Genesis Valley right now.

Her phone trilled, and she lifted it to her ear. "Agent Snow."

"Hello, dear sister. How are you?"

Laurel looked at the darkness outside. "Abigail. I called you earlier but only reached your voicemail."

"I've been busy," Abigail said. "I do have a life outside of you. I still teach at the college, you know."

It was unfortunate the job didn't keep Abigail busy enough. "So you were grading papers?"

"That I was. Today's youth just aren't as smart as we were. Have you noticed that?"

Laurel didn't have time for this. "Have you shot a sniper rifle lately?"

Abigail burst out laughing. "A sniper rifle? No, that's not something I have ever done. Why, do you want to take sniper lessons together?"

Laurel rolled her eyes. "No. Where is Jason Abbott right now?"

"Hell if I know," Abigail said. "I wish you'd go ahead and catch him because I'm tired of looking over my shoulder all the time. You know he's going to come for me."

Laurel wiggled her toes in front of the blissful fire. "Yes, I believe he wants to harm you. Probably both of us, but you first." It made sense. The woman had experimented on Abbott, and he blamed her for his problems. "Did you know he kept journals?"

Abigail fell silent for a moment. "No. What kind of journals?"

Her voice held a different note, but Laurel couldn't read it. Was that concern or hesitation?

"Journals all about your time with him," Laurel guessed. Or maybe he'd detailed his killings. They must hold important information, or he wouldn't have risked the wrath of the FBI to steal them back.

Abigail cleared her throat. "I did not know that Jason kept journals, but I sure would like to read them. Do you know where they are?"

"I do know where they are," Laurel said. "There is no way I'll allow you to read them." She figured Jason Abbott had them, so she was telling the truth. She did know who had the journals, and hopefully he was too arrogant to destroy them. No doubt he'd spent a lot of time detailing his kills so he could go back and relive them by reading through his diaries.

"Now, Laurel, I would very much like to read these journals. Perhaps I can help you decipher what was going on in Jason's head during these last difficult months."

How unnerving the existence of the journals must be to Abigail. What exactly had she done to Jason during those experiments? "I don't think so," Laurel said as Huck crossed around and handed her a bowl of ice cream.

Was Abigail playing some sick game? She could've been the sniper, which meant she already knew about the journals. Yet, did that track? Laurel's temples ached.

"Aeneas, down," Huck ordered. The dog looked at him but obeyed, slinking over to flop down on half of his bed. Fred looked at him and struck out with a paw. Aeneas ignored the cat and shut his eyes.

Laurel looked down at her ice cream. "When was the last time you spoke with Jason Abbott?" she asked Abigail.

"You already know the answer to that. I visited him in jail, hoping to help your case. Now I'm done talking about Abbott." The sound of Abigail drinking something came over the line, most likely a cabernet of very good vintage. "I heard on the news that Haylee Johnson was killed by the river, just like the first still-unidentified victim and that insipid Teri Bearing. Is it true?"

"Yes," Laurel said. "We found her body yesterday."

Abigail chuckled. "I suppose that's one way to end a lawsuit."

Laurel jolted. "Excuse me?"

"Come on, Laurel. That twit was suing us, and now

the lawsuit will go away. I'd say it was a good day for us, don't you think?"

Laurel placed the bowl of ice cream on the table next to the end of the sofa, feeling ill. "No, I don't think it was a good thing, Abigail."

"Well, tomato, tomaaaato. Have a lovely evening, sister. I hope we can get together soon." Abigail ended the call.

Laurel looked at her phone and shook her head.

"What?" Huck asked.

"Perhaps evil actually does exist," she murmured.

Huck rolled over onto his side and punched his pillow, trying to keep from awakening Laurel. So much danger was coming for her right now that he couldn't sleep. That psycho sister of hers was going to make a move sometime, and he had no idea what that would look like. Abigail's interest in the baby bordered on terrifying.

He was in the way. He knew it. Though he had faced plenty of danger in his life, he'd never had something he wanted to protect so badly. Somebody. Laurel Snow had grabbed his heart and held it from the first time he'd met her, although he'd fought his feelings as long as he could. He was grumpy and difficult, and nobody should have to deal with him on a long-term basis. But she seemed to want to stick with him, and somehow, she accepted him with all of his many faults. He didn't deserve her.

But she was pregnant now, and he had to protect her and the baby. No kid of his was going to grow up without a dad as Laurel had. Or the way he'd grown up without a mother. Not if he could help it.

The ring he'd bought was in his sock drawer. The timing had to be right with Laurel, and he knew she wasn't there yet. She had just wrapped her mind around the idea of being a mom. He didn't want to push her. For somebody with a genius IQ, she truly didn't see herself clearly. The woman had more heart than anybody he'd ever met, but she had no clue about that.

He could be patient. She seemed to accept his need to protect both her and the baby, so he could wait forever for the words or a ceremony if that's what she wanted.

His presence in her life was what she needed. His ability to protect and defend. *That* he'd provide for sure.

She rolled over to face him. "You are thinking so hard I can't sleep."

He blinked. "You can feel me thinking?"

She frowned, pursing her pretty pink lips. "I suppose not. I guess from your movements, and your punching the pillow, I surmised that you were having difficulty sleeping. Most people can't sleep because they're thinking or worrying and not relaxing. Hence . . ."

Hence. He loved that. Hence. It was adorable how she explained every situation with logic. He tugged her onto her back and covered her, noting her small smile and letting it fill him. "You think you're so smart," he teased.

"I am smart. Objectively speaking." She scratched her nails down his bare flanks.

Of course she was. She was also fucking gorgeous. Moonlight filtered in, showing those incredible heterochromatic eyes. One blue, one green, both hugely intelligent. The extra starburst in one was just another sign of her being a unicorn among people. If he said that, she'd calmly explain that unicorns didn't exist.

She was wrong.

They most certainly did, and she was one of them.

Her lips curved. "What are you thinking about?"

"You." He kissed her, delving deep, loving how quickly she returned the kiss. Her small body shifted restlessly beneath him. Sometimes the delicacy of her frame caught him off guard. Her brain was so big, sometimes he forgot that the woman was a mere five foot two. He licked along her jawline and down to her collar bone, smiling at her quick intake of breath.

She bit into his shoulder.

Fire lanced through him.

"You bit me." He levered himself up.

She grinned. "You're being too gentle again. I'm perfectly healthy."

Oh, yeah? He shifted to the side, rolled her over, and smacked her perfect ass.

She jolted and then burst out laughing. "You did not."

"I did." He smacked her dead center again.

"Huck Rivers." Laughter and something else sounded in her tone. Need.

He yanked her T-shirt over her head.

She laughed.

He cupped her butt and ran his fingers down and between her legs, finding her wet. "Interesting, Agent Snow." He tore off her panties and kicked his boxers out of the way before pulling her up onto her hands and knees.

"Huck?" she breathed.

"Yeah." He positioned himself at her entrance and then slowly pushed himself in.

She tossed back that wild auburn hair, and it curled across her bare back.

He leaned over her and nipped her delicate nape. She shivered. "Are you all right?" he asked.

"Yes," she breathed.

Good. He lifted back up, grabbed her hips, and pounded into her. Hard and fast he moved, enjoying the perfect outline of his hand on her butt. Heat roared through him, so he switched his angle, feeling her body tremble.

She tensed and then gasped as her body gyrated with an orgasm, gripping him so tightly inside her that he saw stars. He let her ride the waves before he allowed himself to let go, his climax stealing his breath.

He withdrew and tugged her to his side, spooning his big body around her.

She slapped his hand. "I can't believe you spanked me."

He snorted, kissing the back of her head. "That was a love slap. Behave yourself so you don't learn the difference."

She chuckled, the sound sleepy. "I have a gun, Rivers. Never forget it." Then she dropped instantly into sleep.

He held her tight, listening as a punishing rain began to fall outside. The thoughts returned, and he allowed them in this time, content as she breathed evenly against him.

There was no line he wouldn't cross to keep her safe.

Not a one.

Chapter 29

Jason Abbott sat in front of the crackling campfire with his gun at his back, his knife in his boot, and his ax leaning against a nearby tree. He held a flashlight in his mouth as he read through the pages of his most recent journal. The memories came rushing back, and he remembered the sweetness of each kill.

His dick hardened to rock. Where was he going to find black dahlias now?

A rumble started down the dirt drive, and he paused, letting the flashlight drop onto the descriptive pages before setting it aside on a log stump next to him. He pulled the weapon from the back of his waist and stood, pointing it at the bulky car.

Like before, it was an older Cadillac glinting golden in the firelight. The vehicle rolled to a stop, and the door opened, a gun emerging first, pointed at him. Then she stepped out. She slammed the door shut and walked gracefully toward him, tonight wearing all black: sweater, jeans, boots. Even a black knit hat covered her head and a portion of that unreal auburn hair.

"Are the guns really necessary?" Abigail Caine asked, edging toward him, no fear on her face.

He tilted his head. "Where's the sniper rifle?"

"It's in the car," she murmured, drawing nearer. "If you shoot, I shoot. How about we put them away?"

"Why?" he asked insolently, the idea of wrapping his hands around her neck nearly making him come in his pants.

She sighed as if becoming bored. "Would you stop acting silly? We both know you have a much higher intelligence than most people realize. How about you act like it?"

He hated when she spoke to him like that, and yet he also wanted to understand. Why did she always seem to be irritated or bored with him? He was smarter than she was—for sure. "What exactly do you think is going to happen here?"

Her gaze dropped to the journals on the stump. "I thought I could read one of those, and then we have to burn them, Jason."

Fire lashed through him. "We can't burn them. I recorded everything. These are mine." He sounded petulant, and he knew it. He drew in a deep breath and then exhaled slowly. The way she'd taught him.

"If you detailed your kills, then we have to destroy them." She spoke slowly and with a commanding voice, one he remembered from those experiments.

"What did you shoot into my veins during those experiments anyway?" he asked.

She smiled, looking quite lovely in the firelight. She'd look even better dead. "I tell you what. How about we sit, have a nice chat, and I'll tell you? Put down your gun."

He'd wondered for months, truly not understanding. He'd believed when he signed up for her study that she would help him manage his rage. That those injections were vitamin B shots. He now knew otherwise. "All right. You first."

"How about at the same time?" She sounded bored again.

He wanted to roll his eyes but instead stared at her directly. "All right. On the count of three. One. Two. Three."

They both lowered their weapons.

"How about we toss them over there?" she suggested, pointing to a tree close to his cabin.

"Fine." He threw his first. If she'd wanted him dead, she would've killed him when she had him nearly unconscious during those tests. Or rather, yesterday when she'd held that sniper rifle on those officers. He'd been in her sights, too.

"Very good. I appreciate it." She tossed her gun over next to his, and they clinked together.

He retook his seat. She looked around and then sat on a stump to his left.

It had shocked the hell out of him when she'd knocked on his door a couple of days ago, saying that he had told her about the cabin on Viper's Mountain. The cabin couldn't be traced to him, and he truly could not remember telling her about it. Yet she'd shown up, pointed a gun at him, and informed him that his journals had been found—and she had a plan to get them back. She had a source in the FBI.

She looked at the volumes. "How could you have written down anything about your criminal activities?"

"I like to relive them." He saw no reason to lie to her now. He was bigger, and he was stronger, and they were both unarmed. Her outfit was tight, and there was no way she'd hidden another weapon. If she had, it was a knife, and he could easily take it away from her. He hadn't spent his time in jail getting fat. He'd worked out every day and was even stronger and faster than he had been before he'd been arrested.

"Do you talk about me in the journals?" she asked.

"Of course," he said. "What happened was your fault. I never would've killed those women without you."

Her chuckle was low and reminded him of happier times. "That's not true, and we both know it. You were on a path to kill. I tried to help you, Jason."

Fury lashed through him, and he looked toward the guns.

She waved a hand in the air. "Don't be silly. We're in this together now." She crossed her legs, making his mouth water. "What is your ultimate plan?" she asked.

To kill her, that was for sure. "I don't know," he lied. He also wanted a piece of her sister. Then maybe he'd move to a larger city, where he could get lost among the crowds. He missed following his girlfriends, spending time getting to know their schedules, watching them when they didn't know it. Then the leaving of presents, flowers everywhere for them, forcing them to think about him. Only then did he strike.

"I have money," she said. "I can help you get out of town."

"I'm not quite ready to leave."

She stood and started to walk to her car. "Oh, for Pete's sake."

"What are you doing?" He jumped to his feet.

"Would you relax? I'm getting something to drink. We're sitting at a cozy campfire."

He started to reach for the knife in his boot just as she leaned into the car and drew out a bottle of wine and two glasses.

"You brought wine and plastic wineglasses?"

"I'm a woman of fine taste." She sauntered toward him, completely confident. Frankly, it was disconcerting. Then she sat and untwisted the bottle top.

"You don't seem like a twist top." He retook his seat and allowed his shoulders to relax. This time, he would not let her make him uncomfortable. He was in charge.

"There are very good vintages that now have twist tops." She poured them each a glass and leaned over to hand him his.

"Switch me," he ordered.

She frowned. "Excuse me?"

"Switch glasses with me."

She snorted and then handed hers over, accepting his. "All right." Perching on the stump, she took a healthy swallow.

He did the same, now feeling silly. The wine exploded on his taste buds, and he had to admit she was right. It was delicious.

"Your turn," she said.

He reached for the nearest journal and tossed it to her.

Delight lifted her lips, and she opened it, tilting the

pages toward the fire to illuminate them. "Naughty boy. You drew pictures, too, Jason."

"I was an architect," he said. "I like drawing."

She read for a while, sipping her wine. "This is rather detailed."

"I know." His cock wept against his zipper.

She looked at him directly. "You're smart enough to understand that we have to burn these, right?"

He finished his wine, understanding the danger the journals represented. But they were his, damn it. "I suppose so."

"There you go," she said happily, pouring more wine in her glass and then doing the same in his. "I brought an accelerant." She put the bottle on the ground and walked back to her vehicle, pulling out a healthy-sized can of lighter fluid. "I know it's difficult to let these go, but you want to be safe, and you can always rewrite them. You're a genius, Jason. You can remember everything in great detail."

She was correct.

"All right," he said.

She ripped off the front of the journal she'd read and threw it in the fire before tearing out the individual pages and finally tossing the back cover in. Then she opened the can of lighter fluid and poured it all over the papers. They went up instantly, and a swoosh of fire flashed toward the trees.

He could almost hear the screams of his victims.

Thunder rumbled in the distance as he watched his glorious pages burn.

"Now, those two," she said.

He took another big gulp of his wine and then tore

the second journal apart the same way she had before throwing it onto the fire.

She gleefully poured more lighter fluid over it, her lithe body dancing in the firelight.

He finished his wine and sat back. "I could keep just one of them."

She sighed and returned to her seat to finish her glass of wine. She poured herself another one, then walked toward him and dumped out the rest of the bottle in his glass. "Come on, Jason. You know you need to burn it."

"I can't do this anymore," he burst out. "It's too much." The hiding by himself without his dates was killing him. Perhaps taking her life would help him to calm down.

"Do it."

For courage, he tipped back the rest of the wine and then threw the plastic cup into the fire. "Fine."

She'd been correct that he was a genius, and he would remember the kills. In fact, she'd be the first one he recorded in his new journal. His head was swimming from the wine, but he wasn't letting her leave tonight. Almost angrily, he tore apart the journal and threw it on the fire.

She smiled and sprayed more of the lighter fluid.

A light rain began to fall. He'd read that there was a big storm coming.

She retook her seat, and together, silently, they watched the papers burn. "What did you do with the cops' phones?" she asked. "Tell me. I did let you shoot at them, you know."

"The phones are in the cabin," he murmured. "I don't know why you wanted me to take them. I turned them off so they can't be traced." No doubt she had more games to play, or at least she thought she did.

She wasn't going to survive the night.

His eyes blurred as he watched his wonderful drawings go up in flames, and his head swam. Tears rolled down his cheeks, and his vision blurred. His feet went numb, and it took him a moment to realize that his ears tingled. What was wrong with him? Slowly, way too slowly, he turned to look at Abigail. "What did you—"

The world went fuzzy, and he slumped down in his chair, wanting to scream, but then the darkness took him.

Chapter 30

Laurel jerked awake when Huck's phone vibrated, hopping across his nightstand. He shifted his bulk in the bed to grab it. "What?" he snapped into the phone. "Shit, really? All right, thanks." He clicked off.

"What?" Laurel asked sleepily, turning over to face him.

He fumbled on the bedside table for his remote control. "How do I get streaming on this TV again?"

She pushed her hair out of her face and scooted up, reaching for the remote before clicking through to the Internet. "Where am I going?"

"*The Killing Hour*," he muttered, also sitting up and then reaching over to flick on his bedside table light.

She scrolled to the correct app. "Who called?"

"Monty is up late going through case files and had his computer on."

The stubborn man should be getting some rest. "Okay." Laurel flicked through until she found *The Killing Hour*.

"Good evening. I am bringing you a special report even though it's after the midnight hour," Rachel said, looking excited. She appeared more casually turned out than usual, dressed in jeans and a dark gray sweater with her hair pulled up in a ponytail. Even so, her makeup was flawless.

Huck sighed. "This isn't going to be good. I can just tell."

Rachel's voice lowered. "I couldn't wait until tomorrow to report on my most recent news. However, this podcast will of course be available throughout the day, so please like and share, and if you choose to rate our podcast, there are links below to do so. I want to keep giving you the most up-to-date news."

Laurel's eyelids felt heavy, but she tried to concentrate anyway, her back to the solid headboard.

"As you know, we've reported that Fish and Wildlife Captain Huck Rivers is a suspect in the recent murders in Genesis Valley, but we couldn't connect the dots as to why." Rachel's face settled into somber lines. "We have finally discovered the identity of the first victim in the River Reaper case."

Huck groaned and slapped a hand against his head. "The River Reaper. Wow, she outdid herself with that one."

Laurel swallowed.

Rachel's eyes gleamed. "This is going to be a difficult podcast for me, so please just stick with me. The name of the first victim is Delta Rivers. She was in her sixties and once resided in Genesis Valley. You might recognize her last name because, as it turns out, she was the estranged mother of our very own Fish and Wildlife Captain Huck Rivers."

Rachel shook her head. "Unfortunately, the victim deserted Captain Rivers when he was just a baby. We do have to wonder what kind of psychological damage that may have caused him."

"Ah, fuck," Huck muttered.

Laurel winced and pulled the covers up above her waist. The room was chilly, but she'd been toasty and warm cuddling with the captain.

Rachel shook her head sadly as a picture of Huck came up on the screen behind her. He was dressed in his full Fish and Wildlife uniform and looked tough and intense.

"I feel like we need to connect the dots here, but I am not accusing anybody of anything," Rachel said slowly.

A picture of Delta Rivers showed up on the screen, followed by photographs of Teri Bearing and Haylee Johnson. The picture of Huck's mother had been taken years ago, and the scene appeared to be a picnic in Genesis Valley.

"Where'd she get the photo?" Huck asked, leaning forward.

Laurel squinted. "It looks like it's out of a newspaper. We can go back through the archives. It appears as if your mother is just an attendee at the picnic." There was no doubt that Rachel Raprenzi did her research and had excellent sources.

"Now," Rachel said somberly, "there's an obvious connection between Delta Rivers and her son, and who would know better that she'd be back in town just in time to be murdered? She must have reached out to him somehow, but the police are being incredibly quiet about this. Are they protecting one of their own?"

Laurel reached over and turned on her light. This was going to be a rough night.

Rachel pointed to Teri Bearing's photograph, showing the woman smiling with a carnival behind her. "I have exclusive footage that we've already aired on *The Killing Hour*, that captures an altercation between the mayor's wife and Huck Rivers."

The screen behind her shifted to a video that showed the night Huck had arrested the intoxicated blonde. "As you can see," Rachel said, "Mrs. Bearing hit Captain Rivers. Is his ego such that he cannot take rejection by any woman? Please note that all three of the victims are blond . . . like his mother."

Huck drew in a breath but otherwise didn't move. Laurel cast him a glance, then looked back at the television.

"Finally," Rachel said, pointing to Haylee Johnson, "we all saw how Ms. Johnson attacked FBI Special Agent Laurel Snow. It was brutal, and you might ask me what that has to do with Captain Rivers. Snow and Rivers have been in an intimate relationship for months."

Laurel lowered her chin. "Since that's true, we can't sue her for slander. But I would like to know who she's using as her source."

Rachel stared directly at the camera. "Is that the impetus that pushed Captain Rivers over the edge? Allegedly, of course. We're just drawing comparisons between victims here. I am not accusing Captain Rivers of anything, though I have heard that he has been taken off the case by his superiors. One has to wonder, what do they know that we don't?"

Rachel shifted in her seat and pressed her hands onto her plexiglass table.

"In an effort to be fully transparent, I must let you

know that Captain Rivers and I were once engaged many years ago when we lived in Portland. He had a very tough missing persons case there and lost a child. By *drowning*. The same cause of death as these current victims."

Her eyes widened. "I have to tell you, he changed afterward. He lost the light of humanity in his eyes. He broke our relationship off and moved up here to live alone in the woods with his dog." Her shoulders slumped, perfectly conveying concern, dejection, and bewilderment.

Even Laurel could read those expressions on the woman's face. "She's really full of crap, isn't she?"

"Aptly put," Huck muttered. "This is going to screw up the entire case."

Rachel shook her head sadly. "I have to wonder if it wouldn't have been better if everybody had just left Captain Rivers alone to live on the mountain with his dog. Would these women still be alive?"

The screen cut to a commercial.

Huck scraped both hands down his face. "This will go viral within hours. I'm sure an article is already being written for the online version. Do you think we'll see this in the *Timber City Gazette* in print later today?"

Laurel looked at the clock. "It's after midnight, and I bet they've already gone to print, so it's too late to hit the print deadline. My guess is that we'll see an expanded article Saturday morning."

"Great," Huck said. "How soon do you suppose I get charged with murder?"

Laurel pressed the mute button on the remote. "If we're lucky, not for a while."

"When was the last time we were fucking lucky?"

* * *

Abigail watched Jason Abbott slump from his seat and nearly fall forward into the fire. Standing, she stood and planted her gloved hand on his head, pushing him back into the darkness. "Oh, Jason. You always thought you were so smart."

She gingerly removed the vial from beneath the wristband on her right arm. She hadn't used the drug until his final glass of wine. "As if I would put something in a glass that you could switch with me." She tossed the vial into the fire and then poured more of the accelerant on it. The journals were gone, and now so was the plastic. She threw her glass in and then looked at the wine bottle. She'd have to take that home with her.

Humming softly, she walked back to her car and placed the wine bottle in her dark backpack before opening her trunk and lugging the portable generator over to the battered cream-colored truck Abbott had been using.

"See, Jason?" she asked quietly. "You just bought a generator." She shoved it across the truck bed. "Which explains why you have so much gasoline in the back of your truck."

She returned to the borrowed Cadillac and removed containers of gasoline, going back and forth until she had emptied the large trunk. She shut the tailgate of his truck. She let the fire burn because why not?

Keeping an eye on him, she walked past the fire and entered the dilapidated cabin to find the guns and the phones used by the two officers who'd been shot. She jogged out and placed them in his truck. A quick search of the cabin revealed nothing else of interest, so, from the

Caddie she fetched the sniper rifle she'd used and placed the weapon on the floor of the passenger side.

Finally, she returned to Jason. He was slumped over, and she smoothed back his hair with her gloved hand. "It's really too bad. You are quite handsome."

His dark hair was thick, and his handsome face angled. Grunting, she grabbed him by the lapels and dragged him over to his truck. It took her several tries, but she managed to push him inside and shove him over to the passenger side.

The sedative she'd given him would work for hours.

Then she looked back and used a branch to brush away the marks of his dragging heels. More thunder rolled in the distance. There was a hell of a storm on its way; it would eradicate any remaining evidence. Yet, it behooved a girl to be careful. She looked out into the night at Snowblood Peak across the way. It was rather fitting.

Jumping into the truck, she pushed Jason over, then moved the seat closer to the steering wheel. "It's quite convenient of you to have found refuge here in the mountains," she said congenially, driving down the barely there dirt road and then taking a sharp left up toward Widow's Peak. The moonlight shone down as the clouds raced across the sky. It would be completely dark soon.

She didn't much care.

Reaching Widow's Peak, she parked as close to the edge as she could, making sure the truck was perched on flat land. A small ledge protruded below her, and then the cliff dropped off to the river below. Parking the truck, she nimbly jumped out.

She drew the small recorder from inside her jacket

and scrolled through until she found what she needed. Jason had been quite cooperative this evening. She placed one of the officers' phones in her pocket and then turned on the one she believed had been owned by Officer Jill Jordan to key in a number she knew well.

Laurel answered immediately. "Agent Snow."

Abigail pressed the play button. "I can't do this anymore," Jason burst out through the recorder. "It's too much."

"Jason?" Laurel asked, her voice rising. "I can help you. Let me help you."

Abigail ended the call but left the phone turned on. She shoved it into her back pocket and patted his head. "It was fun, Jason. Sorry you have to go like this."

She pushed the seat all the way back, put the truck in Drive, and then shut the door. Taking a deep breath, she walked around to the back. It was good she'd found this flat area. Now all she had to do was give the truck a little nudge. She considered the options and then quickly put two of the gasoline cans in the truck with him—just in case.

Holding her breath, she returned to the rear of the truck and pushed with all her might. The vehicle hitched slightly. Damn it. If he'd stolen a newer truck, the torque converter would most likely propel the vehicle down easier. But not Jason. No. He'd secured this old clunker. She only needed a few inches, and then gravity would take over. Grunting, she set her feet and then pushed hard, using the strength in her legs.

"Jason, you're a pain in my ass." She put both gloved hands against the dented metal, grunted, and pushed. The truck finally moved.

The front of the vehicle tipped over, hitting the lower ledge and jumping before continuing to roll.

"There you go." She gave one more push.

The truck silently coasted off the cliff.

She ran to the edge and looked down into the darkness. A loud bang echoed up and then several glorious crashes beat against the wind. Ooh, it must've gone end over end over end. Finally, the truck hit the bottom and an explosion rippled up.

The fire rose high in the sky.

"Wow." Pretty impressive. Smiling, she turned and broke into a run, heading back to the cabin. It took her about fifteen minutes through the trees. She arrived as the rain began falling in earnest, noting that the drops were already extinguishing the campfire. Shrugging, she reached for the discarded can and quickly squirted more accelerant on the papers. Might as well make sure they burned. Oh, she didn't mind if anybody found his journals as long as they couldn't read them.

She tossed the phones from the downed officers against the rocks surrounding the fire.

Reclaiming her weapon, she surveyed the area and then returned to the borrowed car. Time was ticking, ticking, ticking. She slid inside, ignited the engine, and turned around just as a more punishing rain began to fall and the wind whipped up in a frenzy.

Mother nature was on her fucking side. For certain.

She took back roads and made it to Mr. O'Casey's farm, where she shut off the lights and quietly drove the car beneath his carport. The old guy went to bed at eight every night and rose with the sun. She'd filched a copy of his car keys a year ago, just in case, and once in a while, she borrowed his Cadillac.

He never noticed.

She put all of her possessions in the backpack and made sure the car was exactly as he'd left it before quietly shutting the door and then turning to run.

The distance from the carport to her backyard was only a mile and a half through forest land, so she could easily make it in time to snuggle down in her bed.

Around her, the storm still raged.

Chapter 31

Swirling blue-and-red lights lit up the tumultuous spring storm as Huck rolled to a stop in front of a now-quashed campfire. Laurel jumped out, her gun at her waist, and ducked beneath the crime scene tape, looking around wildly. Fish and Wildlife Officer Monty Buckley strode toward her.

"Where's the phone?" she asked.

Monty pointed to one of two phones partially resting against the stone ring around the campfire. "It's there, left on. We were able to trace it easily. A gun, a CZ, is resting against that tree over there." The wind burst against them, throwing branches around as if having a tantrum.

Laurel ducked and held a hand out to protect her head. Why would Jason leave a weapon outside in the rain? "Have we found anything?"

"No," Monty said. "Jason Abbott has been living here, from what I can tell from the cabin, but I don't see a vehicle. We have people out scouting for it."

None of this tracked. Why would Jason call *her* to say he couldn't go on? Why hang up but leave the phone on?

The man was smart enough to know that the GPS would immediately be traced.

"This isn't good," Huck said.

Monty sighed. "Should you be here?"

Huck shrugged. "So far, there isn't any true connection between Jason Abbott and the three murdered blondes, so right now, yeah. I'm off the drowning cases but not Abbott."

That was quite the ambitious extrapolation. Yet, Laurel wanted Huck there. He was the only one she trusted who was still around, although she was becoming accustomed to working with Monty. "We'll find Abbott," she said.

Monty nodded. "We traced the call as soon as you contacted your techs. It took us about twenty-five minutes to get out here. We hurried, but we didn't find anybody else on the road. There have been no sightings of Abbott yet."

"How many back roads are there from this area?" Laurel asked.

Huck sighed. "A lot. There are many mountain roads, and even trails that a vehicle could have gone down."

"So he may have left the state?" Her head pounded. Why would he call and then disappear? Or had he gone after somebody new?

"Why would he call you?" Huck asked.

"I don't know. It's part of his game." She wandered over to the scraped-clean campfire. He had burned his journals. She would've bet almost anything he wouldn't have done that, but Abigail would. She would've wanted this more than anything. "Did you secure any salvageable pages?"

"No," Monty said. "We gathered all of the ashes, but they were burned pretty good and then got wet in the rain."

Jason would hate for his memories to be burned. Laurel ducked as a pinecone burst through the air. "We need somebody at Abigail's place—now."

Huck jolted. "You think?"

"Absolutely. We have to see if she's home." Had Jason taken her? What kind of hold did Abigail still have on the serial killer?

"I don't have anybody to spare," Huck said.

"Call in the county police or even the city," Laurel said.

He grasped his radio. "Good idea. Just a sec." He loped toward his truck, his body strong and sure in the pounding storm.

Wiping rain off her face, she bent down to look at the campfire spot. The techs had done an admirable job of securing everything. "Nothing appeared readable to you?"

Monty pushed sopping wet hair away from his face. "Smell that?"

Laurel sniffed the air. "Yeah. Is that turpentine?"

"It's an accelerant. We can send these to the lab, what's left, but—"

"We're not going to get anything." Laurel couldn't believe this.

She straightened and walked across the campfire area to a dilapidated cabin with holes in the wood. Jason must've been freezing out here. Moving inside, she stayed out of the way of the crime techs who were already dusting the area. The place held a mattress on the ground with several heavy blankets next to cans of chili and soup. He must've cooked over the fire outside.

Had he fled? Called her to say goodbye to torment her?

She crouched to look at the cans. The most common soup brand. They'd be hard to trace. Right next to the bed was a photograph of Jason with Haylee, both smiling in front of a garden. Why had he kept the picture?

Huck returned. "I have somebody heading to Abigail's now, and we've had a report of an explosion close to the river beneath these peaks."

"Explosion?" Laurel pushed to her feet.

"Yeah," Huck noted. "A group of fishermen camping out, planning to ice fish in the river tomorrow. They saw a huge explosion and reported that a vehicle is on fire right now."

Laurel looked around. "Is there a place that Abbott could have driven a truck off around here?"

"There's Widow's Peak," Huck said. "It's about fifteen minutes from here by foot. Driving, maybe two or three. I'll send a deputy there, and I have people going to check out the scene below. It could just be some kids goofing off."

Experience told her nothing was that easy. She walked back outside with him. "Let's search this area as soon as the techs are finished."

"You bet."

The wind whipped the freezing rain sideways, and she pulled her hood closer over her head.

"Why don't you wait in the truck until they're finished, and then I'll help you search." Huck used the question form, but his tone suggested a command. His overprotective side had just reemerged.

She wanted to argue but couldn't see any reason to stay in the rain, so she ran over to the truck and jumped inside, looking back to talk to the dog. "Jason Abbott isn't somebody who would drive off a cliff," she said, as Aeneas watched her with his soft black eyes. "If anything, he's headed to a city to continue hunting people."

Except that wasn't right either. She knew he wouldn't be able to let go of his fantasies of killing Abigail and Laurel. He just couldn't. It wasn't in his nature. She tried to think through the entire case for a good twenty minutes until Huck returned.

"They're about finished, so we can search. But I have to tell you, there's not much around. The deputy I sent to Widow's Peak didn't see anything out of the ordinary, but the wind and rain have been wild." Huck's radio buzzed, and he pressed the button on the device attached to his dash. "Rivers."

"It's Sheriff York. I headed to the base of the cliff like you asked."

Huck leaned inside, bringing the scent of pine and rain with him. "Hi, Sheriff. What have you found?"

"I found a burning truck by the edge of the river."

Laurel shut her eyes.

Huck exhaled loudly. "Is there a body in the truck?"

"Oh, yeah. There's a body in the truck. It's burnt almost beyond recognition. I've had to call in the state cops on this one. We don't have enough manpower," York said loudly, the wind combatting his voice.

Laurel focused on the radio. "Did you see anything else?"

"I can't get close enough. The truck is still burning. All I can see is a body and a skull on the dash."

"That's all right," Laurel said wearily. "I think we know who it is."

Huck clicked the radio back into place. "Does Jason Abbott seem like someone who'd kill himself?"

"No," Laurel said, every bone in her body aching. "There's no way Jason Abbott would've ended his own life. He was a narcissist, and he was out for revenge. There's only one person I can think of smart enough to kill him."

Huck's phone buzzed, and he lifted it to his ear. "Yeah? . . . Really? . . . All right, thanks. Bye."

She didn't like his tone. "What is it?"

"The Genesis Valley police officer I sent to Abigail's home found her in her nightgown, obviously fresh out of bed. She was irritated to have been awakened and happily gave the CCTV footage from her house to the officer."

"Her camera faces just the front of the home and that whole street but not the backyard, correct?" Laurel asked.

"Yes. I'm having the officer go door to door to retrieve all of the CCTV he can."

She slumped farther down in her seat. "They won't find anything."

"I know."

After an essentially sleepless night, Laurel ignored a call from the deputy director of the FBI as Huck parked in the long field in front of the Genesis Valley Community Church.

He glanced at her phone. "You're not answering George's call?"

"Not right now." She feared he'd pull her off the case, and her blood hummed in the way it always did when she was getting closer to answers.

"Stay there." Huck opened his door and stepped out.

Why in the world would she stay there?

He crossed around the truck and opened her door. "It's icy out here."

Ah, the overprotectiveness again. She held his arm as she stepped down, and her boots did indeed slide. She latched onto his elbow to steady herself. "You weren't jesting."

"I rarely am," Huck said grimly.

They moved back to the main drive and maneuvered the distance to the front of the church among members of the congregation. The storm had been brutal the night before, and branches and mangled pine cones covered the ground. She wasn't one to go on feelings, but the people trudging around them, as well as the very air hanging over them, seemed somber.

They wandered inside the sprawling building and into the narthex, where a woman wearing a long purple skirt handed them a program. Uma stood on the other side of the aisle, also handing out stapled programs. Was she still dating Zeke?

"Thank you." Laurel continued into the nave.

"Where do you want to sit?" Huck asked, his hand at her elbow.

She continued down the aisle and entered the front pew. "Right up front."

"By the aisle," Huck said, sitting instantly.

"All right." She sat next to him and looked up at the currently vacant pulpit. Beyond it lay a chancel and then the altar, with its stunning stained-glass windows framing jagged Orphan's Peak across the river. The name caught her attention. "Who named all of these mountains and peaks?"

"I have absolutely no idea." Huck shifted his weight on the wooden bench.

She looked at him. "Are you uncomfortable?" It was supposition, but based on the rigidity of his shoulders, she likely guessed correctly.

"No, I'm fine." He looked over his shoulder.

Ah, the captain did not like to have people behind him. Whenever they went anywhere in public, he always sat, if he could, with his back to a wall and his gaze on a door.

"Why do you ask about the names?" he asked.

"We have Snowblood Peak, Orphan's Peak, Viper's Mountain, Widow's Peak, Crow Mountain, Witch Creek. Is there a Happy Mountain around here? A Gleeful Mountain or a Cheerful Dancing Mountain?"

He chuckled, the harsh lines in his face relaxing. "Not that I know of, but maybe I can write a letter to somebody."

"I was just curious."

A choir at the far end of the south transept began to sing a hymn that she'd never heard before. The pretty song created a lovely picture about life and a glorious future.

"Hmm," Huck said. "I thought they would've been more traditional."

As did Laurel, but she enjoyed the song.

He grunted. She hadn't learned to interpret all of his grunts, so she didn't know what that meant.

Pastor John Govern soon took the pulpit, dressed in a black robe with a light purple stole. "Hello, my friends." He lifted both hands. "It is good to see you all today." His gaze caught on Laurel and Huck, and he faltered before surveying the crowd.

Laurel looked behind them to see the entire nave full of parishioners. Many people even stood in the back.

"Do you believe in God?" Huck whispered.

She considered the question. "I do believe in a higher power. Otherwise, none of this makes any sense. We can call him God." She had a feeling they had absolutely no idea about the true essence of this higher power, but she'd also seen the intricacies of the human body and the universe at large. They hadn't been created by coincidence.

"Thank you for coming." Pastor John's voice easily reached the back of the church. He appeared commanding and reassuring at the same time. "I've been thinking a lot about community and trust."

Laurel settled in to watch the pastor. His voice rose and fell in a rhythmic cadence that sounded very charming and engaging. He soon had many of the people responding with agreement.

"He's very good," Huck whispered.

Laurel nodded. "I believe that's called charisma."

"I believe it is," Huck said dryly.

Pastor John preached about fellowship, trust, and community, and how important it was for each of the congregation members to watch each other's backs.

"I think he might be creating friends," she whispered.

Huck nodded. "He's definitely hitting hard the ideals of loyalty and small-town community. That's interesting."

Pastor John finished with a flourish and then stepped down to take a seat in the north transept.

Pastor Zeke Caine then advanced to the pulpit, his bald head gleaming, his body looking tight and powerful beneath the black robe. His stole was made up of a darker purple with bright silver threads.

"That was a lovely sermon, Pastor John," he said, his booming voice reaching the highest rafter.

"Whoa," Huck murmured.

Laurel swallowed. She'd never heard his pastor voice, commanding yet comfortable, with a heavy thread of power. Her hatred for him felt red-hot, and she wondered if it was okay to feel such emotion in a church. Probably not. Of course, it wasn't appropriate for a pastor to be preaching after the atrocities that Zeke had committed.

Zeke also talked about fellowship and community, and then he switched topics abruptly to right and wrong, saying that sometimes doing the right thing or saying the right thing could be painful.

Huck slid an arm over Laurel's shoulders and pulled her close. "Buckle up," he whispered.

She could feel something coming but couldn't quite discern where Zeke was going.

He sighed and looked down at the pulpit before placing both hands on the polished wood and facing the congregation. "This is very difficult for me to discuss. But as Pastor John eloquently stated, we are a community, and we must be loyal to each other. A basic tenet of that loyalty is honesty. Do you agree with me?"

Several "yeses" and "you bets" and "of courses" echoed through the crowd.

"Good." He sighed. "We are recording this sermon, although our nationalized television debut has been postponed until this spring because of events happening in town." His face shifted into somber lines. "In an effort to be transparent and honest with my community, I have to unfortunately inform you that our own Pastor John Govern is under investigation for the murders that have happened here recently."

A shocked gasp echoed through the crowd.

Pastor Zeke held up a hand. "Let's not jump to conclusions, and we must be loyal. There are not enough facts, but Pastor John has admitted to having an affair with Teri Bearing, a married woman and a victim of a brutal killer. I believe we all need to be honest about that. How many of you knew about this breach of trust?"

Several people in the parish raised their hands.

"Holy crap," Huck muttered.

Pastor Zeke's chin dropped. "I wish more of you had come to me. I do appreciate the few of you who did. However, as a church, we need to address this situation. Sin is something that needs to be eradicated. Forgiveness, of course, must be granted. We are all human. But first, we need to deal with the sin."

Pastor John jumped up and stormed out of the church via a back door.

Laurel could almost feel sorry for the man.

Pastor Zeke shook his head. "I do apologize for bringing in such negativity today, but secrets are what destroy a community." He stared directly at Laurel as he spoke. "No matter how closely guarded, a secret always comes to light. Also, anybody who sins and fails to adhere to the ten commandments shall pay. 'Thou shall not commit adultery' and 'Thou shall honor thy father and mother' are two good examples."

Huck leaned forward.

Zeke looked away from Laurel and smiled. "We have a wonderful community here. We will get through this together, my friends. I promise you."

Chapter 32

Zeke Caine caught them just as they reached Huck's truck after the sermon. "Hold on a minute, daughter."

Huck turned, standing between Laurel and Zeke as he smoothly opened the passenger-side door for her and made sure his body stayed between them. "I suggest you stop calling her that," he said calmly.

Zeke stepped to the side as several people looked in their direction. "It was kind of you to attend my sermon today."

Laurel paused near her open door and turned. "That was quite the attack you levied on Pastor John. Apparently, he's out of your way now as you take the church onto national TV."

Zeke put both hands in his black robe. "The truth must come out, daughter. When one violates a commandment or is disloyal to the community at large, one must pay."

"Is that a threat?" Huck stepped closer to the man.

"Of course not." Zeke smiled. "That was just a statement."

Huck could not measure the degree to which he disliked this asshole, so he turned and took Laurel's elbow. "Let's go."

She stepped up into the truck.

"Laurel, I would very much like to speak with you and your mother. She won't return my calls," Zeke said.

Huck edged him away from the door and shut it. "She's done talking to you."

Yeah, he was being an ass. Laurel was an FBI agent who could take care of herself, but right now Huck was over this. He'd seen the danger inherent in Zeke Caine during that sermon. Oh, he knew all about the pastor's checkered past and had no doubt there were victims out there that Laurel would find, but watching the man in action had been another thing entirely.

Zeke reared back. "You have no right to get in my way."

That's where he was wrong. Dead wrong. "I don't know a lot about psychopaths or sociopaths or narcissists or whatever label fits you, Pastor." Huck leaned in, staring down at the shorter man. "But I know they all end up where they belong. You want to watch yourself."

With that, he turned his back on Zeke and walked around his truck to slide into his seat. He ignited the engine and pulled out onto the main road as Zeke Caine watched them go.

"Did you get that off your chest?" Laurel asked somewhat dryly.

"Hey, I didn't punch him," Huck noted. "I'll take that as a win."

She chuckled.

His phone buzzed, and he hit a button on the dash. "Captain Rivers," he said.

"What the holy fuck is going on in Genesis Valley?" Deputy Chief Mert Wright yelled.

Laurel winced.

Huck sighed. "I take it you saw *The Killing Hour*?"

"Saw it? Did I see it?" Wright yelled. "I've had fifteen different people send me links. You do realize you were taken off this case? Because you're a possible suspect?"

Huck's jaw tightened. "Of course I realize that. I'm not involved in the slightest."

"The FBI agent you're currently banging is involved," Wright snapped.

Huck stiffened. "You're going to want to watch your words, Deputy Chief."

"Excuse me?" Wright asked.

"I believe you heard me. Agent Snow has done nothing wrong, and you will speak of her with respect."

Silence ticked over the line for a moment. "Or what?" Wright snapped.

Huck's hands tightened on the steering wheel, and he forced them to relax. No way was he letting this jackass upset him. "Or you and I are going to have a little talk, man to man. I don't give a shit about your position within Fish and Wildlife."

He meant every word. If he needed to find another job, then he would, but nobody was going to insult Laurel like that.

She punched him in the arm, and he cut her a look. He was a pretty flexible guy, at least in his own mind, but there were some lines that weren't to be crossed. Wright was real close to stepping over.

Wright cleared his throat. "Captain Rivers, you are officially on notice that you are to go nowhere near this case, or I'll have you arrested for hindering an investigation. You are on leave from Fish and Wildlife. Period. Next week, you'll be interviewed again by me."

Huck turned toward the square in front of Center Diner. Laurel had to be hungry, and he could eat as well. "Is that all?"

"You will be interviewed Monday. Make yourself available." Wright ended the call.

Laurel sat back and pressed her head against the headrest, her eyes closing. "You can't come with me tomorrow to Santa Fe."

"Yes, I can. I'm going, and that's it."

Laurel looked tired. "I think you should hire an attorney before you meet with anybody else. You are a suspect at this point, albeit a weak one. Rachel did a fairly decent job of connecting the dots."

"I noticed," Huck said dryly. "I wish Zeke Caine was a viable suspect, but he has a good alibi for Teri Bearing's murder."

Laurel nodded. "I agree. I found Uma Carrington to be a credible witness, and I believe the alibi she provided."

"What about Abigail?" he asked hopefully. "She's crazy. I can see her killing these people just to mess with our lives."

Laurel kicked out her feet toward the heater. "I could see her playing that kind of game, but it seems like a lot of effort." She placed her phone on the dash and called Agent Norrs on speaker phone.

"Hi, Agent Snow," Agent Norrs said. "I'm wrapping up my cases and will head in your direction to help as soon as I can. We're short staffed here as well."

She swallowed. "I'm sorry, but for my own peace of mind, I need to ask you a couple of questions."

He fell silent for a moment. "Okay. Go ahead."

She tapped her fingers on her leg. "The night that Delta Rivers was killed. On the night of the thirty-first. Do you know where Abigail was?"

"Why?"

Laurel kept still as Huck watched her. "Please just answer the question."

"Fine. Just a sec." The sound of keys typing came through the line. "Oh, yeah. That was the night Abi and I went to *Wicked* in Seattle. Great show. Have you seen it?"

Laurel's shoulders slowly lowered. "Yes. I enjoyed the alternate concept of the *Wizard of Oz*."

He chuckled. "We went out to a nice dinner, saw the musical, and then stayed the night at my place. In fact, we took half of Monday off and watched movies in bed." Then he stopped laughing. "Does that ease your mind?"

Laurel appeared relieved. "Yes. Thank you."

Huck and Laurel had seen Abigail with Norrs the night Teri Bearing had disappeared.

"I look forward to working with you," she said. "Have a nice day."

"You, too." He ended the call.

Laurel sighed. "Abigail was with Norrs the night your mother was killed. For just a second, I thought she might hate you enough to ruin your life and isolate me."

Huck really didn't like that woman. "She is diabolical."

"I think Norrs is in love with her."

"I agree," Huck said. "But I don't see Norrs lying for her, even though he's obviously clueless when it comes to how dangerous she can be."

Laurel stretched her neck. "I concur."

Huck scratched his whiskered jaw. "That leaves us with Jason Abbott as our killer, which means that the murders will now stop. Or . . . there's another killer. One we haven't identified yet."

Laurel sighed. "It's possible Jason learned to change his MO, but to this degree? I am uncertain."

"Unfortunately, we're going to find out." Now all they could do was wait and see.

Chapter 33

After an extremely early flight from Seattle to Santa Fe, with Huck sleeping the entire way, Laurel greeted the young man who'd arrived to pick them up and scooted to the middle of his truck as Huck lumbered inside and sat next to her. She'd been unable to dissuade him from accompanying her, and he was most certainly disobeying orders from a supervisor in doing so.

"There we go. See, there's plenty of room," said the young man, who had introduced himself as Berty Oneworld. He appeared to be about eighteen, with long blond dreadlocks and engaging green eyes. He tossed their carry-ons unceremoniously into the back of the very dusty, dirty truck before levering himself into the driver's seat. "How nice of you to come visit us."

Huck looked outside at the chilly day. "I figured Santa Fe would be warmer."

"Ah, that's a myth." Berty jerked the stick shift into place. "Our days are in the midsixties, and our nights in the thirties. People hear Santa Fe and they think sun, which, you know, is true in the summer." He competently drove away from the airport. "You're investigators, huh?"

"We are," Laurel said quietly. "We're here to talk to your group about Delta Rivers."

"Our whole community is rocked by her death. She was the kindest soul you could ever meet." Berty's shoulders slumped. On the thin side, he wore dusty jeans and a faded T-shirt with a picture of a watermelon on the front. "I liked her very much." He glanced at Huck. "I understand she was your mother."

Huck stiffened. "Supposedly."

"Yeah. I can see that." Berty watched the road through the dirty windshield. "You kinda look like her."

"Tell us about your commune," Laurel said, wanting to ease Berty into talking about more personal matters.

Berty bounced in his seat. "It's more of a co-op. There's a common kitchen and gathering area where we spend time together. We pool resources. We grow some of our own food, and we look out for each other."

"How many people belong to your co-op?" Huck asked.

"We have about fifty people now, at least," Berty said. "Some retirees looking for a better life. Some younger people like me, searching for a family, and then a bunch of middle-aged folks who just got tired of Wall Street and Hollywood and decided to live a simpler life."

"What about demographics?" Laurel asked.

Berty looked at her before returning his focus to the freeway. "Demographics?"

"Yes. Like how many women? How many men? How many kids?"

"I don't know. How do you really tell?" Berty asked. "People are who they are and what they are—why categorize them? I don't think any of that truly matters."

It did when trying to identify suspects.

"How well did you know Delta?" Huck shifted his weight and set his arm by the window.

Berty shrugged. "I've only been with the group for two months, so I spoke with her a few times, and, of course, we shared communal meals. I liked her very much. She seemed kind. Her paintings and drawings brought income to the group."

"She was an artist?" Huck asked.

Berty turned off the main freeway onto a quiet, asphalted road. "Yeah. Now, if you don't mind, I need to calm myself."

Huck eyed him. "What does that mean?"

"I think he needs silence," Laurel answered.

Berty nodded. "Yes. It stresses me to go out in public like this, and the airport was busy. My thoughts need quieting."

Huck cut her a look.

Laurel shrugged, and they both remained silent for the hour drive, heading uphill until they reached open wooden gates.

Berty drove through the imposing arch and wound around several cabins, yurts, and tents to reach an inviting-looking central gathering area. The main hub of the commune consisted of a lodge-type building in front of an outdoor kitchen that included many tables and gathering areas.

A woman bustled out the front door and had already reached the vehicle before they could step out. Huck climbed down and assisted Laurel.

"Hello," Laurel said.

"Hi, how are you? I'm Opal Garcia." She moved forward and grasped Huck's hand with both of hers. She studied him intently, then turned and gave Laurel just as much attention. "Thank you for coming all this way to see us."

Opal appeared to be in her late fifties or early sixties with long, silvery-gray hair and weathered skin. She wore an ankle-length, flowery skirt with a Bohemian top and plenty of beaded jewelry: necklace, bracelets, earrings. "Come in, come in," she said. "Why don't I show you Delta's cabin?"

"I'd like that," Huck said.

Opal smiled. "I can see her in you, Captain Rivers. You have her eyes, and there's something about your bone structure, though definitely not her height. She was barely five foot four."

Huck grunted.

Laurel took the lead. Was this too much for Huck? He had to be experiencing odd feelings. "How long did you know Delta?"

Opal laughed. "Fifteen years. I've lived here for two decades, and Delta came to us about fifteen years ago. She had been wandering through life as many of us do and finally found a community."

"Where had she been?" Huck asked.

Opal shrugged. "We don't really talk about our time before we join the family, but it's my understanding that she worked as a street artist who sold drawings and paintings in Los Angeles, San Diego, I believe Sacramento, and then ultimately made her way to Las Vegas and down to Phoenix."

"We haven't found any sort of criminal record," Laurel said.

"Oh, no. I don't believe Delta ever committed any crimes. I think she was just a free spirit."

Laurel looked around at the quiet surroundings. "Yet she joined your community?"

They walked between several trees and passed small cabins as they spoke. "Yes, you're allowed to stay or leave or do whatever you want here. You can be who you are," Opal said calmly.

"Who was she?" Huck asked.

Opal glanced at him. "She was one of our family members. She kept to herself very often, but she contributed when she could. She had social anxiety and worked in her cabin by herself much of the time."

"Did she date anybody here at the co-op?" Laurel asked.

Opal moved a branch out of the way. "Not here. Not to my knowledge, anyway," she said. "There were a couple of gentlemen through the years who I believe she may have slept with, but there was never any obvious relationship or commitment."

"That seemed to be her style," Huck said grimly.

Opal smiled, not appearing fazed by his statement. "I believe it was her style." They reached a cabin, and she walked up the wooden stairs to open the door. "We haven't changed anything because her spirit is still here with us, and we don't want to offend it in any manner."

"All right," Laurel said, stepping inside. That made zero sense.

It was a one-room cabin with a twin bed against one wall, a small loveseat on the other wall, and a counter across from them that held a hot plate. Several canvases and charcoal drawings leaned against the walls. Paint splatters covered the floor in every direction.

"There's no bathroom," Huck noted.

Opal chuckled. "There's a communal outhouse several yards to the north."

"What about showers?" Laurel asked.

"There are showers there as well. We use natural rain-water and heat it when necessary," Opal said.

Laurel moved toward the one dresser set at the edge of the bed to study several photographs. She lifted one to scrutinize.

"What is it?" Huck asked.

"I think it's her with you." She looked closer. A young Delta Rivers, smiling wildly, held a baby in her arms.

"Huh," Huck said, looking over Laurel's shoulder. "I've never seen that one."

Uncertain of what to say, she remained silent.

"You can keep that if you like," Opal offered.

Huck looked at her. "Thank you."

Emotion passed across the captain's face, but Laurel didn't know how to help him right now. Maybe she could serve as a confidante for him later. Even so, she touched his arm. "I'm here for you."

He kissed her forehead. "I know. Thank you."

She placed the picture back and then looked at the artwork. Delta had used strong lines and abstract forms, creating appealing designs.

Huck grasped another picture. "Is this of the two of you?"

Opal smiled. "Yes. We had one of our visitors take pictures of us."

"Visitors?" Laurel asked.

"Yes, we host weekends sometimes for people need-ing to get away from their busy lives. It's a way for us to make money so we can buy the supplies we can't grow or create ourselves, and every once in a while somebody will take some pictures. We prohibit phones and other electrical devices. But sometimes, as in the case of this man, he had one of those point-and-shoots, so we allowed it. It's good to record our journeys once in a while."

"I see." Huck handed the picture to Laurel. "Who was he?"

Opal's bracelets clanked together when she moved. "Nice guy from Toronto. His name is Bernard Netlabel, and he's one hundred years old. Can you believe it?"

"How current is this photograph?" Huck asked.

"That was maybe last month." Opal ruffled her silvery hair.

Laurel looked at the photograph and jerked before glancing up at Opal. "This was taken last month?"

Opal frowned. "What do you mean?"

"Delta Rivers's hair was brown," Laurel noted.

"Her hair was a dark brown with some gray in it." Opal glanced at the earlier picture. "She was blond when she was younger, but as she became older, her hair turned darker with threads of silver through it."

Huck peered at the picture. "What color was her hair last time you saw her?"

Opal shrugged. "She had dark hair."

"Do you know why she left the commune?" Laurel asked, setting the picture down. She was going to have to take it with them, but she wanted to keep Opal agreeable for now.

"Yes. She flew out almost two weeks ago to meet a man. It was the first romance she'd had in years. I was very excited for her to go meet her Romeo wherever he lived."

Huck jerked and turned around. "Romance? With whom?"

"I don't know." Opal's gaze dropped. "I wish I did, but I just don't have any details. She met a man when she was out selling her paintings in town, and they struck up a romance. Delta was always up for an adventure, and when he invited her to meet him up north, she thought, what the heck? She could take a couple weeks off, get some new ideas for her paintings, and go from there."

"What do you know about this man?" Laurel asked, her heart beating faster.

Opal sighed and looked up as if trying to remember. "Delta grew very excited, and she got that sparkle in her eyes that, you know, we all get during new romances. She said that he was one with the earth and the wind, and she looked forward to her journey with him."

"Did anybody else meet him?" Laurel asked.

Opal shook her head. "No. Unfortunately, Delta remained rather secretive, as if she wanted this relationship just for herself. She met him several times in town."

"Do you know where in town?" Huck asked.

Tears filled Opal's eyes. "No, we don't keep track of each other like that. She would often sell her paintings on different main streets, but I don't know where. She lived her own life, Captain Rivers. I think you would've liked her if you had gotten to know her."

"I didn't get that chance."

Opal sighed again, the sound heavy. "I'm sorry about that. I can't explain it, except that she just lived her life the way she wanted, on her own terms. I'm surprised she stayed here as long as she did, but I think it's because she had the freedom to come and go as she wanted. No obligation, no responsibilities."

"That's not how adults live their lives," Huck muttered.

"Not most adults," Opal agreed.

Laurel cleared her throat. "Let's get back to this mysterious man. Do you know anything at all about him?"

"I have no idea. I'm so sorry," Opal said. "We all refrained from being nosy."

Huck reached for the picture of Delta holding him as a baby. "She never mentioned his name?"

"No," Opal said, tapping her lips. "I figured he was a holy man. The only thing I ever heard her call him was 'the pastor.'"

Chapter 34

After midnight, Huck flipped on the lights in his cabin as Laurel shut the door against the rain and wind behind them. Aeneas stretched from his bed by the fireplace and came to greet him while Fred the cat opened one eye and then shut it again.

Huck reached for a note on the counter from Monty saying that he'd fed both animals, taken Aeneas out several times during the day, and had left a tuna casserole in the fridge for them.

Laurel yawned widely and ditched her boots and coat before wandering over to pet her cat. "We could have stayed in Santa Fe tonight," she murmured.

He shook his head. "I needed to get out of Santa Fe."

"I understand, and after Opal mentioned a pastor seeing your mother, my mind is spinning. Pastor John or Pastor Zeke?"

"Or a different pastor, which I doubt," Huck muttered.

They'd claimed both photographs of Delta Rivers, and Opal had insisted he take several of her drawings. Maybe his kid would want to know something about his grandmother someday. Who knew? At the moment, Huck was too tired to worry about it.

"I think I could sleep for days." Laurel ambled toward the bedroom.

So could he. He felt tired to his very bones.

Laurel's phone buzzed, and she sighed, lifting it to her ear. "Agent Snow and it is after midnight." She stiffened and turned around. "Wait, wait. Slow down, Julliet. Slow down. Okay. What time did they . . . Okay. Yes, I'm here with the captain. I'll have him call in. I'll call you back." She clicked off.

"What is it?" Huck came awake immediately.

"Kate's friend Julliet called her in a panic because her daughter is out on a camping trip. Kate gave her my number since she's in North Carolina. Something about earning a wilderness badge. The kids haven't been heard from, and they should have been back three hours ago."

Huck yanked his phone free of his back pocket and reached Monty.

"Hey, Huck." The sound of wind blowing almost drowned out Monty's voice.

Huck leaned against the counter. "What's going on? We have missing kids?"

"Yes," Monty said. "We started a search two hours ago when the parents notified us. We're over near Sorry Sal Mountain."

"How many do we have missing?" Huck walked to the window and stared at the pouring rain.

"Five. They were supposed to stay close to the road. Spent last night out here and all day gathering and building fires, but they should've been home by nine tonight." Wilderness badges and the procedures for getting them were common in Washington State.

"All girls?"

"Yeah, all around the age of sixteen. I have everybody out searching."

Huck looked at Laurel. "I'll grab Aeneas and join you."

Monty sighed. "We received orders that you are on leave. I wanted to call you, but I don't want to get you fired."

Huck figured there was a pretty damn good chance he was going to get fired anyway. "Tell me where you're searching."

Monty listed the grids.

It was a good search pattern. "No sight of them so far at all?"

"No. We found the area where they camped, but no trace of them after that."

Huck thought through what he knew of the area. "What time did the storm come in?"

"About that time," Monty said. "It would have been easy to become disoriented and lose sight of the road. We did find their vehicle, and it appears fine."

"Did the girls have a radio?"

Monty groaned. "Yes, and we found it in the vehicle."

"They forgot to take the radio?" Huck snapped.

Monty sighed loudly, competing with the wind in the background. "Yeah, they forgot the radio, but they all had cell phones."

"They don't have service out there," Huck burst out.

Monty snorted. "There's some service, but you're right, we haven't been able to ping anybody's phone."

Damn kids thought they could do anything with a cell phone in one hand. "I'm headed out. Don't argue with me. I'll update you on my way."

"Okay. Thanks, Huck," Monty said.

Huck clicked off and whistled for Aeneas. "Come on, bud. We have search and rescue to do."

Laurel stood hesitantly by the sofa. "I'll go with you."

"No, you stay here. You shouldn't be out searching."

"I'm an FBI agent, Huck."

He nodded. "I'm well aware, but this is search and rescue."

The woman had had a long day, and whether she realized it or not, she was pregnant, and it did take a toll. Sure, she could fight if necessary, but right now, it wasn't. He'd go much faster just with Aeneas. His gaze cut to the open laptop on the counter where Rachel Raprenzi's show streamed out live as she stood under an umbrella next to several emergency vehicles. "Rachel's out there?"

"Of course she is," Laurel said, watching the screen. "That woman is everywhere."

"Unfortunately. Lock the door behind me and keep your gun with you." With that, he opened the door and ran into the rain. The temperature was dropping, and who knew how far the girls might have gotten in the three hours they'd been lost.

He had to hurry.

Laurel settled back on Huck's sofa and ate a very late dinner of scrambled eggs, glued to Rachel Raprenzi's live show. Somehow Rachel had planted herself next to dispatch and stood close enough to hear the radio communication.

Laurel's phone dinged from her handbag, and she yanked it out, not recognizing the caller. "Agent Snow," she said.

"Agent Snow, hello. It's Tim Kohnex."

She jerked, the hair on her arms raising. "Mr. Kohnex, how did you obtain my personal cell phone number?"

"The wind spoke to me," he said, his voice a low, calm drum.

She looked out at the pelting rain. "You're telling me that the wind whispered the digits of my phone number to you?"

"Yes," he said. "I know you don't believe, but sometimes fate intervenes. I had to call you. I knew you'd be up. I've been watching Rachel Raprenzi and the search going on. I saw that Huck Rivers is in the woods."

"This is getting downright annoying. Mr. Kohnex, I'm going to tell you once. Do not ever call me on my private phone."

"He's in danger," Kohnex said.

Laurel paused, standing to walk to the kitchen. "Who, Huck?"

"Yes. Everybody you care about is in danger, and I feel you're going to lose him."

She took a steady breath and pressed her hand on the counter. The cool marble calmed her. "If you know something about Captain Rivers, you need to tell me right now."

"Just what I've heard. Just what I've felt and sensed. Just what fate wants me to know," Kohnex said urgently.

Laurel pinched the bridge of her nose. "So you have no concrete evidence."

Kohnex chuckled, the sound slightly hysterical. "There is nothing concrete. That's what I'm trying to tell you. I can see it. I can smell it coming for you, for him, I don't know, for all of you. Please listen to me."

Irritation slid into anger. "Unless you have something of actual importance to tell me, we are ending this phone call."

He sighed loudly. "I just want to help you."

"Then say something that makes sense," she snapped.

He remained quiet for several moments. "I had a dream about you last night. There were veils all around you. Nobody is who they seem, and you're going to lose." His voice dropped to a rhythmic and hypnotic tone now.

"Have you been ingesting drugs?" she asked.

He snorted. "No more than usual."

Her mind clicked through possible scenarios. She had no doubt that Pastor John had her private number. It would be easy enough for Tim Kohnex to get into the church and find it. "I'm not falling for this mysterious act you have going on. If you believe you're psychic, you probably need mental help. And if you're on drugs, you require intervention, but this is tedious." She needed to look at his background more closely. "Where are you right now?"

"Me?" The sound of a door opening came over the line and then the pounding of rain. "I'm at my cabin, out on my back deck, looking at the river. It's a dark night, Agent Snow. There's no moon."

"Do you have anything else to add, Mr. Kohnex?"

"No. I just felt I should warn you. Be careful. You are stepping into pools of darkness that not even you can comprehend."

She clicked off. Her hands shook, and she didn't know why. She didn't believe him. So she quickly pressed speed dial.

"Yo, boss," Nester answered sleepily. "Dude, what time is it?" The sound of him fumbling with something came over the line. "Oh, crap. It's, like, two in the morning. You okay?" He sounded more alert.

"Yes, I'm all right. I'm sorry to awaken you."

"Who is it, Nester?" a female voice asked sleepily.

Nester coughed. "It's my boss. Just a sec. What can I do for you, Agent Snow?"

She listened to the wind whip pinecones against the windows. "Tim Kohnex just called me, and I kept him on the phone long enough for a trace. Call DC and find me his current location as of right now, okay?"

"I'm on it, Laurel. I'll call you as soon as I have something. Also, I'll be back to work on Monday. I just need the weekend here."

It sounded like he had a lady love in Seattle as well. "All right. Thanks, Nester."

Laurel put her phone on the counter and watched the storm. She knew Kohnex was either mentally challenged or on drugs. Even so, she grabbed her phone and dialed Huck just to hear his voice. He didn't answer. She ignored her momentary panic and walked back into the living room.

As she watched Rachel Raprenzi's livestream, Huck walked out of the forest carrying a petite, dark-haired girl who was smiling widely at him.

Relief slid through Laurel's veins. The kids weren't harmed. Huck was safe.

Laurel watched as Huck smiled and said something to the girl, who grinned and waved at the camera. Relief relaxed Laurel's muscles, one by one. The duo appeared perfectly healthy.

At least for now.

Chapter 35

She'd definitely gotten the best footage of the night. Rachel Raprenzi sloshed through the icy mud puddles to reach her vehicle, her heart absolutely singing. She was the only reporter to have hung out in the right spot for so many fucking freezing hours, and it had paid off.

Her cameraman, a solid guy named Roger, had perfectly captured the moment when Huck Rivers carried one of the rescued girls out of the woods, his faithful dog at his side.

Yeah, she'd pretty much accused him of being a serial killer, but the contrast between his dark hour and his hero moment would make for excellent copy. She wanted to do a little dance, but there were still emergency personnel around removing crime scene tape and putting away gear. It turned out the five girls had just gotten lost and had hunkered down in a makeshift shelter until Huck and the dog had found them.

Rachel had pressed close to get an interview, but Huck had told her "No comment." She couldn't decide whether he was friend or foe, but angry makeup sex had always been the best, so she held high hopes.

"Excellent footage. We streamed it live," Roger said, jogging up to her side. He put his camera equipment safely in his van.

She high-fived him, uncaring of the rain drilling into them both. Since she was no longer on camera, she'd ditched the umbrella and now just wore a hood over her head. "I'm freezing. I may spend the next three hours in a hot shower."

"So long as you are in the studio, first thing," he said. "You're actually a live witness to this. Do you want me to interview you?" The guy had been trying to get on camera for weeks.

"No," Rachel said. "I will tell my audience what I witnessed, and then, hopefully, we'll get an interview with Captain Rivers."

Roger snorted and wiped rain off his face. "You're crazy. You accused that guy of killing all those women by the rivers. He's never going to talk to you."

"He'll talk to me if it's in his best interest, or in the interest of the public," Rachel said quickly. And it would be. Rumor had it that Abbott might be dead, but she had a hunch there was still a serial killer out there.

She hadn't been completely serious in accusing Huck, but he did have ties to all three victims. It had been easy for her to make a case against him. Perhaps she should delve deeper into the investigative side of these killings instead of just reporting the facts. If she actually solved a serial killer murder, every podcast she created for the next month would go viral with very minimal effort.

Plus, if she could show Huck Rivers that she was just as smart as that stiff Laurel Snow, perhaps they'd have a chance again. "I'll see you in the studio later this morning, Roger," she said.

"You betcha." He turned toward his van, which he'd parked off the side of the country road.

She shook her head. While around her age, he would never attain the success coming her way. That was hers and hers alone.

The rain increased in force, so she ducked her head and hustled to her compact, which she had parked off the road away from the emergency vehicles. It was much easier to sneak up on a scene on foot than by car. The authorities always waved cars away.

She slid inside and turned on the ignition before blasting the heat. She hadn't realized how cold her fingers had become. Humming softly, she dreamed about the Pulitzer someday coming her way. If she had to destroy Huck Rivers to get there, she would. Although she'd much rather reach that red carpet with him at her side.

It had been a mistake to ruin their relationship in Portland. But considering he was so dedicated to his job that he worked even when supposedly on leave, he should be able to understand how important her job was to her. Righteous anger filled her, but she pushed it away. That wouldn't get her anywhere. She had learned long ago that honey worked much, much better with Huck than vinegar.

She drove slowly on the pothole-riddled road for several miles, noting the storm becoming even worse. Sometimes a rainstorm was more perilous than a snowstorm. When would summer arrive? How wonderful it would be to have the sunshine again. She turned down another road, winding through the forested area.

Why would anybody want to go camping for a day and a half? Who cared about a stupid merit badge?

The truck hit her out of nowhere, zooming from a side road, smashing into her passenger-side door. She shrieked and held on to the steering wheel as her compact spun and crashed into a tree. The sound of metal crunching filled her head as the airbag smashed into her face and then deflated.

Her ears rang and darkness poured into her for a moment.

She blinked rapidly, trying to figure out what had happened, when rough hands grabbed her arm and yanked her from her vehicle. She screamed, fighting, trying to see, but the guy was too strong. He held her against a hard male body and lifted her toward a dark form.

He shoved her face-first against a truck and forced her hands behind her back, quickly tying them. She struggled, trying to see, but her vision remained cloudy. He pulled a blindfold over her eyes. She kicked back, screaming as loudly as she could, her voice competing with the wind. A door opened, and then he easily lifted her up and shoved her into some sort of crate. The metal door clinked shut, and then the truck door shut.

She scrambled around, flopping on her side, having to curl her legs up. The smell of wet dog filled her senses, and she burrowed into a blanket, trying to reach out with her knees. He'd forced her into some sort of small wire crate. She sneezed from the wet dog smell. The truck light came on, but she could barely see from behind the blindfold.

Then her kidnapper hefted his weight into the truck

and slammed the door. He smelled like pine and the storm outside.

"This is kidnapping. Nobody has seen you. Let me go," she said.

He didn't answer. The engine was already running, and she could hear him move the gear shift, and then they started driving.

Terror filled her. "I'm not kidding. Let me go."

She tried to kick out, but the crate was too small. Then it hit her. She was in the back seat of a Fish and Wildlife truck—in a dog's crate.

"Huck?" she asked, her voice shaking.

He didn't answer but instead turned on the radio.

"Huck, I'm sorry. I did not mean to make you so mad."

It was the perfect kidnapping. He had just been a hero on her own show carrying that girl out of the forest.

Where was the dog? What had he done with the dog? She'd probably hear him if he sat in the front seat. Had Huck put him in the back bed of the truck? In the storm?

"Huck, you can't do this. You know you can't do this." Oh, God. Huck Rivers was the River Reaper and his last name was Rivers. He'd made a joke out of his own last name. He mocked them all.

She took several deep breaths, trying to dislodge the blindfold but failing. Her tightly bound hands were starting to lose feeling now. "You have to let me go. You can't do this."

He still didn't answer.

"Huck, the least you can do is talk to me. We were engaged. Remember?"

He hit the brakes, and she slammed against the side of

the crate, her shoulder protesting in pain. He chuckled low, and she strained to listen.

"Huck, I'm sorry. I'll fix it. I promise. You don't have to do this. No one believes you're a serial killer."

He was being stubborn. She remembered that side of him. But she'd never been terrified of him.

They drove over several large potholes, and she bumped up and down, bruising her body against the edges of the crate. Finally, they came to a stop.

She shrieked as loudly as she could. Her senses sharpened as he put the vehicle in Park and opened his door and then the door at her feet. Soon coldness and rain washed over her as he opened the crate and wrenched her out. She screamed, and he slapped her. Her head ricocheted back.

"Don't do this. Please don't do this, Huck."

She was crying, trying to reason with him and fight at the same time. He easily hauled her over frozen ground and tossed her to her knees. The ice cut into her pants. She tried to remember what she had gleaned from the crime scenes. Had he brought her to a river? The sound of cracking ice came through the night. It sounded as if he jumped up and down on the frozen river.

She felt around for any sort of weapon. He hacked for several more minutes, and she tried to crawl away, but she couldn't see anything. He grabbed her by the hair and yanked her back.

"Huck, please don't do this. I'll help you," she begged.

A knife touched her hand, and then the ropes fell away. She tried to reach for the blindfold, but he slapped her hand. She kept her hands down. Okay, she might not be able to see, but she could fight.

Why had he freed her hands? Did he want her to fight the ice when he tried to drown her?

He grabbed her hair and dragged her toward the sound of bubbling water. She gathered all her strength and pivoted on the ice, kicking him in the legs. He grunted and fell, crashing next to her. She punched out as hard as she could, connecting with soft tissue. He howled. Was that his eye?

It had felt like an eye.

She scrambled up and ran, ripping off the blindfold as she went. He lumbered behind her. She could now see that they were at the side of a creek near a forest. Running with all her strength, she barreled into the tree line, cutting and pivoting and turning with every chance she got. She heard something crash behind her. Had he tripped? Had he fallen? She didn't care. She kept going, her chin down, running as fast as she could through the trees, trying to lose him.

Finally, she barreled around an outcropping and ducked down deep in a clump of bushes to gather her breath. She was freezing, but she was alive. Her cheek hurt from where he'd hit her.

Where was he?

She peeked out, watching. Only falling rain sounded around her. She waited for at least a half an hour. In the distance, a truck rumbled. Had he given up? Had he gone away? She stayed perfectly still as the rain beat down on her for another half an hour, maybe more. She lost track of time.

Holding her breath, she finally stepped out of the bushes. Her eyes adjusted to the dark night. If she followed the river the way it flowed, she would eventually reach safety. Ducking her head, she kept moving, stubbornly placing one foot in front of the other. Shock tried to take her, but she staved it off.

How could Huck Rivers be a serial killer? How could she have missed that in him?

She soon came upon a series of cabins that had been closed for the winter. Her breath catching, she continued on until she saw lights in a larger home beside the river. She tripped several times but made it down the long driveway to the front door, where she started pounding. After a while, lights flicked on inside, and then the door opened to reveal an elderly couple in warm-looking bathrobes.

"Help," she said. "I need help." And she fell into their house.

Chapter 36

After a couple of hours of peaceful sleep, Laurel rolled over in the bed to find Huck staring at the ceiling. "You okay?" she asked, snuggling into his side.

"I'm good. It was a relief to find those girls last night. It hit me how easy it is to lose a kid."

She chuckled, happy he'd been able to find them. "Those kids were fine. They went the wrong way, they found a shelter, and they waited for you to save them. You are now that girl's mom's hero for life, though, you know?"

"She did mention in a text that she'd bake me some cookies." Huck slipped an arm around Laurel and drew her near. He kissed the top of her head. "Aeneas did a good job. That is one smart dog."

He was a sweetheart of a dog, too. But he'd been slightly injured in the rescue, so Huck had brought him immediately home. "Is his paw okay?"

"Yeah, it's going to be sore, but I put some medicine on it after I took out the brambles he stepped in. The guy kept going anyway until we found the girls. He's going to have to take it easy for a couple of days."

"That's all right. Monty enjoyed being the hero when he brought the girls home to their families, but we all know it was you."

Huck chuckled. "I don't mind sharing the glory with Monty. He deserves it. The guy should be home in bed for the next three weeks, but he keeps going out on calls."

Laurel cleared her throat. "How much trouble do you think you're going to be in for disobeying orders and attending a search and rescue call?"

"We'll find out," Huck said. "I did disobey a direct order. However, the media recorded me carrying one of the girls out of the woods, so maybe it'll balance out. What are your plans on this fine Sunday?"

Laurel didn't have time to take a day off. "I need to figure out if Jason Abbott was the killer of those blondes. And if so, how he found your mother. Was it just happenstance?" She hated the thought, but it was possible. "Or am I missing something?" She felt as if the truth remained just out of her conscious. "The fact that the killer dyed your mom's hair blond or talked her into doing it is bothering me. Why?"

"Hell if I know. Instead of asking questions, let's come up with a plan."

"I'm bringing in both Pastors John and Zeke to question them. Because Teri Bearing's body was found at the church, I have the right—and because Opal said that your mom headed north to meet a pastor. Of course, all we have is Opal's word that Delta mentioned a pastor. And how many pastors are there between here and

Santa Fe? It's inadmissible. It doesn't mean anything. And yet . . ."

Huck finished the sentence for her. "It means everything."

A pounding on the door had Huck sitting upright. Laurel frowned and slid from the bed to don his heavy sweatshirt over her thin camisole and shorts.

The pounding increased in volume. Huck yanked on jeans. "Stay here." He walked around the bed.

"No." She placed her gun in her pocket and followed him into the living room.

Aeneas barked wildly from his bed by the fire, and even Fred looked up, his body tensing.

Huck opened the door. Laurel leaned around him to see Deputy Chief Mert Wright and Captain Monty Buckley standing on the other side with two uniformed police officers behind them.

"What the hell's going on?" Huck asked.

Monty stared at his boots. "I'm sorry about this, Huck."

Huck looked from one to the other. "What is happening?"

Mert Wright frowned and reached for cuffs. "Captain Huck Rivers, you are under arrest for the kidnapping and assault of Rachel Raprenzi and for the murders of Delta Rivers, Teri Bearing, and Haylee Johnson."

Huck wasn't entirely sure he'd ever been this angry before, so he'd remained entirely silent until he sat on the other side of the interrogation table from Captain Monty Buckley, who looked as if he needed to cry, and

Deputy Chief Mert Wright, who looked as if he wanted to break into song.

"Did you say attack on Rachel Raprenzi?" Huck asked finally, his hands still in cuffs.

"Uncuff him," Monty said.

"Not a chance," Wright retorted. "He's dangerous."

Huck couldn't argue. He was feeling pretty damn dangerous. "What happened to Rachel?"

"Like you don't know," Wright sneered.

Huck focused on Monty. "What happened to Rachel?"

Monty leaned over and released Huck's cuffs, dragging them across the table and tossing them on the floor. "She got kidnapped last night, thrown into a dog crate, and nearly drowned by the river after somebody cut holes in the ice."

Huck stiffened. "When?"

"After the search and rescue operation, which made it quite handy for you, didn't it?" Wright asked.

Huck tried to wrap his head around this new development. "Is she all right?" They were no longer engaged, but he didn't want any harm to befall her.

Monty nodded. "Yeah, she kicked the guy and ran into the forest, eluding him. She also punched him in the face, and I don't see a bruise on yours."

Huck sat back. She'd eluded the serial killer? Sure, Rachel kept herself in decent shape, but this killer operated with meticulous precision. No way a kick-and-punch combo would've taken him down.

"Luck certainly favored her," Monty said.

Huck stared at his friend. "Does that make sense to you?"

"You're not asking the questions here." Wright

slammed his fist down on the table, scrutinizing Huck's face. "Not everyone bruises easily, you know. It's possible she punched you and didn't hurt you. We're going to go through this my way. You are in custody, Captain. Your job is over. Now, we're talking about your freedom."

Monty looked at the empty chair next to Huck. "I think you should have an attorney present."

Wright whirled on him. "It's not your job to give advice to the accused."

The accused. Huck was actually the accused. He shook his head and pressed his fingers against his right eye. He was getting a hell of a headache. "I waive the right to an attorney for now. For the record, I didn't kidnap Rachel."

"She was stuffed into a dog crate. You don't seem to understand." Wright punctuated each word with a chopping motion of his hand. "We have collected dog hair from her coat. Aeneas's fur is on record with Seattle from a case a while back."

Huck thought back. Oh, yeah, during the Snowblood Peak cases. He'd had to give Aeneas's fur for a sample. "Did they match?"

Wright sat back, his shoulders up and his chest out. "We don't know yet. However, I can tell you that I had the sample taken from her coat driven directly to the lab this morning and put at the front of the list. We should know within the hour."

"Huh?" Huck thought back. Since Aeneas had been injured, he'd let the dog sit in the front seat with him as he drove home. He hadn't even looked in the back crate. He usually kept a couple of blankets in there, and he most likely hadn't locked the truck. "Wait a second. If

Aeneas had been in the front seat, she would've heard him. If she screamed, and I'm sure she did, he would've barked."

Wright sneered. "She thinks you put the dog in the back bed of the truck."

This might not be good. Maybe he should have an attorney.

"How angry were you with Rachel Raprenzi for constantly attacking you?" Wright asked.

Huck cocked his head. "I wasn't angry. I just found her to be annoying."

"So annoying you needed to kill her, to shut her up, to drown her, so she couldn't talk any longer?" Wright spit out.

Huck just looked at him. "No."

Monty sagged back in his chair. "I don't think there's any way Huck kidnapped Rachel last night."

Wright hissed. "There was time. You had all disbanded. He could have easily done it. He rammed her car and then tried to kill her, but she got away." He smiled, showing sharp canines. "How does that feel?"

Huck frowned. "Rammed her car? Did you check my truck out?"

"Yes," Wright said. "Those trucks are made to withstand damage. But don't worry, we're going to test the paint on both. That could take a week or so."

Huck sat back and put his hands on his head. This was interesting.

Wright cleared his throat. "When did you find out your mother returned to town?"

"I didn't."

Wright opened a file folder in front of him and took out a stapled stack of paper. "Do you know what this is?"

"No clue," Huck said, looking at the paper.

"This is the GPS record of your phone the night that Delta Rivers was murdered. Your cell phone pinged off the closest cell tower to Snowblood Peak and Iceberg River."

"Well, yeah," Huck said. "We've already covered this. I was across the river on a case."

Wright slammed his hand on the file folder. "We did cover this. You were in the vicinity of all four of the murders . . . excuse me, the three murders and the one kidnapping. Don't you find that to be an incredible coincidence, Captain Rivers?"

Huck actually found it to be pretty damn unfortunate.

Wright leaned toward him, his nose leading the way. "What are the odds that the same guy was actually at the location of every single one of the murders? If I also recall, based on witness statements, you don't have an alibi for Haylee Johnson's murder, do you?"

Huck thought back. Laurel had stayed with her mother that night. They hadn't been together. He looked at Monty. "I would like to get that lawyer now."

Chapter 37

Laurel sat at her office conference table with an uneaten bagel next to her. She stared at the murder board, to which she'd also added Rachel Raprenzi's picture.

"I've got them." Monty hustled into the conference room.

Laurel reached for the photographs. "These are pictures of the crime scene where Rachel had been pushed toward a river?"

"Yeah," Monty said. "Fish and Wildlife officers were close by because of the search and rescue, so when Rachel called it in, they quickly tracked back to where she thought she'd been taken."

"Helping me will get you fired, Monty." But he was all she had. Everyone else was gone.

"Don't care," Monty said. "Plus, it's Sunday. It's my day off. I can do what I want."

Not true. Laurel peered more closely at the broken ice, which appeared as if crampons had been used. The edges exhibited a rough but symmetrical quality. "Rachel said Huck kidnapped her?"

Monty nodded. "But Rachel didn't actually see Huck. She felt a muscled male body hold her and was put into a dog crate in a truck, so she thinks it was Aeneas's crate. But she didn't see him."

"Did she hear a dog?"

"No."

Laurel quickly considered her options. "I'm still on this case."

"Probably not for long."

She nodded. "What do you say we pull Rachel in for an interview? This is a serial murder case, and we do have jurisdiction, especially since this crime occurred on federal land."

Monty had dressed in his Fish and Wildlife uniform. "I would have to take lead."

"I agree. I'll do my best not to interfere."

He lifted his shoulder. "I need Raprenzi's number."

Laurel looked it up on her phone. Rachel had given it to her months ago while asking for information on a case.

Monty lifted the phone to his ear. "Ms. Raprenzi, it's Captain Monty Buckley from the Fish and Wildlife service. I need to interview you about what happened last night." He waited a beat. "Yes, I'm aware you've accused Captain Rivers, and that's fine. But I've been on this case since the beginning and would like to bring you in for an interview."

Laurel held her breath.

He shook his head. "No, I'm not consenting to an on-camera interview. You would come to our offices." He rolled his eyes. "I'm still not consenting to that. Either you come and talk to us, or I will put out word with your competitors that you are unwilling to help in this case and just want to use it to further your career."

Laurel's jaw dropped. She hadn't realized Monty would resort to such a ruthless strategy so quickly.

"That sounds lovely. We appreciate you coming in to see me tomorrow." He ended the call.

"Monty," Laurel said.

Monty took a deep gulp of his latte. "That's the only language she understands. She'll be here to talk to us tomorrow morning."

Laurel wanted to groan. She turned to the screen at the far end of the conference room and quickly brought up the streaming channel.

Somebody buzzed in at the front door, and she stood, hurrying to the reception desk to see Pastor John and a woman on the screen. She buzzed them in, and they walked up the stairs.

Laurel straightened. "Pastor John. Don't you have church services today?"

"I was let go after Zeke firebombed me in front of the entire congregation," the pastor said. "I heard your phone message this morning and thought I would just cut you off at the pass." He pointed to the woman next to him. "This is Lativa Jones, and we were together all last night. So if you're trying to pin the Rachel Raprenzi kidnapping on me, you're way off base."

Lativa appeared to be in her early thirties with curly red hair and sparkling green eyes. "I've never been an alibi before," she said, grinning, "but we were together all night."

Laurel looked at Monty, who'd followed her down the hallway. "All right. Have you been to Santa Fe lately,

Pastor John? Before you answer, please remember that I can track your movements and that it's a crime to lie to a federal agent."

The pastor frowned. "I've never been to Santa Fe." His voice remained level and he did not fidget.

"Are you certain you've never met Delta Rivers?" Laurel asked.

He sighed. "Yes. I promise."

She would have Nester double-check his whereabouts for the last month, but she couldn't create a scenario where he'd killed the victims. "Very well. How about Pastor Zeke? Has he been to Santa Fe recently?"

"I have absolutely no idea where that man has been," Pastor John snarled.

She had leads to pursue and didn't have time to waste. "Would you return tomorrow morning when Agent Nester Lewis is back in the office?" Nester could track them in real time. If Pastor John had an alibi, he'd be cleared of the other murders, considering the same crampons had been utilized at all scenes except for Teri Bearing's. That one kept poking at Laurel's subconscious.

"Sure thing," Pastor John said. "I need to clear my name." He slid an arm over the woman's shoulders. "We'll be back tomorrow." They left with Lativa chattering excitedly about being part of the process.

Laurel hurried back into the conference room with Monty on her heels.

Rachel came onscreen beside a thirtysomething man with curly black hair and greenish brown eyes. "Oh, no," Laurel muttered.

"What?" Monty pulled out a chair

"That's Lucas Carver."

Monty set his elbows on the rough wooden door. "Who's Lucas Carver?"

Laurel shifted uncomfortably. "We attended graduate school together and then were at Quantico at the same time. Whenever any professor graded on a curve, if I had the highest A, he would have the next grade."

"Oh," Monty said, nodding. "So if he had the highest grade, then you—"

"No," she said, "I always had the highest grade." She sat back to look at Lucas. How in the world had Rachel found him?

Rachel smiled prettily, despite the bruise on her face. "So tell me, Mr. Carver," she said, "you're an expert on serial killers, correct? You're a profiler?"

Carver laughed, the tone charming. "We don't really believe in the term 'profiler.' We're more behavioral analysts, if that helps, and please call me Lucas."

Rachel twittered, looking like a heroine from a tragic novel with a bruise over her cheekbone and her blond hair up in a ponytail. She held her right arm against her ribs as if experiencing pain. "I've detailed for our audience what happened to me last night, how I was kidnapped and put into the dog crate but then managed to escape."

Carver reached over and patted her hand. "You did escape. You're a very brave young woman, and you are smart, and you kept your wits. You're the first one to live after facing this brutal killer. You're very impressive."

She smiled, the expression somewhat shy.

"Give me a break," Monty muttered.

Rachel sobered. "I really think the man who assaulted me was my ex-boyfriend, Captain Huck Rivers," she said, her voice hushed, her eyes wide.

Carver nodded. "I can't really say that Captain Rivers kidnapped you, but I can tell you that the person committing these killings is strong, methodical, and very angry at women. From the victims he's targeted, very angry at blond women."

Rachel swallowed and then pulled on her blond ponytail. "I would never have thought I'd be a victim."

"You're not. You're a survivor," Carver said instantly.

Rachel straightened and gingerly touched the bruise on her cheekbone. "You're right. I am. So do you think there's significance to his putting me in a dog crate?"

"Of course." Carver nodded, both eyebrows up. "He thinks women are dogs."

Laurel smacked her hand against her head. If Rachel was put in a dog crate, it was to keep her contained, for Pete's sake. No dog hairs were found on any of the victims. "Every crime scene is the same—the use of crampons, an iced-over river, and an isolated area—except for one. I'm missing something."

On the podcast, Rachel touched Carver's sleeve, as if seeking a connection. "So hypothetically, what if Huck Rivers is the killer? He has been arrested, you know."

Carver stared thoughtfully into the camera. "Let's keep in mind that we need to use the word 'alleged.' But if Captain Rivers committed these crimes, it would be interesting that the first victim was his mother, the mother who abandoned him."

Rachel wiggled in her seat. "Exactly. Isn't that the type of impetus that would propel him to start killing? When we were together, he was searching for a killer who drowned boys, and he saved one, but another died. He never got over that."

Carver nodded wisely. "Then it would make sense

that drowning would be his choice of killing, allegedly," he added at the end. "His mother would be the first target, without question."

Rachel shook her head. "But we broke up."

"Yes, but you were meaningful to him at a time when he was in great pain," Carver said gently. "He might want to end you to end that pain. Allegedly."

Monty sighed. "Tell you what. Why don't I go get some Fireball, and every time that moron says the word allegedly, we can take a shot?"

Laurel shook her head and sat back to watch the remainder of the show. Finally, Carver shook Rachel's hand, and the show went to commercial.

"What a bonehead," Monty muttered.

"I dated him," Laurel admitted.

Monty swung to face her. "You did not date that idiot."

She sighed. "I did. Worse yet, he broke up with me. He claimed I failed to be there for him emotionally."

Monty laughed out loud and then looked down at his laptop. "This guy's all over the Internet. He separated from the FBI in December and now runs his own business looking for missing persons. His initial fee is fifty grand."

Laurel's jaw dropped. "Fifty thousand dollars? This is a publicity stunt for him?"

"I suppose," Monty said thoughtfully, his hands shaking. "This is a big case, and *The Killing Hour* has gone viral. He's probably just gotten himself enough business to last the next five years. Plus, he probably didn't mind sticking it to you a little bit, Laurel."

Laurel studied him. "You need to rest." The color had leached out of his face. She placed too much reliance on

Monty with the absence of her team. He exhibited signs of imminent syncope, and if he passed out, she might not act quickly enough to catch him. "Go home, Monty."

"No. I need to help Huck. Tell me what's bugging you about the crime scenes."

She couldn't force him and understood his desire to help the captain. "I don't like that the ice was broken differently in Teri Bearing's death from the pattern at the other crime scenes."

Monty looked back up the hallway. "You think we have a copycat?"

"The possibility has occurred to me," Laurel said. "We want to look at Teri Bearing's husband as well as lover. Statistically, the killer is usually close to the victim. We know the mayor is an obvious choice because of Teri's affair with Pastor John. But perhaps Pastor John hasn't been truthful about his plans to work with Teri to take the deal from Zeke." Although she hadn't discerned markers of untruthfulness from him.

"Neither man has a decent alibi," Monty said. "But didn't a number of people know about the affair? The cat was out of the bag, right?"

Laurel nodded. "Yes, but not publicly. Not to the point that Pastor John would be ruined nationally."

"I guess," Monty said. "What else is bugging you about this case?"

Laurel breathed out and pounded her palm rather gently against her forehead. "Okay, one thing at a time. It's the dyed hair. Huck's mom's hair. That's the key."

Monty frowned. "I don't understand."

Ideas and scenarios ran through her head faster than lightning. "Me neither. The answer is just out of my grasp."

She only had so much time left to find answers before Norrs rightfully pulled her off this case, and then it'd be too late. "We're need to speak with the mayor again, but first, Monty, have two of your burliest officers go pull in Pastor Zeke Caine. We have to determine if Delta's 'pastor' was Zeke. I would like a show of force when he's brought in."

"Yeah?" Monty asked. "Are you sure? It's Sunday, and he'll be at church."

This could be a colossal mistake. "Yes. Thank you."

He straightened. "Do you want to come with us?"

She exhaled slowly. "No. I want him to wonder why I'm not there. If he asks, tell him I had more important matters with which to deal."

"You're trying to tick him off," Monty noted.

"Yes. He most likely has issues with impulse control. Let's shake him up a little."

Monty rocked back on his heels. "Should we cuff him?"

"Not if you can help it," Laurel said. "I don't want to cross the line, but make the movements public if anybody's around, and look tough. I want him angry when he sits down."

"You've got it," Monty said weakly. "I'll get a couple of badasses."

"Then go rest. Okay?"

He nodded.

How concerning. He'd actually agreed. Laurel sat back, trying to refrain from worry about Huck or Monty.

She hoped she knew what she was doing.

Chapter 38

Laurel sat on the far side of the conference table in front of the murder board that depicted the river killings. Her phone dinged, and she lifted it to her ear. "Agent Snow."

"Hey there, it's Dr. Ortega. I figured you'd be working overtime just like I am today, and I wanted to call you real quick."

She straightened. "Hi, Doctor. Do you have news for me?"

"I wanted to give you a heads-up that we've identified the body of Jason Abbott from his dental records. His teeth were still somewhat intact after the crash and the fire."

Her shoulders dropped. "I'm not surprised, but I was hoping that it wasn't him."

"It's definitely him. Also, I sent over the toxicology report on Haylee Johnson. She was clean. There were no drugs in her system."

That wasn't a surprise. "Was Abbott dead when he hit the ground?"

"I'd say he was alive when the truck went over the

cliff and dead by the time it hit the ground and exploded. I'll send you a complete autopsy report sometime tomorrow."

She didn't see Jason committing suicide. Who wanted him dead? Probably a lot of people. Yet only one most likely benefitted from those journals being destroyed before Jason's death. Abigail Caine. How could Laurel prove that Abigail had killed him? It had to be her. "Switching to the recent drowning homicides. Have you found trace evidence on any of the victims? Any dog fur?"

"Nope. Nothing," Ortega said. "It's like the guy touched them with gloved hands when he dragged them across the ice. We found absolutely nothing. We have no idea where he kidnapped them or how he held them until he killed them. My guess is a plastic-lined trunk, to be honest."

She winced. How terrible. "All right. I appreciate it, Dr. Ortega."

"How's Huck doing?" he asked.

She sighed. "I haven't talked to him yet. He's still being interviewed, but I can't imagine they have any hard evidence."

"It's still your case, isn't it?" Ortega asked.

Probably not for long. "Yes, so far. Why?"

"Then I can share with you that the dog fur found on Rachel Raprenzi's coat does match Aeneas's."

Her chin dropped. "Are you kidding?"

"No. I would never joke about something like that. Somehow this killer got hold of Aeneas's fur or one of his blankets. I mean, she was covered in the fur."

Laurel shook her head. It would have been easy for somebody to steal the blanket out of Huck's vehicle while everybody searched for the kids the night before.

To think that the killer had been that close to Huck. "All right. Thank you, Dr. Ortega."

"You bet. Tell Huck we're all pulling for him." He ended the call.

Laurel texted Nester to apply for a search warrant when he returned so they could dump Zeke Caine's phone—not only for the night before, but for the last couple of weeks. Nester could be very persistent when he wanted, and Opal's mention of "the pastor" might give them probable cause. Maybe.

A ruckus sounded near the doorway, and she straightened, grabbing a notepad and starting to make notations about a poem she'd once enjoyed, anything to keep her focus off the new arrivals. She switched to a different language. It was doubtful Zeke Caine knew Chinese, so she started writing in Chinese.

Soon he appeared at the doorway with Monty and two muscled Fish and Wildlife officers behind him. She kept writing.

"Daughter," he snapped.

She held up one finger from her left hand and kept writing. "Just a minute." She could almost feel the anger pouring from him, so she waited another moment and then looked up. "Oh, hi. Yes. Just bring him inside. Sit him down." She purposely did not address Zeke.

His eyes widened and a red flush covered his face. His nostrils flared. He still wore his pastoral robe with a pink stole this time.

Monty pulled out a chair and pushed him rather roughly into it.

Laurel looked past Zeke. "Thank you, Officers. Sorry to drag you in on a Sunday for a silly matter."

Monty walked around and sat at the head of the table, leaving Laurel to face her father.

Zeke's gaze flicked to the board she'd left revealed behind her, and then he studied the River Reaper board.

"You like what you see?" She tried to sound bored.

He shrugged. "I don't know what I'm looking at."

"Do you like being referred to as a pastor?" she asked.

He looked at her, anger still glittering in his eyes. "Yes. I've earned that moniker. People trust me. I guide them. Without me, they'd be lost.".

No ego there. "I see."

"No, I don't think you do," he spat. "Your goons dragged me away from a large Sunday sermon in front of my parishioners. They pretty much accused me of being a murderer and hauled me away like a common criminal. You will pay for this."

Good for them. They had done exactly what she'd wanted them to do. "Oh, will I?" She rolled her eyes. "You're not nearly as frightening as you want to be. I'm an FBI agent. I deal with serial killers. You're an older pastor who thinks he gets power by talking about God. God doesn't care about you."

His eyes bugged out. "God cares about me more than anybody else. I make this world better for Him."

She chuckled and then looked at Monty. "Did you hear that? This simple man makes life better for God."

Monty snorted. "That's a good one."

Zeke sat straighter, his shoulders going back.

"Do you like crampons?" she asked Zeke.

A small smile curved his mouth, and he looked up toward the cameras mounted on either side of the room. "Crampons? I don't even know what that is."

"Sure you do. You put them on your feet and stomped through ice," she said. "At most of your recent crime scenes." She opened a file folder and took out a picture of Delta Rivers. "You met her in Santa Fe. Remember?"

He tilted his head. "No. I've never met that woman."

"Have you been to Santa Fe?" Laurel asked.

His nostrils flared as he took in air. "I've already told you I won't discuss my travels with you. Period."

They'd see about that. Laurel tapped the photograph. "She had dark hair. You seem to like blondes. Did you talk her into dying it blond, or did you do it for her?"

Zeke looked at Monty and then back. "I have found that women do what you ask them to do if you treat them nicely. But in this case, I never met that woman."

Then he stared at her, a smirk now obvious on his face.

She had studied smirks. She understood the derision behind them. Yet he might just be playing a game with her. Why would he have killed Delta? He had an alibi for Teri's murder. Haylee seemed like an inconvenience for somebody like him. None of this made sense. She took out a picture of Haylee Johnson. "What about this young woman?"

"She was pretty, wasn't she?" He stared down at the picture. "It's quite a pity that Huck Rivers killed her just to protect you. The captain is quite the alpha male, isn't he?"

Would Zeke go to this much evil trouble just to hurt Huck? That didn't fit with his psychopathy. She could see him hunting and shooting Huck, one on one, but not kill him with an elaborate game.

Perhaps she needed to speak with Pastor John again.

For now, she pulled out a picture of Rachel Raprenzi. "What about her?"

Zeke cocked his head. "I saw her show earlier. She is such a brave young woman. How in the world did she escape your boyfriend? Perhaps Huck still has feelings for her and couldn't go through with the murder?"

"Were you at Rachel Raprenzi's crime scene?" she asked.

"I've never been to a crime scene," Zeke murmured.

"Were you present at the search and rescue effort last night?" She needed to tie somebody else to the scene and, from there, to taking the blanket out of Aeneas's crate.

His mouth opened and then closed. "Of course not. I was busy praying at my church when I heard those girls were missing last night."

"Do you have anybody who could corroborate that?" she asked.

He looked sadly around. "No. I worked by myself at the church, then at my cabin. My phone will reflect that, I'm sure."

So he'd left his phone either at the church or his cabin. A man who was smart enough to steal a blanket out of Huck's truck and use it himself wasn't stupid enough to take his phone with him on a kidnapping and murder. Or he actually wasn't the killer. How badly did she want to put him in prison? Could her anger with him be coloring her actions?

He sighed. "Laurel, it appears as if Captain Rivers is a killer with some serious problems. I do wish you'd take heed and protect yourself from him."

"You have access to a lot of trucks, don't you?" she asked suddenly.

"Oh, no, I have an SUV." He drummed his fingers on the tabletop. "You're not going to connect me to any of these crimes, Laurel. I'm a man of the cloth. I would never harm a woman."

She pulled out a picture of Teri Bearing and pushed it across the table. "What about Teri Bearing?"

His eyes flared and for a second, the lines of his face shifted.

She'd have to study the video later to try to determine what that movement meant.

"I'm very sorry about the mayor's wife." He stared as if transfixed by the picture. "I cannot believe Captain Rivers dumped her body outside of our church."

"Hypothetically, if the captain didn't kill her, who do you think did?" she asked. Zeke no doubt knew his parishioners.

"Hmm." His lids lifted and he stared at her. "I don't know. Is there something different about this death?"

She reached for comparison pictures of the holes made in the ice. "The ice is different. The killer didn't use crampons for Mrs. Bearing's drowning."

"Oh, yes, crampons." He nodded. "I do know what that means. Don't you climb icebergs with them?"

"You can," Monty said.

Zeke didn't look at him, keeping his focus solely on Laurel. "Isn't that odd? Don't serial killers often stick to their rituals?" He stared at the different photos.

Laurel pulled back the pictures and shut the file folder. "Yes, they do."

Zeke rubbed his chin thoughtfully, as if in deep contemplation. "I don't really have an answer, but what if somebody wanted to disturb the church? What if they wanted to stop me from going national? It would make sense to leave a body there, right?"

"Go on," Laurel said.

"Or Pastor John was having an affair with this poor woman. He took advantage of her. I would take a hard look at him or at her husband, of course." He shrugged. "Unless somebody just wanted to mess with me and ruin my television debut. You don't suppose Huck Rivers had it in for me, too, do you?"

Laurel studied him. "No, I don't suppose he did. So your theory is that Teri Bearing's killer is either Mayor Saul Bearing, Pastor John Govern, or Captain Huck Rivers?"

Zeke held out both hands and smiled, looking her directly in the eyes. "Well, now, Laurel, who else could it possibly have been?"

Laurel's mind spun after Zeke Caine had left her office. Her emotions might be clouding her judgment. Why would he kill Delta and Haylee, then kidnap Rachel but let her go, and possibly kill Teri Bearing but use something else to break the ice?

She couldn't find his motivation.

The downstairs door buzzer sounded, and then heavy footsteps echoed in the hallway. Laurel took several deep breaths and sat back in her chair, keeping her shoulders straight.

Special Agent in Charge Norrs walked into her office, pulled out a chair and sat. The agent had dark circles under his eyes, which were bloodshot.

"How are the RICO cases going?" Laurel asked.

"Just concluded two of them," he said, and then sighed. "You're off the drowning cases, Laurel. I just spoke with Deputy Director McCromby."

She swallowed. It wasn't a surprise.

Norrs steepled his fingers beneath his chin. "I didn't tell the deputy director that you're pregnant with Captain Rivers's baby, but you probably should give him a heads-up before he finds out from somebody else."

She tilted her head. "Abigail?"

Norrs nodded. "We are dating."

Now wouldn't be the time to tell Norrs that she was fairly certain Abigail had murdered Jason Abbott. She would have to build that case on her own without his interference. He wouldn't believe her anyway.

He sighed. "I'll be taking over the river killings. We're pursuing Captain Huck Rivers as our primary suspect."

Her hands shook. "He is not a murderer."

Norrs shook his head. "Love is blind, Snow."

The irony of that statement struck her.

He flattened his palm on her desk. "I'm going to bring in a small team and we're going to take over your office, okay?"

"That would be proper procedure," she said, noting his slower than usual movements. "You require sleep first."

He shook his head. "There's no time for sleep."

"The conference room is all yours. If you require additional space, you may use the first level of the building to the east. My mother is going to build a tea shop there, but it's vacant for now because she's out of town. You cannot have my office because I'm investigating other cases."

"I don't want to mess with your office. I think you

should reach out to your sister for help. You're going to need support during this very difficult time." His gaze dropped to her abdomen and then up. "I've looked over the case files. We have a good case against Captain Rivers. Unless something else breaks quick and fast, he's going to be charged, and we're going to put him away."

Her stomach rolled.

"We've also received a phone call from Pastor Zeke Caine," Norrs said, his voice almost slurred. "He's suing us for slander and emotional distress."

"What? Because we called him in for questioning?" Laurel asked, her eyebrows rising.

Norrs shook his head. "You didn't catch the last few minutes of *The Killing Hour* just now?"

"No."

"As he left your building, Pastor Caine was attacked by Rachel Raprenzi and her cameraman. They had the whole scoop on how he'd been pulled away from his parish and had basically been accused of murder."

Seriously? What kind of reach did Rachel have? Or had Zeke somehow set this up? "How did they know all of those facts?" Laurel asked.

"Heck if I know," Norrs said. "But he's suing us, and he's pissed."

She thought back to what she knew. Zeke had horribly embarrassed Pastor John in front of their entire church. Perhaps John had taken a little bit of revenge. Not that she could blame him. However, a lawsuit would make her life even more difficult.

Agent Norrs stood. "Where's the case file?"

"All of the files are in the conference room, as are the murder boards. You can take over the entire area if you want." She'd already removed the pictures and notes from the board featuring Abigail so he wouldn't see her evidence.

"Thank you," he said. "I'm sorry about this."

Laurel nodded. "So am I."

He smiled. "The good news is that if I'm here for a while, Abigail will be here as well. You two can finally bond."

Chapter 39

Darkness had fallen as Laurel rode in the passenger side of Huck's truck, idly thinking that she hadn't driven her own vehicle in much too long. It had been at least a week. This was getting ridiculous.

"So they just released you?" she asked.

His grip tightened on the steering wheel. "Not exactly. I called in my attorney, and he pointed out that Rachel could not positively identify me as her kidnapper and that anybody could have stolen Aeneas's blanket from the back of my rig. Plus, there's absolutely no damage on my truck and a lot on Rachel's vehicle."

Laurel cocked her head to the side. "Who's your lawyer?"

"He's an old pal from the military who lives outside of Seattle. That's part of what took so long. We had to wait for him to arrive. You'll like him—I assume we'll be seeing a lot of him over the next months."

Laurel nodded. "They're not dropping the case against you?"

"No. They're going to up the charges. My cell phone

being in the vicinity of all the murders doesn't look good."

She watched the rain beat the ground outside. When would spring come? "You're most certainly their prime suspect."

He set his windshield wipers on a faster speed. "They're definitely building a case. My lawyer convinced them not to arrest me at this time, so long as I relinquish my weapons, badge, and passport. I'm on indefinite leave."

"I'm off the case as well." Her fingers itched to get back to her case files. "I think Norrs is a good agent, and Nester said he'd be back tomorrow."

Huck flicked her a glance. "They're not as good as you."

Her shoulders sagged. The fact that she could get into a killer's mind would always bother her. "You were deliberately set up," she murmured.

"Could it be by Abigail?" he asked.

"She, for some unknown reason, wants a close relationship with me, or at least whatever 'close' means to her. You are in the way." Did it track, though? Abigail wasn't somebody who liked to get her hands dirty, and drowning a woman by forcing her head beneath ice was definitely dirty. Yet Laurel had no doubt Abigail would sink to such lows if the ends justified her means. "We've been looking at this case by asking why each victim was murdered."

"That sounds standard to me."

"What if it's all about you?" she murmured.

Huck looked at her. "The fact that my mother was the

first victim makes that entirely likely, but I don't have any enemies."

She sat back. "Everybody has enemies. You've had a long career, Captain. You've put many a criminal in prison."

"Sure," Huck said, "and I've let people down."

She studied him. "It wasn't your fault that child died in your Portland case."

"I know, but he left behind a great-aunt who hated my guts."

"We need a list of anybody who might want to hurt you and who you think is diabolical enough to go about it in this manner." Just to cross them off. That theory didn't track for her.

He pulled into his drive and parked near the shop. "You haven't had a chance to tell me how the interview with Zeke Caine went earlier."

"I metaphorically poked the beast," she said.

"Meaning?" Huck turned off the truck and looked at her. Silence echoed through the cab.

She swallowed. "He's furious. If he's going to make a mistake or slip up, it's going to be now."

"You think he's the killer?" Huck asked.

"The puzzle pieces won't snap into place." His smirk said he was. Or he was just messing with her head because he could? "If he wants to hurt you, I think he'd just shoot you. So if Zeke is the killer, this actually isn't about you."

"Ug. My head is aching."

She rubbed her temple. "As is mine. To be thorough, we still need a list of anybody who'd want to harm you. We can pass that on to Nester or even Agent Norrs, but Nester won't yell at us when we do."

"Good point," Huck said. "I don't know about you, but I'm starving. Let's go in and find something to eat."

"Agreed." She stepped out of the truck onto the icy ground and shivered when the wind assaulted her. She peered up at the moon shining through gaps in the rain clouds, but looming purplish clouds were sweeping in from the north. "We're about to be impacted by another storm."

"Aren't we always?" Huck reached her side. "I was thinking, after this is all over, let's really take that vacation we've been talking about."

"Somewhere sunny. I could use the vitamin D." She took his hand. "Definitely somewhere sunny."

Somewhere sunny. Streaks of blond. All dead blondes. The puzzle pieces slipped nicely together in her mind. Shock held her still for a moment. How evilly diabolical. The malignant narcissist who'd been thwarted. Of course! She couldn't believe it. "Huck. I've got it. It's—"

A shot cracked out from nowhere, and the captain's body doubled over as he emitted a harsh grunt and then fell.

"Huck!" Laurel screamed, scrambling in her bag for her weapon.

A blur of motion caught her attention, and then a hard body tackled her onto the ice. She skidded several feet. Her purse spun away, end over end, her weapon inside. She looked up to see Zeke Caine's face right before he swung his fist and punched her in the cheek, hard. She'd been right. Her head flopped down again. Her body shook, and she sucked in frigid air, forcing herself to remain conscious. She kicked out, nailing him in the knee.

Grunting, he punched her again in her face, and her head snapped back, hitting the ice. Darkness stole her vision, and she turned, trying to scream for Huck. Was he okay? Was he alive? Was he dead? She scrambled to find him.

Aeneas barked loudly from inside the home, sounding frantic.

Rough hands grabbed her hair and dragged her toward the cabin and then around the side through the scrub brush. She started to fight, but her limbs became heavy and her vision blurry.

"You fucking bastard. I figured it out," she croaked.

Zeke laughed. "You have my brains. Yet I won't accept betrayal from any of my women. Ever."

As they neared the river, Laurel fought to stand. She stood and tried to strike back. He kept his hold on her hair and pulled her along, throwing her down again. She landed on her hands, and pain ricocheted up her arms as agony spread along her scalp. "You couldn't care less about killing blondes."

"Nope. I care about betrayal."

Even though it was dark, there was enough moonlight to see a perfectly cut hole in the ice. A set of crampons had been discarded next to its symmetrical edges. "I knew you killed those women."

"You were right. But don't think you're so smart." Zeke crouched, fury flushing his cheeks a dark red. "I guess we're having our own King Lear moment here, my bitch daughter."

She coughed and searched for a weapon. Those crampons were close. If she could get her hands on them, she might be able to injure him enough to get away. She couldn't think about Huck or the baby right now. She had to focus on survival.

"King Lear?" she mocked. "His actions led to the death of his daughter, but he didn't do it himself. And you're no king." She tried to inch closer to those sharp edges.

He slapped her and she fell back. "All right, then. I guess it's a Titus Andronicus tribute."

She nodded. "He did kill his daughter, Lavinia, but he did it out of love."

"I'm acting out of love." Zeke looked toward the river. "For my life, anyway."

She balanced herself on her tailbone and drew her legs in, searching for the right opening.

He laughed. "I hit you so hard, you'll see stars for days. Don't even think of fighting me. Though I have to admit, I am ready for a good fight. It has been too easy to subdue these weak women."

Laurel coughed, her ears ringing. "All blondes. Do you hate my mother that much?"

He lost the smile. "That bitch. She kept you from me! She deserves to die horribly with her head beneath the ice." His shoulders shook as if with great rage. "Plus, once my church goes national, I can't have her coming out of the woodwork and accusing me of a crime I didn't commit."

"Yes, you did, and you know it." Where were the crampons? She forced her eyes to focus and adjust to the darkness. If she could just keep him talking a little while longer and not think about Huck. How injured was the captain? "The other victims just provided you with a cover?" How evil. She'd questioned its existence before, but now she knew with certainty. Evil existed. All on its own, and it faced her right now.

"Yes."

She gagged. "You killed those women just so you could murder my mother and not be an obvious suspect?"

He lifted his head, hatred glittering in his eyes. "Yes. I want her lungs to freeze as she screams. How dare she keep you from me? *From me!*" he screamed.

Bile rose in Laurel's throat. He was insane. "Why did you take Huck's mother as one of your victims?"

"Why not? I needed to rid myself of that captain, so two birds, one stone."

She ruthlessly swallowed, trying to regain feeling in her arms. He'd just wanted to kill Deidre. Her poor mother. "How did you find Huck's mom?"

"Easily," Zeke said, apparently enjoying the bragging, as most narcissists would. "A private detective out of Texas. It really wasn't that hard. If the captain had wanted to find her, it would've been easy."

"What about her hair?" Laurel asked. If she hit him right in the ankle he'd go down sideways. She could scramble for the crampons and then slash his face.

Zeke winked. "She voluntarily came with me. I told her that Huck had cancer, was dying, wasn't telling anybody, and his dying wish was to see his mother. I suggested she dye her hair back to blond because that was how he remembered her."

She had to keep him bragging until she could grasp the weapons. "You had her fly here and then killed her by Snowblood Peak?"

"Yep," he said cheerfully. "Abbott's escape was a bonus. I was already planning to kill a few blondes to throw suspicion on someone else before I made my real kill. As a true sniveling twit, Haylee Johnson needed to be put down anyway. All I did was knock on her back door, and she opened it. Can you believe it? I knocked her out, and it was that easy to take her. Then, of course, Rachel Raprenzi. Wow, that smart girl got away."

Laurel bunched her body. "You let her escape."

"Of course. She had that stupid dog fur from the blanket I stole all over her. The woman thought she was so smart. I could have murdered her in a second. Not that I won't. Well"—he looked sadly back toward the cabin—"I guess I won't because this is over. Unless they let the captain stay out of prison for a while, but after they find him and your body, he's probably going away."

"So you're willing to kill me? Your own blood."

He paused. "I have to kill you. It's not like you won't turn me in. You're smart. Too smart. I knew you'd figure it out. Take that as a compliment."

The feeling in her hands still tingled. "You're a pastor. Don't you believe in hell?"

He shrugged. "I'm a god, you know. Rarely fail—am quite pissed your mother outran me the other night. I was ready to make a move."

Laurel shivered. "She was too smart for you." Thank goodness she'd gotten Deidre out of town.

He rubbed his hands together, and the wind lifted the bottom of his jacket. "Deidre will die somehow, but apparently not this way. I did love the elegance of this campaign, though, dealing with her as well as Huck, so as to leave you isolated."

"Isolated? By taking some of my team away?" She tried to concentrate. "The raffle for the vacation?"

He snorted. "I paid for that myself. Goodbye, Walter and Ena."

Her stomach rolled. "And Nester's sister?"

He laughed out loud. "Hit that girl with a truck, I did.

Took me awhile to learn her schedule, and I had to hire out for that. But I was the one who introduced her to a bumper."

What a horrible man. Yet Jason Abbott had helped him without even knowing it. "You thought I'd feel alone and come to you?" Laurel asked.

"You would've," he said, his arrogance on full display. "I would've been all you had left once you understood the truth about Abigail."

The freezing wind kept Laurel from passing out. "What about Teri Bearing?"

"Wasn't me," Zeke said. "We both know who it was. Haylee Johnson saw one of you that night, and it wasn't you. Right?"

A branch cracked near the cabin, and they both turned to look. Laurel instantly bunched and attacked, kicking him in both ankles and then jumping up on one foot to nail him in the groin.

He leaned over, grunting.

She dove for the crampons and turned, coming up with them, but he was already on top of her. He grabbed her head and slammed it down against the ice. Her body went limp, even as her brain tried to fight.

"Good move," he growled. Grabbing the crampons with his gloved hands, he pulled her up and spun her around, shoving a gun into her hands.

"What?" she asked.

He put his finger on hers and fired it twice across the river.

His action made no sense.

He pulled the weapon free and tossed it yards away. "Your prints are now on the gun that shot Huck Rivers.

Everyone will think you shot him trying to save yourself from the horrible River Reaper. I fucking love that name. Hopefully he is not bleeding too badly, because I'll need to bring his body up here."

"No!" Laurel screamed as Zeke flipped her over, grabbed her hair and dragged her toward the hole.

She fought as wildly as she could, but her body had gone numb. The first plunge of her face into the river shocked her senses, and she went alert, waking up instantly. She shut her mouth and fought back, and then he pushed her head under the ice. She tried to jerk up and the ice cut into the back of her head.

Panicking, she clawed the ice and river rocks, trying to push herself back. It was a natural response.

She could hear his laugh as he easily held her under. This wasn't going to work. He pushed her harder, and she opened her mouth in response. Freezing cold water poured down her throat. She pulled her knees in and then kicked out as hard as she could, barely hearing his muffled oof from beneath the ice.

Her entire body shuddered. Darkness started to fall. Freezing water filled her lungs. The pressure on her head lessened. She heard a crack and a large boom.

Her lungs compressed, out of oxygen, and she nearly relaxed. A warm darkness enveloped her, and her heart stopped.

She didn't feel rough hands yanking her from the water, but the thump of a fist on her chest brought her back to the freezing world. Gasping, using the last of her strength, she shoved away from the ice. Her lungs screamed. She opened her eyes to see Zeke tackle a bleeding Huck onto the icy ground.

Chapter 40

Huck came to with a jolt, his entire right side screaming in pain. Aeneas barked wildly from inside the cabin, and Huck blinked his eyes, trying to see what had happened as he rolled to his knees

"Laurel?" he croaked. He heard a scream and then a laugh down by the river.

He shoved to his feet, swayed, and went down on one knee. Shuddering, taking a deep breath, he slammed his left hand against his right shoulder, trying to stem the blood, and then gave up the fight as he pulled his phone from his back pocket and stumbled toward the cabin.

"Officer down, officer down," he hissed after dialing 911. "Get everybody out to Huck Rivers's cabin immediately. Fucking everybody."

He fell against the side of the cabin, then pushed on, hearing movement down by the river. In the back of his head he knew he'd been shot, but he could feel Laurel fighting, needing help.

He squinted, trying to peer through the darkness, and saw Zeke Caine holding Laurel's head under the water. With a roar that came from somewhere deeper than his soul, Huck rushed forward and tackled Zeke, throwing them both out onto the ice.

Huck scrambled back and yanked Laurel from the water, flipping her over and pressing hard on her sternum.

Zeke careened into him, throwing them both back on the bank.

Huck struggled, but Zeke hit him in the face. Huck punched him back in the jaw with his left arm, cracking the man's head against the ice. Then he pushed Zeke away and lunged toward Laurel.

She wasn't moving. Then, miraculously, she shoved herself away from the ice.

Huck had almost reached her when Zeke barreled into him from behind, sending them both against the bank again. Huck landed hard, and his injured shoulder screamed agony through his body. Or was it his chest? He wasn't sure. His whole right side was killing him.

Grunting, he flailed around, and his hand landed on a set of crampons. Grabbing them, he turned and swung, viciously swiping the sharpened edges across Zeke Caine's face.

The man howled and fell back.

Huck stumbled to his feet, turned, and side-kicked Zeke in the neck, throwing him several yards. Then Huck dropped to his knees and scrambled to grab Laurel.

Zeke again tackled him from behind and cracked his head on the ground.

Grunting, Laurel pushed herself up, grabbed the crampons, and launched herself forward, slashing them down Zeke's face.

The man shrieked.

Laurel leaned to the side, shuddered wildly, and coughed. Water poured out of her mouth.

Zeke Caine limped away.

Sirens sounded in the distance.

Huck tried to get up but fell back down. The right side of his body had gone numb, but he crawled toward Laurel and gathered her close, keeping her curled on her side as she coughed out more water. Then she went lax.

Zeke disappeared into the tree line.

"Just hold on." Huck smoothed Laurel's hair back with his good arm. "Just hold on."

The sirens came closer.

A light beeping sound filtered through Laurel's consciousness, and she opened her eyes, remaining perfectly still until she recognized a hospital room. The bed was warm and soft, and her elbow hurt. She looked down to see an IV catheter beneath a stretchy bandage. "Ouch."

She glanced to the side to find Huck slumped in the chair wearing a bloody T-shirt. She tried to speak his name, but nothing came out. She swallowed, but her throat was parched. "Huck."

His eyelids instantly opened, and he leaned toward her, grasping her hand. "Laurel, are you okay?"

She blinked. "I don't know. Why am I in the hospital?" she croaked.

He reached for a plastic cup with a straw. "Drink this." He pressed the straw to her lips and pushed a button on the bed, which slowly raised her to a sitting position. She drank, and the water felt soothing.

Water.

Drinking.

In a burst of memories, the entire night came back to

her. She gasped and blinked. He removed the straw and placed the cup on the table next to her. "Did I die?"

"No," he said shortly, leaning toward her. "How's your brain?"

She gulped. "My brain?"

"Yeah, you were out for a while."

She knew she had died. She had felt the life leave her body, something that she wouldn't have thought possible. "I don't know."

He flicked on a small light near her head and peered into her eyes. "What's my name?"

"Huck."

His brown eyes warmed. "How was I named?"

"You were named after your dad's dog, Huckleberry."

"Good," he said. "What's the square root of 1,020?"

All right. Her mind was coming back. "Approximately 31.937."

The tension slowly left his face. "You're okay."

She swallowed and looked at his bloody shirt. "Were you shot?"

"Yeah," he said shortly. "I'm fine."

Her entire body hurt. She looked down at her hands, which were both bandaged. "I scraped the ice."

"Yes. You took off a couple of your nails. You did good. You fought well."

"Not well enough. Where's Zeke? Is he in custody?"

Huck shook his head. "Unfortunately, no. I let him get away. I'm sorry."

She stared at him. He looked exhausted, and his hair had dried curly, standing up on end. Bruises mottled his face, and blood was quite evident on his light T-shirt.

"I think you were probably saving my life." Her chest ached.

"You swallowed a lot of the water."

She looked around the darkened room. "Do I have any permanent lung damage?"

"It's too early to tell," he said, "but since your brain is fine, I assume your lungs are, too."

She liked that logic. "I see." She took a deep breath and looked down. Somehow, she already knew. "The baby?" Then she looked in his eyes.

"No," he said. "I'm sorry." His voice cracked at the end.

Surprising tears filled her eyes. Could she have fought harder?

"It's okay." He leaned in and pulled her against the left side of his shirt as if trying to keep the blood off her.

She shocked herself by crying hard sobs that didn't make a lot of sense. She hadn't realized how much she'd hoped for that baby. She settled her nose into his shirt and let the tears fall. "This is silly," she said. "Twenty percent of women miscarry in the first trimester. I was still in the first trimester. We hadn't even heard a heartbeat yet."

"I know." He kissed her neck, one scalding hot tear sliding from his skin to hers. "I'm still sorry."

She gulped. "So am I. I had big plans for that kid." She tried to chuckle, but the sound sounded like a sob.

"So did I," he said. "I will find Zeke Caine, and he will pay for this."

She forced herself to grow calm. "I know."

"I will find that bastard," Huck said, his voice still quiet. He leaned back and gently wiped her tears away with his thumb. "It's okay to feel sad."

"I do," she said. "Very. I wonder who that baby might've been."

"She would've been perfect," Huck said, kissing her on the mouth and then sitting back down.

That was probably a stretch, but the baby would have been perfect to her.

She might be off the case, but she would use every one of her gifts and IQ to find Zeke Caine and put him in prison, where he should spend the rest of his life.

Movement sounded by the doorway and a woman walked in. "Captain Rivers. It has been long enough," she said.

Laurel blinked to see a nurse with both hands on her hips. The woman appeared to be in her midthirties, with sparkling black eyes and dark hair in a bun. Laurel looked at Huck. "Long enough?"

"He needs stitches from being grazed by a bullet," the nurse said. "The guy's bleeding all over the place. I'm surprised you have any blood left."

Laurel sat up. "What? You need stitches?"

"He wouldn't leave until you woke up." The nurse threw both hands in the air.

Laurel shook her head. "Huck, I'm okay. Go get some stitches."

"They can do it right here," he said, his jaw set.

"No, we can't," the nurse retorted. "We need a sterile environment, unless you want to die of sepsis."

Laurel winced. "Huck. I'm really okay. It'll only take fifteen minutes as long as you listen to them." She said the last part with emphasis. He looked at the nurse and then back. "I could use a couple moments to myself," Laurel lied, knowing it was the only way to get him to go.

He faltered. "Okay. I'll be right back. Can I bring you anything?"

"No," she said. "Just you."

His forced smile cut through her. "I'll be right back." Glaring at the nurse, he stood, his arm bent at the elbow and held against his rib cage. As he followed her out, he paused at the doorway. "I have two guys on the door."

Laurel blinked. "Zeke Caine is not coming back for me. He's running. We need to figure out where he's going."

"Still, two guys on the door," Huck said grimly and then disappeared.

She settled back against the pillows and allowed herself to experience the loss. The baby hadn't been planned, but she'd been happy once she'd wrapped her head around the idea, as had Huck. They had even started to plan. Anger flowed through her, aimed at Zeke Caine. She would find him.

"Let me in right now. I'm her sister," a familiar voice ordered from the hallway.

Laurel sighed.

A young, uniformed police officer poked his head in. "Ma'am, would you like to see your sister?"

"Absolutely," Laurel said with authority.

"Exactly," Abigail said as she swept inside and walked over to take Huck's seat. "I'm surprised you want to see me."

"I definitely want to see you." Laurel pressed the button so she could sit more upright and ignored the pain that clashed through her entire body as she did so. Fighting on ice led to many contusions. "Where is Zeke Caine right now? Tell me, Abigail."

Abigail wore jeans and a black sweater with her hair up in a messy bun as if she'd rushed to the hospital. "I don't know where he is. His face is all over the news, and the entire city's out looking for him. Every cop we have is trying to find him. They will. Don't worry." She patted Laurel's arm. "I didn't think he would go after you like this, or I would have stayed closer."

Laurel looked at the now-empty doorway. "I provoked him," she admitted. "I brought him in and embarrassed him."

Abigail's jaw dropped. "Why in the world would you do that? You know how dangerous he is."

"I figured he'd make a mistake," Laurel said. Which he had. Unfortunately, it had cost her just as much. "We both know that you understand him better than anybody else, Abigail. Please, for once, do the right thing and tell me where he is."

Abigail patted her shoulder. "If I knew, I would tell you. I'll call all the parishioners who still speak to me and see if I can find anything out, dear sister. Do not worry. We will take him down together."

Laurel didn't think Abigail would help unless Zeke's capture served her own self-interest, and right now it definitely didn't. "He admitted that he didn't kill Teri Bearing."

"Is that a fact?" Abigail sat back. "He's a liar, you know?"

Laurel nodded. "He is a liar, but the crime scene wasn't the same, and Haylee Johnson saw you in a truck in the vicinity." Of course, Haylee had thought it was

Laurel, but it was actually Abigail. "What I can't figure out is why you would kill Teri Bearing."

"I wouldn't," Abigail said smoothly. "She was a tepid, silly woman who planned parties all year long. Remember, I was involved in the one for the . . . I don't know. It was one of those charities." Abigail knew exactly which charity.

"Why do you do that?"

"Do what?" Abigail asked.

Laurel sniffed. "Act forgetful or as if you're not as smart as you are. Pretending."

Abigail shrugged. "Habit, I guess. You do the same."

Laurel's chin went up. "I most certainly do not."

Abigail chuckled. "Yes, you do. You dumb down your language all the time."

There might be some truth to that. Laurel didn't think of it as dumbing down, just using more accessible words. "I don't consider it pretending."

"I guess it's a matter of degree, isn't it?" Abigail asked with a catlike smile on her face.

Laurel had never understood that turn of phrase until she'd met Abigail. Now she saw the perfect illustration of it. "Why would you kill Teri Bearing? I'm in the hospital. There are no recording devices. Just tell me the truth."

Abigail crossed her legs and tapped her nails on her knee. "I did not kill the mayor's insipid wife, sister. You are an FBI agent and are perfectly capable of testifying in court as to any conversation you may have, and we both know it, so don't play me for stupid."

"I was hoping to play you for being a decent person,"

Laurel retorted. Though, as the saying went, that ship had probably sailed a long time ago.

Abigail rolled her eyes. "You think I killed Teri Bearing and also Jason Abbott? Tell me, are you going to pin every unsolvable murder on me? Maybe you're just not smart enough to solve them. Perhaps you should join your mother's tea service and just make money."

Laurel studied her sister's expression. Abigail's eyes narrowed and her lips pressed together, revealing classic signs of irritation. Laurel applied more pressure. "I know you killed Abbott. I strongly suspect you of killing Teri Bearing. I know she was dating Pastor John, whom you had dumped a long time ago, but even your ego isn't that big. Of course, the body was left at the church, which ruined or at least postponed the television show. Are you so petty, Abigail, that you would kill a woman just to mess with your father and stick it to an old flame?" Her heart sank as she realized that, yes, Abigail was exactly that narcissistic. "Did you mean to implicate Huck?"

"I'm finished with this discussion," Abigail said calmly. "Besides, when Mrs. Bearing's body was found, nobody knew that the first victim was Huck's mother, did they?"

Laurel sat back. That was true. So, Abigail could have been just copying the most recent murder. Nausea rolled through her, and she felt chilled. She wasn't sure her body would ever get warm. "I think you should leave now."

Abigail stood. "More than likely. Anyway, get better, and we'll make all sorts of plans for that baby of ours. Maybe Genesis Valley isn't the right place for all of us to live."

Laurel blinked and hurt crashed through her again. She cleared her throat. "Abigail, the baby didn't make it."

Abigail reared back. "What did you say?"

Laurel plucked at a string on the blanket. "Our father drowned me. I think I died for a few seconds. The baby didn't survive, Abigail."

Red lanced across Abigail's face, and her eyes sparked a wild blue and green. "Is that a fact? I am sorry to hear it, dear sister." Her voice cracked. She turned and strode out of the room, her boot steps powerful.

Laurel reached out a hand. "Abigail, wait. Wait. Officer, Officer," she called out.

The young officer leaned inside the doorway. "Yes. Can I help you?"

"Yes. Follow her. You have to follow her," Laurel said urgently.

The guy shook his head. "Absolutely not. We have orders not to move. We are not leaving you, Agent Snow. I'm sorry."

"You have to," she cried out.

He disappeared from sight. "No."

"Phone. I need a phone," she yelled out, looking wildly around. She grabbed the hospital phone and started to dial. A buzzing met her ear. "Damn it." She hit nine and then dialed.

"Agent Lewis," Nester answered, sounding wide awake.

She pushed the blanket away. "Nester, it's Laurel. Where are you?"

"I'm at the office, boss. I drove here immediately from Seattle and am on duty trying to find Zeke Caine. Monty and I wanted to come see you, but Huck said it was more important that we find this bastard. How are you?"

"I'm healing," she said. "I need you to ping Abigail's phone right now."

"Sure thing. Do we have a warrant?"

A warrant? "No."

"All right," Nester said. "Just a sec." He was gone for several minutes before he came back. "I have her phone. She's at the hospital."

Laurel's shoulders sagged. "She left the hospital a few minutes ago."

"Her phone stayed there."

Of course it did. She'd probably dumped it out on the ground outside. "I need somebody to follow her."

"We don't have anybody in that vicinity, boss."

Frustration clawed through Laurel. "I need you to start gathering CCTV from the hospital in every direction and track her movements. She's going to lead us right to Zeke Caine. I know it."

"I'll get back to you. Hang in there." Nester ended the call.

Laurel shoved the sheet away and swung her legs over the bed. Taking a deep breath, she pulled out the IV and then winced as blood spurted from her arm. She pressed hard with the elastic bandage against the wound until it stopped bleeding so much. She had to get dressed.

Now.

Chapter 41

At the edge of the Genesis Valley city limits stood a dilapidated, sad-looking apartment complex. One often rented by kids just starting out, the elderly on fixed incomes, and drug abusers. Abigail parked her car in the rear of the eight-apartment complex, even though no security cameras recorded in this dark corner of the world.

Her gun in her hand, she climbed the iced-over stairs to the second landing and walked along the balcony to the far end. It was surprising the thing held her weight—the landlord should probably be shot next.

Without waiting for an invitation, she reached the last door, leaned back, and kicked her leg squarely to the left of the doorknob. The door crashed open. Nobody in this area would bother to investigate a noise. She stepped inside, gun out.

"Hello, daughter," Zeke Caine said, his gun pointed at her.

She reached behind herself and shut the door, then leveled the gun at him, aiming for his chest. "You tried to kill Laurel," she snapped.

Zeke smiled, looking comfortable in dark slacks and

a white button-down shirt with the first couple of buttons open. He had apparently cleaned up after trying to commit murder.

"I think I did kill her," he said congenially, his gun aimed at Abigail's head. "Now, if you want to have a friendly conversation about this, we can. But guns down."

"Very well," she said, placing her gun at the back of her waist.

"Thank you."

She looked around. "This place is disgusting."

"I was in a bit of a rush," he admitted, tucking his gun at the front of his waist. "How did you find me?"

"I know of all your little haunts." A tidily made queen bed had been pushed into the far corner, while a round country-style table took up most of the kitchen, which only had two counters in an L-shape. The fridge hummed quietly, no doubt full of food. And one little couch faced an older TV on a series of boxes. "So this is where you bring your . . ."

"Dates," he said smoothly. "I like to call them dates."

Abigail crossed her arms. "The women you raped."

"It's not rape if they say yes to the drink," he retorted, walking around to pull out a chair. "Sit down, Abigail."

She didn't like the order, but they did need to speak. So she pulled one of the rickety wooden chairs away from the table and sat facing him, clocking the entire room.

His gun was at his waist. The counter held a hot plate, a toaster, a knife block, and several dirty dishes.

She was an expert in geometry and could calculate the distance of every object and every movement in the room. He was smart, but his IQ was nowhere near hers. Yet his narcissism blinded him to that fact.

"I preferred taking them in the church," he said thoughtfully. "There's just something about sex in the church, you know?"

"I don't," she said.

His chuckle sounded like that of a weak man. "Sure you do. You and Pastor John had some fun there, correct?"

She'd completely forgotten, to be honest. "You failed to kill Laurel."

"I kind of killed her." He lifted one shoulder. "But apparently my shot didn't hit Captain Rivers where I'd wanted. I didn't want him *dead* dead. But I needed him to be out for a little while longer."

"You thought he'd be arrested?" Abigail guessed.

Zeke rubbed his smoothly shaven chin. "Of course, I thought he'd be arrested. He was in the way."

"Laurel has it figured out," Abigail said. "She's smarter than you are, by far."

Zeke's eyebrows drew down. For once, he'd taken out the blue contacts, showing his true eye colors. Which matched Abigail's and Laurel's. "She is bright."

"As am I." Abigail had figured it out the second Delta Rivers had been identified as the first victim. Of course, she knew Zeke and Laurel didn't. So it had taken Laurel longer to put the pieces together. "All of this was a lead-up to your killing Deidre Snow, Laurel's mother."

He flicked lint off his pants. "Yes, I suppose it was."

"You meant to frame Huck?"

"He was in the way."

There were much easier ways to get rid of Captain Rivers. "I couldn't agree more," Abigail said. "You underestimated him."

"I most certainly did. I've ruined my life, and now you're going to have to help me, daughter."

"I am?" Abigail asked. "Why would I do that?"

His eyes glittered, probably with anger. Or fear. Who the hell knew. "Because you have a lot of money, and I need to get to somewhere that doesn't have an extradition agreement with the US."

"Ah," she murmured, righteous fury flowing through her veins. "Are we talking the Maldives, Indonesia, or Montenegro?"

He blinked. "You really don't know—there's never been a need for you to know."

"I'm thinking Seychelles," she said. That's where she'd go. In fact, she had plans in place should she ever need to run. He wasn't smart enough to realize that she was giving him this information because it would never matter for him. "I don't plan on helping you."

"But you will." He reached into his front pocket and drew out a small, black USB that he tossed on the counter behind him.

She followed his gaze. "Wow. A USB. That was dramatic. Why?"

His nostrils flared. "Do you honestly think I don't have cameras set around my church?"

Her body chilled, and then her brain took over. "There are no security cameras around the Genesis Valley Community Church."

"Yeah, there are." He smiled. "They're mine, and

nobody else knows they're there. I mainly have them in the trees. They're much like the ones Fish and Wildlife use. Isn't that handy?"

She blew out air and quickly calculated her odds of getting out of this current predicament without having to leave Laurel.

"Yes, dear daughter, I have you on camera. Poor Teri Bearing. But I owe you for that one because it gave me an alibi for the other crimes. It's almost as if you wished to assist me."

She'd had no idea the bastard had killed the first victim. Hadn't had a clue. If only she had discovered the identity of Delta Rivers before deciding to fuck with him. Teri Bearing had seen Abigail with Jason back during her last charity event, and she might've heard Abigail messing with the moron's head. Abigail had been meaning to take care of her for a while, and after the finding of the first body, she figured she'd copy the killing. It was infuriating that she hadn't known the full truth.

Zeke sneered. "I can't believe you wanted to ruin my television show by leaving that woman's body by my church. I could've had a megamillion-dollar church."

She shrugged. Of course she'd wanted to ruin his big moment, which was why she'd dumped Teri's body behind the church. "You don't deserve a television show."

He stared at her. "The USB shows you committing murder. How about ten million dollars wired into this account?" He rattled off the numbers. "We both know you just memorized those."

The rage felt cleansing in her body, causing her blood

to rush faster to her brain. Supplying more oxygen to that brilliant organ. "Of course I did."

"I also need papers, a couple of passports, some credit cards, and a false name. Give me a rich-sounding one. I'm going to need to find dates down there, wherever it is I'm going," he ordered.

"I don't have ten million in liquidated cash, you moron," she hissed, sounding properly angry.

"You own a pot farm, and I know you've invested wisely through the years. Make it happen, or that USB immediately ends up with good old Rachel Raprenzi at *The Killing Hour*. She's very involved in this case, as you know."

"I know." Abigail stood. "Fine. I'll see what I can do."

"Oh, no, no, dear daughter. You won't see what you can do. You will do it." He also stood. "You're lucky you're alive. You're lucky your sister's alive. She's tough."

A rage enveloped Abigail such as she had never felt before. It was shocking, really. She hadn't thought it possible to feel this much hatred for a simple human being. "You killed the baby. Our baby," she spat.

He blinked. "Laurel was pregnant?"

"Yes." The pain felt blinding.

He shrugged. "Whatever."

One word. One simple word. Abigail went stone cold. Icier than those rivers he'd used to kill. "This isn't over." She shifted her weight.

He lifted his hands, laughing. "Of course it's over. I win. I always do."

Faster than he could track, she dodged forward, grabbed a kitchen knife, pivoted, and sliced right into his neck. His eyes widened and he grabbed below his jaw, falling onto the chair.

In a frenzy, she stabbed him over and over again, blood spraying, pausing once to reach for the small USB on the counter and shove it into her mouth. She gagged several times but managed to swallow it before turning and plunging the knife into his eye and his neck and his chest.

Hopefully, the damn USB wouldn't perforate her colon.

He weakly lifted his arms and tried to ward her off, and she stabbed those, too.

"You never should have killed our baby," she yelled, plunging and stabbing until he went limp. Even then, she kept striking.

Huck returned to Laurel's hospital room to find her fully dressed. He shook his head. "What are you doing?"

"Abigail. She was just here. She's going after Zeke Caine. Let's go. Do you have a phone?"

"No," Huck said, grabbing her shoulder, his arm in a sling and his stitches already pissing him off. "You're staying here. You were drowned tonight, and you've just had a miscarriage. You have to be bleeding and in pain."

She looked at him, her eyes luminous. "It doesn't matter. I am bleeding, and the pain will dissipate. I can handle it. Nothing else can happen to me. I don't have anything to protect. We have to go now."

He understood her need to find Zeke Caine because he felt it as well. "Laurel."

"I'm going." She pushed past him.

Groaning, he followed her and nearly ran her over when she halted.

"We need a phone." She looked at the first officer.

The guy handed over his cell phone. "The code is 22789," he said.

"Thanks." She turned and limped down the hallway. Huck caught up to her at the outside door.

She pressed the phone to her ear. "Nester, what do you have? Okay, hospital. Then what?" She groaned. "Okay, then what? Come on. We have to find her somewhere. All right. Think, damn it, think."

They ran out to where Monty Buckley was jumping out of his rig. "Hey, what are you two doing out of the hospital?" he asked, a bouquet of flowers in his hand.

"We need your truck," Huck muttered.

Monty looked from one to the other of them. "You two are certifiable. I'm driving." He tossed the flowers in the back seat.

"You're in front, Laurel." Huck walked around and lifted her in. "I want the heat on you." He was about as pissed off as pissed off could get, and so he slammed her door before jumping in the back seat.

It was going to take him awhile to process this loss, if that's what people did. Processing. He'd never understood the damned word. But right now, the only thing that mattered was keeping Laurel safe.

"Where are we going?" Monty asked.

"North." Laurel listed off different CCTV cameras that had caught Abigail.

Huck thought through what he knew of the area. "There's nothing out that way."

Laurel partially turned to look at him. "I know, but there's a gas station that confirmed the spotting of Abigail's car. She's easy to identify with her hair, and she would've known about the cameras. She wasn't hiding—she wants us to follow. Go there, Monty."

Monty mumbled under his breath the entire time but drove the fifteen minutes to the gas station.

"Stay here," Huck ordered, jumping out of the truck and striding inside. Thankfully, she did as he said. His arm ached like knives kept stabbing him. He couldn't imagine how she felt right now. And Monty should be in bed as well. The guy looked like death had finished knocking and now had entered his front door.

Huck walked up to the clerk behind the counter. The kid was young with a lot of pimples. "Hey, the FBI called you earlier, and you said you had a sighting of a red-headed woman in a black SUV."

"Yeah, man. She stopped for gas."

His shoulders straightened. "Great. Where'd she go?"

"I don't know." The kid pointed north. "She went that way."

Huck looked into the darkened night. "Is there anything out that way?"

The kid chewed on a toothpick. "There's a real crappy apartment complex, but other than that, no. I guess you could go several miles farther and hit a campsite or two."

"This apartment complex, people live there?"

The kid's head hung. "Only real sad people, dude."

"Okay, thanks." Huck jogged back outside. "There's

an apartment complex, but there are also camping areas farther up."

"Morons," Monty muttered, putting the truck into Drive again. They drove for about five miles until they came to a dilapidated eightplex that might've been cream colored at one time. The paint had either rusted or peeled off. The stairs on the side to the top floor appeared as if ready to fall down.

"Looks like it used to be some type of motel," Monty muttered.

Laurel pointed to the far end. "Drive around it. There's parking on the other side."

Monty drove around the back, and Huck caught his breath at seeing Abigail's black SUV. "Holy shit," he said. "All right, you two stay here."

"No way," they both snapped.

"We need guns," Huck muttered.

Monty opened the glove box and handed Laurel a nine millimeter before reaching in his boot to hand back his Glock to Huck. "I'm keeping my service weapon," he said stubbornly.

"Fine. I'm lead." Huck stepped out and walked as carefully as he could to the stairs. "Monty, you take the bottom, I'll take the top. Laurel, you're with me."

Monty started on the lower end.

"Be stealthy. Don't knock on doors. Make no noise," Huck whispered.

"I know what I'm doing," Monty snapped back.

The first three apartments on the top floor remained deadly silent, and Huck caught his breath at seeing the broken door on the fourth one. He nodded at Laurel, and she angled around him to see.

"I go high," he whispered.

"Affirmative," she whispered back.

He moved to the other side of the door, his weapon in his hand, and kicked it open. He slipped in fast to find Abigail Caine covered in blood, her hand on a knife.

Zeke Caine was slumped in a chair next to her, blood flowing from every visible inch of him, his head down and his chin on his chest.

"Drop the knife, Abigail," Huck ordered loudly.

She dropped the knife, her bloodied hands in the air. The spray had caught her across her hair and face and entire body. She blinked, her eyes wide and dazed. "It was self-defense. He tried to kill me."

Chapter 42

Two weeks later

Laurel changed into heavier socks in Huck's bedroom as the sounds of voices hummed through the wall. She had not been able to get her feet warm after her near drowning. One would think her lungs would feel cold, or even her face, but it was her feet, always chilled.

It had been two weeks since Zeke Caine's death and Abigail's arrest.

Laurel quickly read a text from her mom and then looked at the beautiful pictures of the herbal gardens Deidre had sent. After receiving the bad news, her mom had offered to fly home immediately.

It had taken Laurel awhile to convince her to continue her journey and actually enjoy it. Finally, her mother had decided to extend her visit for two weeks, and Laurel had heartily agreed. The adventure would do her some good, and there was no reason to return home quickly.

Laurel's phone buzzed, and she lifted it to her ear. "Agent Snow."

"Hello, Agent Snow. It's Tim Kohnex."

She sat on Huck's bed. "Mr. Kohnex, I've asked you not to use this phone number, and yet you persist. This is your last chance. If you call me again on my private number, I will have you arrested for harassment."

"I do apologize," he said formally. "I am sorry. I just wanted to call. I've been watching Rachel Raprenzi's reports as well as the news, and I feel as if I could have warned you about your loss."

She took the hit and felt it deep in her body, but nobody knew about the baby. "Excuse me?"

"Your father. I know he was not a good man from what I'm learning, but his death still represents a loss. I knew you would face that, but . . ."

"But what?" Laurel asked.

"I just felt your loss would be more personal, you know, something innocent about it, but I must have been wrong. Anyway, I was hoping that perhaps I could sit down with you for an interview."

She paused and looked at the thinner socks she'd discarded on the bed. "An interview? For what?"

"I would very much like to consult with your team. I think I could be a valuable asset. In addition, I'm writing a book on my experiences. An interview with you would make that really sing."

She swallowed. "Mr. Kohnex, I have no interest in speaking with you, either for your book or for my cases."

His sigh was heavy across the line. "All right, but I can tell you already, I know there are forces coming for you. You may think you're out of the woods, but Agent Snow, the evil has just gotten started. I see another threat, from an area you can't even imagine."

"Call me again, and I'll arrest you." She clicked off and shook her head. The last thing she needed was to deal with a wannabe psychic, and yet his words chilled her. Was there any truth to them?

She shook off her unease and walked back into Huck's living room, where Nester and Kate were cleaning up after an impromptu lunch of chicken tenders and pizza. Her entire team had returned, and she finally felt settled again.

"We just had to come see how you were doing, boss." Walter finished his beer with Ena at his side.

Ena nodded. "We've been worried about you two out here by yourselves for the last two weeks and had to get a visual. It's lovely to see you healing nicely. Do you know when you'll both be reinstated?"

"We were, yesterday," Laurel said. "I imagine we'll be back to work soon." Her body still ached, and her soul felt tired, if that were possible. Now she was becoming maudlin. "Though it's my understanding you've all been doing an admirable job."

Monty Buckley walked in from the bathroom. "Everyone's been doing a phenomenal job, but we would like you back soon. Even with Officers Tso and Jordan back at part-time desk work at Fish and Wildlife and bringing us cookies once in a while, it's been a little quiet."

"What's going on with Abigail?" Kate threw paper plates in the garbage.

Laurel looked at Huck. "She was arrested. We have her for killing Zeke Caine, though she has a decent self-defense claim. We're also still looking for evidence against her in the Jason Abbott killing."

"And Teri Bearing's death," Huck said grimly. "Haylee Johnson saw Abigail that morning, so it's possible somebody else did as well. I feel like there's evidence out there."

"We can't underestimate her," Laurel said, "but we'll do what we can. She voluntarily chased Zeke Caine down that night, and it's her word against, well, a dead man's, that she killed him in self-defense. Had her terror been authentic, she would've called the authorities."

Walter straightened his shoulders. "I am looking forward to pursuing the case."

"As am I," Huck said. "She's out on bond right now, so we have somebody following her 24/7. She'd be smart enough to know that, however."

Laurel smiled. "It was nice of you all to bring us food."

Aeneas barked happily from the corner. Fred, the cat, looked at him and turned his back, going to sleep again. He slept near the fire often.

"Yes, it was very nice of all of you," Huck said, pointedly standing.

Walter chuckled. "All right, buddy. We'll leave you to your peace." He stood, and everybody ambled out.

Huck frowned as he shut the door. "Was that rude?"

"No," Laurel said. "All you did was stand."

He grinned. "Yeah, that's all I did. I like our teams, but that many people in my cabin . . ."

She nodded. "It's too many people. We're better off dealing with all of them at work." She walked over and sat on the sofa.

He sank down next to her, put his arm over her shoulders and extended his feet, crossing his ankles on the coffee table. The fire crackled merrily in front of them. "So."

"So," she murmured, leaning into him and snuggling. It felt good to be warming themselves by the fire. Although it was nice to have everybody come to check on them, she liked the quiet, especially right now.

"I'm tired of the rain. I'm tired of the snow, Special Agent in Charge Laurel Snow," he murmured.

The rain pattered outside. "As am I."

"Good. I've taken a ten-day leave of absence, and I'm hoping you'll do the same."

She angled her head on his shoulder to look up at his face. "You have?"

"Yes. I booked us a stay at the Hacienda del Sol in Cabo for ten days. It's all-inclusive. We can eat all we want, drink all we want, and get all the sun we want. We can heal in every possible way."

Part of her still felt frozen inside, and the idea of stretching out on a warm beach held a lot of appeal. They did need to heal, and not just physically. "I miss the baby."

"Me, too." He held her closer. "We can say goodbye to her on the beach in the sun. Then maybe we can plan."

She blinked. "Plan?"

"Yeah. We're alive, we're almost healthy again, and we're together. The two of us will get through this and find something good and new." He turned his head and kissed her temple. "Both of us understand that life is never easy. But we can make it good, Laurel. I promise."

She believed him, even though nobody could control life. "The two of us planning, huh? I could get on board with that."

He chuckled. "Listen to you using colloquiums."

"Listen to you making actual plans that involve more than you and your dog." She snuggled closer to his hard body. "Let me at least help with the plane tickets."

He shrugged. "I haven't bought them yet because they're nonrefundable and I wanted to make sure you could go."

"I have enough points that we could fly first class," she said, perking up.

He looked down at her and grinned, his eyes mellow in the afternoon light. "First class? That sounds great. All you can drink. What do you say?"

She snuggled into him. "I say yes. Let's go chase the sun for a while, Huck. We deserve it."

Keep reading for a special excerpt
of the new book in the thrilling new dark romance
series, a dark reimagining of Snow White,
set in a world where information is power
and those who control the flow
of information live like gods.
Billionaires play games of insult and influence,
and one woman will stop at nothing
to win the game herself.

ONE DARK KISS

Rosalie

Alone, I cross my legs again beneath the intimidating metal table secured to the floor, feeling as out of place as a raven in a nursery rhyme. The heat clunks and whispers from a grate in the ceiling but fails to warm the interview room, and when the door finally opens, the heavy frame scrapes against the grimy cement floor.

My spine naturally straightens and my chin lifts as my client stalks inside, his hands cuffed to a chain secured around his narrow waist. He doesn't shuffle. Or walk. Or saunter.

No. This man . . . stalks.

His gaze rakes me, and I mean, *rakes* me. Black eyes—deep and dark—glint with more than one threat of violence in their depths. He kicks back the lone metal chair opposite me and sits in one fluid motion. The scent of woodsy male wafts toward me.

I swallow.

The guard, a burly man with gray hair, stares at me, concern in his eyes.

"Please remove his cuffs," I say, my focus not leaving my client.

My client. I don't practice criminal law. Never have and don't want to.

The guard hesitates. "Miss, I—"

"I appreciate it." I make my voice as authoritative as possible, considering I'm about to crap my pants. Or rather, my best navy blue pencil skirt bought on clearance at the Women's Center Thrift Store. I don't live there, but I'm happy to shop there. Rich people give away good items.

In a jangle of metal, the guard hitches toward us, releases the cuffs, and turns on his scuffed boot toward the door. "Want me to stay inside?"

"No, thank you." I wait until he shrugs, exits, and shuts the door. "Mr. Sokolov? I'm Rosalie Mooncrest, your new attorney from Telecom Summit Law Group."

"What happened to my old attorney?" His voice is the rasp of a blade on a sharpening stone.

I clear my throat and focus only on his eyes and not the tattoo of a panther prowling across the side of his neck, amethyst eyes glittering. "Mr. Molasses died in a car accident three months ago." Molasses was a partner in the firm, and he'd represented Alexei in the criminal trial that had led to a guilty verdict. "I take it he wasn't in touch with you often?"

"No." Alexei leans back and finishes removing the cuffs from his wrists to slap onto the table. "Don't call me that name again."

I frown. "Sokolov?"

"Yes. It's Alexei. No mister."

Fair enough. I can't help but study him. Unruly black hair, unfathomable dark eyes, golden-brown skin, and bone structure chipped out of a mountain with a finely sharpened tool. Brutally rugged, the angles of his face reveal a primal strength that's ominously beautiful. The deadliest predators in life usually are.

Awareness filters through me. I don't like it.

Worse yet, he's studying me right back, as if he has Superman's x-ray vision and has no problem using it. He lingers inappropriately on my breasts beneath my crisp white blouse before sliding to my face, his gaze a rough scrape I can feel. "You fuck your way through law school?"

My mouth drops open for the smallest of seconds. "Are you insane?"

"Insanity is relative. It depends on who has who locked in what cage," he drawls.

Did he just quote Ray Bradbury? "You might want to remember that I'm here to help you."

"Hence my question. Not that I'm judging. If you want to do the entire parole board to get me out, then don't hold back. If that isn't your plan, then I'd like to know that you understand the law."

It's official. Alexei Sokolov is an asshole. "Listen, Mr. Sokolov—"

"That name. You don't want me to tell you again." His threat is softly spoken.

A shiver tries to take me, so I shift my weight, hiding my reaction. I stare him directly in the eyes, as one does with any bully. "Why? What are you going to do?" I jerk my head toward the door, where no doubt the guard awaits on the other side.

Alexei leans toward me and metal clangs. "Peaflower? I can have you over this table, your skirt hiked up, and spank your ass raw before the dumbass guard can find his keys, much less gather the backup he'd need to get you free. You won't sit for a week. Maybe two." His gaze warms. "Now that's a very pretty blush."

"That's my planning a murder expression," I retort instantly, my cheeks flaming hot.

His lip curls for the briefest of moments in almost a smile. "So, do you know the law? Usually women who look like you aren't expected to use their brain."

My eyebrows shoot up so quickly it's a shock a migraine doesn't follow. He did not just say that. "You are one backassward son of a bitch," I blurt out, completely forgetting any sense of professionalism.

"Fuck, you're a contradiction." He flattens a hand on the table. A large, tattooed, dangerous-looking hand. "As a rule, a beautiful woman is a terrible disappointment."

Now he's quoting freakin' Carl Jung? "You must've had a lot of time to read here in prison . . . the last seven years," I say.

"I have." A hardness invades his eyes. "You any good at your job?"

The most inappropriate humor takes me, and I look around the room. "Does it matter? I don't see a plenitude of counsellors in here trying to help you."

"Big word. Plenitude. I would've gone with cornucopia. Has a better sound to it."

I need to regain control of this situation. "Listen, Mr.—"

He stiffens and I stop. Cold.

We look at each other, and I swear, the room itself has a heartbeat that rebounds around us. I don't want to back down. But also, I know in every cell of my being, he isn't issuing idle threats. A man like him never bluffs.

Surprisingly, triumph that I refrain from using his last name doesn't light his eyes. Instead, contemplation and approval?

I don't like that.

My legs tremble like I've run ten miles, and my lungs are failing to catch up. I suppose anybody would feel like this if trapped with a hell beast in a small cage. There's more than fear to my reaction. Adrenaline has that effect on people. That must be it. I reach into my briefcase on the floor and retrieve several pieces of paper. "If you want me as your attorney, you need to sign this retainer agreement so I can file a Notice of Appearance with the court."

"And if I don't?"

I place the papers on the cold table. "Then have a nice life." I meet his stare evenly.

"My funds are low. I don't suppose you'd take cigarettes or sex in trade?"

Is that amusement in his eyes? That had better not be amusement. I examine his broad shoulders and no-doubt impressive chest beneath the orange jumpsuit. How can he look sexy in orange? Plus, the man hasn't been with a woman in seven years—he'd be on fire. A little part of me, one I'll never admit to, considers the offer just for the no-doubt multiple and wild orgasms. "I don't smoke and you're not my type. But no worries. My firm is taking your case pro bono until we unbind your trust fund."

He latches on to the wrong part of the statement. "What's your type?"

I inhale through my nose, trying to keep a handle on my temper, which doesn't exist.

"Don't tell me," he continues, his gaze probing deep. "Three-piece suit, Armani, luxury vehicles?"

"Actually, that's my best friend's type," I drawl. Well, if you add in guns, the Irish mafia, and a frightening willingness to kill.

Alexei scratches the whiskers across his cut jaw. "Right. When was the last time you were with an actual man? You know, somebody who doesn't ask for guidance every step of the way?"

That fact, which I don't remember, is not one I'll share. My thighs heat, and my temper sparks. "Was this approach charming seven years ago?"

"Not really. Though I didn't need to be charming back then."

True. He'd been the heir to one of the four most powerful social media companies in the world before he'd gone to prison. Apparently, his family had deserted him immediately. "You might want to give it a try now."

His eyes warm to dark embers, rendering me temporarily speechless. "You don't think I can charm the panties off you?"

"All right. You need to dial it down." I hold out a hand and press down on imaginary air. "A lot."

"Dial what down?"

"You," I hiss. "All of this. The obnoxious, rudely sexist, prowling panther routine. Use your brain, if you have one. It's our first meeting, and you're driving me crazy. You want me on your side."

"I'd rather have you under me."

I shut my eyes and slam both index fingers to the corners, pressing in. This is unbelievable.

"Getting a headache? I know a remedy for that."

I make the sound of a strangled cat.

His laugh is warm. Rich. Deep.

Jolting, I open my eyes. The laugh doesn't fit with the criminal vibe. It's enthralling.

He stops.

I miss the sound immediately. Maybe I am going insane.

Using one finger, he draws the paper across the table. "Pen."

I fumble in my bag for a blue pen and hand it over.

He signs the retainer quickly and shoves it back at me. "What's the plan?"

The switch in topics gives me whiplash. Even so, I step on firm ground again. "The prosecuting attorney in your case was just arrested for blackmail, peddling influence, and extortion . . . along with the judge, his co-conspirator, who presided over your trial and sentenced you."

His expression doesn't alter. "So you can get me free?"

"I don't know. Best guess is that I can get you a new trial."

"Will I be free for the duration?"

"I'll make a motion but can't guarantee it." I tilt my head. "Your family's influence would be helpful."

His chin lowers in an intimidating move. "I don't have a family. Don't mention them again."

I blink. "One more comment."

"Go ahead."

"I'm sorry about your brother's death." His younger brother, rather his half brother, was killed a month ago, probably by my friend's boyfriend, if one could call Thorn Beathach a boyfriend.

Alexei just stares at me.

I feel like a puzzle being solved. "There's a chance his death was part of some sort of social media turf war against Thorn Beathach, who owns Malice Media."

"So?"

"Thorn is currently dating my best friend, so if there's a conflict of interest, I want you to know about it." Not that anybody would ever catch Thorn, if he had killed Alexei's brother after the man had injured Alana. I'm still not sure he was the killer anyway.

"Are you finished mentioning my family?" Alexei's tone strongly suggests that I am.

"Yes," I whisper.

He cocks his head. "How many criminal trials have you won?"

"None," I say instantly. It's crucial to be honest with clients. "I haven't lost any either."

His head tips up and he watches me from half-closed lids. "You're in charge of the pro bono arm of the firm?"

"No."

"Why you, then?"

It's a fair question as well as a smart one. "I've never lost in trial, and the partners assigned me your case."

"Why?"

"Because I'm good, and they want you free." I shrug. "This is positive exposure for the firm." Which is what my boss, Kay Ramstead, told me when assigning me to the docket. "We have several verdicts being overturned because of the judge's corruption, and yours came up, being the most high profile. The loss of your case hurt the firm seven years ago."

His nostrils flare. "The firm? The loss harmed *the firm*?"

"Yes." Damn, he's intimidating. Do I want him free to roam the streets? "This is a chance to fix the damage caused."

"And promote you to partner?" he guesses.

My life is none of his business. "I'm good at my job, Alexei." Yeah, I don't use his last name. "You can go with outside counsel. I'll rip up your retainer agreement if you want."

"I want you."

I hear the double entendre and ignore it. "Then it's my way, and you'll follow my directives."

Now he smiles. Full on, straight teeth, shocking dimple in his right cheek.

Everything inside me short circuits and flashes electricity into places sparks don't belong.

He taps his fingers on the table. "I signed the agreement, and this means you work for me. Correct?"

"Yes." But I call the shots.

He moves so suddenly to plant his hand over mine that I freeze. "You need to learn now that I'm in charge of every situation. Do you understand?"

I try to free myself and fail. His palm is warm, heavy, and scarred over my skin, with the hard metal table beneath it a shocking contrast. My lungs stutter and hot air fills them. "Whatever game you're playing, stop it right now."

His hand easily covers mine and his fingers keep me trapped in sizzling heat. "I don't play games, Peaflower. Learn that now."

"Peaflower?" I choke out, leaving my hand beneath his because I have no choice.

"Your eyes," he murmurs. "The blue dissolves into violet like the butterfly pea flower. A man could find solace from everlasting torment just staring into those velvety depths."

I have no words for him. Are there words? Scarred, barely uncuffed, and intense, he'd just whispered the most romantic words imaginable. And he's a killer. Just because the judge was corrupt doesn't mean Alexei hadn't committed cold-blooded murder. Two things can be true at once. "We need to keep this professional, if you want me to help you."

He releases me and stands. "Guard," he calls out.

My hand feels chilled and lonely.

Keys jangle on the other side of the door.

"Rosalie, this is your out. If you tear up the retainer, I'll find another lawyer. If you stay, if you continue to represent me, this is gonna become a lot more personal. Tell me you get me." Fire burns in his eyes now.

I stand, even though my knees are knocking together. "I'm doing my job."

"Just so we understand each other."

The door opens and the same guard from before moves inside, pauses, and visibly finds his balls before securing the cuffs on Alexei, who watches me the entire time. He allows the guard to lead him to the door.

Once there, he looks over his shoulder. "I hope you stick with me in this. Also, you might want to conduct a background check on Miles Molasses from your firm. He was a co-conspirator to the judge and prosecutor." His teeth flash. "How convenient that he had an accident. Right?"

Look for *One Dark Kiss*, on sale in Spring 2025.

Visit our website at
KensingtonBooks.com
to sign up for our newsletters, read
more from your favorite authors, see
books by series, view reading group
guides, and more!

Become a Part of Our
Between the Chapters Book Club
Community and Join the Conversation